D1041440

EDITED AND WITH AN INTRODUCTION BY

Clifford E. Trafzer

Anchor Books

New York London Toronto Sydney Auckland

New Native American Storytellers

# Blue Dawn, Red Earth

AN ANCHOR BOOK

PUBLISHED BY DOUBLEDAY
a division of Bantam Doubleday Dell Publishing Group, Inc.
1540 Broadway, New York, New York 10036



*Book design by Jennifer Ann Daddio*

Many thanks to the following for permission to reprint excerpts from copyrighted material included in this book.



Library of Congress Cataloging-in-Publication Data
Blue dawn, red earth: new Native American storytellers / edited and with an introduction by Clifford E. Trafzer. —1st Anchor Books ed.
p. cm.
1. Indians of North America—Folklore. 2. Indians of North America—Social life and customs. I. Trafzer, Clifford E.
E98.F6B59 1996
398.2'08997—dc 20
95-35195
CIP

ISBN 0-385-47952-2



Printed in the United States of America

An Anchor Paperback Original

First Anchor Books Edition: February 1996

1 3 5 7 9 10 8 6 4 2

# Acknowledgments

"The Witches of Eufaula, Oklahoma" copyright © 1996 by Craig S. Womack. Printed by permission of the author.

"Names" copyright © 1996 by Lorne Simon. Printed by permission of the estate of Lorne Simon.

"Darlene and the Dead Man" copyright © 1996 by Anita Endrezze. Printed by permission of the author.

"The Reapers" copyright © 1996 by Jim Barnes. Printed by permission of the author.

"Spirit Curse" copyright © 1996 by Annie Hansen. Printed by permission of the author.

"What's in a Song" copyright © 1996 by Maurice Kenny. Printed by permission of the author.

"So I Blow Smoke in Her Face" copyright © 1996 by Laura Tohe. Printed by permission of the author.

"Beets" copyright © 1996 by Tiffany Midge. Printed by permission of the author.

"The Last Rattlesnake Throw" copyright © 1996 by Ralph Salisbury. Printed by permission of the author.

"Never Again" copyright © 1996 by D. L. Birchfield. Printed by permission of the author.

"Talking Things Over with the Boiler Man" copyright © 1996 by Duane Niatum. Printed by permission of the author.

"A Jingle for Silvy" copyright © 1996 by Richard G. Green. Printed by permission of the author.

"Roma and Julie: Indians in Duality" copyright © 1996 by Barney Bush. Printed by permission of the author.

"Rocking in the Pink Light" copyright © 1996 by Gloria Bird. Printed by permission of the author.

"El Sol" copyright © 1996 by Guadalupe J. Solis, Jr. Printed by permission of the author.

"The Mystery of the White Roses" copyright © 1996 by Vee F. Browne. Printed by permission of the author.

"A Belated Letter to Christopher Columbus" copyright © 1996 by Georges E. Sioui. Printed by permission of the author.

"The Atsye Parallel" copyright © 1996 by Lee Francis. Printed by permission of the author.

"Grampa Ramsey and the Great Canyon" copyright © 1996 by Darryl "Babe" Wilson. Printed by permission of the author.

"Looking for Hiawatha" copyright © 1996 by Andrew Connors. Printed by permission of the author.

"Dreamland" copyright © 1996 by Jason B. Edwards. Printed by permission of the author.

*For My Mother*

*and*

*In Memory of Lorne Simon*

# Contents

Clifford E. Trafzer, a mixed-blood Wyandot, is professor of history and Native American studies at the University of California, Riverside, where he is also director of the Costo Native American Research Center. He is active as chair of the Chancellor's Native American Community Committee, regional director of the Wordcraft Circle of Native Writers, and vice-chair of the California Native American Heritage Commission, which protects sacred sites and remains. He is the author of many articles and stories about Native Americans. His books include *The Kit Carson Campaign*; *Looking Glass*; *Renegade Tribe*; *Mourning Dove's Stories*; *Yakima, Palouse, Cayuse, Umatilla, Walla Walla, and Wanapum Indians*; *The Nez Perce*; *American Indians as Cowboys*; and *Chief Joseph's Allies*. In 1992, Anchor Books published *Earth Song, Sky Spirit*, which he edited and which won the Pen Oakland Literary Award for fiction. His short stories have appeared in *The Raven Chronicles* and *Talking Leaves*. Trafzer lives in Yucaipa, California, with his wife and three daughters.

Clifford E. Trafzer

# Introduction

Blue Dawn, Red Earth *is a collection of fiction, and it is introduced to readers through an imaginative story about tribal librarian Agnes Yellowknee, a fictional character and composite of people I have known and respected.*

AGNES YELLOWKNEE LIVED IN A BLACK OAK TREE GROWING in the middle of the reservation. She had lived there as long as anyone could remember, and she knew the tribal stories that made us a community. Agnes was old. She had always been old. Her face looked it, too. Deep, dark lines ran across her face in every direction. My father used to say that her face looked like a road map, but to me her face looked more like a relief map I had touched in school. All of the lines in her face ran to and from her eyes, and it was her eyes that I remember most. Agnes Yellowknee had narrow, expressive brown eyes. Bright brown eyes that danced and laughed, eyes that let you enter her heart and come to know her.

Agnes Yellowknee was a tribal personality, a one-of-a-kind woman of the old-time mind. She spoke the ancient language, but she had taught herself to read and write English. She did so after running away from Carlisle Indian School, where white teachers and matrons tried to destroy her word shadows and trickster temperament. Every child on the reservation knew Agnes Yellowknee through heard stories from their parents and grandparents. They knew her through the stories she told and retold, the books she read to them. She kept tribal stories about the reserve, even though she never thought of herself as a reservation Indian. She knew the remembered history of the People, traditions and stories that unlocked secrets about ourselves, the very stories the matrons tried to beat out of her at Carlisle Indian School.

Agnes knew the power of word shadows, stands of sentences, and pregnant paragraphs that gave birth to new life. Through Agnes Yellowknee, I came to know the value of told and untold stories. They were representations of the real tribal memory, segments of the past and present that could be understood through word masks. I heard her say often that "words and stories free you so that you might know your own long shadows." When I was young I thought Agnes Yellowknee created such rationale out of her own mind. But she admitted to me that she had learned such things from an Anishinaabe author named Gerald Vizenor.

"Reading *Manifest Manners: Postindian Warriors and Survivance* changed my life," Agnes Yellowknee once confided. "I had never given word shadows and nicknames a second thought until I read that book." Agnes was moved by Vizenor's postmodern views of modernism, American Indian activists, and profound professors working in the field of Native American literature. As a result of her interest in Vizenor's book, President John Fitzgerald Kennedy invited Agnes Yellowknee to the White House to give the keynote address when the President awarded Vizenor the National Native American Literary Award. This is the highest honor bestowed on American Indian writers, and Agnes felt it was one of the highlights of her life to give Vizenor a crystal *oshkiwiinag* and a generous check. When I asked Agnes who donated the money for the awards, she told me that the statue and money came from native volunteers who generously gave of their time to raffle tickets for a sacred turkey pelt to New Age writers attending the Wood B. Shamans Ceremonial Pow Wow in New York City the summer before the Rose Garden celebration.

Agnes Yellowknee's home housed the tribal library, which featured works written by Indian writers. Her library was the focal point of the reservation, the center of tribal activities. Some reservations had concentrated on other forms of development, building huge bingo palaces to generate funds for housing, water, agriculture, police protection, scholarships, and the like. Our reservation added a large room onto the home of Agnes Yellowknee and built a multistory library with books, magazines, scholarly journals, government documents, videos, and oral histories. Agnes Yellowknee, who served as head librarian, spent most of the yearly budget buying books written by Mourning Dove, Charles Eastman, Joy Harjo, and D'Arcy McNickle. She surrounded her home with books by N. Scott Momaday, Linda Hogan, Louis Owen, James Welch, and Diane Glancy. Books by Louise Erdrich, Michael Dorris, James LaMotte, and Paula Gunn Allen were featured in weekly book reviews, which first were heard Saturday nights in the library auditorium and published the following Monday in the tribal newspaper, *Teondeon*.

Spirits were much a part of Agnes Yellowknee's life. She often said she lived with spirits, and we believed her. There were spirits within the oak tree where she lived, and I heard them speaking and singing sometimes when I was alone with Agnes Yellowknee. Agnes said that these spirits chased each other around the reservation at right angles behind our daydreams and résumés. She'd tell us to watch for spirits in our dreams and cans of commodity soup. Agnes saw spirits in everything from puppies to pigs and Ford station wagons to John Deere tractors. She found spirits in books, too.

"Just listen and you'll hear them," she used to say. "Paper spirits live in books about Indian people, and they stick to your mind like glue made from your own blood." Agnes Yellowknee believed in blood memory. Native American writers write from blood memory, creating new shadows and new traditions through the written word. Agnes insisted that paper spirits swirled around us at right angles like silent, unseen winds so that we could draw on them, use them in our own writing.

Agnes saw one value of storytelling—it helped us make it through the struggle of daily life. Stories convey good and bad alike. Whether or not we wanted to admit it, bad things happened to all of us. When bad things happened to us children, we'd go to Agnes Yellowknee for help. Her advice was as soothing as salve on an open wound, and she'd always know how to help.

Once I talked to her about my maternal grandfather, who was

working as a janitor at the Lower Lights Rescue Mission, an agency that helped homeless public servants. Grandpa was the head janitor, and he had an administrative assistant who was caught soliciting funds on behalf of the mission and then pocketing the money. Before getting caught, the assistant had given me money to buy Bazooka bubble gum, Twinkies, Tootsie Rolls, and orange soda pop at Scangaresse's Store. She liked me. I was her boss's son. She had given me a lot of money for those days, and I had used it to treat my entire fourth-grade class. When my grandpa found out what I had done, he made me pay back all the money. I was a child and I was ashamed. So I went to Agnes Yellowknee and told her my troubles. She wiped my tears and prayed over me.

She called on my ancestors for help. Using the language of our people, she summoned the power, and I felt it move through me like an electrical charge. It came to me through the soft spot on the top of my head, and I felt it go deep inside me. Agnes asked the spirit people to come. She asked them to help me with my problems, to help my grandpa get through the ordeal, and help the administrative assistant to learn from the mistake. While she prayed, Agnes Yellowknee closed her eyes and told me what she heard and saw.

"I see your grandpa walking through the woods," Agnes reported. "I see the rain pouring down on Will, and he's tired and cold. He's walking in mud knee-deep, and he's having trouble walking. He's all alone, but he keeps going. Now the rain has stopped and he walks better and comes out of the mud. He still has some mud on his boots, but it hardens and falls off. He's going to be okay."

While she said this, I had my own vision that someone or something was flying on each side of me, picking me up and carrying me above a bunch of people who were jumping up trying to grab me and pull me down. The people kept trying to get me, but each time I went higher to escape their grasp.

I felt better after spending this time with Agnes Yellowknee. She helped me get a paper route and collect soda bottles to earn money to pay back the Lower Lights Rescue Mission. She set up a special fund at the library so that tribal patrons could contribute to my retribution. I worked off some of the money serving bowls of soup to homeless men and women at the mission and by washing the same bowls after the sermon and dinner. I spent each morning for four weeks washing gray sheets before school. The rest of the money I earned trapping gophers for farmers and firing a shotgun to scare off red-wing blackbirds around Agent Amos Glasscock's berry bushes. I paid back all of the money, and the story belongs in the collective tribal memory.

"I'd hate to get into a fight with you," Agnes announced unexpectedly one day. We were the only people in the library, and I was surprised at the severe tone of her voice. At the time, I was flipping through Charlotte Heth's book, *Native American Dance,* but I put the book down and turned my full attention to the ancient woman. Agnes's words caught me off guard.

"I see spirits standing behind you tonight."

I looked behind me but I saw no one.

"You have People with you," she said. "Right there they are, and I see them. Don't you see them?" she asked. I shrugged my shoulders and turned around again. I saw nothing, but the hair on the back of my neck went up. Something *was* there.

"There are four of them," she said again, peering at the silent air behind me. "They say they're with you all the time these days. They're gonna help you with your life."

I looked behind me again. I saw nothing, but the words scared me. I looked again. We sat in silence for a long time. Then Agnes asked what I was going to do when I grew up. I told her the truth. I told her that I planned on playing professional baseball for the Cleveland Indians, since the tribe had lost the World Series and needed some help. She suggested that I work real hard so I could play two sports and help the Washington Redskins, too.

Actually I was afraid of the future, because I didn't know exactly what I was going to do. I thought I'd make a good teacher. My grandpa had taken me to a university once, drove right up to Old Main and had parked the car.

"When you grow up," my grandpa had said, "I want you to go to college. I think you would be a good lawyer." I didn't know what to say. He had attended school for six years and my parents had only completed the eighth grade. I was in school, but no one in my family had ever gone to college. To think that my grandpa thought I was college material bordered on the absurd. I probably nodded my head as we drove away.

Like my grandpa, Agnes had faith in me. She told me I ought to go to college and study hard. She didn't think I had much of a future in professional baseball or football. She warned me, saying, "You shouldn't join the Indians 'cause they are going to go on strike just before they reach the World Series, and you'll be out of a job." She was prophetic that way. After that night I started seeing silent people hiding in trees and heard songs. Words and stories swirled in my head. I heard Wolf, Antelope, Eagle, Hawk, and Black Phoebe. This was something I kept to myself, except for Agnes Yellowknee. She knew the ways of these people. She was host to paper spirits, tribal ghosts brought to life by Indian writers.

Agnes Yellowknee lived in a world of words and stories where books and told words melted together into a listened fabric. She kept the best books close to her, honored the volumes by displaying them on metal racks where her patrons could handle them, feel their weight, and consider their value. One book in particular had greater value to her than all the rest. *Blue Dawn, Red Earth* was a book Agnes Yellowknee loved above all others. She loved this book because of the variety of native stories and because so many Indian writers had written into the work. She thought so much of the book that she had given me a copy when it had first appeared. I treasured it as much as Agnes. And when I think of *Blue Dawn, Red Earth,* I remember the last time I saw Agnes Yellowknee.

She was sitting in the tribal library on the tattered orange couch holding the book close to her chest. It was open, resting against her breasts. Sunlight set her silver hair aglow, and her head was turned slightly toward the morning sun. Dark green leaves of the live oak tree formed a perfect background, and I thought she made quite a picture. I captured the scene in my head and promised myself to keep this image of Agnes Yellowknee in my heart forever.

My presence broke the spell. When she noticed me, Agnes spoke kind words and gently patted the couch with her brown, wrinkled hand.

"What'cha reading?" I asked, already knowing the answer.

"Some of *Blue Dawn, Red Earth,*" she said with a smile.

I looked at her quizzically. I'd seen her read that book at least a hundred times, maybe more, but it seemed she never got enough of it.

"I know, I know," she answered, waving both hands in the air. "I've read this book many times, but I get something new from it every time."

*Blue Dawn, Red Earth* was a book of short fiction by Native American writers. The stories were all original, and except for a few, most of them were written by Indians who were not well known but who had created wonderful stories out of their minds and experiences. Agnes Yellowknee liked to talk about that book, tell stories into and out of it. She loved to tell you all about it, or enough of it that you'd want to read it. She shared the book with everyone, just as she had shared it with me when it was first published.

"There's a story in here," she began pointing to the cover of the book, "about witches written by Craig S. Womack, who's a Creek-Cherokee from Oklahoma. He writes all about 'The Witches of Eufaula, Oklahoma.' You'd like reading about Lenny, Sammy, and the other losers on that res who wasted their lives using drugs and alcohol. They decide to witch old lady Bowlegs but get the surprise of their lives at her house one day. The spirits swirl around that story, as well as Lorne Simon's tale called 'Names.' Simon is a Micmac from Canada who tells us how Andy sees a spirit that his dad calls Amalegne'j. It's one his dad's seen before and he helps Andy deal with the thing.

"There's playful humor in a story by Yaqui writer Anita Endrezze. The story about 'Darlene and the Dead Man' makes you laugh. Darlene and Marlene are sisters who find a dead man on Darlene's Ford Pinto. They handle the situation themselves, and Darlene gets all tied up with that dead man. In the end, Darlene and Marlene deal with things as best they can, but that's not so in the story written by Choctaw writer Jim Barnes. His story is 'The Reapers,' in which a salesman gets in trouble with a farm family out to do a dangerous ritual. There's also danger in Annie Hansen's story 'Spirit Curse.' She's Lenape and has spirits around Jimmy in his 1962 Chevy car. Jimmy is haunted by a dark hooded spirit, but he uses his Indian prayers to call on the power to break the curse."

Agnes Yellowknee sat forward on the orange couch, placing *Blue Dawn, Red Earth* between two wooden bookends. A large round coffee stain had appeared on the cover since the last time I'd seen the book, and the sun cast a long deep shadow on the book. Agnes sat back in her seat, staring far off into the shadows of the library.

"I know Maurice Kenny," she announced, breaking the morning silence. "He's Mohawk and he's been writing a long time. His story in *Blue Dawn, Red Earth* is called 'What's in a Song,' and it captures his heart, the way he thinks and lives. He writes about a man who feels music in his bones, hears the song of the river and a tiny chickadee. Animal people still teach us, you know, but you have to listen. Cherokee writer Patricia Riley tells us that in her story called 'Wisteria.' In that story Justine listens to her grandmother, Eddie T., pass along Cherokee traditions—including the belief in little people who dance at the edge of the woods.

"The woods is the home of little people, stick people, and bears. Great bears also live in your dreams, but they only appear to certain people. That's what happens in Métis-Cree writer Misha's story 'Memekwesiw.' A woman sees bears during the day and night. She's all mixed up with dreams and life and bears until she draws her own blood and sees her inner self. We learn through stories, learn about ourselves and others, learn about love and hate. Stories tell us about hatred and jealousy, life and death. That's what Diné author Richard Van Camp shows us in his story 'Sky Burial.' It's about the last day of a tribal elder who thinks back to an owl and unwraps the secret hair of a girl before passing on to the next world. The other side and love is also part 'Midnight at the Graveyard' by Ojibwe writer Penny Olson. There's high adventure for children in her ghost story about the golden arm woman and a body that appears at a local graveyard.

"Sometimes Indian people today will use old stories to tell new stories. That's what Cherokee-Shawnee writer E. K. Caldwell does in 'Cooking Woman.' She weaves an old tale about Cooking Woman into a modern-day story about love and broken circles. Sometimes Indian people tell stories about things today, as when Onondaga author Eric L. Gansworth deals with 'The Raleigh Man,' a white salesman that everyone likes but no one wants around when the tribe's out hanging dummies that they are going to set on fire. That story has something to do with tribal ritual, but not as much as 'Bagattaway' by Mohawk writer Chris Fleet. His story is about a spirit that ties Iroquoian people to the Great Mystery through lacrosse, a game that is ceremony, ritual, story, and prayer all wrapped into one. His story keeps bringing a character back to his own people, and that's what Chippewa Kimberly M. Blaeser does in 'Growing Things.' It's a story within a story, weaving a woman named Spanish with her grandpa and family. It's a tender and poignant story tying yesterday to today. The story is deep and magical. It will awaken the 'kitten blood' in anyone who reads it."

Agnes Yellowknee laughed, at first just a little and then a lot. She laughed until she cried. I couldn't help but laugh, too. But I didn't know why.

"What?" I asked. "What's so funny?" I asked again, trying hard to hold back my own laughter. Agnes took out a small white hanky from between her breasts and wiped the tears from her eyes.

"That Gerald Vizenor," she exclaimed, quickly regaining her composure, "that Anishinaabe has a story set in the center of the book that's the best he's ever done. It's about tribal trickster and dentist Gesture Browne and how he ended up with the Naanabozho Express. There's a nurse who's got lots of names and finds *oshkiwiinag,* a crystal trickster that gives sexual pleasure to Girl Scouts, crossbloods, and full bloods while they ride the tribal railroad."

Agnes Yellowknee began laughing again, and between breaths tried to compose herself.

"There's serious stories in *Blue Dawn, Red Earth,*" Agnes reported, tightly clenching the used white hanky in her right hand. "Laura Tohe is Diné from the Southwest and her tale is about a Navajo girl and her cousins going to school at a government boarding school. She calls the story 'So I Blow Smoke in Her Face' because the young girl has such contempt for the government Indians working at the school. She cannot keep her mind on school because her thoughts drift off to Dinetah, the land of the People. That's where her mother and family live by ranching cattle in the shadow of the Chooshgai Mountains. That's serious business, you know. Tohe's story tells true things. Growing up Indian is hard for people to understand, even when you're a native person. Ralph Salisbury is Cherokee, and he says as much in 'The Last Rattlesnake Throw,' which deals with some crossblood boys who get involved in snake thowing.

"The danger of throwing rattlesnakes is you can get killed. You can also die if you go hunting in bad weather. That's what happens in a story called 'Never Again' by Choctaw writer D. L. Birchfield. Two brothers nearly die in an adventure that takes them deep into the woods of eastern Oklahoma. We can all get into deep trouble through our own mindless actions. Stories tell us about that all the time. The key is to stay out of trouble. But if you get into it, get up and get going again. But that's a lot easier for me to say than for me to do. I like Tiffany Midge's story called 'Beets' because she's a Lakota writer who's taking us into and out of trouble with two girls who sell the food their father grows in the backyard. The story moves from Indians of the past to those of today in a humorous tale that will make you laugh. There is something serious about that story, as well as Duane Niatum's story 'Talking Things Over with the Boiler Man.' The Klallum Indian writer tells about a Black Irish boiler man who gives wise counsel about a love affair gone bad. The boiler man has been secretly adopted by Young's Coast Salish clan, and he tries to help Young navigate one of the trials of life. Jump ropes, a deck of cards, and a basement deep inside the earth are all part of this story.

"Sometimes stories in that book go from serious to sad. I'd say that's so, but so is life. It swings like that from good to bad times. Mohawk writer Richard Green does a story called 'A Jingle for Silvy,' about Marcie and Silvy, two girls who do jingle dances at powwows until Silvy moves away from the reservation to the city. The story is not so much about moving away to urban areas as about a new stepfather who's sexually abusing Silvy. That happens too much, I'm afraid, but we can't ignore it and pretend it doesn't go on. It seems to me the older I get that there's really a pull between good and evil, or the things that are right and wrong. We have to make choices, you know, that's what Shawnee writer Barney Bush says in 'Roma and Julie: Indians in Duality.' It's hard for Indians to sort out what's traditional and new, what we'll take of the new and save of the old. Lots depends on individuals like Roma and Julie. It's not real clear if they sort it out, and I don't know how clear it is for any of us. Look at me, living in a tree house and working at a library where we have books written in the language of the Wootowquenauge. Think of that for an old Indian woman.

"We don't have all the answers. I'm not even sure we've asked all the questions. The stories say we should think, use our wisdom, grow by experiences, and be mindful. Each day is important and there are fine miracles in small things. They say we need to sort things out as best we can. Spokane writer Gloria Bird does that in 'Rocking in the Pink Light,' a story about bringing a baby into the world and dealing with one relationship that is brand-new and promising while dealing with another that is complicated and incomplete. Guadalupe Solis, Jr., is Aztec Indian, and he does it too in 'El Sol,' a story about love and death. This is a touching story about inner voices that speak to all of us if we listen. Navajo author Vee F. Browne offers an enchantment through her voice in 'The Mystery of the White Roses.' She writes about a hitchhiking Navajo marine, returning home to the res. Vi picks him up and takes him home to Ganado. Along the way, a friendship and future develop between the two until Vi learns the truth about Stuart Chee Love. There is mystery in 'The Atsye Parallel' by Laguna author Lee Francis. His story is like an echo from the past and present through the life of Martha, a woman known in her Pueblo community of New Mexico as Like-A-River. Martha returns to her home and immediately re-creates her relationships with her place and people. She grieves a loss, is troubled by a dream, and takes her place as mother of Rock Clan.

"Like Martha, we believe that we are part of this earth, that we always have been and nobody discovered us. We discovered ourselves through our stories, and we repeat the creation every time we tell the stories. That's why I like the story 'A Belated Letter to Christopher Columbus' by Georges E. Sioui. He's Wyandot-Huron—one of the people—and he tells the truth about our home here on Turtle Island. He tells us how white people have gotten it wrong about Columbus "discovering" America. The history of our people is found in heard words, and that's what Darryl "Babe" Wilson says in 'Grampa Ramsey and the Great Canyon.' Wilson is Achuma-We and Atsuge-We. He writes about a young man who learns the old story from an old master storyteller, and he promises to pass it along to future generations. That's also a point in Andrew Connors's story 'Looking for Hiawatha.' Connors is a Bad River Ojibwe. In his story, a white anthropologist thinks he knows so much that he comes to the Chippewas looking for Hiawatha. The real Hiawatha lived among the Haudenosaune or Iroquois, not the Anishinaabe. That girl, Snow Dancer, tries to teach him about the Shinaab beliefs about spirits in trees and stones, but he just doesn't get it.

"Indians today take from the heard words of their youth, and they write new stories based on new experiences. That's what Blackfeet-Blood author Jason B. Edwards does in 'Dreamland,' a story about Tom Losteagle, who is trying to find himself but becomes involved with lots of street people in a big city. He's a veteran of the Vietnam War, a Blackfeet of the Pikuni Tribe. He saves a life through his courage and knowledge of how to deal with violence. It's a fitting way to end *Blue Dawn, Red Earth* 'cause there's little courage among people today. I see boys and girls, men and women all around me who run from trouble, afraid to stand up to good and right and just things. To do that might hurt them somehow, so it's easier to run or hide. They pretend at being brave, but when the chips are down, they don't stand up for the People or themselves. In the last story, Tom stands up for someone, saves a life. It could have cost him his life. We need more of that, doing things for others, standing up to evil and bad things that take the People away from places like this library."

It was nearly noon, and I had listened patiently to Agnes Yellowknee. Although I had read *Blue Dawn, Red Earth,* it was wonderful to sit with Agnes and listen to her soothing voice as she discussed her favorite book. But now I wanted lunch and she sensed it. Agnes was perceptive that way and put her handkerchief in the "dust catcher" between her breasts. She moved forward on the couch and took *Blue Dawn, Red Earth* from the bookends. Agnes took the book lovingly in both brown hands and held it close to her chest.

"Let's go to the kitchen and I'll fix you lunch," she suggested.

I nodded, adding, "Good idea!"

"We can go outside and eat," she said. We moved out of the library and into her home. "We'll get some fresh air and have some food. You know your mind doesn't work without food."

She fixed two tuna sandwiches with tomatoes, pickles, and lots of mayonnaise. She handed me an unopened bag of Eagle brand potato chips and two cans of Classic Coke. We traveled down the wooden steps out of the tree house and onto the grass around the base of the tree. I led the way and turned to watch as Agnes Yellowknee stepped from the tree to the earth. No sooner had her right foot touched the ground than I heard her gasp loudly and fall forward. I watched her, as if in slow motion. She crashed to the ground. At the same time, I moved in slow motion, too, tossing the Cokes and potato chips and stretching my arms out to catch Agnes before she hit the ground. I tried to catch her and break her fall, I really tried. But I missed her and she hit the earth with her face full force.

I was by her side in a moment, reaching for her left shoulder to turn her over. I held her head in my lap and pushed her thick gray hair from her face. I felt the deep lines that crisscrossed her face to her brown eyes. I gently caressed her worn face. Only my fingers felt the change at first, then my heart. Her eyes were closed, and I knew she was dead. Tears ran down my face, warm silent tears that came from deep within me. The warmth of my tears turned cool as a wind came up and dark clouds gathered above my head.

I bent over and lightly kissed her cheek as a small wind swirled about us, taking her soul skyward. I remember rocking Agnes in my arms, holding her body close. Through my tears I saw that in one hand she still gripped the tuna sandwiches. In her other hand, she tightly held on to *Blue Dawn, Red Earth*. I took the book from her hand and brought it close to me. The stories of this book had touched Agnes Yellowknee so deeply they seemed almost hallowed to me. The stories had transformed Agnes, forever changing her life. There was something good and magical here that might be given to others.

Craig S. Womack is a professor of English at the University of Nebraska at Omaha, where he teaches Native American literature. A Creek-Cherokee, he is an accomplished young writer trained at the University of Oklahoma. His scholarly works have appeared in the *Native American Culture and Research Journal* of the University of California, Los Angeles, and the *American Indian Quarterly* of the University of California, Berkeley. In addition, he has published creative work in *The James White Review, Christopher Street, Callaloo, The Raven Chronicles, Windmill, News from Indian Country,* and *The Evergreen Chronicle,* as well as the Anchor Books anthology *Earth Song, Sky Spirit.* Womack has completed his first novel, dealing with various aspects of his own Creek people of Oklahoma.

Craig S. Womack

# The Witches of Eufaula, Oklahoma

"DID YOU BRING ANY DOPE, LENNY?"

Lenny shrugged his shoulders and lifted his hands. "Clean out, man. Everybody's tight. Next week I can get some." Lenny waved at the smoke in front of his face and rubbed his eyes. A small breeze came up and wisps floated out over the scrub oaks. Around Sammy, Lenny's voice was small and piping like a bird's, and during these meetings he would try to scratch around for the right words and answer the questions in tones Sammy liked to hear. Lenny looked away from the fire, blinking from the smoke. Out of habit, he messed with the zipper on his brown leather bomber jacket. Unlike Sammy's, it was cheap imitation vinyl; he had bought it at the Wal-Mart in town. Sammy's jacket was heavy black leather with a three-inch belt and metal buckle. He had ripped it off from a leather shop in Oklahoma City while Lenny had kept the clerk busy. Lenny raised his long, thin fingers up to his face and looked up at Sammy on the other side of the fire.

Sammy started in ragging on him. "Should have figured. You're more useless than your faggot cousin, Josh. At least he's gone back home and we don't have *him* trailing after us. He'd fuck things up for sure." Lenny shrugged, not feeling particularly responsible for his no-count cousin. Out of sight, out of mind. Sammy went on. "Shit. You're always smoking my stuff. Same ole story. 'Everybody all dried up, but I'll have some really killer shit, Sammy, next time.' Jesus Christ." From the steel-riveted pocket of the black leather jacket, Sammy pulled out a little one-hitter and tamped it down into the weed. He took a long toke and started it around while continuing to gesture, as if still speaking; he held the smoke deep in his lungs. As he exhaled, a cloud swirled and rose above his head, and smoke and song lyrics bellowed out of his mouth as he grinned and sang "We don't smoke marijuana in Muskogee."

Sammy took over the meeting and started laying out the plans. As the boys warmed their hands over the puny blaze they had started, the sound of humming locusts filled the night woods. Before he spoke,

Sammy placed his hand on his chest over the Harley emblem on his ragged T-shirt, just inside the jacket, and stood up straight. Lenny grinned and thought, Christ, he thinks he's Napoleon. Lenny watched the fireflies flicker in and out among the trees as Sammy spoke. "Okay," he said, "we all know about Martha Bowlegs, my grandma's gossip partner. Everyone in town has heard she don't trust banks. Rumor is that ever since her old man died, and he ain't around to force her to deposit her horde, she's taken to hiding it somewhere in her little shack." Sammy paused and pushed his thin, stringy hair off his shoulders. "Okay, Lenny. Here's how you can make yourself useful. You're gonna find out how to make those *stikini* scratches from your grandpa."

Lenny had just taken a hit, and he raised his hands to signal that he couldn't talk at the moment. Finally, exhaling smoke and words at the same time, he said, "Look, man. Why me? You know how me and him don't get along. Always harping on me about straightening up. You can't talk to the old bastard; it's impossible. All he does is start rattling on about a bunch of old stories."

"You dumb fuck." Sammy's face tightened as he clenched his fist and moved closer to the fire. "That's exactly what we want. A *story*. We want one of these old geezers to tell us a story of how they put people to sleep. Let him tell *stories* all day long until he finally gets around to telling you about *stikini* scratches. It can't be that hard because we already know part of the secret. But we got to find the right kind of thorn and the right words to say because that's what makes these old guys think they're under the spell."

Lenny looked skeptical. "How do I know he'll ever get around to telling me about *stikini* scratches?" he asked. Lenny remembered the time he went to see his grandpa the previous summer and had to listen to him ramble on all day, a bunch of stuff about the old days. The old man never seemed to have made it into the twentieth century.

"Guidance," Sammy said. "You just lead the old farts along. You pretend like the story they're telling you is the most fascinating thing you've ever heard. While you sit there wide-eyed like you're soaking it all up, you wait to ask the right question."

"Like what?" Lenny asked.

"Like, 'Hey grandpa, rumor has it that some of you old people know how to make folks go to sleep,'" Sammy replied in a mock-innocent voice. "If anybody knows how to make those scratches, Lenny, it will be your grandpa. Man, I grew up hearing all that shit. How powerful old man Henneha was. Aunts and uncles, Grandma and Grandpa talking all the time. Always saying, 'Sammy, stay away from that old man. He's gotten a hold of some powerful medicine. When he was young, he put a girl to sleep and raped her out by the spring. Her sister found her passed out on their front porch stoop.'"

"Oh, Christ," Lenny said, sounding bored. "I've heard that old story about Grandpa raping what's-her-name's sister a million times. Every old lady around here tells that one. I'm telling you; the old man is harmless."

Sammy continued, ignoring Lenny, "'The old witch, Henneha, goes about as a dog,' my grandpa says. My grandma says he's an owl, and Uncle Tony says he's a bear, man!" Sammy made his voice wheeze and rattle: "'Now, young man, listen to your old Aunt Bertha. Don't even get close to the witch's house because he can shoot an invisible medicine arrow that'll make you sick, and we'll have to take you to the *hilis heya* to have him remove the poison with the sucking horn. You listening, Sammy? The man-owl sneaks about and puts people into a deep sleep. Then the *stikini* sucks out their heart. Through their mouth. He takes the heart away and cooks it in a little iron kettle he carries with him. For every heart the *stikini* eats, he adds two or three years on to his own life. That's why old man Henneha looks so young.'" Sammy laughed as he contorted his face to resemble his aunt's wrinkles and leaned over on an imaginary cane.

Jimmy Harjo, the youngest one in the group, fidgeted nervously at all the talk about the old people. Jimmy looked down at his feet and pulled on the strings dangling from the holes in the knees of his Levi's. Jimmy spoke up. "Hey, if we want to rob someone," he asked, scratching his head, "why mess with all this mumbo jumbo? Why not just break into somebody's house?"

"First of all," Sammy said, "we might fuck up and leave fingerprints. Second, in this one-horse town everybody already knows us. Word gets around. You know how my grandma's always going on about this no-good gang of scum I hang out with that don't have jobs or anything better to do than hem-haw around every day. We'd be the first ones everybody'd suspect. The *stikini* scratches are much better. We'll go over to Martha's when my grandma sends me to her house with that fancy Seminole dress she's sewing for her. You know how much Grandma hates going way out in the country herself. So we, being the gentlemen that we are, will volunteer to deliver it to Martha, that sweet little old widow woman. No one will think anything of it, since my grandma's always making me tote *sofki* and cornbread over there. Martha being too old to cook much and all.

"When she invites us in, one of us will have to sit next to her at the little table in her kitchen, and he'll make the scratch marks on her arm. She won't know what hit her. Then we'll look through the house until we find the money stash, but we won't steal anything. Not yet. When we find where the money's hidden, we'll just put that handy piece of information on the back burner to use a little later. We'll lay Martha out on the sofa. Leave a note saying, 'Gee, Mrs. Bowlegs, we really appreciated the cookies, but you seem to have nodded off on us, and we had to leave.' Since nothing will be missing, she won't be able to call the cops, even if she suspects us.

"Now, here's the best part of the plan," Sammy continued, tossing his head and throwing back his hair over his shoulders. "We know that all the old geezers go to town the morning of the first to cash their Social Security checks and stand in line and bullshit about their hemorrhoids. We'll go back to the house and rip her off, and it will be a month later. She'll have no way of proving that we were the ones who did it. I mean, what's she going to do? Call the county sheriff?"

Sammy pretended to dial and then pick up the telephone, blurting out Martha's excited broken English. " 'This p'lice station, ennit? Uh, hello, Officer, Martha Bowlegs, me. Sir, money I'm missing from my house, and who did it I know. Yes, sir, Officer. *Stikini* witches month ago past. Three man-owls flew over to my house and put me to sleep with some thorn scratches. My money they found it, snooped it up round my house. Well, sir, found it they did and flew over here back month later, making off with it. Mr. White P'liceman, even though month been gone here at my house since robbing them hoodlums, they the ones.' "

The boy's laughed at Sammy's mockery. Jimmy said, "She doesn't talk that bad; she speaks better English than your grandma, Sammy."

"Shut the fuck up, dickhead!" Sammy shouted. "I'm the one who has to go on errands all the time for my grandma and take stuff out to her house. I should know." Sammy stirred the fire, and a column of sparks rose up the night sky. "All we need now," Sammy said, looking at Lenny, "is for you to visit your grandfather and find out what kind of thorn to use and what words to say over Martha to put her out like a light. We gotta get it right because, even though we don't believe in this crap, the old folks know if it ain't done the right way."

The porch boards sagged and creaked as Lenny walked up to the door of the shack later that evening. Looking back over his shoulder at the thick stand of oak and cedar trees that hid the place, he thought, Great place to grow dope. He knocked and waited.

"Just minute," a voice called out from inside. The door opened slowly, and an old man motioned Lenny in. Lenny thought that there certainly wasn't anything particularly witchlike in his grandfather's appearance, and he was glad he put no stock in the local superstitions. Lenny cleared his throat while cracking his knuckles nervously. "*Stonko,*" he said, hoping the old man didn't hear the break in his voice. He shifted his weight, stuck out his chest, and, as he stood outside the door, tried to look like nothing unusual was up.

Grandpa Henneha said nothing. He left the door open and wandered off into the kitchen, where he sat down at the speckled Formica tabletop and rolled a cigarette. After lighting up, he took a deep drag of smoke and stared at his hands. Finally, he said, "Well, you standing out there or coming inside?"

Lenny walked in and pulled up a chair at the table. The old man's brow furrowed, and he put the can of tobacco back inside the pocket of his bib overalls. As he slicked back his gray-black hair with both hands, he asked, "This time how much you want? Only show up when you needin' something. Why you shaking? Maybe you b'lieve what they say about me."

"I don't believe in witches if that's what you mean. That's a figment of you old folks' imagination. Too much time on your hands. Don't y'all have anything better to do than daydreaming?"

"Like breaking and entering?" asked Lenny's grandpa.

"I don't want money this time. I have a question."

"Advice? You listening at me now? Long time ago grandsons come to their grandfathers or their clan uncle on their mother's side. Which clan you in, you even know? Ind'ns let things go by like that now'days. We never think about it or ask about it, we just let things go by. You never show no interest in anything I tell you till now. This don't seem like you."

Lenny came right out with it. He blurted, "About *stikini* scratches." Lenny squirmed in his chair, having just forgotten all of Sammy's tactics for priming the old ones for stories.

The old man straightened up and set his burning cigarette down in the ashtray. Lenny fidgeted in the silence and tried to think of something to say next, but nothing came. He sneered, "I've got something in a Ziploc bag, old man, that'll make you give up Bull Durham forever."

"Show some respect, or I won't tell it. I don't know anything you're interested in anyway. Where you hear bout *stikini* scratches?"

"Sammy's grandma is always going on about being witched every time she finds a shirt buttoned unevenly or the hem of her dress turned up in back," Lenny said. "She really shit a brick when she found out Sammy got busted for trying to rip off the Git 'N Go. She'll be warding off bad medicine for a year, man. Sammy pretending like he had a gun under that ragged leather jacket, what a dumb ass. You should've heard Sammy hollering in Creek. Would've made you old folks proud. '*Eufaula talofan leykit omes,*' he's screaming at the officer. Shit, Sammy don't speak no Creek. That's the only phrase he ever learned. He's always playing stupid when he gets in trouble. Besides, he's from Weleetka, not Eufaula. Yeah, I mean, that young white policeman grabbed Sammy's arm, you know, the one with the biker tattoo? Has the cobra curled around a bleeding lamb, with a dripping knife in the snake's mouth? Well, anyway, the cop twisted Sammy's wrist, hollering 'You Indian bastard' until he brought his arm around his back and cracked those cuffs. He led Sammy like a balking steer, trying to shove six skinny feet of kicking legs and flying hair through the back door of that squad car. Sammy straightened up like a board. Braced himself against the frame, but the cop slugged him in the gut. When Sammy doubled over, the policeman kicked him through the door with his foot. Anyway, like I was fixing to say about Sammy's grandma. One time she started telling us about you."

He eyed his grandfather, looking for a response. The old man didn't move and stared at the ashtray in front of him. "She said I should stay away from you, grandpa or not. All because of something she claims happened to her sister. Said her sister used to have a thing for you when y'all was young. Sammy's grandma claims that one night you took her sister down by the spring to get her alone out there beneath the trees." Lenny grinned.

"So, her sister figures she got a little more than she bargained for and decides she's had enough. The sister shoves you off her and starts hurrying back toward home, with you following behind begging her to come back. Saying you only wanted to love her up a little. The faster she walks, the more she notices she's getting sleepier, and that's the last thing she remembers. When the sister wakes up on her front porch, she notices some god-awful smell like a dead cow in a ditch or something. You're nowhere to be seen, but someone has pawed all over her and messed up her clothes. She notices she has four scratches on her breast. She's laying next to the porch rail; she looks up and there are entrails hanging off of it, and that's where the rotten smell is coming from. Now, here's the funny part. She hears an owl hoot, and she looks up and sees a horned owl circle above the house, then fly off into the woods.

"Sammy's grandma says her sister was put to sleep by a *stikini* witch, a man-owl," Lenny continued. "She says you're the one who took advantage of her sister. The rotten smell was that bunch of old guts, and you had to leave your human innards behind before you could change into an owl. A couple days later Sammy's grandma and her sister woke up in the middle of the night when they heard something scratching around on the front porch. The sister kept wanting to go back to sleep. Them scratch marks you made on her was to make her drowsy, so the next time you wanted to have your way with her, she'd be in your power. You'd have a little easier time with it instead of having to chase her all night around the woods. Well, Sammy's grandma gave her sister some strong black coffee to help her stay awake and kept shaking her while she burned some cedar leaves and cudweed on the stove. The medicine was supposed to help them resist you. Keep 'em from sleeping. Thataway you couldn't sneak in and have both of them." Lenny placed both of his hands on the table and sat there grinning at the old man as if he'd laid down a trump card. He thought about all the trouble he was going through just to find out for Sammy how to make the scratch marks. "Sammy's grandma says that her friend Martha—the elderly lady she cooks *sofki* and corn bread for —always suspected you of being the witch because she always sees owls sitting in that little patch of woods out here by your house. Martha's always telling Sammy when he's on one of his errands delivering food to her from his grandma, she says, 'Sammy, be sure to burn some cedar when you get back home, since you have to pass that old man Henneha's house.' "

The old man laughed and got up to get some more coffee. "So, what you make of that old long-ago story, Grandson?" he asked.

"Crock of shit. I think Sammy's grandma dreamed the whole thing up."

"Why you here then? 'Cause someone say your grandpa use to turn himself to dog, owl, or something and witchcraft people?"

Lenny pulled out a Marlboro and tapped the end of the cigarette on the Formica tabletop. He lit it and cleared his throat. "I want to learn how to make them *stikini* scratches."

The old man bent over and began to convulse with laughter. Because of the tears running down his face, he had to leave the table, and he got up and went to the bathroom to blow his nose, all the while speaking. "Grandson thinks it's 'bullshit,' but wants *stikini* scratches from the old man. Well, don't that beat all."

He sat back down. "Listen, Lenny. I know stories. I remember them. I tell them to whoever it is who'll listen. I learn new ones sitting on the porch listening at whippoorwills whenever the sun goes down. People all move off nowadays. Long time ago neighbors use to brought food and help with chores, but now, even if you paid them, you can't find no one to do that now. Grandkids don't come by; your cousin Josh Henneha moving out to California with his parents; they only send him to see me summertimes. I don't know how to make bunch of witch stuff, only stories. Why you wanting to learn all this medicine?" His lined face turned down into a grimace. "What you wanting to know about this witchery for? I got things to do. I promised to help mow and clean up the stomp grounds. I'm fixing to leave." Lenny's grandpa got up and pulled his coat off the hook near the door.

"Whoa, wait up a minute," Lenny called, sensing the conversation was slipping out of his hands. "Lighten *up*, man. Have a seat for a second. *Lekibus*," Lenny said, pointing at a chair and thinking that throwing in a little Creek might improve his grandpa's mood. "It's not like I'm gonna put some kind of spell on no one. It's just that I ain't been sleeping so swift with all the worries about being on probation and all. Figured maybe if I knew how to make those scratches I could finally get some rest at night." Lenny thought about how bogus this excuse must sound. He tried again, hoping to eventually stumble upon the right words. "I won't have to worry about witching myself," he continued, "because I got better things to do than believe fairy tales. I just figure that the thorn Sammy's grandma says you witches use prob'ly has some kinda chemical for sleeping."

"You think you needing *stikini* scratches?" The old man leaned over the table and stared straight into Lenny's eyes. His voice rose. "You're already covered with snakes and arrows." He grabbed Lenny's upper arm with the tattoo of the bleeding heart pierced with an arrow; half of the left ventricle and the feathered shaft protruded from beneath the sleeve of Lenny's T-shirt. "You? Not worried about witching yourself? I tell you something, tell it real good, too!" he said, shouting. "You're already witched. How many them stories I told you when you were little you still remember? How many words, besides *stikini*, you know from your own language? Can't even talk it no more, I reckon. Come in here talking to old person this way. You're *beyond* witching. They've got you just where they want you, and they don't need any witches' help."

Lenny groaned, "Here you go again. Spare me, old man. I know the one you're fixing to tell. I heard it a million times from you when I was a kid."

But it was too late. The old man had already started. "The end will come like this here. The people will forget the herbs where we came from. They'll forget that one time our people had no friends. The animals, the birds, everything was against us. But the herbs came together and said they would protect us, take care of us, if we named them the right way, remembered them, spoke to them often. They brought us and the animals together. They got together trying to help out one another. That's where our name comes from; we are herbal people, and there's cure for everything from the herbs. But when we forget, when we forget our language and how to tell the stories, we won't know the cures anymore. We won't remember how we name the herbs to use them. We'll get sick. When language goes, there goes people, too. The loss of the language and the neglect of the ceremonial grounds was all told years ago."

The old man looked at Lenny. "You have become this story."

Lenny slammed the screen door behind him and headed out past the trees toward his car, parked on the side of the dirt road.

"What did I ever ask from him?" he grumbled to himself. As Lenny started the car, he remembered his god-awful boring Oklahoma history class in high school. Whenever his pretty young teacher spoke of "Oklahoma's Indian heritage," she always had a bright smile on her face. The only reason Lenny pretended to listen to this lecture was because the teacher always stared at him and the other Indian students when she said it. She was quick to remind them that the culture had vanished and that the rich legacy of curious folklore and quaint superstitions had passed away. As Oklahoma's Indians had blended in with their white neighbors and become farmers and ranchers and businesspeople, they had disappeared. Indian people were quick learners, and they had wisely put behind the past and looked toward the future. Now

Indian people were free to be just like their white friends and on an equal footing. Lenny thought, Good God, if she could only see my grandpa, she'd wipe that silly grin off her face.

"Well, what'd ya find out, Lenny?" asked Sammy.

"Man, you know how it is. He rambled on all day long about everything from the old days, and how I had forgotten what he taught me. When I finally brought up the *stikini* scratches, he knew something was wrong. I never bothered to ask about the old times before, and he guessed I was up to something."

"Well, this don't surprise me," Sammy said. "You prick, you got over there and froze up. You didn't ask him the right way. Man, we can't even rely on you to do something as easy as collect a fucking *story*? Jesus, Lenny. So, we're back to square one. Look, let's put our heads together about what we already know. We know it takes a thorn, four scratch marks, and you have to say some stupid words over the person about sleeping. Look, what would happen if we just use any old thorn?"

"Shit, I don't know," said Lenny. "We don't even know if the medicine works anyway. You're right, what's the difference? Things happen for reasons, not because of stories. People get sick from germs and go to sleep when they feel like it."

"Exactly," said Sammy. "We aren't gonna present that thorn to Martha for inspection before we scratch her. When she sees the scratch marks, she'll automatically think she's been witched, and it won't occur to her whether or not we did it the right way. Her own superstition will carry off the rest of it for us because she'll *think* she's been witched and her imagination will kick into gear. After that, we won't need the right words because she'll be swooning into a sleep from her own ignorance." Sammy was gaining new confidence. "We've got more than enough to work with," he said.

. . .

"Well, hello, boys. I was expecting y'all," Martha giggled as she wiped her hands on her apron. She patted Lenny on the back and ushered them in the front door.

"You were?" Sammy said.

"Sure 'nuff. I figured your grandma must have been finished with that dress by now, and I know how much she dreads coming way out here in the country like this. I guess your cousin Josh already gone back to California, huh? I see they let you out, Sammy. I hope you learnt something. You about worried your grandma plumb sick. All y'all sit down."

*"Lekibus cey,"* she said, pointing to the tattered tweed sofa. "Y'all sit while I get you some cookies. I surely appreciate y'all bringing the dress way out here." The boys scrunched up against each other and coughed as clouds of dust rose up from between the uncovered sofa springs.

"When's the last time anyone sat on this thing?" asked Jimmy.

"Let's see," Martha said. "Harold died in '72. Well, generally I have guests sit in the kitchen, but you boys can't all fit at the table. Where's my dress?"

"Oh, here." Sammy handed over the bundle his grandmother had neatly wrapped and tied.

Martha clutched at the dress with her gnarled, arthritic hands. A wisp of gray hair had fallen down in her face and bobbed in front of her nose every time she nodded her head. Fingers that once had been agile painfully untied the dress, and Martha held it up close to her black glasses in order to see it. She looked over the rim of the glasses, which had almost fallen off of her nose, eyed the dress, and examined the stitching. "Oh, yes. Very fine. Sammy, your grandma always does such a nice job. Now, you'll be sure to tell her thanks for me, won't you?"

Sammy forced a smile and said, "Yes, ma'am. I certainly will. Um, how about those cookies, Mrs. Bowlegs?" Martha's slippered feet were thumping time on the hardwood floor to some music coming from an old record player on top of a dresser missing half its drawers.

"My God, that's Jimi Hendrix. 'All Along the Watchtower.' Where did you dig up that old relic? It's like ten years old." Jimmy looked over at Martha, puzzled.

"Seven," Martha corrected. "Oh, well. Donny, my son, played it all the time before he volunteered in '69 for Vietnam, and when he didn't come back, I never could quite get myself to throw the thing away. I dig it out and play it every now and then. Record player's his, too." Martha's eyes had clouded over, and she sniffed once or twice. She showed them Donny's picture, his infantry unit, Donny as a handsome army soldier in a uniform who looked nothing like Martha.

Lenny looked over at Jimmy and winked. "Don't you have any Led Zeppelin?" he laughed.

"You mean the music group?" Martha cackled, recovering quickly. "Any you fellows care to dance?" Martha said, beaming a wide grin, two of her missing upper teeth revealing a gaping black hole.

The boys all stared at each other in amazement. Lenny cleared his throat. "Uh, no, ma'am. I don't think so. We just came by to bring you the dress. We'll still take some of those cookies, though. I bet they're delicious. What are they, persimmon? That's what my mom always bakes, you know." As Sammy jabbed Lenny in the ribs with his elbow, he patted Lenny's pocket where the scratching thorn was. Lenny looked at Sammy and said, "Oh, yeah. Right. Sure, Mrs. Bowlegs, I'll dance." Martha hurried off into the kitchen and came out with the plate of cookies, which she stuck in the boys' faces, and they each took one. Then she set the plate down on the kitchen table and went over and cranked up the volume of the record player so loud that the music started to distort from the speakers and rattle a line of empty Coke bottles that was collecting dust on her windowsill.

Lenny finished his cookie and stood up, holding his hands out to do his best at a respectable foxtrot with the old woman. He turned red with embarrassment as it dawned on him that he was fixing to dance with an old lady. But before he could take her hand and put his arm around her back, Martha grabbed him by the hips and started to bump and grind to the lyrics. She turned him round and round, laughing loudly at Lenny's clumsy feet trying to keep up with her. Lenny had to shout over the music, "Mrs. Bowlegs, I'm getting dizzy. Could I sit down for a while?"

"No," Martha cooed, "not yet, young man. Why don't the rest of you boys join us?" Sammy winked at Jimmy and said "Come on, what the hell?" as he felt in his own pocket for the scratching thorn that he had brought for reinforcement if Lenny botched it.

"Now watch your language, boys," Martha said.

Sammy and Jimmy stood up, planted their feet on the hardwood floor, and started to gyrate to the lyrics. Martha, shifting like a diesel into high gear, began rubbing her crotch tightly against Lenny's, moving her hips in wide circular arcs, joining the two of them at the waist like enmeshed rotating sprockets. Lenny thought, Christ, I knew this was bullshit. These old people are plumb crazy. The old days, old ways, this is what happens when you dream up stories. Get crazy. Lose touch with reality. Can't be yourself, have to be a story, live in the past, spin out lies. Lenny turned pale and began to stagger dizzily as Martha turned him, winding and twisting like a snake coiling and uncoiling, all the while clutching him by the waist and pulling him through her mad loops. She started singing under her breath along with the lyrics, " 'There must be some way out of here,'/ said the joker to the thief." Swinging Lenny in a 360-degree circle, she shouted into his ear, " 'There's too much confusion, / I can't get no relief.' " As they watched in horror while Martha ground her hips against Lenny, Sammy motioned Jimmy to move forward cautiously, to crouch, to prepare to pounce. Martha threw back her head, groaned with pleasure, rolled her eyes back wildly.

Jimmy looked over at Sammy in disbelief and started toward the door. Sammy grabbed his arm and jerked him back. "Don't be a pussy," he said. "Just because the old lady's a little loony don't mean we have anything to worry about. Hang tough, we'll get her."

"A *little* loony?" Jimmy shouted back in disbelief. "Look at her; she's in another world. It's like she doesn't even know we're here while she's practically banging Lenny!"

They moved a little closer and waited for the best moment to jump, but the room started spinning out of control, and they staggered from wall to wall like passengers on the deck of a ship in a great storm.

"Oh, yes, I know you're here, boys!" Martha screamed over the music.

Jimmy said "Oh, God, I'm gonna be sick," grabbed the arm of the old sofa, and began to throw up all over the dusty tweed. Jimmy gave up trying to help grab Martha, looked up from the floor where he was lying, and watched the lyrics floating in the air, the words of the song rolling and curling above them like smoke rings.

"Jesus Christ, Sammy. What was in that shit we smoked in your car? Do you see what I see?"

"Fuck, man. Feels like we're on acid," Sammy said. Martha pirouetted with Lenny, laughing in glee, Lenny reeling, beyond speech. As she turned, her long gray hair fell out of its bun and flew behind her. Her glasses fell off and crunched under Lenny's boot. The Hendrix lyrics spooled out of her pursed lips like thread from a bobbin, and the words wrapped around Sammy, who tried to steady himself against the rickety furniture in Martha's living room. " 'No reason to get excited,' " Martha sang louder in Lenny's ear, "the thief he kindly spoke." During the distorted guitar solos, Martha looked over her left shoulder and spun herself into a whirling eddy like a dog chasing its tail.

Lenny made a frail effort at speech. "Please, Mrs. Bowlegs, make it stop," he pleaded, struggling to free himself from her grip.

"Shut up, you pansy," said Martha, wrapping her arms more

tightly around him and pulling him closer. Sammy lunged toward Martha and grabbed her wrist, making one large scratch down her forearm. The blood started to ooze out of the wound, and Martha began to howl like a mad dog in the moonlight. She twirled Lenny even faster and broke Sammy's grip. She threw back her head, bayed toward the ceiling, and sang, "Outside in the distance, / a wildcat did growl. / Two riders were approaching, / the wind began to howl."

The faded yellow curtains in the house were blowing as a rush of wind sent papers flying off the kitchen table; they circled in a whirlwind in the living room. As Martha sang, Lenny could see her words spinning from her mouth. He wondered if he was seeing things from the dizziness.

Sammy just stood and held on to the couch, waiting for things to slow down. He knew he shouldn't have got so high, mixed pleasure with business. Sometimes too much dope made him so paranoid, but this was ridiculous.

Martha started chanting her own lyrics to the distorted guitar wails, singing exactly in time to the Hendrix words. "You thought you could fool the old ones, you don't have no respect. There are those among us who think old stories are jokes." Then Martha started chanting over and over, started singing each of her successive stanzas in a higher key, completely ignoring the record player accompanying her, as she pulled Lenny through each of her loops. The room darkened and grew hazy with fog, and the boys felt a centrifugal force spinning them closer and closer to Martha, who now was lunging violently up against Lenny like a hound dog jumping in frenzy against a trunk where it has treed a raccoon. Sammy grabbed at Martha again. As she turned loose of Lenny, she bit Sammy on the shoulder. Lenny crumpled to the floor in a dead faint like a piece of wadded-up paper; Martha stood erect. Sammy dropped her arm and grabbed at his shoulder. His piercing scream matched note for note one of the guitar wails floating through the room.

Sammy couldn't believe it. He rubbed his eyes and stared at the haze in the room. He looked out the window. It didn't look dark outside. Sammy hadn't planned ahead for all this confusion, for lack of a better term. He felt his legs shaking. He saw Jimmy looking at him, wondering what they were supposed to do next. He looked away, trying to get his thoughts straight, and hollered, "Now we're really gonna get you, you old bitch!" He rushed her, but when he brought her down to the floor, she slipped out of his arms and backed up on all fours into the corner of the room, where her eyes glowed red in the darkness. Sammy rubbed his eyes again when he saw Martha, who had long trails of saliva hanging from the sides of her mouth. Her lips curled back. She bared her teeth and snarled at the boys, alternately rushing forward and biting at their legs, then backing into the corner.

A smell like a rotten carcass filled the room and Jimmy screamed, "Jesus, does the old woman keep roadkill in the kitchen?"

"Shut up; you're losing it," hissed Sammy. "Stay cool, and we'll get her. We should start watching who we buy dope from! This goddamn house is so dark you can't really tell what's going on anyway. It's probably a setup. The old woman got wind of what we were up to and is playing a trick on us. She knows what's up now anyway; we might as well go ahead and take the money from her. Christ. She's just a little old lady," he said. Jimmy could hear the waver in Sammy's voice. Martha's shape seemed to shift in the darkness. At times they could see the loose folds of her apron dangling between her legs, then, just when they thought their eyes had adjusted to the blackness, the apron looked like the penis of a large black mongrel. Martha backed into a half-opened closet door, which slammed behind her. The boys heard a steady low growl. Sammy said, "We got her now. No way she can get away. Jimmy, you go in the closet and scratch her four times."

"Fuck you, man. I ain't opening that door," said Jimmy.

"Me neither," groaned Lenny. He had come to on the floor.

Alone, from the dark of the closet, from the depths of the blackness that hung in the room, Martha's voice, rising, chanting, singing rhythmically, sounded against the scratching of the Hendrix record. When it reached the end of side one, she began to tell her story:

many years ago it happened
i followed two lovers
through the woods
because i loved the man
and hated his sweetheart
years of longing
nights of hatred
many days i had watched them
holding hands and making love eyes
the man made love magic by her cabin
imitating the song of the mourning dove
he sang her lonesome call and pointed to the
bedroom
*Paci ho we, Paci ho we*
dove go there, dove go there
i hooted from a nearby tree to no avail
i swooped around the cabin's chimney but
the man's words sent the dove
to the woman's bedroom
the bird repeated the haunting call of love
and quickly made away
unharmed

each day i grew sick with envy
until one night pulling handfuls of hair
in fury
i hid behind rocks and trees
sneaking along behind the couple

until they reached the spring
they laid down in the grass
i heard their pleasure
i tore the bark from the tree where i hid
i bit my lip to keep from shrieking
until the blood ran down my chin
the woman shrank back in fear
from my magic
i hissed in delight
she ran down the path toward home
the heartsick man behind her, pleading
"come back my darling
you frighten me with this strange behavior"

i swooped down on the man first
scratching him four times
then i flew after his girlfriend
she ran from my claws
but i caught her
she was soon asleep
i pulled back her dress
to tear out her heart and eat it
but the man had strong medicine
in the past he'd seen me watching
and peering out from rocks and bushes
he'd worn a pouch of cudweed and cedar
around his neck
he knew stronger words than my black
  chantings
he spoke himself awake

he chased me away
and carried his lover home

The Witches of Eufaula, Oklahoma

he left her on the porch and ran
not wanting to shame the girl to her sister
who might think
a man had torn her clothing

two nights later i returned to the girl's shack
in human form
to finish my black work
i stood on the front porch and knocked
pretending to be a lady from the Baptist church
inviting them to a hymn singing
i knew the girl was already scratched and in my
power
i could easily make her drowsy
and for the sister i had brought some bad
medicine
to slip in her coffee

but the lover had waited for my return
with power i knew not of
he hid beneath the porch where
he'd prepared a special arrow to kill a witch
fletched with owl feathers
notched with small grooves near the point
full of strong medicine
but my undoing was his words
words laced with strength
beyond any arrows
stories
when he heard my footsteps on the creaking
boards
he jumped from his hiding place

he overcame me with a story
about naming the herbs
he said i had become the old prophecy
of the people
he weakened me with this
damned truth

i flew off carrying his arrow in my flesh
and dared not go back ever since
i do not have power to counter this man
in my hatred i struck back as i could
spreading rumors among the busy old hens in
  town
that he is the witch
when all along
it is me

With these last words, the closet door flew open and an owl circled the room as if she were darting with raised wings above her own brood, about to drop food into their mouths. "You boys wishing you hadn't smoked all that dope?" the owl seemed to say. As the boys looked up and felt the rush of air from her flapping, their mouths were agape in astonishment. Sammy couldn't think of anything to explain this. She hovered in one place, just below the ceiling, wings raised in benediction. In a shrill cry she demanded, "Say it! Now!" and she swooped at their heads, claws extended. They covered their faces with their hands, and Jimmy and Lenny dropped to the floor. Sammy grabbed an old lamp and did his best at fending the owl off. She hooted in rage, lowered her beak, and began to drop scat around the room. Sammy finally fell on his knees and covered his head. She became gentle for a moment, her voice calling out the soft *o* implicit in her name. "Whooo, whooo, who is the owl? You are. You all are. Blend into your surroundings. Lose yourself in me. Forget your own voice. I will hide you, enfold you in my wings."

The boys leaned toward the floor and covered their heads as she beat her wings about them. Although they could feel their energy draining away into her, they were afraid for her to leave them, as if they would slip from her wings, out into the furious wind in the room.

"Are you hungry?" she screamed, her voice barely audible over the rushing wind that whipped their hair and clothes.

Their jaws moved together like rusty hinged machines. "Yes. Feed us. We're starved." She hooted in rage, lowered her beak, and dropped scat in their upturned mouths.

"Let your voice die on the wind," she proclaimed, and the boys crouched down on the hardwood floor like small birds being blown about on a limb. She raised her wings in a final blessing. "There is an even greater power than the *stikini* scratches. In this manner you can obtain it. Turn loose of the past. Strike out on your own. Be your own man. Do not believe you are the result of those who came before. Then you'll have power. Then you'll create yourself in your own image. Then you'll be free of all that is already dying."

She flew backward as if she were going to make a final swoop on them, and, in a blur of motion, rushed forward on all fours, snarling and biting Lenny's leg, her head shaking furiously, whipping his pant leg back and forth until it ripped in a long tear. Lenny took advantage of the situation and abandoned the torn part of his Levi's, slowly backing out of the house, afraid to turn his back on Martha. He reached behind him for the door handle, pulled it open, and light came flooding into the room. Lenny didn't wait for his eyes to adjust to see if the sunlight would clear up what he had witnessed. He backed onto the front porch and called out to Jimmy and Sammy, "Hey, let's give it up, man." They both followed him out the door, not able to see anything inside the house in the glare of the new light. They walked hurriedly to where they had hid their car up the road. Sammy was drenched in sweat, and he wiped it from his eyes. "Whose dumb fucking idea was this anyway?" he said. None of them looked back until they had reached the road.

After a while, a horned owl called out in the darkness. It had landed in an old slop trough in Martha's hog pen. The sows snorted, jumped up together, and rushed toward the far side of the enclosure. The owl flapped around among the rotten garbage in the trough. Someone in the house had turned over the Hendrix record.

The words "Purple Haze running through my brain" floated through the tree branches and blended in with the hum of insects as distorted guitar wails fell down like rain around Martha's house. Hendrix growled out, "Lately things don't seem the same," and Lenny felt the words swirling around his feet and slinking their way up tree trunks. The lyrics carried him away through a cave of words where Hendrix's voice dripped down red-streaked walls. His own voice ran beneath his feet, covered with dank, cold moss, leaking out from him like a river of meaning that flowed down gullied ridges toward a womb of darkness. Confusion washed over him, and he walked faster toward his rusted-out '64 Dodge Dart.

Lenny looked over his shoulder at Sammy. Lenny wished he would hurry up, but Sammy lagged behind, talking to himself in a daze, trying to work out what he'd just seen. Sammy was mumbling incoherently to himself, and Lenny couldn't make out a word of it. He'd never seen Sammy at a loss for words before, even for a moment. Finally, Sammy managed to blurt out, "Fuck these scratches, man. If we could learn what that old man knows, we could do a lot better than just robbing these old ladies. Christ, we could own this fucking town. Lenny, next time *I'll* go visit your grandpa. Do it the right way." Sammy's voice was getting less shaky, and he started sticking out his chest and pointing in Lenny's direction. "I won't let the old man get me off track. Gotta admit he is one slick old bastard."

"Be my guest," Lenny replied. Lenny tried to think, hold down the panic, get his head clear. He had always heard about the witch stuff from the local gossip, which he knew better than to take seriously. Now what should he think? What was it about his grandpa? Even Martha, who seemed able to do unspeakable things, admitted she was no match for the old man. What did it mean to have somebody who could do shit like that for a relative? Would any of it rub off on Lenny? What the hell would he do if it did?

Sammy went to get Jimmy, who was lagging even farther behind and walking around in circles in a clearing. Sammy turned him, pointed him toward the car, and said, "That way, Jimmy."

Turning back toward Lenny, Sammy said, "Can you believe that story Martha told, man? What a trip. She must think we'd believe most anything. I'd still like to know how that old man got her to believe those fairy tales, though."

"I gotta admit," Lenny replied, "she sure had everything planned out pretty good to try to scare the shit out of us. Christ, let's get out of here. I hate those old songs." They left the Hendrix lyrics behind and headed toward the car. Sammy and Jimmy climbed in silently. Lenny fired up the starter. "Sammy, do you have any dope, man?"

"Jesus, here we go again. Always mooching off of me."

"Well, I've got some rolling papers," Lenny replied.

Lorne Simon was a young and talented Micmac Indian author and storyteller, a student and friend of Maurice Kenny. He was born in Big Cove, an Indian Reserve Nation, on October 10, 1960, and was tragically killed in an automobile accident on October 8, 1994, while swerving to miss a deer. He was a student at the University of New Brunswick, where he was majoring in education. He left a rich collection of short fiction and poetry, including his short story "Names," which appears in *Blue Dawn, Red Earth.* Simon had recently worked with other writers from the First Nations of Canada at the En'owikin Center of Penticton, British Columbia, where he had received the Simon Lucas, Jr., Award. His first book, *Stones and Switches,* was published in 1994 by Theytus Books of British Columbia. Simon's mother, Sarah, and his family are preparing many of his other works for publication so that the creative writings of Lorne Simon may be shared and enjoyed by generations to come.

Lorne Simon

# Names

TWO BOYS AND A GIRL SAT AROUND THE SMALL SQUARE table made out of two pieces of pine plank that sat atop a stump. The children had shards of glass wrapped in small rags of leather in their hands. They were shaving axe handles that their father had made the night before. Their father was outside the log cabin splitting ash. The children could hear the pock of the axe smacking into the juicy hardwood and then the long tearing and sucking sound of wood splitting cleanly. Good wood, free of knots, could be split fine enough to make a deck of cards, their father liked to say. Although they had not seen the sun all day, the children knew that it was setting behind the clouds and that their father would soon step inside to continue working. He would row with the drawknife all night long—leaning forward over the work bench, pulling back, scraping wafers of white wood from the axe-hewn pieces—all night until dawn.

A comforting heat emanated from the wood-burning stove. Wi'sis, the gray tomcat, lazed under the stove just below the oven door. His large furry head sat on the floor between his square paws, one slit eye rolled back into the strange world of dreams and the other leisurely monitoring the shadows moving in the cabin.

"I bet you guys don't know why you have your names?" Andy asked his older brother and younger sister. Although his inflection contained an invitation to unravel secrets, Andy did not look up from his work. Andy's lap was draped with an empty burlap bag. Strands of wood as fine and curly as his hair covered the burlap. The sweet moist scent of sap rose from the downy shavings. It was an essence as subtle as the mystery implied in Andy's remark. Grant and Celia looked at each other.

"*Ei'oqa!* That's stupid," Celia pronounced. "Everybody knows we have to talk. That's why we have names—aye, Grant?"

Andy, keeping his head down, rolled his eyes toward Celia and stated patronizingly, as if he were a store clerk looking over the rim of a pair of reading glasses, "That's not what I meant, Celia. C'mon, now."

Celia glanced at Grant, who had already capitalized on the opportunity to set his axe handle aside and begin rolling a cigarette. Grant had a head like a chopping block. He was thirteen, a year older than Andy. But while Andy was slim, Grant was stout. In spite of his robust stature, though, Grant was unsure of his strength. His disproportionately small hands and small feet made him self-conscious. Grant often marveled at the easy way Andy carried his body. Andy was an acrobat, capable of doing a back flip that ended with his feet squarely landing in the same place they had been.

Grant licked the paper's edge and sealed the cigarette before setting it on the table next to the piece of glass he had been working with. All the while, Grant kept his eyes screened with slitted eyelids and thick lashes. He methodically and sedately whisked the shavings on his leather-draped lap into a pile, which he then packed into a ball. Grant slowly stood up with the ball of fine shavings in his palms. The square patch of leather slid from his lap and dropped to the bare wooden floor. He walked to the wood-burning stove, opened the grate, and tossed the ball of shavings into the fire. The gray tomcat rolled on his back, inviting Grant to scratch his stomach.

"*Na!* That takes care of that," Grant asserted. "No more shaving for me tonight."

"Dad'll get you to sand, then," Celia said.

"Don't care," muttered Grant as he slowly walked back to his seat. "Just won't shave no more."

"Mum gave me my name," Andy announced as casually as he could.

This time Andy studied Grant's response. Grant quickly put the cigarette into his mouth and sat down. He searched his shirt pocket for a small box of wooden matches. The box slipped from his fingers several times. Grant could hear the matches jostling inside the box and he felt his fingernail scrape against the striker on the box. Finally he jabbed his hand into the pocket, tearing the corner, and fished out the matches.

Celia's lips tightened. Her brows pinched obstinately, squashing the anguish that momentarily glazed her eyes. She worked so fast with the glass that its edge quickly dulled and she had to pick up another piece from the tin can on the table. The chip of glass was brown and curved—part of a beer bottle.

"Last time Dad got drunk and had his friends over and I came back from the Gagnon's to get my watercolors, I heard him talking and crying," Andy said, "and he talked about Mum and he was sorry for beating her. He said that he was never strong enough to get over his jealousy. Then he said Mum named me after her godfather because he always treated her good. And that's where she is now."

"Where?" Celia pounced, but immediately turned back angrily to her work.

"With her godfather in Maine," Andy answered. "He's got a large family there and Mum's helping them out—"

"But not us!" Celia snapped.

*"Ei'oqa,* Celia! Dad would have killed her," Grant declared, flashing at Celia as he struck a match and lit his cigarette. Even when he was upset, Grant spoke slowly. "I'm happy she's not here. Dad always came back from the logging camps and beat her for nothing, just because that old witch Ginny always talked and made up stuff. *Nisgam nuduid!* Dad should have beat her up instead."

*"E'be."* Andy nodded in agreement. "Mum never did nothing wrong. Dad knows that, too. But Ginny gossiped so much Dad had to show people he was still boss."

"He was scared what people would think if he didn't beat Mum?" Celia asked, amazed. Her brows crinkled in revulsion as this terrible insight into masculine nature hit her.

"You shouldn't be listening, Celia!" Grant snarled.

Andy whispered, "You know what else?"

Andy looked as if he were suddenly ill. His jaw hung slack and his lips were dry. He had to swallow before he spoke again. He closed his eyes and rubbed his forehead with the back of the hand that held the glass flake. A strand of shaving fell loose from his sweaty palm.

"Dad was crying because . . . because he heard," Andy mumbled.

Celia's stomach grew queasy. Grant inhaled and nodded lightly as he blew the smoke out.

"He heard that Mum's getting married," Andy finished.

The door opened and their father stepped in with a bag full of split ash. He emptied the bag in the middle of the room near a square block of wood. The sticks were over thirty-four inches long and about four-by-one inches in thickness. Their father was short and wiry. His hair was cut almost to the skin at the sides and greased back at the top. His face was long, with small cheekbones, thin lips and a prominent nose. His glinting raven eyes were startling in contrast to his pale complexion. He quickly unbuttoned his black woolen jacket and shook it off with a brisk, jerky flurry of arms. He hung the jacket on a nail in the wall near the door and then immediately set to work shaping one of the sticks into the rough mould of an axe handle. He had a contract to provide CNR with axe and pick handles.

"*Nahe'*, Grant, light the other lantern," the man ordered, masterfully manipulating the axe. "And hang it from that beam. Open the damper and the vents on the stove, Celia, and don't put any more wood in the fire. Andy, get the whetting stone. I left it outside. Bring the other axe in, too, and sharpen it."

A glaze of perspiration gleamed on the man's high forehead. Several strings of curly hair shook free from the waxy and flattened hairstyle and grazed the man's thick brows. He tossed the rough-cut to one side and picked up another stick, set it on the square block and started shaping it. Grant pumped the pressure into a gas lamp. Andy stepped outside and returned with a whetstone and an axe. And the cool air that followed Andy into the cabin made Wi'sis, the gray tom, lean his head over his forepaws and growl. Celia made a few adjustments on the stove and then gathered all the axe handles they had shaved and placed them on a rack behind the stove.

"It's starting to freeze, Dad," Andy said.

"*E'be.* Winter's going to be early this year," the man replied.

"Did something blow off the clothesline?" Andy asked, sweeping his disheveled curly locks back into place. "I saw something white out there near the woods."

Grant got up from the table to look out the window. He said, "I hope it's not the dress shirts Paul Gagnon let me borrow."

Grant peered out. Wi'sis left his niche under the oven door and issued another low growl as he slowly ambled forward. Darkness had already begun to smoke the sky. "Where is it?" Grant asked.

Andy placed the axe on the table and stood beside Grant.

"There," Andy answered, touching the glass with his right index finger. "Don't you see it?"

"Where? What're you pointing at?" Grant asked.

"There. Near the split pine. Just to the right of it."

"Is it small?"

"*Nisgam!* You don't see it? You growing blind, Grant."

Celia walked over to the window.

"You say it's near the pine that was struck by lightning?" she asked.

"Yeah," replied Andy, exasperation beginning to creep into his voice. "It's sorta fluttering a bit."

"Maybe it's too dark," Celia said.

"Oh, c'mon!" Andy cried. "Maybe you need glasses."

"*Ei'oqa,* he's just pulling our legs!" Grant told Celia and he walked back to the table.

"I'm not!"

"Well, I don't see nothing either," Celia said.

Their father stopped his work and looked at Celia and Andy. Wi'sis stopped, whipped his tail and snarled.

"I'll go and bring it in," Andy said.

"Wait a second, son," the man said. "Let me have a look first."

The father walked to the window. He placed a hand on Celia's shoulder and gently pushed her aside.

"What does it look like, son?"

"Well, don't you see it either, Dad?"

"Tell me what you see, son."

Andy stared at his father, pinching his brows, and then he looked out the window again.

"Well, it's right there, near the trunk of the blasted pine," Andy started. "It looks white. It flutters a bit. I think it's a blanket caught on the bushes."

"Does it glow? Is it brighter than everything else?" his father asked.

Andy was surprised. "Yes!" he said. "Strange, isn't it?"

Celia strained to see over her father's shoulder. Grant got up from his chair and walked back to the window. He stood between his father and Andy. "I still don't see a thing," Grant murmured, shaking his large head from side to side and drawing his lips tightly in.

"*Bana, Nisgam,* I can't see at all," Celia complained.

"Celia, put some fresh wood in the fire," her father said.

"You said you didn't want no more wood in the stove," Celia complained.

"Andy, I'm going to walk with you out to where that thing is and I don't want you to get scared."

"Why should I be scared?" Andy asked, alarmed.

"We can't see what you're seeing," his father answered, "but I know what it is. When you get close to it, it will try to frighten you. You mustn't run away."

"But it just looks like a blanket."

"Is Andy getting sick?" Celia asked.

"Bring the axe, Grant," the man ordered. "We're going outside."

"What's going on, Dad?" Grant asked as he put his coat on.

"Somebody is calling for Andy's help. Somebody we know is in trouble and Andy has to help," the man answered. He lifted his black woolen jacket from the nail in the wall and put it on. There was a troubled expression on his face, and his brows twitched uncontrollably. His complexion became paler and his jet black eyes glittered.

"What do I have to do?" Andy asked, and his question was a whisper and his eyes didn't want to know.

His father walked to the door, opened it and then yelled over the cold air rushing in, "You have to embrace it!"

Balls of shavings blew in circles over the planked floor. Wi'sis arched his back and hissed, spitting saliva toward the open door, before retreating under the stove again.

"But what is it anyway?" Grant shouted.

"Amalegne'j!" his father answered. "That is the Micmac name for it! Amalegne'j! It is a spirit!"

His father stepped outside. Grant followed him. Andy glanced out the window again. Whatever it was that he was seeing didn't look like a spirit to him. It was just some clothing stuck to a bush. And just because it glowed somewhat didn't really matter. A white bucket at the edge of the field glowed as much. Or was that only when the moon was full?

"You see it—don'tcha, Celia?" Andy asked his sister, who had returned to the window and was intently peering out.

"I'm trying real hard," she answered, brushing aside the long brown strands of hair that kept blowing across her face. "I never seen a spirit before. Why can't I see it, too? Is it wearing chains?"

Andy turned away in disgust. He didn't bother to put his jacket on. He glanced at the blazing lantern and walked straight out the door, oblivious to the frosty air. The image of the lantern followed him out the door as a splotch of violet superimposed on the blackness he stumbled into. For a few seconds he was blinded and then he could make out his father and Grant waiting for him. Grant looked terrified. His small bulging eyes stared at his father, as if looking at anything else would drain his lingering courage. Andy, after stepping outside, sensed a difference that he could not quite distinguish at first and for a moment he smiled foolishly at his father. Then it hit him. He felt that he was in another world—a world that resembled the ordinary world but was thick with the attendance of supernatural whispers and unsettling caresses. The wind was blowing, making the dry branches click together and the waves lunge against the rocks to spray the grassy bank. And the wind had a sheen to it. Andy could see its innumerable tentacles curling or rushing or stretching up to the treetops.

His father spoke but Andy didn't hear him. His father walked up to him and rasped into his right ear. "I know where it is," his father said. "I can see the bushes shaking. Go over to it. I will be close behind you. Do not run away when you get close to it. It will look at you. It has a terrifying face. No matter how scary it is, you have to put your arms around it. You have to embrace it. Nothing will happen to you."

Andy walked toward the apparition. His father followed behind him. Grant remained close to the door of the house. Celia's head darkened one corner of the window. As Andy got closer to the image, it became more distinct. The figure was just a bit over five feet tall, the same height as he. It was hunching slightly, its back to him.

"Son," Andy heard his father shout behind him, "Amalegne'j will turn its face to look at you once you get close to it! You can't look away from it! Just don't run away! Don't get scared! Embrace it, no matter how you feel! Somebody close to you needs your help—remember that!"

Andy was so numbed that his fear felt unfamiliar, yet a part of him was indifferent and curious to see what the spirit looked like. The last few steps were a blur to him. He no longer felt his legs and his motor skills functioned on their own. When he got to within arm's length of it, the spirit spun its head around and Andy felt an attack of nausea surging in his guts.

Amalegne'j appeared to have no face at first. But Andy quickly realized that this impression was due to the fact that its lips and eyelids were sewn shut. No sooner had Andy comprehended this bizarre feature when the seams that sealed the eyelids burst open, revealing two enormous eyes that pulsated and squirmed and were coated with a slimy film that reminded Andy of washed-up jellyfish going bad and turning yellowish gray. The eyes were like two yolks broken open from eggs that had matured and there was the color of blood and milky yellow in them. The pupils were mere specks of scarlet from which red veins discharged, cracked and wriggled. And the eyes were larger than a man's palms.

Andy recoiled from the unrelenting, piercing eyes, but even though he quickly snapped his head to his left, the eyes followed him and he felt as if he were impaled to his very core by their penetrating scrutiny. He shut his eyes and almost doubled over but the huge sickening eyes of the creature followed him behind his cupped hands and sealed eyelids. He wheeled around and yelled "Father! Father!" and flailed with his arms and still he could not escape the eyes. His fear escalated into panic and he was about to begin swinging wildly at the maddening eyes when he heard his father shouting, "It will disappear the very moment you embrace it, son! Do not run away! Do not strike it! Embrace it! Turn around and embrace it!" Andy reached out with his open arms trembling and stepped forward and he felt the wind streaming down his open collar and puffing out the back of his shirt. "Turn around! Turn around!" his father yelled.

Andy tried to yell, "I want to embrace the damned thing and be done with it but where is it?" He could not utter even a word, however, because his breathing came in fast, short gasps. He turned stiffly, making a perfect about-face, his back straight and his arms extended as if he were holding a boulder. With strained, bent legs, he staggered toward the fiend. He noticed that its head was once again joined with its body; and so, fearing that this opportunity to end his nightmare might mysteriously slip away from him, he lunged at the horror and threw his arms around it. He thought he heard the cat scream. Perhaps it was the wind. The thing he clung to shook violently for a moment and then its strength expired with a brisk wind that blasted through Andy's ribcage. Something moaned in the woods. A second later it moaned again and the moan was fainter, coming from deeper in the forest.

"Well done, son!" Andy heard his father yell. It took him a while to realize that his eyes were sealed shut. The darkness was never so welcome. He kept his eyes closed. He kept his head bowed. He did not dare to peep out from the corners of his eyes. Then he felt his father shaking him by his shoulders.

"Get up, son. You have to chop off this bush now."

Andy opened his eyes. He realized that he was hugging a willow bush. The wind had subsided. He was drenched in sweat and the muscles of his arms ached. Painfully he stretched his fingers out of their fisted curls. Slowly he straightened up and took in a robust chestful of the damp night air.

"Grant, bring the axe over here!" his father yelled.

Grant walked over from the house with the axe, and his father seized the axe from him and gave it to Andy. Grant stared at Andy. "*Nisgam nuduid,* you better put my coat on or you'll get sick," Grant said, taking his coat off and handing it to Andy.

"Well, you go back in the house, then, and make sure there's a good fire going in the stove," the father ordered Grant.

"Okay," murmured Grant, giving Andy one last looking over before walking back to the house. Andy stood still for a minute, his arms hanging limply at his sides, the head of the axe resting on the ground and its handle held loosely in his fingers.

"What happened here, Dad?" he finally asked.

His father wiped his lips with his fingers, stretching the sides of his mouth, and then scratched the stubble under his jaw. "I'll tell you what I know when you get back inside," his father said. "Make sure you chop that bush off right down to the ground. Then bring it inside."

Andy watched his father's back as he walked to the cabin. He saw his father unbutton his jacket, pull out a package of cigarettes from his shirt pocket, light one and then walk on, hunched and thoughtful, blowing out shapeless clouds of smoke and not the perfect rings he exhaled when he was relaxing.

Andy chopped the bush down and dragged it into the cabin. It was warm and very dry inside. Celia stared at him from the far end of the table. Grant had his right side to him, pumping the gas lantern that was on the table. His father was smoking and pacing the floor.

"Chop it up and throw all the pieces into the fire," his father told him.

Andy walked over to the square block and began to chop up the bush. He removed Grant's coat and hung it next to their father's jacket and then continued chopping the bush into small pieces. When he was done, he opened the door of the stove and threw the pieces of the willow bush into the blaze. Wi'sis raced out from under the stove and jumped onto Celia's lap. To Andy's surprise the fine willow sticks were not immediately consumed. They sat untouched over the flaming logs for a minute like thin rods of metal and then suddenly blackened and crumpled into ashes.

"It takes a strong fire," his father said.

Andy shut the door of the stove and returned to his seat next to the table.

"Now you two didn't see anything and you would like for Andy to tell you what he saw," his father said, eyeing Celia and Grant. "Hand me that chair, Grant. Thanks. I'm going to tell you what happened to me when I was a young man so you'll understand what happened tonight. It'll take Andy a long time for him to say what he saw because it's so hard to describe these things. Before I begin, I think we should all have some tea. Celia, bring out the cups and, Grant, you pour it out. I think the pot's too heavy and hot for her. Oh yeah, and don't forget to turn the damper a bit. We don't need a blazing fire now. Look at that, huh! *Me'gadu!* The stovepipe's just glowing red! Boys, it's hot in here. *Mogua,* don't open the door, Andy. Not for a while anyway. A little sweat is good for us. Fire cleanses. Thank you, Celia. Okay, that's good enough, Grant."

Their father drank a mouthful of black steaming tea. Grant, after pouring tea into all the cups, set the teapot on the part of the stove farthest from the fire. Their father stared at the floor, collecting his thoughts, and the children sat perfectly still, waiting. The delicious flavor of willow bark permeated the room. Their father lit another cigarette and then told his story, pausing for a drag every so often. From the very start, his voice was heavy and reluctant and his eyes stared out over his listeners' heads, glancing at them only occasionally.

"I was thirteen when I started working in the woods," he said. "I learned from your grandfather, my father. When I turned fifteen, I was already very smart with the axe. I went to work. There was a logging camp in the Miramichi. I found work there. I thought I was going to work as a logger but they made me a cook's assistant instead. Well, that was okay. Got to eat real good food and the lumberjacks liked my cooking. I didn't like it at first, though. The guy in charge of the mess hall had me peel all the potatoes. I did that for one week and I was ready to quit. I knew how to use the axe and I could cut as many cords as the next guy, I figured. When I threatened to leave, Dutchie—that was the head cook's name—a short man but almost as wide as he was tall, and I don't mean fat either, but just plain big-boned and husky—well, this Dutchie come up to me and put his big hairy hand on my shoulder and asked me if I could cook. And I told him, sure I could. I cooked a few dishes that I knew and the guys enjoyed it but Dutchie taught me quite a bit more about cooking than I knew. I got to be good friends with Dutchie. He didn't live in camp. He had his house across the river. I went to visit him all the time.

"Now Dutchie had a wife and a daughter. The girl was eleven. She had long dark hair and big round eyes. She really got to like me. Every time I paid Dutchie and his family a visit, I would bring along some present for the girl. She was like my baby sister. She even started calling me Uncle Jimmy. She was a very special person. She could tell stories just like an adult. Both Dutchie and his wife would listen to her when she told her stories. *E'he.* I can still see them sitting in that cozy living room they had. It was funny—Dutchie's wife was taller than him. Their daughter talked about things I never had, like going to school and talking to teachers and learning to read and write. I was young and sometimes I walked back to the camp thinking about learning all that stuff. I'd tell myself that I still could do it 'cause I wasn't old. *Nisgam,* I had crazy daydreams but I liked it. Seemed like a whole new world was just an arm's reach away.

"Winter times I could walk across the frozen river instead of going the long way around and using the bridge. I wanted to pay Dutchie and his family a visit but a storm blew over. I heard that his daughter was sick. I bought some things for her—you know, sweets and stuff—but I couldn't take it to her. I had to wait for the storm to blow over. And it stormed for about five days straight, I think. The last day of the storm wasn't freezing cold. It was a wet snowfall. Perfect for making snowballs. Bad for snowshoeing. When the storm was over, I waited all day for this wet snow to freeze over so I could walk over it. By nightfall I figured the crust was hard enough. I started walking across the wide river straight toward Dutchie's house. I hadn't seen Dutchie all week. Another fellow took over for him. The same guy that had set me to work peeling potatoes when I first started there. I missed Dutchie. It was a dark night. The frozen crust held me up pretty good.

"Now I got to about halfway across the river when I noticed

something white and shiny, sorta flapping in the breeze a good ways ahead of me. I didn't know what it was. It was right in my way, so I kept on walking toward it. When I got close to it, I thought it was a man wrapped in a white blanket. Of course, I became concerned for the poor fellow. Maybe he was lost and freezing. That's what I thought when I seen that blanket. But it wasn't a blanket. It glowed. I didn't think nothing of it, though. You know, when something strange comes up to you, the first thing you try to do is make it into something you know. That's what your mind does, see. Even if something isn't quite right—if your mind thinks it has figured it all out, well, then it'll just ignore all the little things that aren't right. So there I was, thinking I could help some guy who was lost and freezing in the middle of the river. I even figured that it would be shorter to take him back to camp than to go the rest of the way to Dutchie's house.

"So I walked right up to the guy. He looked like he was crouching a bit. That only made me more sure that he was shivering. 'Hey, are you okay?' I said and I reached out for him. Then he turned his head around so fast that I almost choked on my heart. He wasn't a human! He was the scariest-looking spirit I had ever seen! Its mouth and eyes were sewn shut. Then its eyes flew open, and the busted seams fluttered around like so many twisted eyelashes. *Nisgam nuduid*, and the eyes! It had eyes the size of saucers. Big yellow eyes that glowed. They beat like hearts! They looked shiny and sickening. Red veins ran all over them. The pupils looked like blood clots in the centers of those slimy eyes! And they stared right into my soul! Stared with hard, angry eyes! I was so shocked that I didn't even think what I was doing. I just punched the creature's head. I just reacted. Then I took off back to camp and I didn't even look back once."

The man paused to drink more tea and light another cigarette. Again he studied the floor for a long time, then he raised his head and looked past his young listeners. His gleaming black eyes looked pained. He squinted, shielding his eyes from his children.

"I knew what it was. Right after I had swung at it, I knew what it was," he confessed. "But I took a shot at it without even pausing to think—so I haven't changed, humph! Yes, yes, yes . . . I prayed all night but it didn't help. How could it? I was sick to my stomach, knowing I would find out something horrible the next day. I had heard stories about the spirit called Amalegne'j, the Sheeted One. When I finally fell asleep, it was very late, so I woke up late and I had to rush to the mess hall and get to work. It wasn't long before word got to us at the camp that Dutchie's daughter had died. I walked away from camp. I walked out to middle of the river. There was a snowman standing there with half of its head on its shoulders and the other half on the snow beside it. I cried. I cried. I cried and I swore that if I ever had a daughter that I would name her Celia. That was Dutchie's daughter's name—Celia. Amalegne'j appeared to me because Celia needed my help and she felt I was the one who loved her and was brave enough to save her. But I got too scared."

The man paused again.

Celia's eyes were wide with revelation. She whispered, "Love needs courage, then."

"But why are its eyes sewn shut, Dad?" Andy asked.

"Amalegne'j, the Sheeted One, is one name by which it is called," the man replied. "The other name for it is Eli'sasid, the Sewn One. Many of our people still prepare the corpses. The only way they can close the mouth and eyes is by sewing them shut."

"Brrrr!" Celia shuddered.

"When you were born," their father continued, looking at Celia, his voice now detached and matter-of-fact, "I kept my promise to that girl and I named you Celia. As for what Andy's done tonight, I have only to say that we'll probably never find out who of our loved ones he saved. Our people are scattered all over Nova Scotia, New Brunswick and Maine at this time of year and we won't be getting together again till early summer. Now light that lantern, Grant, and hang it up on that beam. I need more light here if I'm going to see what I'm doing. And then I want all of you to start sanding the pieces you've shaved so far."

Grant struck a wooden match, stuck it inside the glass of the gas lantern and turned two valves. The gas leaked out in a hiss and then a ball of blue fire swelled inside the glass before the flames gathered into the mantle and became a white, blinding ball of light. The incessant snoring of two gas lanterns brought a lull to the cabin. The sandpaper scraping the hardwood was barely audible. Only their father shaping another rough-cut with the axe and the sparks popping in the stove could be heard.

"Who do you think it was?" Andy finally asked, and for a moment he wasn't sure if he had only thought the question. The breathing of the gas lanterns hushed everything else. Neither Grant nor Celia responded. They had their heads bowed and their hands intently worked smoothness into the wood.

Andy's father paused from his work. He let the head of the axe rest on the square block, then he turned his head while still bent over and looked at Andy and said, "I don't know, son. You did the right thing . . . Maybe it was your mother." Then he went back to work, shaping the hard white stick of ash.

Anita Endrezze is an award-winning Yaqui Indian writer who received a master of arts degree from Eastern Washington University. Her book *at the helm of twighlight* won both the Weyerhauser/ Bumbershoot Award and the Washington Governor's Writers Award for the best book of poetry in 1992 and 1993, respectively. Her poetry and short fiction have appeared in publications in France, the United States, and Canada, including *Words in the Blood, Anthology of 20th Century Native American Poetry, Poesie Presents, Zyzzyva,* and *Poetry Northwest.* In addition, her work has appeared in the Anchor Books anthology *Earth Song, Sky Spirit* and in Joy Harjo's much-acclaimed *Reinventing the Enemy's Language.* Endrezze has recently completed a collection of short stories entitled *The Humming of Stars and Bees & Waves.* She lives with her family in Spokane, Washington, where she is a well-known professional writer, teacher, and storyteller.

Anita Endrezze

# Darlene and the Dead Man

I COULDN'T FIGURE HER OUT. MY SISTER DID EVERYTHING wrong: ate too much chocolate, drank too much whiskey, had too many lovers, and she was happy, slim, and beautiful. I dieted, drank herbal tea, and had been married to Sonny for twenty-eight years. I was often sad, bewildered by life, whereas Darlene was always laughing.

Sitting across from me at the dining room table, she tapped her finger impatiently against the side of a card. We were playing gin rummy. This was our "girls' night." Sonny was out bowling and Darlene was talking about her latest, Guy.

"He told me he was taking me to Moscow for breakfast," she said, picking up the nine of spades. "I was so excited, you can imagine. I was trying to figure what to wear. I mean, isn't it pretty cold there all the time? Anyway, when I told him that I didn't know he spoke Russian, he looked at me kinda funny."

I laid down four queens. As I discarded, she continued.

"Well, I told him I didn't have a passport, and that's when I found out he was only taking me to Moscow, Idaho!" Darlene laughed and laid down her last card. I picked up all the cards and started shuffling again.

"I thought I had finally hit the jackpot with Guy," she went on. "I mean, he seemed rich. He drove a BMW. But I found out he had just rented it to impress me. He really drove an old Chevy truck. Who wants another cowboy?"

"Don't you think it's kind of sweet, Darlene, that he was trying to impress you?" I asked.

As I dealt, Darlene took a sip of the iced herbal tea I had made. Sonny doesn't allow alcohol in our house, because his dad was a drunk, so Darlene has to dry out one night a week when she comes to visit me. She grimaced as she tasted it, or maybe it was her response to my question.

She waved her hands. "I expected honesty. How can you build a relationship if there's no honesty?"

I assumed this was a rhetorical question, since Darlene practiced situational ethics. Her ideas on what was right and wrong certainly differed from mine. She usually jumped into bed with a man on the second date. I couldn't understand that at all.

"Well," I said, "you've only known Guy, what, a month or so?" When she nodded, I went on: "So you didn't really get a chance to know him very well."

Since this was what I always told her, she ignored me. Because I was the older sister, I felt it was my duty to point things out to her.

"Darlene, can't you just take things a little slower? Get to know a man before you become intimate? Then you wouldn't always get so disappointed."

She groaned. "No lectures, Marlene, let's just play gin."

So we played quietly for a while. I thought about how different we were. Just look how we dressed. I was wearing an old sweatshirt and stretch jeans. She was all dressed up in a low-necked red dress and red high heels. I suspected she was meeting someone after our evening together.

It's not that I begrudged her some fun. She worked as a teacher's aide most of the year for low wages. In the summer when school was out, she was a waitress at a tavern.

I did some part-time work, cleaning two local businesses, but I didn't really have to work. Sonny's office supply business was doing pretty good. We had some lean years, of course, in the beginning, but now things were okay. Darlene never seemed to resent my success; I always felt a little guilty about it, though. I guess it was because she was my little sister. I still wanted to take care of her.

Finally, she stretched and shoved her cards into a pile. "Gotta go. Thanks for a fun evening, sis."

She stood up, looking around for her purse. Then she gave me a peck on the cheek and let herself out the door. I gathered up the glasses and the bowls we had used for the popcorn, put the cards back into the case, and thought about checking on my son, Gary, who was upstairs watching a video in his room.

Suddenly, though, there was a banging at the door and Darlene was screaming. I opened it quickly, frightened. She pushed her way in, slammed the door shut, and locked it, her teeth chattering.

"Darlene! What's wrong?"

Her mouth opened, but nothing came out. She pointed at the telephone.

"What?"

She took a deep breath. "Call the police! There's a dead man in my car!"

"Have you been drinking?" Had she been sneaking some liquor into the tea? I wondered.

"No, you idiot! There's a dead man out there!"

She punched in the numbers for 911 and spoke quickly to the operator. I didn't know what to think. I looked out the windows, but it was dark, of course, and there was no way I was going out there by myself.

"What am I going to do?" she said, coming over to stand next to me. "I just washed the car yesterday. What if he's bleeding? Or he puked? Oh, I can't believe it. What's he doing in my car? Well, he's not *doing* anything, he's just being dead in my car. But what can he be thinking? It's *my* car!"

I thought she was hysterical, but with Darlene you can never be sure. She kept on chattering, while I wondered whether I should slap her or throw cold water in her face. "I mean, I never win anything, and now look. It's my fate to end up with a dead man for a date."

"You mean you know him?" I asked. Maybe there was some sense to this.

"No, of course not," she said. "But it must be my karma to be surrounded by dead men. Most could pass for dead in bed if I wasn't giving mouth-to-mouth, know what I mean?"

I shook my head.

"What is it with guys these days? Where are all the good men?" she wailed.

This was a familiar song, but not what I wanted to hear now. Where were the police? We both stared out the windows, waiting.

Years ago, when Darlene had just gotten divorced, she went hunting for a car. We offered to go with her, but she wanted to do it herself. As usual. We shrugged and crossed our fingers.

Two days later, she called up. She'd found her car.

"It's an old one-eyed, half-rusted, sway-backed, exhaust-poppin', bumper-knockin', tail-draggin', seat-saggin' '76 Pinto." After taking a breath, she added, "With possibilities."

Since she was dating a country music singer at the time, I took her description with a grain of salt. I did ask her, though, if she'd test-driven it.

"Well, sure, and the windshield wipers work."

"Darlene, what about the engine? What kind of shape is it in?"

"It has an eternal combustion engine," she reported proudly.

I laughed. "That's internal, not eternal."

"Okay, so I'm not up on all that technical stuff." She sounded annoyed. "But the radio works and it has a blue battery."

"Darlene . . ."

"Look, I'm coming over in ten minutes, sis."

I heard her nine minutes before I saw her. There was a sound in the air like a St. Bernard coughing up a hair ball. Then followed a stuttering burst of hiccups. Finally, she chugged into the driveway, her body swaying forward as if she were Betty Rubble, pedaling her Stone Age car with her feet.

When she stopped, the Pinto burped a few times and then shuddered, rust and dust floating down around it until there was a perfect outline of a car in my driveway. The Pinto was partially primed. I thought it looked diseased, leprous and scabby. I carefully looked into the window. The seats were cracked vinyl. Wires hung down from under the dash. There was a bullet hole in the passenger window.

I inspected the tires. Slick as the salesman who had sold it to her.

I tugged on a door until it opened. She warned me about looking inside the glove compartment.

"A mouse and her family live in there."

I jumped back a little. She admitted that the floor was rusted out in spots. Lifting the driver's side floor mat, she revealed a piece of cardboard. Under that was nothing but the driveway!

"Don't worry," she assured me. "I've got plans for this car."

A week later she drove up again, surprising us just as we finished dinner. We rushed out to the porch.

Darlene stood by her "new" car, face beaming. She'd had a vision, she said, that this car was full of good medicine. It had revealed its Manifold Destiny; its spirit was strong and walked in beauty.

"It's a machine," Gary scoffed.

Darlene rolled her eyes, remarking, "Gary's at that difficult age, isn't he?"

I sighed, my shoulders sagging. Apparently, she'd sprayed the car white, then painted big russet-brown blotches all over. She walked around it, talking, slapping the "rump," and showing us the tail made from a cheerleader's old orange pompom that was fastened over the rear license plate.

She'd covered the seats with old saddle blankets and hung a feather from the mirror. The floor was meticulously clean except for the bottles of Jim Beam in the back, which I suspected was the spirit part of her spiritual revelation. "Whaddya think?" she asked. We were silent, lost in apparent admiration, she thought.

"Look, Mom!" Gary pointed to the two eyes she had painted on the hood. Sonny and I bit our lips to keep from laughing. He started choking and ran into the house, mumbling about a drink of water.

Darlene stood tall and proud. "Nothing bad will ever happen to me in this car," she prophesied.

Now, I knew why there were no medicine women in our family. Generations of displacement from our original homeland had left us sadly lacking any kind of spiritual connections. We were city Indians, clueless and innocent, believing that any belief was better than nothing. Darlene's prophesy was wishful thinking, ghost-shirt thinking, and left us unprepared for what was happening.

There was a cop in my yard. His car came to a fast stop and he got out cautiously. Suddenly he jumped. He was looking at a car that was looking back at him.

Darlene cracked the front door open and called out, "There's a dead man in my car!"

The cop jerked at the driver's door. When it opened, a body rolled out. The cop fell backward, hitting his head on Gary's bicycle. As the officer tried to get up, he got one hand stuck between the front-wheel spokes. He shook the bike, slipped and fell down again.

I nearly screamed when Gary muttered behind me, "Hey what's that cop doing to my bike!"

"Go back to bed, Gary," I ordered. The last thing I wanted was for my son to see a dead body.

Darlene grabbed his hand. "There's a dead guy out there," she announced.

"Darlene!" I was irritated with her.

"Cool, can I see?" asked Gary, craning his head for a view.

"I think he rolled under the car," she said. "I can't see it, er, him."

"Go to bed Gary!" I told him.

"Maybe we should help the cop look for the body," he suggested. I gave in. He never listens to me; he's fifteen.

The three of us crammed our way through the doorway, stepping out onto the porch. The cop was standing up, confused. He looked all around him. Nothing. He got on his knees and peered under the car. No body. Slowly, he got up and turned to face us. We stared, mouths open, looking incredibly stupid.

The next half hour was chaotic. More cops showed up and asked us too many questions. Darlene offered her sympathy to the cop who had lost the body.

"I didn't lose it," he insisted.

Gary told them all about a sci-fi movie he'd once seen where a corpse disappeared from a coroner's table, only to turn up as a bride in a wedding procession. And I just told them what happened, the "plain facts, ma'am," and nobody listened to me, either.

The cops were suspicious of us at first. I thought they were spending an awful lot of time with Darlene, but I guess they had to check her story. Finally, they started leaving.

Only one cop hung back, talking to my sister, but he soon left, too.

Darlene strolled over to us, smiling. "He asked me out this Friday. Isn't he cute?"

Gary grinned at her. "Is that the one who asked you about your priors?"

Darlene tried to shush him, but I wanted to know what he was talking about. "Priors, as in prior *arrests*, Darlene?"

She made a face. "Oh, that."

"Talk." I think I must've sounded like Mama because she took a slight step back, thrusting her hands behind her the way she used to do when she was hiding forbidden sweets.

"Okay, well, it's no big deal, really. Once I was arrested for protesting the clear-cutting up at Baldwin's Mountain."

I considered this. Sounded worthy. Even noble. But, no, wait, this is Darlene we're talking about.

"What happened?" I asked.

Gary answered for her. "I heard her say she was dressed up like a tree and threw herself on the mercy of the loggers."

"Well . . . it was actually only one logger and he didn't get hurt too bad. We're friends now and everything." I gave her a questioning look. She explained, "See, my costume was made out of green lightbulbs and some of them broke when . . ."

"Never mind," I said. "I shouldn't've asked. So, what else?"

"The other arrest was just a silly thing, not worth talking about, really," she stalled. I finally managed to drag it out of her. She'd been arrested for defacing private property. Apparently, she'd spray-painted a tavern called The Town on Main Street.

"Why?" I asked, not sure I really wanted to know.

She managed to look both smug and embarrassed at the same time. "I was painting the town red."

Gary hooted, then ducked his head when I glared at him.

It's never been easy having Darlene for a sister. There were just the three of us after Mom got divorced, and we moved around a lot. Mom had to work all day, sometimes even weekends, and I was responsible for Darlene. She did whatever she wanted and then I got in trouble for not watching her. I remember there were times when I *hated* her. As I looked at her now, both in fondness and exasperation, I wondered if she had ever grown up and if that was such a bad thing after all. Excitement seemed to follow her like a puppy off a leash.

When headlights turned in at our driveway, we thought at first it was the police returning. Then we recognized Sonny's car.

"Uh-oh," muttered Darlene.

Gary ran out to meet his dad, trying to tell him what had happened. Teenagers aren't noted, though, for their logical train of thought, and his highly mangled version ended with this statement: "And then the police lost Darlene's body."

Sonny stared in disbelief. "But she's right here!"

"No," Gary explained, "not that body, her other body!"

"Somebody better tell me what's going on," Sonny suggested. We all marched into the house. I told him everything quickly. He kept shaking his head.

"And you actually saw a body, Marlene?" he finally asked. I noted that he hadn't asked my sister or son.

"Yes, I did. Whether he was dead or not, I don't know, but a body rolled out of her car."

Suddenly Gary jumped up from the sofa. "Dad! Dad! What if he's a zombie and in our backyard?"

"Don't be ridiculous, Gary." Sonny thought a moment. "On the other hand, what if this guy was just drunk and wandering around. I better check the house."

He grabbed his bowling bag and unzipped it, taking out the midnight-blue ball with the pearly swirls.

"You girls stay here," he ordered, then added, "You, too, Gary."

"Awww, Dad!" Gary protested.

"For Pete's sake," Darlene said. She flopped down on the sofa.

Sonny gripped the ball in the classic bowler's position, fingers in the holes and tight to the chest. He began to patrol the house. First we heard him in the kitchen, opening the refrigerator, then the oven and pantry.

"Bet he checks the toaster," Darlene said. Then she asked me if I had any cooking sherry. I shook my head.

"I'm getting my bat and helping him," said Gary. I put my hand on his arm. I could just see him coming around a corner and scaring the bejesus out of his father.

"You stay here," I told him as I heard Sonny check the bathroom (toilet flushing) and the bathtub (curtain sliding). Then he went upstairs. Doors slammed. Drawers banged shut. The old floors creaked and groaned.

Our Siamese cat came skidding around the corner, paws slipping on the hardwood floor, tail fluffed up like a bottle brush.

Finally, Sonny returned. He wiped the ball down carefully before putting it back into the bag. Then he stood up, sucked in his stomach, and announced that we were safe.

The next day I returned home from grocery shopping and found Darlene sitting on my porch steps. She had a magnifying glass in one hand and Gary's baseball bat in the other.

"And just what are you up to?" I asked, sounding more and more like our mother every day. But I knew Darlene was doing something stupid. I saw a can of talcum powder at her feet and figured she was playing detective.

She raised her chin. "I was out looking around. Did you know someone's been camping in the gully?"

She pointed to the northeastern part of our property. The gully was thick with wild rose bushes, tall maples, pine trees, and sour Oregon grape. On the other side, basalt cliffs rose one hundred feet up to a mesa where new houses were slowly being built. We lived on land once owned by a pioneer doctor. He had built our house as a vacation retreat, someplace in the woods he could visit, away from his busy practice.

"It's probably just kids playing," I replied. I started taking sacks out of the car.

"Let's go check it out," she suggested.

So, after we put away the groceries, we tramped over to the gully. I was worried, though.

"What if some bum's camped out there, some guy on speed, or just out of the mental hospital?" I stopped walking.

Darlene raised the bat and shook it. "Hey, are we warrior women or not?"

"Not," I said. "Maybe we should call the police."

"Sure, and whaddya think? They'll come all the way out here to look at an old campfire?" She stared at me.

Okay, she had a point. "Come on," I said. As we walked, I asked her what she hoped to find.

"See if I can find some fingerprints on some rocks or something, and compare them to one I found in my car."

"But . . . isn't it kinda hard to compare fingerprints, Dar? I mean, you can't just look at them and tell, can you?"

"Oh, just come on, will ya?" She hated it when I was logical. I shrugged and followed her.

We slid down the grassy slopes, grabbing on to tree limbs, until we found a faint trail. Darlene went first. I was thinking about the dangers of forest fires and hoping whoever was using the site as a camp had some common sense.

We found the spot. It wasn't much, just a few fire-burnt rocks in a circle with a metal grill over them. A couple of beer cans, some candy wrappers. My sister stirred the ashes with a stick. Then she spread the talcum powder on the grill and rocks, knelt down, and gently blew. Of course, nothing remained but sticky talcum and ashes.

"Oh well," she said, her mouth turned down at the corners. "Guess you were right. Let's go back. I'm thirsty."

I followed her again, noticing how she still had a nice figure. Her jeans looked good on her. I'd been working my way up the sizes until I was too embarrassed to reveal what size I wore. I struggled up the path.

The rocks, chunks of basalt, crumbled underfoot. I grabbed a clump of grass to steady myself, when all at once the clump broke loose and I tumbled backward. I fell on my hip, then slid, rolling over.

"Geez, sis, are you okay?" Darlene scrambled down to my side and helped me up.

I felt a little shaky. My hands were scraped raw, dirty and bloody. My pants were torn on one leg where a sharp rock had slashed through to the skin, leaving a long and painful cut. I could feel tears running down my cheeks and wiped them awkwardly on my shoulders. It hurt to bend my head. With Darlene holding on to me, I hobbled back to the house, using the bat as a crutch.

We washed the cuts. Everything stung. I felt awful. I hate looking at blood or bruises. I always think I'm going to faint. I was never any good at tending to the kids' injuries; it was Sonny who had bandaged and comforted them when they were little.

Darlene looked at me. "Now's the time when a little booze might help."

"Boy, don't I know it." I thought for a moment. "Okay, just this once. I have a bottle hidden behind the clothes dryer."

She sat down next to me at the kitchen table. "You know, this is your house, too. Why does Sonny have to dictate your life? Why do you have to hide the liquor?"

I didn't answer. We'd been over this before. The bottle of wine behind the dryer was for those days when Gary drove me crazy or I was feeling a little low. I'd put it there a month ago and it was still half-full.

She shook her head, then got up and left. I limped into the living room, moving stiffly, and settled down on the sofa.

When she returned, she had the bottle and two water glasses. She sat down in the chair across from me, placed the glasses on the coffee table, and poured the wine. It was a merlot from a regional vineyard. I loved its dark red color.

"Sis, let me ask you something." Darlene cocked her head. "Are you afraid of Sonny?"

I laughed. "No! How could you think that? Sonny's the gentlest man I've ever known, and you should know that, too."

"Then why do you let him tell you what to do?"

"If you're talking about the wine, then it's because I'm sensitive to his fears." I took a sip. "Look, you know how his father was drunk all the time. He hated it. But he was always worried that he might turn out like that, too. So I don't think it's a great hardship if we don't have liquor in the house."

"Yeah, but . . ." she paused, not looking at me.

"What?"

"I thought that you two had a great relationship, but you're lying to him. You're not being honest when you hide the bottle."

I put my glass down. "You're right. I should tell him. I know by now that he won't turn into an alcoholic and he knows it, too. On the other hand, Dar, even though we have a good relationship, I don't tell him everything."

"You don't?" She was amazed. She took a big swallow of wine, by now a tad sour. "Hmm. Good wine. What don't you tell him?"

"Oh," I said vaguely, "just things." When she raised her eyebrows, I continued. "Well, like my feelings. Sometimes I don't tell him what I'm thinking because, oh, because it's just better that way."

"What do you mean?"

I talked slowly, sipping now and then. "Sonny and I are close, but I still am me. We're a couple, yes, but I have my own thoughts and feelings and sometimes I don't want to share them. I don't want to lose myself. I don't want Sonny's opinions to be mine. I want my own ideas."

She nodded. "Okay."

We were quiet for a while, drinking, listening to the silence. What I hadn't told her was that I'd found early in my marriage that Sonny couldn't understand all my feelings. Whether it was because he was a man or because of his bad childhood, I didn't know. And part of me was glad at my discovery. I liked thinking my own thoughts. I'd never been a talkative woman anyway.

Darlene poured a little more wine into my glass. She filled hers up to the top.

"Hey," I cautioned.

"I'm okay. I can handle it."

"I'm more worried about you than Sonny," I admitted. "You seem to drink too much."

"Me?" She gave me a look of mock surprise.

"Yeah, you. Let me ask *you* a question." I waited for her to nod. "Why do you drink so much?"

"Well, first of all, I don't drink too much."

"Darlene, your car's always full of bottles, the hard stuff. I get so worried and mad, thinking you'll kill yourself—or someone else—if you're drunk while you're driving."

She looked startled. "Those bottles are from work!"

I was puzzled. "So?"

"Roger gives them to me. See, I take them over to the recycling center and cash them in. Some months I get an extra hundred bucks that way."

Roger was her boss. I couldn't believe I'd been so stupid. Why hadn't I asked her about this before instead of assuming the wrong thing? I could feel my face flushing.

"Gee, Dar, I'm sorry, I thought . . ."

"Yeah, yeah. I know. You think I'm the party-hearty girl." She sounded bitter. "It makes it easier for you that way."

I frowned.

"Sure," she went on. "You're the good girl. I'm the bad girl. Makes life simple, doesn't it?"

"Wait a minute!" I tried to sit up. My knee ached. I groaned. "I think you're way off base here."

"Am I?" She took another swallow of wine. "Think about it. When we were growing up, you and Mom always talked things over together. I was left out. You didn't want to listen to me. Nobody did. So I made sure I got your attention, one way or another."

I was stunned. "Darlene, Mom and I talked about things because we didn't want to burden you with problems. I was old enough, Mom thought, to know that life wasn't easy. She needed someone to talk to. Mom was all alone, you know, except for us. I guess she thought you were too little. She wanted to make your life a happy one. If you want to know the truth, I hated her telling me how hard things were. I got so scared. We never had enough money and she was always worried. I wanted to be a little girl, too, but I never had the chance."

We both looked at each other. She spoke first.

"I never knew you felt that way."

I was close to tears. Thinking about it had brought back the memories of Mom crying at night, her thin shoulders shaking. I remember rubbing her back, trying to comfort her, offering her my milk money. She'd only cry harder at that, her head bowed down over her folded hands.

I took a drink. "Well, that was a long time ago." I tried a smile but it didn't quite work.

Darlene came over to me. She gave me a hug. "You know," she whispered, "I do drink a little more than I should. I just get so lonely. And I remember Mom crying, only for years I thought it was part of the night. 'Cuz that's when I heard her, at night, when I was sleeping, and sometimes now I'm afraid to go to sleep. I take a little drink, then another, trying to sleep."

"We thought you didn't hear us." I held on to her. "Mom waited until you were asleep to tell me about the bills or the guys that bothered her at work or about how afraid she was that she'd die and there would be no one to take care of us girls."

We sat holding each other's hands, thinking about those times.

We'd move from one house to another, sometimes in the middle of the night. No rent money, you see. Once I'd left my favorite doll in the backyard but we couldn't go back to get it.

We drank quietly. She poured some more for me. I kept drinking. I didn't really care if I got a little tipsy. It felt nice.

We were Yaquis, living in Spokane, Washington, far from our tribal homeland in northern Mexico. For generations our family had been on the move. South to Durango to work in the silver mines. East to hide in the Sierra Madre Mountains, where the Mexican soldiers couldn't follow. West to the coast, where our grandfather traded his goods from the backs of burros. And finally north to the United States when conditions in Sonora got so bad that the only choice was to leave or die. Then the constant search for work: in the fields, orchards, and fish canneries of Southern California.

Now, my children would have a better future. I should have been able to relax, to stop worrying, but I couldn't. Maybe it was genetic by now. A worry gene. In spite of myself I giggled.

"What?" asked Darlene. When I told her, she smiled, nodding. "That's what makes us strong, you know. We remember the past."

We clinked our glasses together. The bottle was empty. How did it get that way? I blinked. The room seemed to be on rockers, tipping and tilting first one way, then another.

"Dar . . ." I started to speak but she shushed me, looking at the window. She got up and inched her way to the curtains. She parted them slowly and peered out.

"Marlene! He's back, the dead guy's back!" She dropped the curtains and flattened herself against the wall.

I tried to stand up. My knees were making little circles that my feet couldn't follow. I put my hand out where the wall should've been, but someone must've moved it. I lurched forward.

"Cripes," Darlene said. She grabbed my hand, steadying me. "I forgot you're not used to drinking."

"I'm not drunk," I protested. "I never get drunk."

"Yeah, right." We walked side by side to the window and looked out. She was right. There he was, sprawled out on the front hood of her car.

"Wha'll we do?" I asked. "Poleesh?" I swallowed and tried again. "Po-lice?"

"They'll think we're crying wolf again. No, I have a better idea."

She started for the door. I grabbed her T-shirt.

"Wait! You can't go out there. There's something fishy . . ."

She pulled free and went out the door, so what could I do but follow her?

He was a big man, Indian, wearing a red ribbon shirt and old blue jeans. He wore his braided hair long with strips of red cloth. He was spread-eagle across the hood, right between the painted-on eyes. His own eyes were closed. He looked peaceful. I guess if you're dead, you don't mind Darlene's car so much.

She was rummaging in the trunk. I edged away from the dead man and went to her.

"I'm going to take him to the police, then they'll believe me."

I tried to shake my head, but it hurt. "What do you mean?" I asked.

"I'm going to tie him to the hood and drive him to the police station."

"You mean, the way hunters tie up deer?" I must have been really drunk. It sounded like a good idea.

"Yep."

We walked around to the front of the car. She threw the rope over him and I caught one end.

"Tie it to the bumper," she said.

My knee hurt. I couldn't kneel, so she did it for me. I stood back up, dizzy. I thought for a second that he moved.

"Darlene!"

"Here." She threw the rope over him again. I pulled it tight across his chest.

"Hey!" I yelled. "He groaned."

She finished tying the knot. "Dead bodies make all sorts of noises. Something to do with gases and decomposing."

I gagged.

"Okay," she said. "Let's go."

She got in the car, but my door was warped and wouldn't budge. She stretched her legs across the passenger seat and kicked the door open. The dead guy shuddered. His head was on the windshield. I could see his right ear. The sun was shining through the top curve and it reminded me of a reddish seashell I'd once found.

Darlene stuck her keys in the ignition. The car trembled, then coughed and died. Muttering, she pumped the pedal, pulled out the choke, and pumped again. When it started, the car felt as if it had the dry heaves. I clutched my stomach.

"Adjust the choke," she said. As I reached over, the car bucked and I fell against her. Her elbow knocked the windshield wiper button. The wipers began sweeping back and forth, beating against the dead man's ears. His head swayed slightly from one side to the other. Then the car died again. I sensed a weird relationship between the man and the car.

"Well, shit," Darlene said. "C'mon."

"Now what?"

"I have to check under the hood." She opened her door. "We gotta untie him and roll him off the hood."

"No way." I shook my head. "No way."

We looked at him. He was older than I'd thought at first, but maybe I was just getting sober. His face had settled into his bones, so that he seemed sharper, more in focus. It was a strong face, with deep lines from the corners of his nose to his mouth. Graying eyebrows, skin wrinkled around the eyes, and a day's growth of white hair on his jaw.

Now that I was thinking better, I knew something was wrong. What was he doing up there? Who put him there? How did he die? Or, I said to myself as I saw his chest move, was he really dead?

I squinted. I was sure his chest had moved. There! It moved again, the braids rising slightly.

"Look!" I pointed at him.

Darlene was busy with the knots. "Hmmm?"

Before I could say a word, she threw the rope to me. As it arced over his head, he opened his eyes.

Darlene's mouth fell open. I gasped. We grabbed each other. He lifted his head a bit and blinked.

"Am I dead yet?" he asked. "I thought it was a good day to die, like they say in the movies."

I gulped.

A tear trickled down his cheek. "I wanted to die." His head fell back with a small thud.

My sister pulled the last of the rope off, letting it fall to the ground. He stared up at the sky, continuing to talk.

"I'm not dead, am I? No, I can see clouds and sky. And I'm still me." He touched his chest and thighs. "I wanted to die and be a horse. Some people say you can do that, you know, die and be reborn."

"A horse?" I couldn't believe my ears.

"Yes. A horse made of clouds and thunder, belly like a drum, hooves like sparks of black moons." He had a deep voice. "I want to be beautiful."

Darlene put her hand on her hip. "Get off my car."

He lifted himself up, leaning on one elbow. "This here Pinto car is a sign, see? It's pointing the way toward my rebirth."

"Bullshit!" Darlene hollered at him. "It's my car. You can't die on it. Now get off."

He tried to sit up. "Aww, my ears hurt." He looked puzzled. I stole a look at Darlene. She had picked up the rope and was coiling it around her arm.

"You're drunk," she said.

He shook his head. "There's lots of spirit horses here." He gestured widely, taking in my yard and house with the sweep of his hands. "This is a holy place. I feel the spirits talking to me."

"You're drunk," she repeated.

"I have visions, always have." He started crying. "Wanted to be a medicine man just like my grandfather, but the wind won't stand still and I forget things." He rubbed his eyes. Slowly, he sat up, legs dangling off the hood. His head hung down. "I want to do great things. Help people. Be someone. Even trees have hearts and a place to grow strong. But me, I don't have roots and my heart's sawdust."

Darlene was thoughtful. "Say, what's your name?"

He sniffed. "Arnold Lost His Horses."

More like Lost His Marbles, I thought. Our family didn't have any colorful Indian names, just Mexicanized ones like Hernández and Ortiz. His name sounded phony to me.

But Darlene's eyes widened. "You're Arnie? Hey, I've heard about you."

She whispered to me. "He's a hermit, lives in the hills, wherever. He's harmless, kinda holy, but only out of simplemindedness."

I was doubtful. "Is that really his last name?"

She nodded. "Way I heard it, one of his ancestors was a gambler. Lost all of the family's horses, and they got so poor, the women had to beg at the forts. From that point, the family went downhill. 'Course, the way they were pushed off their land by the Homestead Act was part of their troubles." She lowered her voice. "He was the oldest of five kids, and his mother died of TB when he was seventeen. His father was killed in some kind of mill accident the year before, so Arnie was left with all those kids to take care of. Then, I think, one of his brothers was killed in Vietnam. A sister disappeared, never saw her again. Another brother died in a car accident. I don't know what happened to the others, but he's the only one left."

She walked over to him and offered him a glass of water. "You stay here and I'll be right back."

He nodded without looking at her. We both hurried into the house.

"Look, Dar, I don't like him out there. He scares me. I don't want him hanging around here. I'm sorry about what happened to him in his life, but he seems a little 'off,' you know, and I got my family to worry about . . ."

In the kitchen, she let the water run awhile until it got cold. Then she filled up a glass while I called the cops. She tried to talk me out of it, but I was worried.

I followed Darlene back outside. He made me nervous. I didn't want to think he was lurking in the bushes while I was home alone. I tried to explain this to my sister, but she wasn't listening. She was too busy looking for him.

He was gone.

Only one cop showed up, a woman with a wary look on her face. She heard us out, then started searching the grounds. We sat on the porch steps and waited.

Half an hour later, she returned.

"I found some footprints in the garden," she said. I said they could've been Sonny's or Gary's. She shrugged.

"Your son a joker, ma'am?" she asked.

"What?"

"Well, at first the footprints were from a big man, but then they changed into a horse's hoof tracks. I followed the tracks into that gully there, down a path, up to the cliff. Then they completely disappeared. No ordinary horse could do that. I'd say you better have a talk with your son."

I shook my head. "Gary didn't do that."

She shrugged again. "Some other kids then, playing tricks."

Darlene and I looked at each other.

"No," said Darlene softly, "just a good day for beautiful horses."

Jim Barnes, of mixed Choctaw-Welsh descent, was born and raised in Oklahoma. In the 1950s he moved to Oregon, where he worked as a lumberjack for ten years before returning to Oklahoma to earn a bachelor of arts degree. He completed his Ph.D. at the University of Arkansas, and for the past twenty-five years he has been a prolific author of poems, essays, short stories, and translations. Barnes is an internationally recognized and award-winning author, and his books include *Summon and Sign: Poems by Dagmar Nick* (winner of the Translation Prize for 1980), *The American Book of the Dead* (Honorable Mention in the Before Columbus Foundation's American Book Awards), *The Sawdust War* (1993 Oklahoma Book Award), *The Fish on Poteau Mountain, A Season of Loss,* and *The La Plata Cantata.* His poems have appeared in thirty anthologies and numerous literary publications, including *Harper's Anthology of Twentieth Century Native American Poetry, Carriers of the Dream Wheel, The Pushcart Prize, The Nation, The Kenyon Review,* and numerous others. Barnes has been awarded fellowships by the National Endowment for the Arts and the Rockefeller Foundation, as well as a Fulbright Fellowship. He is professor of comparative literature at Northeast Missouri State University, and he is the editor of *The Chariton Review.*

Jim Barnes

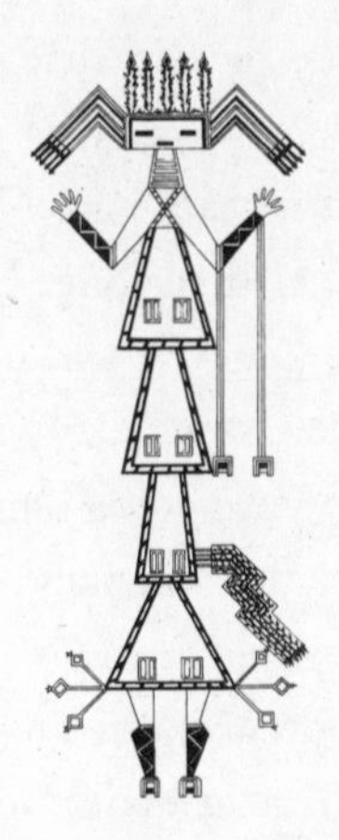

# The Reapers

*The corn-spirit is supposed to lurk as long as he can in the corn, retreating before the reapers, the binders, and the threshers at their work. But when he is forcibly expelled from the refuge in the last corn cut or the last sheaf bound or the last grain threshed, he necessarily assumes some other form than that of the corn-stalks which had hitherto been his garment or body . . .*

*Certain persons, especially strangers passing the harvest field, were regularly regarded as embodiments of the corn-spirit, and as such were seized by the reapers, wrapt in sheaves, and beheaded, their bodies bound up in the corn-stalks, being afterwards thrown into water as a rain-charm.*

—Sir James Frazer, *The New Golden Bough*

THE SUN DROPPED TOWARD THE JAGGED MOUNTAIN IN THE west. The car moved rapidly along the dirt road bordered by net and barbed wire fence. A heavy, dirty fog boiled up behind it. Delaville cursed his luck. He wondered whether the eroded county road would ever come to an end. He knew he shouldn't have listened to the jumbled directions of the proprietor of Simon Jones Gro & Sta. But this was a new route, and it was essential that he save all the time he possibly could, especially today, since he had that standing date in Linusburg. This road, if he hadn't made a wrong turn somewhere, would junction with State 7. He glanced at a road map. No indication at all. He had already gone two miles farther than Jones had said. The road was bad, bad as he had ever seen. He knew he was driving too fast, but, damn it all, if they kept adding on new stops to his route, pretty soon he would have to take a plane. He ripped open a sample pack of a new menthol cigarette he was pushing for the company. The smoke was cold in his lungs, as cold as the frost earlier in the day.

The road became smoother momentarily as he came into a long, sloping valley. He pushed the accelerator down. The heavily loaded car labored, then picked up speed. Suddenly the car swerved toward the ditch; he didn't hear the blowout, but he could tell it was the right front. He fought the steering wheel back to the left, being careful not to brake until he had control.

He threw the door open. He felt like killing something. He spat the cigarette into the ditch. "Son of a bitch," he muttered, going round to the trunk.

Across the ditch in a cane field, three field hands were working. Their heads were bent. They worked slowly, rhythmically. For a moment he watched, his trunk key dangling from one finger. He noticed that one of the workers was an old woman. A bearded man swung a scythe. Another man, middle-aged as best he could make out, gathered the mowed stalks into his arms and carried them to where the old woman was tying stalks together to make a great upright shock. Hundreds of these sheaves dotted the field. Delaville saw that the field was almost completely mowed flat. All that remained was a corner near the road. He watched the reapers, fascinated. Slowly, steadily, the bearded man with the scythe slashed the cane to the ground. Finally, only one scythe-full remained standing. The mower stopped abruptly and pulled himself up sharply, looking back over his shoulder toward the other two. For a moment the three stared at one another. Then the man who had been picking up the stalks walked over to the reaper. It looked as if they were arguing. Delaville couldn't hear all that was being said. He started when he felt the old woman's eyes on him, but he continued to watch. The bearded man was shaking his head. The other jerked the scythe from his hands and with one rapid swoop felled the remaining clump of cane. Then the bearded man broke into a cracked, rasping laugh, which stopped as suddenly as it had begun. The two men had seen him.

Delaville was embarrassed. He dropped his glance toward the ground, fumbled with his key, and opened the loaded trunk. He felt their eyes on him as he stacked carton after carton of cigarettes on the road behind the car. At the same time he discovered that he didn't have a jack, he heard the fence creak. He looked up and saw the two men climbing over the fence.

"Evening," Delaville said. The middle-aged man nodded almost imperceptibly. The man with the beard—who, Delaville noted, was, like the woman, quite old—squatted by the flat tire. His rasping laugh suddenly irritated Delaville. The old woman was standing on the far side of the fence.

"Delaville, tobacco salesman," Delaville said, putting out his hand. He immediately cursed himself. The farmer would have to take two steps at least to shake.

The man seemed unaware of the hand. "Longbaugh," he said flatly. For long seconds silence prevailed.

"I'm kinda in a fix," Delaville said. "No jack." The squatting man rasped and spat a brown stream into the dirt. "I wonder if you might be able to help me out."

The farmer looked at the squatting man, then at the old woman. "I had me a jack one time, I reckon. In the barn, I guess." The reapers climbed back over the fence. Delaville stood undecided until the old woman made two quick gestures and nodded. Delaville hurriedly re-packed the trunk and followed them.

Catching up to the others, Delaville commented, "Real good job on the cane." He meant it. The stubble, he noticed, was cleanly cut two inches from the ground. Longbaugh glanced at him without comment.

"Sorghum?" Delaville asked.

Longbaugh shook his head. "No. Stock cane."

The old man had fallen behind. Delaville had forgotten him until he heard the rasp. He glanced back. The old man had swung at a lone half-stalk that had somehow escaped the blade before.

"That's Mr. Linney," Longbaugh said. "Hired hand."

As they left the field and started down a deeply rutted road toward a farmhouse, barn, and pigsties, Delaville suddenly shuddered in the coolness of the approaching night. The sun had disappeared behind the broken rim of the mountain, on the other side of which, he reck-oned, lay State 7, and farther on to the west was Linusburg. He dreaded the thought of being on the road at night.

The stench of the barnyard ran through Delaville's nostrils like a knife. Longbaugh started for the barn. Delaville followed him. The hulk of a rusted Ford leaned against the building.

Longbaugh turned. "Go in the house," he said. "It may take a while."

"I need to get on," Delaville said.

"You'll stay for supper," the farmer stated flatly.

Stepping onto the front porch, Delaville could see, through the open door, the old woman kneeling at the fireplace, stirring the coals.

A blaze sparked up as she added dry kindling, then a quartered log. She hummed through wrinkled lips until the fire took hold. Then she looked out at him and grinned between blackened teeth. "Come in. Take a chair," she said. She seemed amused at something. She went into the kitchen. Delaville watched her. She dropped chips into the stove, shook kerosene on them, and tossed in a match. A slow flame climbed up, and she shoved the stove lid over it. The rear door opened and Mr. Linney came in, whispered something to the old woman, and took two tin pails from a large pan on the stove. Delaville saw him wipe them with a greasy-looking rag. Delaville shivered. He heard a rasping laugh as Mr. Linney left.

Longbaugh came in with an armload of wood. He laid it carefully down on the hearth. He brushed the bib of his overalls and said, "I ain't found that jack yet. But I'm pretty shore I know where it is." He went into the kitchen. Delaville turned his backside to the fire. Longbaugh came back in with a stone jug. "Corn," he said. "Melt the frost off." Delaville could see a hard intensity in the man's eyes.

"Say, now. That's real good. Appreciate it," Delaville said. Something cold began to settle on his shoulders. He felt ill at ease.

"You go ahead," Longbaugh said, handing him a glass. "I've got some more chores to do. Go ahead. Drink. I'll be back directly."

Delaville poured himself a generous helping. Longbaugh looked toward the kitchen and called, "Josie, bring Mr. Delaville some water."

Delaville took the water and chased down the hot whiskey. He felt the whiskey seep into the marrow of his bones. He was suddenly numb, then just as suddenly completely relaxed. That was just what he had needed since leaving old Jones's place. The chill that he had felt was now gone, and in its place was an odd sense of well-being.

He sipped the whiskey. It was much too hot and had an acid bite to it. Carbide, he thought. But then surely they knew better than to use carbide. He concluded that it was just his imagination. The whiskey was good. It was probably just as good as anything that he would be drinking in Linusburg anyway. Still, he wished he were there, a good water-high in his hand.

He must have fallen asleep, for only slowly did he become aware of the sound. At first he thought he was back on a familiar road with the tires slicing across black oily spots on the asphalt surface. Then he realized that the sound wasn't quite right. It was more like the old man's laugh. He was suddenly jarred fully awake, and the rasping was behind him. Mr. Linney sat on the high hearth whetting the scythe. The sound of steel on steel was the same as the old reaper's laugh.

"You was asleep," Mr. Linney said, continuing with his task.

"Guess so," Delaville said. But he wasn't sure. Mr. Linney was humming under his breath. The melody was almost inaudible, but for Delaville it was somehow familiar. He tried to remember. He was no expert on folk songs, but he did pride himself on his knowledge of the country people. God knew he had had to deal with enough of them.

Longbaugh came in the front door, carrying a rusted crank-type jack. One of the early ones, it seemed to Delaville, that was designed for the axle.

"I found it," Longbaugh said. "It don't look any good, but maybe it'll work." He sat on the corner of the hearth opposite Mr. Linney, who was still whetting. "Get me the coal oil can, Mr. Linney." The old man didn't seem to hear. "Get me the coal oil," Longbaugh repeated, his eyes narrowing. The old man looked at him for a moment, then rasped from deep down in his throat.

"Coal oil ain't going to help that thing," he said as he propped the scythe up against the massive stone fireplace and started toward the kitchen. Longbaugh's eyes followed him.

The old man came back with the can and set it down. "There. But it won't help."

The muscles standing out on his neck, Longbaugh looked at him hard. The old man shrugged and again began whetting the scythe.

Longbaugh poured the kerosene into the jack. Delaville went over to the hearth and squatted beside him.

"It's giving," Longbaugh said. He struck the base of the jack against the great flat stone hearth. He began working the crank slowly back and forth until he was able to make a complete turn, then another. Finally the screw of the jack started rising slowly up from its housing.

"It'll break," Mr. Linney said.

Longbaugh did not reply but kept working the apparatus until the rust began to melt away and metal appeared. "That ought to do it," he said, wiping his hands on the knees of his overalls. "We'll go down after supper and finish it." He took up the stone jug and drank from the neck.

The old woman came to the doorway of the kitchen. Delaville judged that she must have been at least seventy. She wiped her hands on a soiled cloth. "It's ready," she said. She turned back into the kitchen.

"Supper," Longbaugh said.

"Could I wash up?" Delaville asked.

"Pan's on the back porch," Longbaugh answered. He pointed toward the kitchen. Delaville went out as the two men sat down at the table.

On the open porch he could see the silhouette of a bench. A hound lay beneath it. "Get out," he said, shoving the dog off the porch with his foot.

The night had become bright and cold. The moon was up—a new moon, with a star close to the bottom tip. Delaville could even see the field that had just been harvested. The shadows of the shocks stood out like black rocks on a naked plain. A certain loneliness crept through him. The water was cold on his face and hands. He used his handkerchief as a towel. He could hear a cow lowing in the barn. Why did these hill people keep hanging on? he asked himself. He didn't understand. He had got out early. He had seen that the old way was no longer good enough. The land was barren, and if you didn't work yourself to the bone, sedge grass would take over in less than a year's time. It wasn't worth it. A man ought to have some freedom. On a place like this . . . Well, it wasn't his concern. He went back into the kitchen. The reek of kerosene hung about the gloomy room. The lamp on the table was smoking. As he sat down, Delaville looked over the familiar food—corn bread, fried potatoes, turnip greens, and coffee. He had been raised on these foods and did not hesitate in filling his plate. The old woman sat on a stool by the stove watching the men eat. She seemed on the verge of saying something.

The three men ate in silence. Delaville could remember that at mealtime, even when he was a boy, silence was almost sacred. It was a custom that he followed most of the time, not from choice but from necessity, since he was on the road constantly. But he had broken with most of the old traditions, or forgotten them. He couldn't remember which.

Longbaugh and the old man finished before he did. They shoved their plates back and waited, watching him finish. When Delaville was through, Longbaugh lifted the jar from the floor by his foot and laced his coffee. He gave the whiskey to Delaville, who in turn passed it on to Mr. Linney.

The old woman was at the table filling a plate with what food there was left. "I'll take a glass of that, Mr. Linney," she said.

The old man laughed, glancing sideways at Longbaugh. But the farmer was looking out at the night. The old man laughed again as she lifted the heavy container and poured. "You'll dance us a jig, Josie. You'll dance us a jig if you ain't careful," he said, starting to hum the same tune he had before, only livelier.

"Never seen nobody dance to that," the old woman said. Delaville again saw an amused look in the old woman's eyes. Something seemed strangely familiar. The whole evening—the reapers, the field, his being there, the meal and the drinks—the whole thing seemed to fit into some sort of pattern. Still, though, it had no real meaning for him.

The old woman continued, "Mr. Linney, what was it Old Mother Hicks used to say about strangers? For the life of me, I can't seem to remember."

Looking askance at Longbaugh, Mr. Linney answered, "Don't rightly know. She used to prophesy so much stuff."

"It weren't any of her prophesying. It was a ditty, I think."

Mr. Linney was silent, but his eyes appeared to glow. Delaville sipped his whiskey and watched Longbaugh. The farmer wasn't sipping. He drank by gulps, and after each there was a long pause.

Mr. Linney went into the front room and in a few seconds returned with his scythe. He continued whetting the curved blade.

Longbaugh broke his long silence. "Mr. Linney used to be champeen cutter hereabouts."

Delaville was startled by the words. Longbaugh had been silent a long while as the two old people were talking, and Delaville had been thinking about the day, mentally figuring up his commission.

"Champion cutter?" Delaville asked, not understanding.

"Nobody could keep up with him. He don't look like it now, does he?"

Delaville looked at the bearded old man at the stove talking in hushed tones to the old woman. No, he didn't look like it, Delaville thought. Time could make a difference. In twenty, thirty years, he probably wouldn't look like a tobacco salesman either.

"Folks all liked to have him in the field," Longbaugh went on. The liquor seemed to have slackened his features. The jaw hung loose. But there was still a cold intensity about the eyes. "No cutting was complete without Mr. Linney, Mr. Salesman. I've seen him cut down much bigger men than him. Nobody could keep up with him. They used to come from all over to challenge him. That used to be a real thing. The haymaking, then later on the cane. And the Halloween dance. Some folks used to say it was in his honor."

"It was!" Mr. Linney said. He had come back to the table and was standing by his scythe. "It was a harvest dance and I was the champeen!"

By the stove the old woman cackled. "Tell them what the old folks used to do with strangers in the field, Mr. Linney. Tell them!"

"Hot damn, Josie!" Mr. Linney cried. "Them was the good old days."

The old woman cackled again and began to dance around the table. The old man followed her. The hum that Delaville had heard before broke into full song from the rasping throat of Mr. Linney:

> "The day is down, the barns all full,
> And the scythes make a heavy load.
> Draw back, and swing, and pull,
> The last one must be mowed!"

"Shut up, you drunken old bastard!" Longbaugh shouted at the dancing figures.

Delaville grinned at Mr. Linney's attempt at song and dance.

"Goddamnit, sit down and shut up!" Longbaugh roared.

Mr. Linney stopped. He wasn't smiling. "I know why you're mad, Longbaugh. I know."

"You're pretty goddamned smart, ain't you, Mr. Champeen?"

"He tricked you, Longbaugh. He tricked you good. Go on, say it," the old woman chanted.

"You cut the last bunch, Longbaugh. You did it!" the old man screamed. His voice sounded like rain on a tin roof. He broke into hysterical laughter, a mad laughter.

"You shore did, Longbaugh. You was in such a hurry when he stopped, you forgot. You cut the last bunch, Longbaugh. You're the nigger baby! It's up to you to see we get a crop next year!" the old woman hissed. Both she and Mr. Linney were doubling up with drunken laughter.

Delaville began to laugh; it seemed the thing to do. It rang loud through the house. He suddenly stopped. Something was wrong. The others were not laughing now.

"You son of a bitch," Longbaugh spat at him across the table.

Delaville staggered to his feet. "Now, wait a minute, Mr. Longbaugh. I didn't mean—"

"You know what the old folks used to do to strangers in their fields, mister?" the old woman said. Her voice was now cold. "Tell him, Mr. Linney."

The old man stooped slightly and picked up the scythe. He began to hum.

"Now wait a minute!" Delaville tried to clear his head. He didn't understand what was happening. This was crazy. The old man came around the table toward him slowly. Longbaugh rose, his hard eyes piercing Delaville's. The old woman stood motionless. This couldn't be happening to him. He could think of only one thing to do. He ran for the door.

"Catch him, Longbaugh. Get him!" the old man rasped. "You got to."

Delaville broke into the yard at a dead run, his whiskey heels pounding hard against the rough earth. Past the barn he ran, and into the deep ruts of the road leading to the field. Behind him he could hear the sound of running voices. He looked back over his shoulder. He saw the glint of the scythe and heard the old man's rasp and Longbaugh's curse. In the name of God, what is this? he thought.

His breath coming hard, he raced into the stubble of the field. The sweet smell of the cane hung over the land. The sharp stubs bit through his thin-soled shoes. He ran headlong into one of the great shocks. Frantically he picked himself up and saw the glint of the scythe flash on toward him. His chest ached; a tortured sob broke from his throat. He ran. On across the field, forcing himself to hold to the furrows, trying to miss the knives of cane, he ran.

At the fence finally, he rolled over, heaved himself over by sheer force of will. His strength was gone. He fell into the car. The key, he thought frantically, the key! Oh my God! For a moment he knew the key would not be there in his pocket. His labored, putrid breath came unevenly and with pain. He pushed down into the pocket and his cold fingers closed about the key. He had it.

The fence screeched. Delaville jerked his head around, his eyes wide against the night. Balanced, it seemed, on the topmost strand of wire was the figure of the old man, the scythe held high. Delaville heard the rasp and a cackling laugh.

He forced the key into the switch, pressed it hard to the right, rammed the accelerator down. He leaned forward on the wheel with all his might as the car jerked forward, as if by mind alone he was making the car come alive. The wheel shimmied in his hands. The tire, he thought, the tire! How far could he get before the rim went? To State 7? But he was lost! Maybe he could get far enough.

More speed, he must have more speed. He pressed his foot to the floor. The car swerved, he lost control. No! He had control, he was only going down, down. The night got blacker. He was going down.

He couldn't understand what was happening until he heard the splash and water fell on the windshield. He was in the ford of a creek. The car died. He tried to start it. It was dead, drowned out. Pull it to the other side with the starter, he thought. But then he knew that with the flat he would never make it. "Calm down, calm down," he told himself aloud. He forced the door open. Water flowed in on his feet. It was icy. He wet his hands and touched them to his face. He held his breath and listened. Far back in the night he could hear the sound of running men. There was only one thing to do. Run. He broke across the icy water to the far side, which was as black as the creek itself. But the light of the moon shone through the willow tunnel of the road, and he ran on, struggling up the steep incline of the bank. Out of the creek bottom he ran, trying not to think of the pain in his chest, trying not to think of anything except keeping his feet going on and on and on. Behind him, he knew, was the glint of the scythe. Ahead was the horned moon.

Annie Hansen is of Lenape and Norwegian heritage. She is a fiction editor for *The Raven Chronicles,* published in Seattle, Washington, and the author of several creative works of her own, particularly short stories. Her story "Sun Offering" appeared in Anchor Books' *Earth Song, Sky Spirit.* She has written many stories based on her protagonist Jimmy One Rock, and she is completing a novel based on this unusual character. She has published her fiction and essays in *Carolina Quarterly, Duckabush Journal, The Kenyon Review, The Raven Chronicles, Akwe-kon, Northwest Ethnic News,* and *Caliban.* Hansen lives on the Suquamish Reservation in Indianola, Washington, where she is a long-distance cold water swimmer in addition to fiction writer and poet. An engaging public speaker, Hansen is often asked to read her works to those interested in contemporary Native American literature.

Annie Hansen

# Spirit Curse

When Jimmy came to on his bed in the little cabin, he at first had no idea of what had happened, or how he had got home. And the pain was so blindingly strong it felt like a drug coursing through his veins, carrying him down, down. For several days, he slipped in and out of consciousness, unreal moments of Mary, Roy, his sons, darkness, light, the sound of waves crashing below the cabin, and horrible deep silence all twirling and spinning around him.

The deepest, strongest grip of the pain had passed. The memory of his rage, the fight on the dock, falling in the water, being pulled out and dragged to the Impala and home by Roy, was beginning to take shape in his mind, to become a story. And the story would become almost like a bright, hard object in his hands. Something to hold, to look at, to pass around. And finally to laugh at.

Jimmy and his brothers were quick on stories. Sometimes the story would form in their hearts before the experience was even over. They went into their days looking for a story, sniffing it out like bloodhounds. They lived by the story. Telling and listening to each other's stories gave them breath, saved their lives and connected them deeply to each other. They recognized each other and their kinship by their stories.

But this one, this fight, took a little longer in becoming a story. The physical pain was as bad as any Jimmy had experienced. And the memory of his own rage at such a pitiful man was so strong he could still taste its bitter poison in his mouth.

And finally that became the center of the story, that Jimmy could get so angry at such a little weenie of a guy, a screwed-up, lonely man who didn't know shit, but wouldn't shut up. All in full sight of the biggest, meanest tug operator in Puget Sound, a fucking Green Beret just back from Vietnam, who had just been waiting for Jimmy's slightest move to pound the crap out of Jimmy's brown face. And did.

And pretty soon, Jimmy and Mary's bedroom was full of cousins and relations all wanting to see the fresh red scars, hear the story and bring bits of other stories of the man in the short black coat, of the tug operator, of the docks and other fights. And these bits of stories were offerings to tie on to Jimmy's story and pain like tobacco bundles. And Jimmy's story grew with his healing and became that bright, hard object to pass around until it had a life of its own and could be lifted off Jimmy's chest.

And unexpectedly, Jimmy's story became a lifeline and his cabin a haven for the men on the reservation to hold on to as they saw their own families gripped by a sorrow, a tragedy that no one could ever imagine even whispering as a story. Each telling, each memory, would peel their hearts like a sharp knife, bleed them again and again.

In the two short months since Uncle had died, four young men had committed suicide, in cars, with whiskey and guns. Each death struck deep, bringing up old stories of the dead taking young men as companions on their long journey home.

Families were split, torn open, by stories that had become twisted and changed at the missionaries' altars over the years, making Uncle's family feel suddenly defensive that anyone would think that Uncle would steal a son, a child. And with each progressive death, the confusion and fear grew.

Jimmy watched the women cook and talk and try to comfort each other. They rose early and were busy all day and went to bed late in that comforting. Their hearts and their bodies were occupied with the living. And Jimmy watched the men go silent, move away from each other and come together only on days they fished, or around Jimmy's bed to hear some story that didn't cut into the vein of their powerlessness, their sorrow.

But finally it was Aunt Ethie who called the meeting. She said she woke from a dream deep in the middle of the night, remembering the meetings of the women, the aunties and grandmothers of her childhood. And she knew that that was what should be done. It came to her like a vision and a gift, that to stop the death the women should meet.

Whether her vision dream was from memory or from love, it was strong and real and true.

With only a couple of exceptions, there were women from all the families on the reservation crammed tight into Aunt Ethie's little cabin, around the cookstove and cups of strong black coffee. And the women from those families who did not come were forgiven; some feuds are best left alone for a while. And Ethie understood. Once, when one of the anthropologists had visited the reservation asking questions about the culture of the people, the religion, the food, the work, he asked Aunt Ethie about the role of women in the Salish culture, and she answered, straight-faced and sincerely, "To keep the feuds going." Of course, everyone laughed for years at her answer to that anthropologist, but no one disagreed.

But Aunt Ethie knew she had spoken only a piece of the truth, had tricked that anthropologist with just a little bright thread of the whole cloth. She knew it was also the women's job to get together, to talk.

Aunt Ethie understood that things were out of balance, and that to return the balance the women needed to pay attention to what they loved. There were spirit words for what was going on. There were prayers to call for spirit help, to lift the spirit darkness. There were stories to explain and help.

After a long night of tears, talking and prayers, Aunt Ethie gave the women some healing herbs for their families and asked them to keep close to the children, keep everyone in after dark. She said that they would understand when the spirit darkness had passed.

Jimmy knew this, and he felt comforted by the protection of these fierce women. And Jimmy was feeling stronger in the day now. He'd chopped some wood and split a few shakes to repair the roof. He had kept close to Mary and the boys since Aunt Ethie had gathered the women together. And twice a day he walked up the path to Aunt Ethie's house, to check on her and Joey, sometimes bringing Joey and two or three other cousins back with him. But when the sun went down, some of Jimmy's pain and broken pride returned, and he'd go to the bedroom alone and escape into the comfort of a dog-eared paperback western.

With some of the money from fishing, Roy had bought the boys a used TV and hooked it up to an old generator he'd rebuilt. It pleased Mary because she wanted the boys in at night now, out of the darkness, out of harm until the time had passed. And for a couple of hours each night the drone of the generator and the quieter hum of the TV seemed to fill the cabin and the whole dark clearing. But a tree that fell in the storm the night before had crushed the generator, leaving the night quiet, returning the small, heartbeat-like sounds Jimmy liked to hear from his bed: Mary, the boys, the snap of pitch wood in the cookstove.

"Jimmy," Mary's voice called from the other room. "Jimmy, I'm going to the store." Jimmy could hear her footsteps come to the door and the door open.

"Jimmy, we're out of bread, and I told George I'd make sandwiches for him to take when he meets Roy and FloLo at the dock in the morning. I think George and FloLo live on doughnuts unless Roy cooks for them. And Roy's working so hard I thought I should send food. But I have to go up to the store to get bread."

"Alone?"

"The boys are on the mattress reading comics. And I don't want them out yet. I will be okay, but I want the boys here. You listen for them, keep them in, I'll just be gone a minute."

"I don't want you out alone."

"But we can't both go."

"I'll go."

"Are you sure? Do you feel good enough?" Mary knew how spooked Jimmy could get alone at night. For Mary, this staying-in time was a reminder of what they needed to care about. It wasn't so much that she was afraid of what was outside in the dark night as it was what she cared about inside the house, inside the houses of her relations. But with Jimmy, Mary understood the power of his fear, what he knew, what Grandma One Rock had taught him.

In the first week after the fight, seeing Jimmy so hurt, so strangely broken, Mary had been a little afraid for him in a way she couldn't wholly understand. During the time Jimmy was drinking so hard that he finally ended up in jail, there was a stubborn edge to him. It had been easy for Mary to leave him then, to walk away from Jimmy and his path for those months. But maybe there were more years between them now and she could read his pain better. Or maybe Uncle's death, followed so quickly by these suicides, cast everything in a different light, made this breath, this life, seem much more fragile. Mary felt strangely protective of Jimmy, as she would a son, in this staying-in time. She knew it would pass, that Jimmy would be strong again. But she used this time to be careful of Jimmy.

While Jimmy dressed, he could feel his body protest, the pain of his healing wounds rise up, a shiver rise on his skin as he pulled on his cool, rough clothes. He wanted to be in bed, his naked skin next to Mary's soft naked skin, the smell of her in his nostrils as he fell into a dream. But at the same time, Jimmy felt an odd exhilaration at going out in the night, as if getting this loaf of bread were truly an important, difficult task.

Out in the yard at the Impala, Jimmy opened the door, then he stamped his feet to warm himself. Instead of getting in, he stopped and looked back at the cabin, the warm yellow lights in the tiny windows. He was transported for a moment by the stillness of the night, by the knowledge that that cabin held Mary and his children against the darkness, the wind and the crash of the waves.

It had stormed the night before; the sky had been lit with lightning for hours before the rain and wind started. Then it hit the cabin hard from the water, pelting the roof, the windows, the thin board walls. All night the sound of the storm was around them, cracking and felling branches and trees.

Now the yard was littered with cedar and fir branches that, heavy with the summer growth and rain, had been blown far from their trees. Even after the storm quieted, the rain continued hard all day. And now the air was fragrant with all the smells: the rain and cedar and fir and wet fallen maple and alder leaves and the ripe, rotting apples under the ancient tree.

Jimmy knew that with this storm the season had changed. These last few weeks the early-morning fog, the pale yellow in the leaves, the low white sunlight across the water—these had been only gentle reminders of its coming. The storm brought a time of passing and change. Not that there would be a harsh change in this place, Jimmy understood that. In this place of water and rain and green, the changes were subtle. There would be warm days still, soft rain, sun, but there would be no mistaking it for summer now.

Standing at the open car door, he saw how small and fragile the cabin looked against all that blackness of the sky, the cedars, the small clearing. And Jimmy understood that maybe that was what Aunt Ethie and the ancestors of this place wanted him to feel from these weeks of staying in, a sense of themselves, small and fragile and together in this dark clearing, a sense that these families belonged in this place.

For many years Jimmy used to separate his ancestors in Oklahoma from Mary's ancestors here. But as the years passed, he had tried and then begun to see them all as his ancestors. Gradually, over the years, he heard the stories, the names of the Old Ones gone before, and began to feel the rhythms and the seasons of this place. And when the first elders he knew passed on to the other side, he began to know who those ancestors were and that, for him, there was finally no separating the ancestors of his people from the ancestors of this place, these people.

Jimmy shivered at the damp cold that had penetrated his clothes while he had been lost in the night and his thoughts. He rubbed his hands along his arms, then slipped into the driver's seat of the '62 Impala. It started right up. The deep hum of the engine gave him a renewed sense of purpose. Jimmy glanced at the tiny cabin, feeling as he had the times he and Roy passed the cabin on the water as they left to fish in Uncle's boat.

As he drove from the clearing, he left the warm familiarity of the cabin. He moved into the dark overhang of cedar branches along the winding road, where the high beams of the Impala seemed to be sucked up, lost in all that darkness, in the black puddles of the gravel road, in the black patches of the moonless night woven into the tall cedars.

It was only at the last curve, under the dim blinking streetlight before the big hill, that Jimmy had a sense that something wasn't right, had a strong sense of a presence near him, behind him, and his eyes caught the white glow in the rearview mirror. Jimmy's blood froze, his breath caught.

Jimmy saw the image in the mirror take shape, white glowing eyes beneath a black hooded shape, before it faded away. It was there, in his car. Jimmy gripped the wheel and drove up the hill, expecting, knowing, understanding that he would be next.

Jimmy's mind raced as he watched the dark road fly by and saw the image grow, then fade again, the black hooded figure staring at him with those cold white marble eyes. He tried to remember, what had Mary told him that Aunt Ethie said to do? Pray. Pray. What prayers?

Jimmy started praying, loudly: "Dear God. Creator. Grandfather. Spare me. Spare me."

Then he thought, panicked, it was a Salish spirit. He tried but could not, in his fear, remember any of Uncle's prayers. He called out random words, hoping to at least get some sympathy from the black hooded figure.

*"dtalə. q̓il'bid. ʔal ʔal."*

And then he remembered and shouted, "But I'm Lenape." Tears

were streaming down his face now; all thoughts of all ancestors being his ancestors were gone. "I'm Lenape. Oh God, are you Lenape? Coming to find me here. *Getemaktunhe. Wineweokan.*"

By the time Jimmy said the Lord's Prayer and started his Hail Marys, he was crying, calling out in gulps between the prayers. "I've been good. Oh, I *will* be good. Don't take me now. Mary. Jesus. God."

But the black hooded shape just came closer, moving toward Jimmy until Jimmy could almost feel it at his neck. There was a red glow now below the white eyes.

Jimmy took the last curve at close to ninety miles an hour, panting, leaning into the steering wheel. Seeing the lights of the little store ahead, he tried to slow down. But feeling a cold breath on his neck, he steered the Impala straight for the low picket fence around MacDougall's chicken yard next to MacDougall's Store. As he hit, and the sleeping chickens woke midair, with feathers, fence, straw and splintered boards flying everywhere, Jimmy leapt from the Impala, rolling, rolling, as he saw the black shape follow out the door and become Aunt Ethie's old black pointed-eared dog, Bart.

And flat on his back, chickens everywhere, screen doors already slamming, porch lights coming on, Bart licking his bloody face, Jimmy knew the prayers had been answered. The spirit curse was broken. Jimmy knew everyone would be out tomorrow. Because sure as hell, there wasn't a person on the whole reservation who wouldn't come out to see this mess.

Maurice Kenny is the renowned Mohawk author who has spent five decades writing and publishing poetry and short fiction. He is recognized internationally as one of the foremost voices among people of the First Nations of Canada and the United States. His work has appeared in more than seventy-five magazines and thirty-one anthologies, including *Earth Song, Sky Spirit,* published by Anchor Books. Kenny has received numerous literary awards, including the American Book Award and the Hodson Award. Two of his works have been nominated for the Pulitzer Prize. He has written numerous books, including *Dancing Back Strong the Nation, I Am the Sun, Between Two Rivers: Selected Poems, Humors and/or So Humorous, Lost Mornings in Brooklyn, Rain and Other Fictions, The Mama Poems, Tekonwatonti: Molly Brant, Poems of War, 1735–1795, Greyhounding This America,* and others. Kenny has taught at the University of Oklahoma, the University of Wisconsin–Oneida, and St. Lawrence University. He is an accomplished speaker, a special storyteller who has captivated audiences everywhere. Kenny lives in Saranac Lake, New York, and teaches at North Country Community College. "What's in a Song" is a story that Kenny has dedicated to Harold Katchenago, at Menominee.

Maurice Kenny

# What's in a Song

MARTIN FELL FAST ASLEEP WITH HIS HEAD RESTING NOT SO very comfortably against a sleek log, his feet nearly to the river edge, his arms akimbo but stoutly holding a flute. He hadn't actually come to the river to sleep. That was not his purpose, yet there he was, snoring as loudly as any crow could caw in the cedar rising over his head. When he'd arrived that morning, considerably earlier, he carried a small bag of cold corn bread and a glass jar of water. The river's freshness could not be trusted anymore. After eating and sipping the water, he simply leaned back against the log and fell sound asleep. The warmth of noon cuddled around him, heavied his arms, weighted his eyelids. The yawns arrived softly at first and then protruded rudely into his revery.

Summer flies began to dance about his ears, then attacked his rather pug nose. Hands flew out to subdue the insects' buzzing attacks, but to no avail. They continued to snip at his nose; one had the audacity to light on his lip, where a tear of water from the jar stealthily clung to the fleshy corner. He swatted and swatted. The flies continued to annoy the sleepy young man. At last he gave up the battle, settled back with his round derriere firmly planted on the earth, then covered with last autumn's leaves. He slowly allowed his head to find some comforting spot on the log. The first snore, light and musical, gobbled from his open mouth, where a last fly entered. The breeze of the snore was strong enough to evict the fly. His mouth shut, tight. The fly, having lost the battle, flew off and gave Martin the moment to rest which, it would seem, he needed.

Martin had not gone to the woods and the river that late spring morning merely to eat cold corn bread and sleep. He could more comfortably do that at home on the sofa, or on the grass beneath his leafy apple tree. He had an important reason for his trek to the river, a far more imaginative reason. The night before, he had felt music in his bones, as he would have said had someone asked. His spirit was twitching, he also might have suggested. Notes and rhythms were floating in his inner ear but not making a true composition. He lay awake most of the night hearing notes and the rush of water, a river in his ears. The house he owned with Matilda was a goodly distance from the river. There was no water leaking in the tub or sink, or rain running off the roof. At 4 A.M. he knew what he must do. He should rise early with the dawn, pack a light lunch, and trek to the river to see exactly what would happen.

It was the loveliest of mornings: the sun was bright, and warm as bread Matilda might take from her oven; robins were singing, a red cardinal flew before his view to a telephone wire and sat there watching his move across the meadow to the woods; clouds, thin and lazy, hung in the bluest of skies; the meadow was covered with wild blossoms—black-eyed Susans, daisies, fleabane—and one ruby-throated hummingbird hovered before a single common tickweed. He felt good; he felt music in his feet, in his itchy fingers, and his head swirled with notes so immediate he thought he could see them in the air. He carried his two flutes in a deerhide bundle strapped to his back. He carried his lunch of corn bread and water, but he also carried tobacco. He lunged across the meadow as though wading through deep water; he plied waves, though the waves were a field of forgotten wheat. Plunge that he did in his hike, he thought he walked as spiritedly as a dancer, lightly on the earth, touching the center, the earth, as though a drum of beaten hide, soft as skin, undulant as clouds floating above his head. He was light and airy, almost dizzy with expectation. He knew that morning he would have a new song, a song of the river, as the waters had called him in the night to come and freely take their music.

Shortly, he entered the woods. The river was only a quarter of a mile farther into the trees. Birds and squirrels hopped from one branch to another. An elderberry bush, black fruit hanging, dangling in a shaft of sunlight, took his glance. Witch hopple, now barren of flowers, tripped him as he ambled through in a daydream. He staggered but, confident in his mission, he paid no attention and stumbled on to the river, which he could now easily hear. He was so excited that he ignored the morning dew dampening the moccasins Matilda had sewn for him only this past February. They were wet and loose. He thought of the new song, a fresh, original composition, the creativity, the making of notes, order from chaos, beautiful rhythms which would flow from his flute so thrillingly . . . He failed to see a chickadee flitting about his path. It would perch and flit, flit and perch, fly off into the leaves and then return to perch on a pine branch directly over Martin's head. It sang "fee-bee, fee-bee," the second note much lower in tone than the first. Martin, of course, did not hear the bird's "fee-bee." It flew down to the path where the young man hiked. He nearly stepped on the feathery bird. When he realized his foot had nearly killed the chickadee, he awoke at the very edge of the river. Thin ripples washed to the grasses and stones sitting out from the shore.

A heron, which stood in the shallows, heard Martin's approach and flew off into the air, leaving circles of waves fanning to shore. He wandered downriver looking for a rock, a large stone where he could sit, meditate, hear all the notes of the new song. Half a mile downstream he found such a rock, a foot high, a foot wide, and fairly flat. He placed his lunch bag safely away from the water, shook off the hide bundle which contained his two flutes, pulled off his moccasins, and dropped his feet into the water, where the river tickled his hot toes. And he listened. And listened and listened. His toes curled the water, made a slight noise, but not the noise he had come to the river to hear. He pulled his two feet out of the coolness of the slow-moving waters and held them out to dry in the sun on the grasses surrounding the flat stone. And he listened and listened. He could not hear the river, he did not hear his new song. The chickadee clucked and sang: "Chick-a-dee-dee-dee, dee-dee-dee, chick-a-dee-dee-dee, dee-fee-bee."

"Go away, chicky. Go away. I came to hear the river's song . . . not your silliness. I can't make a song from 'dee-dee-dee.' Go away."

The chickadee, indifferent to his command, continued to peck the earth for insects and to sing as she pranced about Martin on his rock.

"Chick-a-dee-dee-dee," the bird sang, and the song seemed to grow louder and louder, to the point that nothing of the water's rhythms, the river's music, could be heard at all, even though a few yards upriver huge stones jutted out of the riverbed and caused rapids not only to spray the flow's surface but to make loud music, shrill and deafening. Martin was not able to concentrate on the rapids' music. All he heard was the song of the chickadee.

There was a powerful song in the river. Powerful. Magical. He had to hear it. Didn't it keep him from sleeping most of last night? He had to capture the power of the river. It was speaking, singing to him . . . or would, if that damned chickadee would go away.

"Shush, shu, shuuuuu. Get out of here. Go away."

She wouldn't leave, but continued circling his stone. She hopped up on his flute bundle. "Get off my bundle. Get off my flutes, you nasty bird. Go away."

And he listened, and listened and listened. The river made no gurgle, offered no song, seemed to have lost power, its magic. His flutes remained tied in the bundle. It was then he decided to eat his breakfast, the cold corn bread, and have a swallow of water. As he opened his plastic bag, a sweet scent of baked corn bread careened into the air. The chickadee caught the smell and made a fast rush to Martin's feet. He began to feel guilty, having food in his stomach yet not knowing whether the little bird was hungry. Her white cheeks and pale gray belly feathers looked bedraggled and thin; her wing feathers, tucked to her side, appeared ragged. Martin tossed the chickadee a small hunk of bread. With a cluck she thanked him and pecked away at the corn. "Now go away," he requested gently. As if she understood his words she left, left Martin alone on his rock, munching his lunch, satisfied with his altruism, content that he was not only a good Indian but a thinking, feeling human, a man of respect and sensitivity. Now he would listen to the river, the powerful music of the waters, and compose his song.

And he listened and listened and he continued to listen some more.

The sun was moving higher in the sky. Shadows shortened. The birds of the woods sang less and less. A breeze that had wafted across the morning stilled. It was quiet. So quiet that he could easily hear the powerful song rise from the river. But it refused to rise. Refused.

From the rock, he strolled along the river edge. A water snake slithered off the shore and sank into the river. He watched as a gray-white kingfisher perched on a thin dead tree stump rising a foot out of the shallows. No fish, minnow swam into the bird's ken. He shrilled and rattled loudly, rattled more, and took off from the stump to hover a few moments over the flowing water, then quickly disappeared into the vast sky.

Martin knew he could compose the song of the kingfisher, or the song of the hummingbird, the bird he'd heard earlier in the morning on his trek to the river. He knew he could accomplish that. Not difficult at all. But no, no, no. He came for the river's powerful song. He wanted a big song. A huge song for his flute. No kingfisher's rattle, no hummingbird's mouselike twitter. He'd as soon record the raucous caw of the bluejay or crow. No, he came for the river. Wasn't the sign the water? Wasn't his sleep disturbed by the rush of the river? Yes. He'd wait.

He ambled back to his stone, but the sun was now straight overhead and the stone was too hot for touch, as he found when he dropped his hand to test the rock. He spotted the sleek log, bereft of bark, a young beech caught in a lightning storm and brought down to the earth. He strolled to the log, dropped his plastic bag and his hide bundle, took a seat on the earth cross-legged, and awaited the song from the river. And he listened, and listened, and . . .

"Chick-a-dee-dee-dee. Dee-dee-dee. Dee-dee-dee."

Startled, he awoke. The chick perched on his moccasined toe. He could hear the river. It grumbled. He took up his bundle, untied the thong, and pulled out one flute, the flute which he had carved with his own nimble hands, fingers. It was carved like the head of a loon, the waterbird. It was handsome, and the music from its mouth was always beautiful. Today his flute yearned for the music of the river. He held the instrument straight out before him. Placed the lip against his mouth and blew. It grumbled the same as the river now was grumbling. His flute seemed angry as the river seemed angry and disturbed. He took the flute from his lips, held the loon-shaped instrument to the sun now passing into the southern sky. He lowered the instrument, and as he did, the chickadee flew up and perched on the slender flute's arm and stared Martin directly in the eye. He made no motion of tossing her off, though verbally encouraged her to hop down. "Go away. Get off my flute."

She continued to stare him down. "Dee-dee-dee," she said softly, mellifluously. "Dee-dee-dee." She hopped down and flitted into the woods, off from Martin, now sitting straight before the log, the flute in hand, raised to his lips. And he sang his new song.

The chickadee tried so hard to tell him, to give him a gift. He continued to ignore her, to push her off, to chase her away. He was blind. He was not only sightless, but deaf, stone deaf. He heard nothing, even though he listened, and listened and listened. He listened to the wrong voice. He listened to the river, which did not want to sing that day. He failed to hear the black-capped bird with the silly song, "Dee-dee-dee." A song was a song, all given by the Creator. As each creature was unique, each of their songs would be different. But that did not mean they had no beauty . . . even the hummingbird singing its mouselike twitter, or the sheer rattle of the kingfisher, or the ugly caw of the crow, and certainly the chickadee. Her charm was magic; her magic was his song.

He heard. He blew, and blew sweet air into his instrument, the carved loon flute. He blew and blew and magic filled the air. No, it wasn't as powerful as the river song he had come to obtain, but the "Dee-dee-dee" had its own power, a power which was pleasing and light and delightful.

He played his song over and over until it was memorized forever.

He finished eating the corn bread and drank a deep swallow of water from his glass jar. The sun was beginning to move down the sky. A light wind was rising. He felt a late-afternoon chill on his shoulders.

Martin pulled out a small soft hide bag from his pants pocket. Pulled open the strings and pushed fingers into the bag. He extracted some fine tobacco and dropped it where he had sat when the chickadee hopped onto his flute. He spread the tobacco as though he were spreading corn to the birds. Shortly he had his flute tied into the bundle, and he left for home.

That night, Matilda had a surprise supper ready for Martin: macaroni goulash, his favorite dish. After the excellent food, he took out his flutes and entertained Matilda by blowing a wolf song, a bear song, and the new song of the chickadee. She was pleased, delighted, and thanked Martin, for he had played the new piece to his wife for her fine cooking. He put down the loon flute and patted the round of his belly, contented . . . for the time being. Martin really loved good food. Maybe tomorrow he would go to the woods near Duck Creek to gather mushrooms. Maybe he'd hear a song, a song of bears eating blackberries. You never could tell, it might be very powerful. Or maybe just some squeaky song of a red fox.

Patricia Riley is of Cherokee and Irish ancestry and a mother of two children. She completed her Ph.D. in Native American literature at the University of California, Berkeley, and she is currently assistant professor in the Department of English at the University of Idaho. She teaches courses on Native American literature, and she is known as a storyteller. Riley is the editor of a new anthology, *Growing Up Native American,* and she has published several scholarly articles in various journals and other anthologies. Her creative works have appeared in *Northeast Indian Quarterly, ASAIL,* and Anchor Books' *Earth Song, Sky Spirit.* Her essays and criticism have also appeared in the much-acclaimed *Fiction International* and *Looking Glass.* She has written a major study of the novels of Louise Erdrich and plans to publish it in the near future. Riley lives in the heart of the Palouse country in the university town of Moscow, Idaho.

Patricia Riley

# Wisteria

IT WAS HALF PAST SEVEN IN THE MORNING AND EDDIE T. was already up and stirring an enormous black pot full of the bright yellow squash she planned to can that day. She hummed absentmindedly as she wiped the perspiration from her ancient face with the edge of her rose-embroidered apron. Though the hour was early, the kitchen already had the feel of midafternoon due to the hickory fire that blazed inside the antique wood stove where Eddie T. continued to do all of her cooking. In the storage shed behind the garden, a modern "radar range" languished new and never lifted from its crate. It had been a gift from her daughter-in-law, Jessie, but Eddie T. mistrusted the new stove's shiny chrome and doubted its ability to brown the crust just right on a fresh loaf of bread. She felt this way, at least in part, because Jessie had chosen the appliance. Everyone within smelling distance of Jessie's farm knew that she burned most everything she turned her hand to. Eddie T. never ceased to be amazed at how far the charred smell of burned beef and biscuits could travel on an evening breeze. It only made sense that such a person could not be relied upon to make an intelligent decision about something that was meant for cooking.

Justine crept up to the back door, pressed her face softly against the screen, and quietly watched her grandmother's preparations. Eddie T. moved back and forth along the kitchen counters with thoughtful precision. Carefully, she poured boiling water from a copper kettle into the tall round jars that sat like sentinels in dishpans of battered enamel. Justine knew she had to wait until Eddie T. was completely engrossed in her work or she wouldn't have a chance of making it past her undetected. If luck was truly with her, which it never had been before, she would be able to sneak inside quietly, make her way to the table unobserved, and be there, sitting smugly, when her grandmother turned around from the sink. It was a kind of cat-and-mouse game the two of them played whenever Justine came to visit, which was almost every day, except for Sunday. These days, Jessie kept her daughter to her self and away from Eddie T. on the Lord's day.

Justine blamed the enforced Sunday boycott on the TV preachers her mother had listened to during a two-week bout with the flu. Before that, her mother had been a fan of three, sometimes four, soap operas that she somehow managed to work into her hectic daily routine. Being ill, however, changed all that. Confined to bed, her mother had little else to do but watch whatever came on the TV. She had started out by intending to increase her soap opera consumption, but then something happened. Something that her mother reverently referred to now as "the mighty hand of God." On day three of the flu, three for the Trinity, her mother swore, an unprecedented thunderstorm of the most severe electrical variety had hit Harrison County and knocked out the local programming. When the ozone finally cleared, the only station that remained operational was a religious network broadcasting from out of Tennessee. It had to be a miracle.

Justine's father, Tom, told her that he figured the combination of the flu and the thunderstorm must have put Jessie in immediate touch with her own mortality because by day seven of vomiting and the green apple trots, Jessie had suddenly acquired what could only be described as a religious personality and rapidly converted to three-times-a-day Bible study and absolute churchgoing on a strict Sunday basis. This practice, as designed, was no doubt intended to be spiritually beneficial. However, in Jessie's case it provoked an intolerant streak a mile wide and five hundred years deep. After six steady weeks of study groups and Sunday sermons, the hellfire-and-brimstone kind, her face took on a fevered expression and her eyes began to gleam with unnatural light. At the drop of a hat, she would launch into long and impassioned sermons to whoever was within hearing distance, willing or otherwise, on why Eddie T.'s was no fit place for a young girl on Sunday mornings. In fact, Justine knew that if her mother had been allowed to have things entirely her way, visits with her grandmother would be limited to Saturday afternoons, when the rest of the family dropped in to check on the old woman and have their traditional Saturday family suppers. Those visits, at least, could be controlled, taking place as they did under Jessie's newly righteous and ever watchful religious eyes. She eagerly oversaw every suspected nuance or contrary word in a conversation with the protective tenacity of a bulldog guarding the sanctuary door. Justine's father, Tom, sat on the other side of the fence. He continued to insist that no harm was being done and that as far as he was concerned, Justine should spend as much time as possible with her grandmother.

In his secret thoughts, Tom regretted ever having listened to the disparaging things his schoolteachers had said about his people and their ways. They had made him feel backward and ashamed of who he was and where he came from. Most of all, he wanted Justine to grow up proud of herself and her people. He knew his mother had a lot to offer on that score and he thought he ought to give a listen to the things she said more often himself.

Jessie naturally took a dim view of her husband's attitude. She rebuked him regularly, called him "stiff-necked," compared him to some Philistine people, and prayed to God not to smite him. In her eyes, his failure to capitulate put all their souls in jeopardy. The entire state of affairs left her flustered because even though Tom professed to be a Christian, nothing she could say, do, or quote from Scripture would convince him that his mother was a heathen.

Often, late at night, Justine lay in bed listening to the endless, usually one-sided, argument over whether or not Eddie T. was an endangerment to Justine's tender young soul.

"Why, Tom, Eddie T. don't even pray to God," Jessie cried. "I myself have come upon her a number of times standing in the woods, waving her hands about and calling on the sun and moon and stars. Even the river, one time. God only knows who or what else she calls on. Anybody that does that is a heathen and a heathen's domain is no place for my daughter on Sunday mornings. Or any other morning for that matter. And I will say it. I don't care if she is your mother. I have a right to my opinion and a right to raise my child as I see fit. A heathen is a heathen and children need to be protected from that kind of thing."

"She prays to God, Jessie. She just does it in her own way is all."

Justine's father seldom answered his wife's diatribes directly, though he often shook his head over them. He hated most any kind of conflict, pure and simple, and avoided it as much as possible. Usually, he just listened until Jessie blew herself out and then went off on a walk somewhere while she simmered down. But even though he eventually compromised with her about the Sunday visits, purely for the sake of the temporary domestic peace, he remained firm about Justine's freedom to visit every other day of the week.

Eddie T. always looked forward to Justine's visits. She enjoyed the little games they played together. They kept her on her toes, and let her know that even though she was almost eighty-seven years old, she still had her wits about her. From the corner of her eye, she could see Justine's shadow now as it fell across the doorstep and into the room.

"Mornin', Liz." Eddie T. cackled and turned to face the small girl, who had tried so hard and unsuccessfully to make herself silent and unobserved. "Durned if you don't look like the spittin' image of Liz Taylor this mornin'."

"It's the haircut." Justine smiled at the old woman and opened the screen door. "Mama had it done. I liked it long, myself, but you know Mama. She says it tangles too much and, besides, long hair isn't stylish these days. She told Arleen at the Beauty Barn that she wanted something particularly stylish and this turned out to be it."

"Well, it looks okay, so don't get yourself worked up. Anyway, we got more important fish to fry. I found somethin' special out back of the yard this mornin'." Eddie T. looked sideways at her granddaughter and motioned for Justine to follow her back outside. "I can show you, but you got to promise not to mention it to your mam. You know how she feels about some kinds of things. It'll have to be our secret."

"Okay, Gramma," Justine said and smiled. It seemed as if they shared a lot of secrets these days since her mama had gone over to the TV preachers.

The old woman crossed the overgrown expanse that she called "the yard" and stopped beside a huge, out-of-control wisteria bush, heavy with pungent lavender blossoms.

"Mmmm, last blooms of the season. Smell that perfume. Sure smells good, don't it?" Eddie T. smiled at Justine, revealing toothless gums, which she quickly tried to hide.

"You came so early I didn't get a chance to put my choppers in," she said.

Justine took a deep breath of the flowered air and held it in as long as she could, reluctant to let go of the heavy, sweet smell.

"Gramma," she said, "you know I don't care if you got your teeth in or not."

"Yeah. You might not, but I do. I used to be pretty once."

"Still are." Justine tugged at the old woman's skirt. "Prettiest old lady in three counties, I bet."

Eddie T. chortled behind her hand. "We won't ever know the truth of that one, Miss Priss, since they ain't no beauty pageants for old toothless ladies in these parts."

"We'll start one of our own. It'll be a first."

"Um-hmm, I can see a king-size pitcher of that already."

The old woman took Justine's small hand in her own and led the way through the thick tangle of undergrowth behind the yard and on into the bordering woods. The tall oak trees provided shade and home to a wide variety of creatures and served as a kind of an outdoor pharmacy for the old woman. Eddie T. had taken the girl there many times and taught her where to look for roots and plants that were good for healing any number of common complaints from sore throat to fever.

"Somebody sick?" Justine asked. She knew that her grandmother was often asked by some of her neighbors to gather and prepare plant remedies. Most of the people Eddie T. knew couldn't afford the price of a town doctor.

"No, not this time. I told you this was somethin' special. Somethin' you almost never see."

"Did that old mama squirrel finally have some squirrel babies, is that it?"

Justine's eyes jumped with excitement at the thought. That was something she could tell the kids about at school, and her own mama, too. Then again, Justine thought she probably ought to keep that one to herself as well. Her mother could go on for hours about how squirrels carried rabies and wasn't it just like Eddie T. to expose her daughter to the perils of familiarity with savage disease-carrying rodents.

"Look over there where that blackberry bush is twinin' around that stump and you'll see what I'm talkin' about."

Justine scrunched her eyes and studied the area, but all she could see was an old broken-off oak tree and blackberry vines trying to turn brown from the summer's heat and not enough rain.

"I don't see anything so special about a tree stump and some dying berry vines, Gramma." Justine kicked at the ground in disappointment. "What am I supposed to see?"

"Look beside the stump, Justine, not at it. See that circle of grass all mashed down?" Eddie T. pointed at a spot about two feet in diameter that appeared to have been deliberately trampled down.

"Uh-huh," Justine said, still not seeing anything special about a spot of mashed grass.

"There's little people out back here, Justine, and sometimes they get together and hold a dance. They must have had one of them dances right there just last night."

"Little people? Really? Mama says there ain't no such thing as little people, Gramma."

"Well, I'm not gonna say that your mam is wrong, Justine, 'cuz that wouldn't be right. I guess for some people, and your mam's probably one of 'em, that there ain't any. That's 'cuz they let them die inside their minds a long time ago, I expect. But there's always been little people livin' in these old woods since time immemorial. That's what the old folks told me when I was a girl and I know it's true. Sometimes late at night I could hear them singin' songs. They must have been dancin' back then, too. I used to get up out of bed and go to the cabin door and see way off in the woods little lights flickerin' through the leaves. Those old-time Cherokees always said they was there. They called them the Yunwi Tsunsdi."

"If you been knowing this such a long time, Gramma, how come you never told me before today?"

"Well, mostly because I always get in trouble with your mam, or get you in trouble with her, but also because I wanted to wait until the time was right to tell you."

"How come now is the right time to tell me, Gramma?"

"Well, I'm not as young as I used to be, Justine. I'm an old lady. I have had a responsibility to these little people for a long time now. I remember them, you see. It's our obligation to do that."

"How do you remember them, Gramma? What does that mean?"

"Oh, I leave things for 'em. Little snacks of food mostly, sometimes tobacco and beads when I got 'em, and wisteria flowers when they're bloomin'. They like them blossoms. My mam called them things offerings. Just to let them know that we ain't forgot about 'em. That we know they're out there livin' on. But like I said, Justine, I'm gettin' to be an old lady now and I know I won't be on this old earth much longer."

"I wish you wouldn't say things like that, Gramma. You make me sad."

"Shush. Ain't nothin' to be sad about, child. Things got to grow old and die when their time comes, just like them wisteria. And dyin' ain't all that much anyway. It's all a part of the cycle. What's old just naturally got to make room for them that's new. It's the way things is. If it weren't there'd be too many things walkin' around chokin' up the earth. Us what's old just got to move on and make a place for you to stand in this world. All things gotta die, child, that's just the way of it. It ain't as bad as all that, because nothin's ever really gone even when it dies. It's kind of like a snake sheddin' its skin: you just wiggle on out of the old dried-up part and leave it behind. You wipe them eyes. We'll go on back to the house now. We got Saturday supper to think about, but you got to promise me to remember them little people when I'm gone, Justine. And bring 'em some of that wisteria once in a while. They like that."

Justine grabbed the old woman's hand and held it as if she never wanted to let go. "I promise, Gramma," she said, "I promise."

Late that night, the weather turned and a wind blew up out of the north that keened around the doors and rattled the windows of Eddie T.'s house. It thundered so hard and long that jelly jars tumbled off the cellar shelves and broke on the old stone floor.

Safe at home, Justine stretched and snuggled, warm beneath the quilts her grandmother had given her. She watched the long oak branches skitter and scrape against her bedroom window and thought about how they sounded like nightbirds calling to each other across the darkness. The last thing Justine remembered before she fell asleep was the wind whispering secrets to her in a language she couldn't understand and a streak of light that blazed and sped across the southern sky.

The next day, Eddie T.'s kitchen stood quiet and empty. The usual open door remained closed and locked. And for the first time there was no smell of fresh-made coffee hanging in the morning air. The ashes in the ancient black stove stood gray and cold. In the tiny room next to the kitchen, the old woman never stirred. And way out back of the house, near the woods, something small sobbed as it moved slowly and heavily among the suddenly silent trees.

Richard Van Camp is an exciting young native writer, one of many associated with the prestigious En'owikin Center of Penticton, British Columbia. He is a member of the Dogrib Nation in the Northwest Territories, and he is currently a student at the University of Victoria. His creative works have been published in *Whetstone, Descant,* and *Gathering I, II,* and *III.* His first book, *The Lesser Blessed,* is scheduled to be published by Theytus Books of British Columbia. His talents have been recognized by CBC television, which has hired Van Camp as a script consultant for "North of 60." The author has dedicated his story "Sky Burial" to the memory of Lorne Simon.

Richard Van Camp

# Sky Burial

(Dedicated to the Memory of Lorne Simon)

THE OLD INDIAN STOPPED WALKING AND STARED AT THE bird. The mall screamed past him. A stroller barked his leg and a parent growled, "The helloutatheway!" The old man kept looking. He didn't know its name but was awed at how bright the feathers were. The bird was dying.

Parakeet? Parrot? No, he knew it wasn't the tribe's name and he wished he knew. The bird deserved worship. He thought of all the shampoo bottles his daughter Augustine used and chose the one that smelled the best.

"Papaya," he said, "I will call you Papaya."

The pet store that boasted the bird had it in a cage. The bird measured three feet from black beak to bright blue tail, yet the cage offered only four. A sign read DO NOT TAP CAGE. There wasn't a name for the bird, anywhere. The bird was upside down, shitting yellow on itself and biting at the chain that sliced into its leg.

"Are you a woman?" he asked. He was sure she was a woman. The bird was panting, its black tongue licking its bleeding foot. It hung, rested, tried to bite at the chain, fell back. It looked as if it were drowning. The Indian watched the bird and felt under his shirt where his ulcer was bleeding inside. He grunted and went to open the cage.

"Macaw," she said.

"Huh?"

"It's a macaw." Joseph turned to look at the wielder of such a firm voice. It was a child. A girl. Tall, slim, an elf almost. She was beautiful. Her eyes were a question; they were large and round. She wore a T-shirt with a huge white owl with yellow eyes on it. A younger boy came up and started banging on the cage and the girl left as fast as she had appeared. Joseph wanted to talk to her but he was hit again with pain. He looked down. There wasn't enough light in the mall for shadows, but he imagined if there were, the bird and he would look glorious.

. . .

He bought coffee and a doughnut at Grandma Lee's. As he sat, the pain bit again and again, as if a red whip were let loose inside his belly and were lashing all around. He winced, put his head down, and through his braids saw his new old shoes. He took a breath, biting the tip of his tongue.

"Chinaman did a good job on polishing them up," he breathed and wiggled his toes.

The pain struck again. He took a bite of the doughnut, thinking the meat of the dough would soak up the blood inside him. His shoes were so polished they looked like black glass. In the reflection he watched the shadows and saw a man walking toward him.

"There you are," Harold said and sat beside him.

"Cocksucker," Joseph whispered and looked up. The noise of the mall rose around him: the metal whine of blenders; children hollering for toys. Harold had a tray of Cokes and tacos. The smell was thick and sweet. "We were looking for you."

Joseph stared out the window at the mall parking lot. A blond child stood crying in the middle of the pavement, her red balloon flying away. One of her shoes was off; Joseph squinted but couldn't see a parent.

"I see you got your shoes fixed. What else?" Harold took the paper bag and looked inside.

Joseph glared at him for not asking first. "Safes," he grumbled. "Suzy Muktuck's in town." He studied Harold's throat; his sharp windpipe would be easy to crush.

Harold pulled out a pair of new black shoes.

"Joe." Harold blushed. "Nobody calls them *safes* anymore. Did Augy say you could afford these?"

Augy can kiss my ass, Joe wanted to say.

"I don't understand why you got those fixed up," Harold scoffed. "You don't even have enough money for next week. Christ, you've been eating at our place the last four days . . ."

"Gotta look good," Joseph explained.

"If I hear another Vietnam war story, Joe, I don't know what I'll do," Harold said.

"Doc says I gotta talk about it."

Harold rolled his eyes and bit into the taco. Tomato sauce gushed out the bottom. Joseph closed his eyes. The sauce was blood to him, Augustine's blood every time she tried to have a baby. It was also the blood in his piss and the blood on the snow.

Harold, with a full mouth, went on talking. Joseph nodded and pretended to pay attention. He sipped his coffee and waited for Harold to quit chewing.

"Where's Augy?" he asked.

"She's your daughter. Prob'ly looking for you." Harold bit into the taco again and Joseph looked for the little blond girl. She was gone, nowhere.

"There you are," an exhausted voice heaved. Augustine huffed toward them: her bad perm, pink track pants, jean jacket, dusty runners. She sat down and grabbed the other taco, elbowing Harold for a sip of his Coke. "And you!" she scolded. "This is cold."

She bit into it anyway. Joseph studied her and her husband. He looked at her dyed-black hair, her dreadful perm, and thought, Spider legs, thousands of spider legs.

The couple gabbed. Food toppled out of their mouths. Their noise was muffled and lost to the crowd. Joseph looked around.

"Oh." A breath lit from his mouth and he caught himself. It was the young girl he saw, the one with the owl shirt. Augy and Harold kept talking, taking turns sucking at the dry Coke, biting into each other's tacos.

A spirit, Joseph said inside. A wood spirit.

Her long black hair was what caught him. He watched her. She was with a white woman who walked behind her. They had hot dogs and drinks. They sat down out of his view and he shifted to see them better.

". . . And the lady, Dad, said we could visit Sundays and we could bring you home-cooked food. Oh, it'll be so good for you to be with others your own age." Augy giggled and ate while Harold listened and nodded. "Joe, the move will be good for you."

Joseph nodded and looked for the young girl. A young couple was in his way. They had their lower lips pierced, and whenever they kissed, Joseph could hear metals clicking, clicking. Their fat, sloppy tongues ate into each other's mouths, which looked like yellow tractors smashing and sharing dirt.

Savages, he thought and caught a flash of her hair, and his heart brightened.

He squinted and saw her. She was nodding, listening to the white woman speak. Oh, her eyes were so wide!

Joseph sat straight up and almost spilled his drink. He brought his hand up over his lip and caressed the whiskers. She is the one, he thought; it was her shirt that did it. The white owl she wore was the white owl he killed in '79. Those were his drinking days: his and Stan's.

"I'm Stan the man with the nine!" Stan would cry to the women that drank with them. "When I die, there's gonna be two boxes: one for Stan and one for the nine!" The women would giggle and Stan would always throw Joseph a wink.

Joseph, that winter, was taking a leak outside a party when he looked up and saw a huge white owl looking down at him. What he remembered most was the eyes. They were yellow and there was fire behind them. The owl hissed at him and he ran back to his shack. He grabbed his .410 and Stan followed after him.

"Take a look at this fuckin' owl!" Joseph hooted. "Take a look!"

They were both drunk and Stan made the sign of the cross when he saw the owl.

Stan yelled, "Someone's gonna die! Don't shoot it!" But Joseph aimed and fired, *not meaning to hit it,* he would say later, and all they saw was an explosion of white feathers. Stan slapped him hard across the ear and Joseph fell down. Stan ran into the snow to help the bird but it was dead.

Neither of them buried the bird and Stan didn't speak to Joseph ever again.

The next time Joseph saw the owl, it was in a dream. He dreamed that he was walking in the snow to the old trapline he and Stan had shared when they were kids and that owl landed in front of him. The eyes of the owl had changed. They were Stan's.

Joseph woke up to Augy's running into his room saying that Stan had died. A stroke had taken him during the night.

The pain hit again and Joseph bit his cheek so he wouldn't scream. "It's gettin' closer," he whispered.

He thought of the lake.

In his dreams, Joseph walked into the lake by his home as he died, releasing himself to it, disappearing.

On CBC this morning, the Dogrib leaders were telling everybody to boil the water twice before drinking it. Nobody knew why.

He shook his head. "We can't drink it, but we bathe in it."

It was true.

He took a long breath, stood, and walked in the direction of the table. He knew he was the last of the old-timers and he could taste blood in his saliva.

"Where are you goin'?" Harold asked.

"Refill," Joseph answered and he began to sing under his breath.

His lips moved and he felt the wind gather around him. He walked in his polished shoes and there she was. She and her mother were eating their hot dogs. The girl was the first to see him. "Mommy," she said, "look at his hair."

The mother gawked toward him and warned, "Now, honey . . ."

"Scuse me," Joseph said, all the while hoping he'd have enough time. He sat beside them. The mother began to look around, perhaps for Security, but the girl watched him. "There is something in your daughter's hair."

"What!" the mother squawked. "Where?" She went through her daughter's hair. "Oh, Mindy . . ."

Mindy wouldn't stop looking at his hair. "It's so long. Can I touch?" she asked, holding her hands out to him.

"Go ahead."

"Honey, no!" the mother scolded. The top of her lip had curled in, revealing yellow bleached teeth.

"It's okay." Joseph smiled. The young girl took his braid and felt it.

"Did you tie this yourself?" Joseph fell into her eyes. They were so big!

"I get my daughter to do it. She's over there." He did this more for the mother, who looked at and studied them.

The mother's eyes went wide when she spotted the couple.

"Yes"—Joseph shook his head and chuckled—"the one with the perm."

"That's some do. Zat her husband?"

"Yes," Joseph said, singing loudly inside, roaring the call.

"Oh," Mindy apologized and pulled her hands away from his braids, "some came out."

Joseph smiled. "*Whatsee da.*"

"What?" she smiled and he loved her for it.

"It means 'Let's see.' "

"Ahh." She gave him his hair and he took it. *"Wot seee doh,"* she tried.

"Well," the mother exhaled, "I can't find anything."

"It's right here," Joseph explained and felt through Mindy's hair. He felt the waves of a hot lake, the down on a duck's belly, the underflesh of a thousand petals.

"Look," he said and brought back a bright blue feather. He pulled a hair from her head when he pulled back the feather.

"Oh my"—the mother grinned—"oh my!"

"Oh, Mommy"—Mindy clapped—"it's beautiful!"

"For you." Joseph offered to Mindy. "A macaw," he said.

"The macaw!" Mindy beamed.

"When a woman gives birth to a girl," he offered, "the girl is the father's teacher."

Under the table, he wrapped her hair around his fingers.

"I'm Daddy's teacher?" Mindy asked.

"You're the one," he finished. Yes, he would teach her. He sang. He called it forth and it came. The young girl giggled and covered her mouth. A hand grabbed onto Joseph's shoulder, almost snapping the song.

"Here he is!" Harold hollered. "Over here, Augy!"

Joseph looked down.

*"Dyae kae khlee nee,"* he whispered and looked over to Mindy. "Remember me."

"Can I keep the feather?" she asked.

"It was always yours."

"Say thank you to the nice man," the mother said.

*"Mahsi."* Mindy smiled and held the feather up to the light.

"Dad!" Augy said and came over. "I'm so sorry," she apologized to the woman, "my father wanders." She cleared her throat and lowered her voice: "He's . . . confused."

Joseph sank into his seat but sang louder now and began moving his lips. He wished he had his wolf rattle. He felt the song push against the back of his teeth and run its fingers through her hair. He looked into Mindy's eyes and sent part of himself: the good part. Mindy's eyes went wide as she registered his power. She wasn't scared and that was good.

He sang. He unraveled her secret hair from his fingers. He sang. He had strands of his hair in his hands as well and under the table pulled them together. He waited, sang, he looked down. He looked down to make sure all their shadows were touching.

He sang her name with a breath and all she heard was "*Deeeee* . . ." as he pulled their hair together until the strands snapped.

Like trip wires, he thought and Joseph left his body. Mindy received him: the macaw's blue feather in her hand; her mother pulling her close; Augy, her bad perm blocking out the sun.

"Dad? Dad!" she called but he did not meet her eyes.

He was swallowed by the hottest lake,

flying,

an explosion of white feathers . . .

Penny Olson is an Ojibwe who lives with her family in Michigan's Upper Peninsula. She earned her bachelor's and master's degrees in English from Northern Michigan University and emphasized Native American literature in all her studies. Olson published her first short story in Anchor Books' *Earth Song, Sky Spirit,* and she has prepared a manuscript entitled *The Circles of Life,* which she plans to turn into her first novel. Currently, Olson is an instructor at Bay Mills Indian Community College and Lake Superior State University in the eastern Upper Peninsula. She teaches English and courses dealing with her specialty, American Indian literature.

Penny Olson

# Midnight at the Graveyard

"LIGHTNING STRUCK!" MEGAN VARIED HER PITCH, SHIFTing like the wind before a storm. She brought her fingers gently together at the nape of Sean's neck and watched him shiver. "Chills climbed up the murderer's spine, like a spider spinning a web."

"That's enough, Megan," Sean's voice cracked as he jerked away from his cousin. Ever since she had come back from Girl Scout camp two weeks ago, Megan had been giving him the chills and telling ghost stories. "I don't want to hear any more."

"What's the matter, chicken?"

"Naw, it's just a silly ol' story." Sean looked down and watched himself dig a hole in the dirt of Gram's flower bed with the toe of his gym shoe. He cringed, still feeling the aftereffects of Megan's fingers creeping across his neck. "Are ya goin' to do it tonight? Are ya?" he asked, trying to change the subject.

"Why not?" Megan grinned. "After all, Gramps said there would be a full moon tonight. That's the best time to spend a night in a graveyard, isn't it?"

Sean looked at Megan and gave her a watery smile. Nothing scared his cousin. Sean believed that Megan was the original tomboy. Her auburn hair had been long at the beginning of summer until it got in her way at a baseball game and she chopped her pigtails off. Her lip was split from when she fell off her skateboard. Although most people would describe her as tall and thin, Sean thought of her as just being skinny. Megan was ten years old, about eighty pounds, and almost five feet tall. About three feet of that five was leg, and what wasn't leg was arm.

Everyone said how much Megan looked and acted like her mother. Sean didn't really remember his Aunt Elizabeth. He had been only five when she died along with her husband in a motorcycle accident, but Megan did look like the pictures of her mother that were in Gram's photo albums. And from the stories that Gram and Gramps told, Sean could see why people said they acted the same.

"What was my mom like when she was little?" Megan would ask Gramps.

"Kind of like you." Gramps would smile and watch Megan as he told the story. "One time, she and your Aunt Mary wanted to sleep outside in the tent. Gram and I said it was okay, and that I would get the tent down from the rafters in the garage after supper. Well, your mother couldn't wait that long. She snuck outside and climbed up there to get the tent down. While walking back across one of the rafters, she lost her balance and fell. She broke her arm in three places and got a concussion out of the deal." Gramps paused for a second. "When she landed, the tent fell on top of her and pinned her underneath it. It muffled her screams and cries for help. If Mike hadn't come over to look at the stock car, I don't know when we would have found her. Just like you, Meggie, patience was not one of her virtues."

Sean's older brother, Bill, joined the two younger children. "So, pick a night to pass the initiation ceremony yet, Meggie?"

"Sure did." Megan faked a punch to Bill's midsection as she took what she imagined to be the stance of a prizefighter. Then she closed one eye to become a swaggering pirate with a shifting grin. "Tonight, me bucko, under the full moon. Will you be joining us, matey?"

"Aye, you old dog, someone has to go along to keep you honest." Bill played right along with his younger cousin before reaching over to grab Sean in a headlock and rubbing his brother's stubby brown crew-cut. "And what about you, little brother, are you going to last the night in the bad old cemetery?"

Sean was definitely the most timid of the three children on the Dowds' front lawn. He was also the smallest and quietest of the three. Sean was the one Meggie and Bill depended on to remember to bring the bat and ball down to the field so they could play baseball. He was the fall guy for most of their practical jokes. Sean was the one who got bound and gagged when the three of them played cops and robbers, and then forgotten in the attic when Meggie and Bill got bored and went out to play. He was the one who made sure a path was left for Gramps through the bikes and toys, and he always helped Gram bring groceries in the house after shopping.

Every summer Bill and his friends would allow Megan and Sean to hang around with them only if they performed some outrageous act. This summer they were to spend two hours, right around midnight, in the graveyard.

"C'mon, Sean, don't be a Jiminy Cricket," Megan chimed in with Bill, referring to the Disney character who served as a conscience to Pinocchio. "You want to hang around with the big guys this summer, don't you?"

"Yeah, but . . ." Sean paused. "Well, how are we going to do this? Mom and Dad will hear us sneak out, Bill. And Gram will have a heart attack if she finds you missing."

"That's why you're going to ask Gram if we can put the old umbrella tent up in the backyard and see if the three of us can sleep out here tonight." Megan grinned. "Gram never says no to you. You're her baby. And we don't have to worry about Gramps; he's going to Baraga tonight to help Mike Dakota get the stock car ready for the race next Saturday night."

"You've got it all figured out, don't you?" Sean still had some doubts. "Well, what if we get caught? What if . . ."

"Enough already! Either you're with us, or stay at home." Bill never had much patience with his younger brother. "I don't care one way or another."

"All right, I'll ask Gram if we can use the tent."

"I knew we could count on you." Megan raised her hand above her head. "High five!"

"We'll see if you're this happy about this around midnight." Bill practiced his best Count Dracula impression. "You never know what or who lurks in a graveyard."

Megan put her arm around Sean's shoulders. She wasn't about to let Bill worry her. If she showed Sean that she wasn't the least bit scared, her nine-year-old cousin might lose some of the worry plastered on his face. She puffed out her chest a little. "Let's go get the tent, Sean. You can help me put it up. Then we'll call Aunt Mary and see if you and Big Boss Man can spend the night. C'mon, I'll race ya."

Bill let Megan and Sean run into the house while he shuffled behind them. *I'll show them. I'll get Jeff to help scare the heck out of them tonight. They'll run back here screaming. It'll be worth getting in trouble just to see the look on their faces.* He heard a car in the back and knew that Gramps must be back from the store. *I'll have to find a way to call Jeff when everyone is busy and won't hear our plans.*

"How ya doin', Billy Boy?" Gramps handed Bill a bag of groceries to bring in the house. "Meggie and Sean went runnin' in the house, yelling something about sleeping in the backyard tonight. What kind of mischief do they have planned?"

"Ah, nothin', Gramps. You know how little kids are."

"No, I'm not sure," Gramps said. "Why don't you tell me. I'm going out to Baraga tonight to help Mike with the stock car, and I might spend the night at Great-Grandma's, depending on what time we finish up. I don't want to have to worry about you three behaving yourselves. Okay?"

Bill took the groceries into the house to avoid his grandfather's question. Gramps took the boy fishing, taught him how to ride a horse and gave him the medicine bag that Bill always wore around his neck to protect himself. He would not risk Gramps's trust by lying to him.

Gramps shook his head and wondered even more about what his three grandchildren were up to as he followed Bill through the banging screen door.

Gram met her husband at the top of the stoop. "Did you get the carrots?" she asked. "I'm going to make some venison stew for supper and for you to take to your mom and Mike."

"Yeah, I got your carrots, my girl." He put his free arm around his wife as they entered the kitchen. "What do you think about these kids' plans for tonight?"

"I think that they'll be in the house and in bed with me before the first owl hoots. Don't you?"

"I'm not sure," Gramps answered, remembering how Bill had avoided his question. "Do you want me to stay home tonight? Or should I take Bill up to Baraga with me? That would be one less monkey that you would have to worry about."

"If you need his help, take him." Gram found the carrots and took them over to the sink to clean. "But don't worry about me handlin' these three rascals. They can't be any worse than their parents were."

"Okay, I won't. Hey, you three!" Gramps yelled into the living room. "Come help Gram put these groceries away and I'll go and get the tent down."

"You're too late, Gramps," Bill told his grandfather. "Meggie and Sean just went out the front door. They said something about going to the garage."

Gramps ran out of the kitchen, slammed out the back door and headed for the garage, hoping to cut off Megan and Sean. As he reached the back door of the garage, he heard Sean's frightened voice.

"Meggie, are you sure you should be getting the tent down that way?"

Gramps looked in the small window of the garage door. He saw his granddaughter perched on one of the rafters carrying the tent as if it were a pole and she were on a high wire in the circus. He knew if he rushed into the garage he would frighten the girl. Gramps quietly opened the door and stood underneath his granddaughter.

"Drop the tent into my arms, Megan Elizabeth," he began in a slow, even voice. "Then you get over to the loft and climb down from there."

"Oh, hiya, Gramps." Megan's voice was about half an octave

higher than usual. "I thought I'd get the tent down so we could sleep out back tonight. Gram said it was okay."

Gramps heard his wife catch her breath as she joined him and watched Megan continue across the narrow rafter, fifteen feet above the garage's concrete floor. He knew that Gram was seeing Megan plummet to the concrete just as her mother had done twenty years ago. As soon as Megan reached the loft, they both started to breathe again. Before Gramps could say anything, Gram rushed to the ladder and started climbing. He wasn't sure if Gram was going to hug the child or strangle her.

"Young lady, I may have told you that you could sleep outside in the tent tonight, but I specifically told you to let Gramps get the tent down. What are you trying to do, give me a heart attack?"

"Geez, nobody got hurt, Grams." Megan put her arms around her grandmother. "I just couldn't wait any longer. Don't be mad."

Gram just shook her head. She looked down at her husband and shrugged her shoulders. She gently slapped Megan on the butt and said, "Okay, let's get down from here now."

"Megan." Gramps spoke in a stern voice that Megan knew meant trouble. "Why do you think I told you that story about your mother?"

When there was no answer, Gramps continued. "It was a way for you to learn a lesson. It wasn't meant for you to try the same stunt."

Gramps rubbed his forehead and looked at Gram. "I guess I learned the lesson," he said. "From now on the tent stays on the landing."

When Megan heard Gramps say that, she asked, "Gramps, can you help Sean an' me put the tent up?" She gave her grandfather a smile he couldn't refuse. "It smells kinda funny. I think it needs some fresh air."

Bill was standing on the concrete block as they brought the tent out of the garage. "I'll help the kids with it, Gramps," he said.

"Are you anxious to get rid of us?" Gramps looked closely at his oldest grandchild.

"Naw." Bill took his grandfather's corner of the tent. "I'm just trying to help. That's all."

"Hey, Bill, do you think Jeff would want to sleep out with us?" Megan asked. Jeff was Bill's best friend; usually they did everything together.

"Naw, I already asked him," Bill answered. "He's got something else planned tonight."

"When did you ask him?"

"When you were trying to break your neck getting the tent down. Jesus, Megan, sometimes I think you enjoy scaring the crap out of Gram and Gramps." Bill came as close to swearing as he dared. He couldn't believe the things that Megan did. If someone dared her to do something, she would definitely try it.

The three of them struggled with the tent for over an hour. They almost had it up when they discovered the pole for the middle was only half there.

"I'll go get it." Megan headed for the garage.

"One more step and you can forget about sleeping out," Bill said. "Gramps'll skin you alive and me for letting you go up there again. Sean, go tell Gramps we need his help."

Sean hurried into the house and Bill stared at Megan.

"What are you looking at?" Megan asked.

"I'm just trying to figure you out," he answered. "You knew Gramps told you that story about your mom so you wouldn't go up on the rafters, yet you did it anyway. How come?"

"I do a lot of the things that Gramps says my mom used to do." Megan looked down at her feet. "I offer tobacco at night instead of the morning because that's the way she did it. I play baseball instead of softball because she did. When I can do something that she did, it's like she's still here. Gramps says that she must be watching over me, taking care of me so I don't get hurt when I do things that she did as a kid."

"What about your dad? You hardly ever talk about him."

"I miss him, too." Megan started scuffing up the dirt with her shoe. "But he was gone so much. You know he was only home from the navy three months when they got killed. I was mad at him for a long time."

It had been quiet for about fifteen seconds when Bill asked, "Why?"

"If he hadn't taken my mom on that stupid motorcycle"—Bill couldn't believe the anger in Megan's voice—"they might be alive now and I wouldn't have to go to the graveyard to spend time with them." Megan angrily swiped at her eyes with the back of her hand.

Gramps and Sean came up behind Megan. Gramps put his hand on Megan's shoulder. "Are you okay, Meggie?"

She shook her head.

"Want to come help me get the rest of the tent down?"

"Uh-huh."

"Your father and I used to go on fishing weekends," Gramps said as the two of them went into the garage. "Most of the time we'd throw back what we caught. We would only keep what we could eat. You know that was before your parents were even married. Then your mom started coming along. One time your dad threw one of the fish that she caught back in the lake. It was the biggest one that had been caught that day. Your mother was furious."

"Is that the time she tipped the canoe over?" Megan smiled.

"Let me finish the story," Gramps said. "Yes, she tipped the canoe over in the middle of the lake. She told your dad that he had better find her fish before he got out of the lake. At seven o'clock the next morning your mom woke up face to face with a ten-inch lake trout on her pillow. It wasn't the same fish, but it was close."

Gramps was glad to see Megan laugh. "Megan," he began, "we talk about your mother because we knew her better. But, child, believe me, you are an awful lot like your father, too. You laugh like he did and at the same things. You wouldn't be Megan if it hadn't been for him."

"I wish we could have a bonfire in the backyard," Megan said wistfully as they left the garage. "That was my dad's favorite part of camping. He loved to cook hot dogs on a stick and roast marshmallows." She smiled at Gramps. "I like doing those things, too."

Gramps helped them put the tent up. The kids put out their sleeping bags and were having a pillow fight when Sean stopped everything with a simple question.

"When are we going to go to the cemetery?"

Bill started to speak, but ended up just clearing his throat. Megan looked at both of the boys and started to giggle. The laughter just bubbled inside of her. The boys were trying to look serious, yet they only looked as if they were in pain. Megan tried to take a deep breath to control her laughter. She ended up gulping the air, burping, and laughing all the harder. It felt as if someone were tickling her from the inside out.

Sean and Bill got caught up in Megan's laughter and started to giggle, too. Finally, when all three were gasping for air, Megan choked out, "Midnight, of course."

Gram had come out to the tent to call the kids in for supper. "What will happen at midnight?" she asked.

"Uh," Sean started stuttering.

"Nothin'," Bill said.

"Ghost stories," Megan replied.

"And who's going to tell these stories?" Gram asked.

"Me, of course." Megan was still trying to get her laughter under control. "You always say I'm the best storyteller, Gram."

"That you are, Meggie. Now come in and get washed up for dinner. We need to get Gramps on the road."

After supper, as Gramps got ready to go, Megan went outside and picked a sprig of cedar for her grandfather to carry with him. Gram had told her a long time ago that cedar helped make a journey safe for travelers. At the same time, Megan took some tobacco out of the small pouch she always carried with her, held it in her right hand and said, "Thank you for the cedar. I know this will keep Gramps safe. I'm also hoping that by giving you this gift of tobacco that my mom and dad will be with me tonight, watching over me, keeping me safe. I know that we will be by their graves, so they will be close by. Thank you, Creator, for a good day."

Megan sprinkled the tobacco in her hand around the cedar tree. Then she took the cedar branch to her grandfather and gave him a kiss.

"I'll see you in the morning, Gramps," she told him.

"Ask Mike if we can be in the pit next week at the race," Bill said, "please, Gramps."

"Yes," Megan and Sean chimed in. "Ask Mike, Gramps."

"We'll see," Gramps replied. "Behave yourselves and I'll check on you when I come back either late tonight or early tomorrow morning."

About nine o'clock Gram came out to tuck them in their sleeping bags, listen to prayers and give them that last glass of water.

"The back porch light will be on," Gram said, kissing the tops of their heads one last time. "And the back door will be open in case you need to come in. Good night now."

"Night, Gram." The three childish voices combined, creating a harmony that made Gram smile as she left the tent. She zipped the tent flap closed and went into the house.

The lightbulb on the back porch cast eerie shadows on the tent walls. As Sean traced the monsters created by the light on the tent wall by his pillow, Megan began speaking in a low voice.

"This is a true story that I heard at Girl Scout camp about a very rich man who had to have the best of everything. He drove a Corvette during the week and a Rolls-Royce on the weekends. He only ate steak.

He had three mansions with a TV in every room in all three of his houses. One day he decided it was time to get married." She lowered her voice even more so the boys would have to come closer. "The woman he fell in love with was the most beautiful, kind, loving and talented woman in the world. She had won Miss America and Miss Universe. She could play Bach and Beethoven on the piano, and she had adopted three children to live with her. She gave all her winnings from the beauty pageants to charity."

Bill looked at Megan and shook his head. "Why would she do that? Didn't she need that money to support those kids? Was she nuts?"

"Shut up and listen." Sean elbowed Bill.

"The man asked the woman to marry him and she agreed. They both were happy until the day of the accident." Megan took a dramatic pause.

"The woman was in a horrible car wreck," Megan continued. "She lost her right arm and was in a coma. Her husband stayed by her bedside night and day waiting for her to wake up. He told her that he would even get her a solid-gold arm to replace the one she had lost, if she would only wake up. She woke up and he spent millions of dollars to get her this golden arm that would work just like a real arm. But it wasn't enough." Megan stopped again.

"Just tell the story," Bill demanded. "Quit stopping all the time. You're making me mad."

"The woman got sick again and died. The man was devastated. He started gambling at casinos and drinking all of his fortune away." Megan stopped again. "I think we should go now."

"Oh no you don't." Bill grabbed Megan's arm. "Finish the story."

"I will at the graveyard." Megan gave a sly smile. "It will be better there."

The three of them went to the side of the house and grabbed their bikes. The full moon cast enough light that the children's eyes quickly adjusted to the semidarkness. The back entry of the cemetery was a mile and a half away, and it would take about ten minutes to get there. As they rode past an empty field, Megan saw wild daisies glow in the moonlight.

"Stop," she told her cousins. "I want to put some of those daisies on my mom's grave."

"Hurry up," Bill grumbled. "If we get caught, it's all your fault."

"We won't get caught. It'll only take a minute."

"Quit your complaining, Bill." Sean stopped his bike and had a threatening tone to his voice that was unusual. "It'll be fine."

Megan quickly picked the flowers and got back on her bike. "Let's go," she said.

When they got to the cemetery, they followed the road around the curve and found the big maple tree where Megan's parents were buried. Megan dropped her bike and went over to the headstones. She traced the writing first on her mother's, then on her father's.

Beloved Wife, Daughter, Mother
ELIZABETH KATHLEEN KENNEDY
Born: May 14, 1955
Died: August 15, 1985

Beloved Husband, Son, Father
ROBERT MICHAEL KENNEDY
Born: January 29, 1955
Died: August 15, 1985

When she finished, Megan placed the daisies below her mother's headstone. Wild daisies had been Elizabeth's favorite flower. Megan, too, liked the wild ones better than the daisies bought in the store. The wild ones seemed fragile, yet they had a toughness that allowed them to survive. She sat down and leaned against the old maple.

"Okay, boys, you ready for the rest of the story?"

"Yeah," Billy answered. "Are you?"

"Come closer, big mouth," Megan said in a stage whisper, "and you'll find out."

The boys sat down one on each side of her and waited for her to continue.

"Soon the man lost everything. He had no home, no job, no money, and no food. In fact, he owed people money. All he could see was his beautiful wife. Her blue eyes followed him everywhere. He was haunted by the memories of her golden hair, soft alabaster skin and ruby lips. When he had reached the lowest point of his life and was living in the gutter, he remembered . . ."

"What?" Bill had been caught up in Megan's telling of the story. "Remembered what?"

"His wife's golden arm." Megan's eyes narrowed. "The memory of her gold arm became his salvation. He plotted and planned going to the graveyard to dig up the body of his dead wife and take her gold arm from the grave."

Megan looked at both her cousins to make sure they were listening before she continued.

"Late one night, a night like this one with a full moon, the man went to the cemetery. He found his wife's grave and began to dig, and before long he heard the sound of the metal of the shovel hitting the brass of the casket." She paused. Bill dug at the ground with a stick and wasn't watching Megan at all. He was also muttering something that Megan couldn't quite make out. Sean, on the other hand, was watching his cousin intently. Usually he was bothered by stories like this; however, this time he seemed captivated by Megan's performance.

"The man jumped in the grave next to the casket." Megan licked her lips. "He grabbed a crowbar and slowly pried the casket open. There lay what was left of his dead wife. Maggots had eaten away part of her skin. The beautiful clothes she had been buried in had turned to rags. With bones showing through rotting skin and hair dulled by dust, his wife looked like one of the zombies from *Night of the Living Dead.*"

Sean was now biting his lower lip. Bill dug faster and deeper with the stick.

"That's enou—" Bill started to say, before quickly changing his tone to sarcasm. "Are you almost done?"

"Shh," came from Sean.

"Her golden arm was the only thing that hadn't changed. It glowed as bright as the day he had given it to her," Megan continued as if there had been no interruption. "He quickly snatched it out of the coffin, slammed the lid, threw dirt back in the grave and went home. When he got home, he threw the arm under his bed and tried to go to sleep. An hour later, a figure appeared at the end of his bed. 'W-who a-are y-you?' he stuttered, trying to control his trembling. 'And what do you want?' 'Don't you recognize me, my dear husband? I'm your dead wife, the one you visited tonight at the graveyard.' "

Megan glanced at the two boys to find out if they were really listening to her. " 'If you're my wife,' the man asked, 'where are your bright blue eyes?' 'Gooone in the grave.' " Megan dragged the moan out for as long as she could.

" 'What about your sun-gold hair?' 'Looost in the grave,' the ghost answered."

Megan's moaning and groaning was making Bill's skin crawl. He dug faster and harder, sending dirt everywhere.

" 'Where are your alabaster skin and your ruby lips?' 'They're all gone,' the ghost answered, 'gooooone in the grave.' " This time Megan howled.

" 'Well, if you are my wife' "—Megan stopped for a second before continuing in a whisper—" 'where's your golden arm?' "

As Megan grabbed Bill's arm and yelled " 'You've got it!' " a shadow from behind one of the large tombstones became a body.

Bill jumped up and screamed with all of his might. He hit his head on the tree trying to get away from the figure that had popped out from behind the tombstone. Megan and Sean laughed until they, too, saw the body standing there. They started screaming, too. Bill ran to his bike still screaming. The body was coming closer; it was saying something.

"Guys, will you stop your yelling. It's me, you idiots, Jeff."

Megan and Sean stopped and started to laugh. Bill, on the other hand, continued to scream while he got on his bike. Suddenly an arm reached out and grabbed his shoulder. It was old Mr. Larson, the night caretaker. Bill folded to the ground in a dead faint. Megan and Sean instantly stopped laughing. Mr. Larson shined his big old spotlight on them. Megan, Jeff and Sean ran over to where Bill lay.

"Could you tell me what the hell is going on here?" the caretaker asked.

"Mr. Larson," Megan said, "I'm worried about Bill. I can't tell if he's breathing."

Sean was almost in tears. "Is he dead?"

Bill moaned and Jeff started laughing. "I will never let him forget about this one."

"I'm waiting for an answer." Mr. Larson did not sound amused.

"We were going to spend a couple hours here on a dare," Megan tried to explain. "I told a story, and it scared Bill half to death. Then Jeff here popped out from behind a tombstone. I bet Bill and him were going to try and scare Sean and me."

"Well, it worked," Jeff piped in.

"Let me finish." Megan glared at Jeff. "Anyway, Bill started screaming and then you showed up."

"Well, Miss," Mr. Larson said, "I guess I'll have to call your grandfather to come and pick you three up."

As soon as Mr. Larson said the words "call your grandfather," Sean jumped into the conversation. "Please, Mr. Larson, don't call the house.

Gramps probably isn't even home and you'll only upset Gram. We'll just go home and you can call Gramps tomorrow." Sean stopped to catch his breath.

Bill had come to and chimed in with "Please."

"Not this time, kids," Mr. Larson said.

He rounded the four kids up and walked them back to the office. They sat and waited in the outer office while Mr. Larson made the telephone calls.

"I can't believe you forgot I was coming down here," Jeff said to Bill. "I have never seen you so scared."

"Megan's darn story didn't help," Bill muttered. "If she hadn't done that, our plan would have worked."

"Yeah, right," Sean said. "You just can't stand the fact that we passed your stupid initiation."

"We passed it all right," Megan said, "and I think we're all going to live to regret it."

They were surprised, ten minutes later, when Gramps showed up in the truck. He didn't say a word. He picked up their bikes, put them in the back of the truck and opened the passenger door of the truck for them to climb in.

"Bye, Jeff!" Bill yelled from the truck. "I'll talk to you tomorrow."

"Don't count on that, William Patrick," Gramps said. They knew they were in trouble.

"Gramps," Megan started as they left the cemetery. "I . . ."

"I'm sorry, Gramps." Sean spoke next. "I knew better."

"Yes, you did, and so did these other two."

Megan tried to change the subject. "When did you get home? I thought you were going to stay at Great-Grandma's."

"I had a problem with the truck." Gramps's voice was flat. "So I came home. I'll go tomorrow."

Bill didn't say anything at all. He didn't even try to look at his grandfather. He kept his eyes on the truck floor out of respect.

"I guess I'm at fault, too." Gramps sighed deeply. "I gave Bill too much responsibility that he just wasn't ready for."

Gramps feeling guilty made the three culprits feel even worse. They were all relieved, a few minutes later, when the truck pulled into the driveway. The children walked slowly into the house as their grandfather put the truck away. Gram was waiting there with a cup of herbal tea for each of them. Sean hugged her and mumbled into her chest about how sorry he was. Megan sat down and drummed her fingers on the table.

Bill stood in the corner and nervously clanked his spoon against the side of the teacup. What had started out as an adventure had turned into a disaster. Bill didn't want his grandfather to feel responsible for his mistake. Gramps walked into the kitchen, sat down at the table and drank his tea. He looked at each of his grandchildren, smiled and shook his head. A deep chuckle escaped from down in his chest. The children looked at him in surprise.

"At least," he said while laughing, "you didn't knock over any headstones like I did when I was your age."

Gram laughed, too. "I remember your mother taking your freedom away for two weeks and how miserable you were. What do you think, same punishment for these three?"

"That sounds good enough, seeing as they'll have to give up the stock car race next weekend." Gramps nodded his head, knowing how much the three of them had wanted to be in the pit.

"Aw, but, Gramps," the three of them started to protest.

Gramps cleared his throat and looked through his grandchildren as if they had disappeared. The three of them stared at the floor and said, "That'll be all right."

"Funny." Gramps smiled at Gram as Sean, Meggie and Bill gave them a hug and kiss and went upstairs. "I knew they'd see it our way."

Penny Olson

Misha is a mixed-blood Métis-Cree who lives in eastern Oregon, where she raises the draft horses she uses to plow her small farm. She is a gifted musician, playing and recording the flute and saxophone. In 1989 some of her work was performed by Australian musicians who won the Prix D'Itila Award. Misha herself is an award-winning author: her first book, *Red Spider, White Web,* won the Readercon Small Press Award for 1991. Her other books include *Prayers of Steel* and *Ke-Qua-Hawk-As.* She is currently completing a novel, *Yellow Jacket.* Her creative work has appeared in dozens of anthologies, including *Looking Glass, Storming the Reality Studio, Derrissimbimmel, Illuminated History of the Future, Unterdiebaut, Witness, Bone Saw,* and *Hard Times.* Misha is an artist who draws on her Indian heritage to create her poetry, short stories, and novels.

Misha

# Memekwesiw

*The drum in a dream pounds loud to the dreamer.*
—Carl Sandburg

THE MOON IS A FIRE DRUM POLISHING THE ANTHRACITE sky in silent booms. She stands before a steel cage that holds this week's exhibit. A white bear with muzzle of frost. Cold blue light crackles around its spirit pelt. The sheer bulk of the bear punches through her chest and leaves a cavelike hole that sucks her through herself into the bowels of the earth. Still, she watches her hand, the silver key strobing in the starlight, as it stretches forward and unlocks the door. There is a long moment of dead silence after the solitary click. She turns to run and is frozen by the sheer volume of bear roars. The bellow whirls her around to face the bear just as it strikes out and slaps the top of her skull off. It's a skull juggler. Her scalp flaps away into the night. Before the woman can fall, the bear sinks its massive jaws deep into her chest and begins to chew her; smacking and crunching, it rips the flesh from her bones. A bear hungry as fire licking her bone dry and white under the taut moon drum. She is screaming and screaming, horribly conscious of all the pain, the black blood and grayish fat flying in moonlight, as the bear rends her alive. The bear stands full height and roars, its muzzle frozen with crystallized gore. A small ivory chip of a bone seed spins slowly on the black ice. It reverses direction, spins faster, and explodes once again into a woman clothed in flesh.

She bolts upright with a sharp intake of breath. Slaps her palms against her chest. Sheets of moonlight fall through the window on the cream-colored Pendleton blanket. Her husband stirs beside her. "What is it?"

"Horrible," she gasps, feeling her flesh, brown hands covering her naked self, feeling light-headed, newborn.

"Dreaming of bears again?" He turns, ever the therapist, even with his own wife, especially with his own wife.

"I felt it. It hurts. I was eaten alive by a bear, and I felt every bite, every slice of claw." She was breathing in great heavy gasps. "It was real."

He leans up on the pillow. His voice is calm, dry, his Mongol eyes gleaming silver in the moonlight. "You're going to have to face it."

"What?" she gasps, still feeling the prickly fur in her mouth, the musky smell of bear pelt in her eyes and ears, all of her trembling.

"Your Native self," he says, rolling back into the blanket, his Slavic/Mongol form, itself bearlike, falling back into snores of ursine contentment.

She crawls off the floor mat onto the bare particleboard floor. Reaches for a light, a wisp of smoke. The moon lights up the drum above her bed; she makes out the ghostly form of her dun draft horses outside the window. "My drum is my horse," she says to the horses out the window; they nicker back to her.

In the morning a young grizzly cub sits by the refrigerator licking milk from its nimble paws. The kids are yelling, "Can we keep him?" But she grabs the cub by the ruff and drags it, bawling, across the floor and throws it out the door. It's crying like a child outside the door and she feels sorry and pours it another bowl of creamy milk. That night, the bear grows huge and rips the shack door right off its hinges. She is trying to hold the door back, but the bear is too strong.

"Why don't you do something about your Native side?" Her husband steps around the bear, shakes his head "No, no" at it, sits at the table with his paper, ignoring its huge bulk, its savage odor of blood and dung.

As soon as she sees the black bear, she knows it is coming for her. Its sleek hide galloping as fast as her horse can run. She takes the kerosene lantern from the hook above the lintel, swings it at the bear, but it only circles her warily, keeps coming back. Not to maim or kill, but to embrace her. Her husband stands silently watching, the red glow of a cigarette dangling from his lips. "You can't fight truth with illumination," he says cooly. She stops swinging the lantern and the bear snuffles her palm with his wet black nose.

Later that week, paddling away from the steep sloped sides of the

Minam, she looks up at the slate rock cliffs and sees the mother grizzly. Two red cubs are smacking their lips and standing on their hind legs. They swim out to the green canoe. The mother is as long as the boat. She slides noiselessly into the Minam, her amber pelt cutting the cream of the rapids into her own dark whirlpool. The woman tries to hold off the bear with the paddle, but, lightning fast, the bear knocks it away with a single swipe. The woman watches the paddle skimming through the air like a slender wooden bird. The bear heaves her bulk into the canoe, capsizing it. The woman wakes up on the stone bank in the arms of the bear and cubs. "There, there, it's not so bad," the woman says to the griz, "it's not so bad."

The husband scratches the bear under the muzzle and she faintly purrs. He understands things ursine, black and hairy under layers of human flesh.

Her Oglala friend takes her to a sweat. "You'll understand your bear dreams," she promises the woman who keeps dreaming of bears. But at the lodge there are protesters. Only enrolled tribe members, the signs say. Go away wannabes. The woman is stricken with horror. No papers for the daughter of a Métis, no papers from a white man guaranteeing her Indian blood. She turns under the scorn of racial purism, preferring the fury of bears to the contempt of picketers. Her tribe is scattered bone seeds. Each one springing up into a new chimeric monster, scorned by both red and white people, welcomed only by the animals.

The bears dig roots in the moonlight. By day she claws the earth loose from those roots and hangs them to dry over the woodstove. The house is filled with the odors of sage, sweetgrass, and drying herbs. At night she hears the bears padding softly around the house. They scratch at the door, but she only pulls the covers around her ears, refusing to answer.

She becomes ill, her body paralyzed and her face twisted into a false face mask. The white doctor shakes his head. Says he doesn't know what causes it, what is a cure. After three weeks of agony she goes to a white bear, he hands her a piece of topaz, gold and sticky, puts the sweet comb to her mouth, and she becomes well.

Pieces of bears come in the mail. A claw from her cousin, a scrap of fur from a sister, a jet bear with a red arrow from a Zuni friend. From Arizona her brother brings her a bear carved of onyx. All these things she puts on the shelf, ashamed of dreams that keep pouring into her daily life.

The first strike of her drum calls the bears from the four corners of the earth. Lightning shaped into a bear paw claws down five of her neighbor's cows. She says nothing but thinks of it often. The dream books tell her that dreaming of bears means some one unbearable is in her life. But the only thing she dreads is the savage sounds of bears. Bear grunts and snorts, steamy bear breath, bear wallows, bear claws prying up rocks, sliding across the tin door, heavy bear paws groaning across the porch and clasping her to wooly breasts.

At night she is afraid to sleep, so she walks to the top of the hill on the farm. Her drum horses watch her go with questioning eyes. These ponies are not Native ponies, but ponies from the land of berserkers, also her white ancestors. Everywhere she goes she sees the bears. At the top of the hill she climbs a big pine tree; halfway up she sees that it is painted with vermillion horizontal stripes. She keeps climbing past little streamers in the colors of the four directions. As she nears the top of the tree, she finds a bear skull. It is painted with Cree chin stripes like those of her ancestors. At the top of the tree the wind is blowing from the west, and she turns and faces the skull direction, east. She takes a buckknife from her pocket and slices it deep into the skin of her forearm. She expects to find mixed blood, pink and thick as Pepto-Bismol, raises her arm toward the raw red sun. But the blood is crimson, streams from her uplifted arm, and covers her in a blanket of scarlet. Memekwesiw speaks to her from the black earth below.

He says, "Now you have found your dream."

E. K. Caldwell lives in Depoe Bay, Oregon, where she writes for *News from Indian Country,* doing special feature interviews and news reporting. She also writes for the New York Times Syndicate, including interviews for its multicultural wire service. Caldwell is of mixed Cherokee, Shawnee, Celtic, and German blood. Her poetry and short stories have been anthologized in the United States and Canada. She recently completed a children's book for first-grade readers that will be published by Scholastic in 1996. She is a feature writer for *Inkfish Magazine* and serves on the National Advisory Caucus for the Wordcraft Circle of Native Writers. Caldwell is a skilled professional writer known throughout Indian country as one who mentors young people in the art of creative writing.

E. K. Caldwell

# Cooking Woman

SHE DIDN'T COOK FOR HIM ANYMORE. HE FIGURED THE time was getting closer now. Probably should start gathering up the few belongings he called his own before they ended up in the yard, thrown into a pile as jumbled and muddied as his very own mind. As he wandered through the trailer, listening to the rain beating that staccato rhythm that only comes from rain against thinned metal, he remembered another time, and the story she told him as they walked a sunny beach on the central coast. She had been laughing that day as the wind tore at her braids, loosening stray and secured hairs alike, her eyes shining in a way they had only when she was beside the ocean. They were talking about the future and how it would be with them. He wanted her to make a forever promise. Now that he thought about it—today, with the rain pounding in his ears—she never really did make that promise. Instead, she had pulled him out of the wind and into the protection of a pile of storm-deposited driftwood, and kissed him hard.

"I have a story for you. You wanna hear a story?" He nodded and she began.

There was this Woman a Long Time Ago—might even have been First Woman, but I don't know for sure. She gave a lot to The People. Her favorite thing was feeding people. She really liked to feed people—the pot at her camp was always bubbling with something that would waft its aroma through the camp and get people's attention. When people came around, she always insisted that they have a big bowl of whatever was boiling in that pot. And it tasted good to The People and they were glad she lived in their village. And one of the most amazing things was how everything she cooked came from one big pot, but when you filled your bowl, you would find that you had a variety of things to eat and they all complemented one another so well. You might be having a strongly pungent deer stew and suddenly taste a hearty corn soup. And your next bite might be some sweet spring greens and then bean bread. Oh, this was some good food and The People loved it.

And this Woman, she loved words almost as much as she loved cooking. Always talking about everything and why things were the way they were. And if she didn't have the words for talking, she would sing out her songs, sometimes strong and bold, but most times half under her breath, or she would hum or just make her private sounds. When she was really concentrating on her cooking, she would hum and sing.

Somebody asked her once why she always cooked so much food and she said, "Well, people need to eat. No matter what happens in a person's life, they shouldn't have to go hungry. To hunger for some things can be okay, I guess, but you better watch out for what a belly twisted with hunger will make a person do." And when they asked her why she talked so much and sang so much, she would answer, "The cooking spirits like talking and singing. It lets the food know it is loved and appreciated. And it tastes better and it does more for you. Besides," she would laugh, "I think I just like to talk and sing because it feels good being with The People and seeing them smile with a full belly."

So The People ate her food and listened to her talk and her songs. At first The People were grateful for her generous meals and her generous heart. They would give her small gifts and her dark eyes would warm and her laugh would sing through her. Another's hand pressed to her own sustained her and replenished her.

Each morning she would wake before the Sun. She would make offerings in the predawn light to all those who had visited her in the Dreamtime, and then her song would shift as the Sun's light touched her face, singing in gratitude to the new day that was blessing The People.

Then she would stir the embers of her cooking fire and feed it into a tidy blaze for heating the stone pot just right. And the day's cooking would begin. Her song and the pot's aroma would soon have her camp filled with hungry people.

This went on for many seasons. So many seasons that, after a while, The People just figured she would feed them and they stopped taking care of themselves in other ways. The men didn't hunt the way they used to and the women spent more and more time in the Woman's camp and less in their own. They stopped being grateful and expected the Woman to feed them and look after the children and take care of them as if they, too, were children not yet grown. The Woman saw this and she tried not to let it bother her. She knew it wasn't really that The People did this on purpose. It just happened and she wasn't sure if maybe it just might be her own fault for not saying something about it. She convinced herself that she would not really be affected by it in the long run and that it was probably just a phase The People were going through and that it would be all right.

She was determined not to let her feelings bother her—but some people did notice that she was singing less when she cooked.

And the meals started changing. They didn't taste the same—some of The People started complaining about bellyaches and bad dreams.

Now, not a one of those people gave a thought to the Woman and what trouble was in her heart. They didn't give one thought to the simple fact that no one was contributing to the bubbling pot with fresh game or tender greens. It had been months since anyone had pressed the Woman's hand or brought even so much as a softly colored river stone for her. Her round body sagged from lack of hugging and her shoulders got stooped from so much work.

Then she quit talking altogether, but she still kept cooking. Her eyes looked vacant on the surface, but if The People had taken the trouble to look in her left eye, they would have seen the fear and loneliness and bewilderment she was having in her mind and in her heart. The bubbling pot grew caked and crusted with her fear and her mounting bad thoughts about why The People didn't love her anymore.

It took a lot of concentration just to tend the fire in these times, and she was feeling very tired inside.

One morning around breakfast time, some of The People noticed there was no smoke showing itself from her cooking fire, announcing the first meal of the day. No wonderful smells sang through the encampment. They stood around for a while and looked at each other. Finally, someone figured they should look around and see where the Woman had gone. They couldn't find her anywhere around the camp, and, oh, you should have seen them then. At first they refused to believe that she was gone and they sat around until their bellies were grumbling. Still she did not return. Then they got cranky, as hungry people will, and started whining around and being mean to each other.

One of the younger men said he was going off to find her and make her come back to feed them. Others joined him and off they went, looking in all directions for her. And at the river's edge they saw her sitting huddled and silent, facing West. This scared them pretty good because she always faced East in the morning hours and it was unlike her to turn her back on the Sun before it reached its zenith. They shook her, gently at first, telling her it was time to come back and that The People were hungry. She didn't move a muscle, didn't say a word. The young men started to panic and began shaking her and hollering around at her to stop being so stubborn. When she didn't respond, they got frightened and angry and began hitting her and then started dragging her from the river to the camp. The Woman didn't say a word. She just looked hollow-eyed and sad.

Once they had returned her to her camp, they sat her in front of the cold cooking pot and demanded that she fill it with her magic. She looked around slowly without moving her head and saw their faces twisted with anger and fear. Her heart heavy, she slowly reached for the slivers of kindling and gently stirred the cold ashes. A quiet song brought one cold ash to a glowing ember and she blew softly, singing the fire into a small circle of flames. The People were sullen until they saw the first bubble roll to the top of the pot, and then they raised their bowls in expectation. She silently filled their bowls and went off to sit away from them as they stuffed their bellies, complaining about the taste being so ordinary, as they ate until they could eat no more.

By nightfall The People were getting sick and looking puny and ailing. They started to die, big round swollen bellies sticking up all over camp as they fell on their backs, moaning and cursing her, calling out that she was indeed a witch who had been planning to kill them off all along. No one survived, except the Woman. She watched The People die all around her and she wept bitterly as they cursed her with their last dying breath. She questioned within herself if maybe she had, in some way, some inattentiveness, opened herself to the witch's moon and had killed The People on purpose. The grief tore at her heart and left her feeling a gaping hole where her spirit once resided. She ate little and spoke not at all.

One night when Winter was upon her, she had a dream that lasted until Spring. She saw herself as she had been in the beginning, trusting the spirits and loving The People, smiling into the Sun, singing and laughing. And she watched the circle of time shift and saw The People becoming lazy and resentful, like spoiled children, demanding as their right what had been a most sacred gift. And she saw that she had allowed it without questioning herself. She rode the tides of this dream throughout the Winter and saw many things in its variant rhythms. As Spring approached and she felt the sunlight that stirs life, she shook herself awake slowly, stretching her hands tentatively toward warmth.

Her heart was not healed but was beating again, accepting life. She knew now that it was her mistakes that had contributed to the death of her People, but it had not been her intention and she had not been overcome with the pull of the bad medicine of causing harm to others. She had been dragged within her own confusion about events and intentions. She had offered herself as a never-ending replenishment, expecting others would know instinctively to make appropriate return for the good of all of them. She had taught no one the lesson of reciprocity and had leaked her life into that cooking pot. No young woman had learned how to sing the cooking songs—no young man had learned the value of his contribution. The Woman was saddened by understanding, as understanding is not always an occasion for happiness. She knew now she could have stopped cooking before her breaking heart and bad thoughts made their way into the bellies of others. It became clear to her that when the spirit sickness of one touches the spirit sickness of another, life is taken, leaving unsatisfied bellies bloated with confusion, internal roots choked and twisted. Yes, she understood her responsibility now and it brought a silent solace in knowing what she must do.

She walked to the river and stood on its bank, listening to the current rushing with melting snow and loudly singing. She made the first offerings she gathered to the East direction and the rising Sun. For four days and nights she honored the spirits in her ceremony. She called out to the restless spirits of her People that they must go on their journey and that they need wait for her no longer—that she was making preparations to join them.

And with the setting sun on the fourth day, she cooked a small meal and offered it to the ancestors who would come to meet her as she began her journey. She sang the loving songs the spirits had brought her so long ago, and she felt full and happy for the first time in so long. She unbraided her hair, letting it hang loose around her, its strands silvered by the rising moon. She stood in her skin, raising her hands to the darkened moon, its newness cloaked in the night sky, and she opened her throat to her death chant, going to her People.

Her words floated back and shivered through him this chilled and rainy day. That day he had shivered, too, and had told himself it was the ocean wind and the evening coming. The seriousness in her eyes disturbed him, although her laughing voice had teased him, saying, "So, if a woman stops cooking for you . . ." He had answered, "Guess I better make sure I know how to cook for myself." And they had both laughed and headed back to her dilapidated trailer.

That had been over two years ago. He refused to allow memories of long evening walks and of feeling her heart in her eyes. He couldn't allow himself this wandering around in a mind already cluttered with past debris, stirring the confusion, clouding his perception. He refused himself remembering how, after the fishing went to hell, he started using it as an excuse for the drinking that had had a foothold in his reality long before the fishing gave out. He would not see the first time he had left bruises on her upper arms and the sad understanding in her eyes after he had apologized and said he would quit drinking and never lay a mean hand on her again. The nights of hurting her blurred into hazy fog, backlit with glare and ill-defined edges. The silence between them had many roots twisting and tangling.

And one morning he had awakened earlier than usual and she was not beside him. He smelled no brewing coffee. He stumbled out of bed into the tiny bathroom and leaned against its only window, his breath foul with whiskey, the cool pane on which he rested his head damp with morning. He wiped another pane and saw her there, facing away from him, toward the ocean, toward the West. The dawn lighted the back of her head. Damn her! What was she trying to do now? All those damned ceremonies and rituals she put so much energy into—didn't she know this was a different time?—man, that stuff was ancient history now. And even he, who professed disdain for the ways their People used to be, felt a soured fear churn in his belly. Remnants of the story she had told him on the beach tugged at his mind, but he resisted and wrote off the sour belly to cheap whiskey and stale tobacco.

He walked down the skinny hallway, using the trailer's age-warped walls for support. Blinking into morning light that flooded the kitchen, he was startled by how clean everything looked. She had gone over that kitchen from top to bottom and it reeked of sterile cleanliness, further irritating his uneasy stomach. He shook a cigarette from the pack on the counter and sank onto the couch, his legs folding in on themselves.

She hadn't come home for four days that time. He told himself he didn't care where she was, but he felt his heart quicken when he heard her car in the muddy driveway. He convinced himself he had the right to be angry, and grabbed her roughly from the doorway, slamming her into the wall, cursing her. "Bitch" was the kindest thing he called her. He raised his fist, and the look in her eyes froze his arm.

"I will not die for you."

He still didn't know if she'd actually said it out loud. But he knew he couldn't move his arm that day, and in the brief weeks that followed she did not make him as much as a cup of coffee.

It's raining today like it was that day. The trailer shakes with bursts of thunder. His mind won't remember all the things that have led to this moment. But the story is there—stark with clarity it did not have in the first telling. He opens the door into a gust of salted rain and doesn't look back when he hears it banging against the side of the trailer. His pack is heavier than when he arrived—he feels the brand-new stainless steel cooking pot poking into his side. She had left the pot for him on the kitchen counter. Hell, maybe she didn't really hate him after all—maybe she was just trying to save both their lives.

Eric L. Gansworth is Onondaga and was raised on the Tuscarora Indian Reservation of western New York. He received his associate's degree from Niagara County Community College and his bachelor's and master's degrees in English from State University College at Buffalo. Gansworth is a versatile and creative writer, painter, and photographer. His story "The Ballad of Plastic Fred" appeared in *Growing Up Native American,* and his poetry has appeared in *Slipstream* magazine. In addition, his poetry is featured on *Roadkillbasa,* a performance audiotape released by Slipstream Productions. His paintings have been widely shown at many exhibits, including "Keepers of the Western Door" at Buffalo's CEPA Gallery and at the World University Games and "In the Shadow of the Eagle" at Niagara University's Buscaglia-Castellani Gallery. One of his paintings appeared on the cover of Sherman Alexie's novel *First Indian on the Moon.* Gansworth is an instructor of English at Niagara County Community College, where he teaches freshman writing, American literature, film as literature, and contemporary Native American literature.

Eric L. Gansworth

# The Raleigh Man

I PASSED HOOVER THE DAIRY MAN LAST SATURDAY ON my way home from the grocery store. His red-and-white truck rumbled along the road. He moved closer to the ditch so we could both fit on the road. He stuck his arm out the open accordian door of his truck and waved as we went by. I think he knows just about everybody on the reservation. I raised my fingers a few inches off the steering wheel in response. He was making his Saturday run, which was shorter than his weekday deliveries. He delivered to only a few people on Saturdays, those who had been on his route since the time when the white scarecrow burnings were happening. That was about the time we lost The Raleigh Man.

The Raleigh Man used to come on Saturdays, too. They must have been Saturdays. Everybody was always around and it was the middle of the day. He must have come by all year round, but I remember him only in the summers. We'd all be playing in the mountain when we'd hear his weird horn.

His car horn wasn't like the usual kind. It didn't just honk. Instead, it played this little song. Years later, I heard these sorts of horns all over the place, mostly on customized vans and trucks with the monster tires. But back then, The Raleigh Man was the only one who had a horn like that.

As soon as we heard it, we always just left our plastic Indian tribe in the mountain and ran to the big open space between my mom's house and my aunt's. That was where he always used to pull into.

I hadn't thought about The Raleigh Man in years. I saw Hoover just down the road from my family's plot of land, and as I stood in our driveway, and before I headed to my trailer, I stopped into my mom's house for a second. She was sitting on the couch doing some sewing.

"Hey, what did The Raleigh Man sell, anyway?" I asked. I couldn't really remember what his main goal in visiting us was.

"Oh jeez, lemme think," she said, setting her material down after poking the needle through it. "It seems like it was mostly cleaning stuff. Sponges, cleaners, scrub brushes, and some funny things, too. Spices. I remember this one time I was right in the middle of cooking some spaghetti, and I needed some oregano. Just then The Raleigh Man came pulling up like clockwork, and I sent Kay out to buy some from him.

"But I didn't have enough money for it, and when Kay came back and told me that, I was just gonna skip it. But then The Raleigh Man showed up at the door and said I could have it as long as he got to eat some of that spaghetti. I think that was the first time a white person was ever even in here. He even poured himself a drink from the water pail. He didn't seem to mind that we didn't have running water. What made you think of him?" she asked, smiling.

"Just thinking," I said and walked out the door. I was kind of baffled by that answer. I didn't remember any of that. I must not have cared too much about that kind of stuff. What I remember most about The Raleigh Man was the little red radio-controlled car and the cat masks. He kept these, with all of his other stuff, in the trunk of his car.

As he pulled up into the clearing, all of us kids crowded around his trunk. Even now, the smell of exhaust fumes weirdly excites me. The Raleigh Man always got slowly out of his car. He was a pretty old man to have this as his job. His skin was really pale, and his silvery hair was almost all gone on top. The few strands there always floated around in the breeze whenever he moved his head.

He wore a suit. I'm not sure, but it seemed as if it was always the same suit. Either that or he had a whole closet full of dark gray suits with pale yellow shirts. The suit was always kind of crumpled-looking. He brushed at it with his thin blue-veined hands as he got out of his car and walked slowly toward us. It never did any good, but he brushed away as if his hands were irons, magically straightening the material.

The Raleigh Man was something else. It wasn't that we never saw white people. We saw them at the store and places like that, and they sort of looked like The Raleigh Man, but we never talked to them. And the white people we did know didn't look anything like The Raleigh Man, at all.

They all lived in trailers. Most of them wore dirty white T-shirts that were stretched across huge beer bellies and work pants that didn't fit too well. They were always hiking their pants up, even if they were wearing belts. The bottom halves of their faces were always gray with stubble because they didn't shave too often. They also usually had these really nasty dogs tied up right near their trailers.

They had been living on the reservation since the days when the state built the dike. They had come in to work on its construction, and after it was done, some of them must have liked living with us, because they stayed. But not everybody was too happy with this. The state had taken a big part of our living area, and now because of them, we had to share what we had left with those who had helped take the rest away. When we asked the state to get rid of their old workers, they told us they didn't have any jurisdiction out here.

We tried to discourage the old workers from living with us, asking them if they wouldn't like running water better. But a lot of them, when you asked them this, would simply crack another beer and say that pissing on the ground was just as easy as pissing in a bowl. So some people tried heckling them, I guess. They did things like driving cars in circles on the lawns where these men had settled, making big dough-nuts in the grass.

With one particularly sickening guy, they shot out the transformer that kept his electricity connected. That seemed to work, and the guy left within the week. But this was not all that practical. When they shot out the transformer, about eight other houses lost their power, too. But people had gotten the right idea. We had to scare them off. Giving them hints wasn't working.

Someone got the idea to burn some dummies dressed up like the trailer guys. A lot of people went down to the "Dig-digs" to see if they could find some clothes that looked like the trailer guys' clothes. They found some old work pants and T-shirts, and Mel's mother, Vonnie, even donated one of her only good white sheets for the dummies' faces and hands, so no one would miss the point. They stuffed the bellies extra full and painted big red mouths on the faces.

They selected a clearing down on Walmore for the burnings. That way they wouldn't have to worry about catching someone's field on fire. My mom wasn't planning on going. She was worried that the trailer guys might do something back and she didn't want us kids there. Then Kay offered to watch me if my mom really wanted to go down. She said okay, maybe for just a little while.

I really wanted to go, but my mom said that it might be too dangerous the first time, and besides, there were going to be plenty more. I'd have my chance after she checked it out. I complained, but she reminded me that I was only six, and that she could decide that I couldn't go to any burnings until I was grown up and could make the decision on my own. As she left, she also reminded me that it was Raleigh Man Day.

I went outside and sat on the porch, watching my mom as she drove out and headed toward Walmore. My cousin, Innis, from next door saw me and walked on over, to see if I wanted to go and play in the mountain. I shook my head, not interested. He said that he had some new ideas and this would be a good one, but I didn't take him up on it. He went to the mountain and brought the plastic tribe to our porch. We started playing and eventually we did move over to the mountain.

The hours disappeared as we gave our plastic Indians a whole new war to fight. Innis was right. We hadn't thought up this one before. He had boosted some Barbie doll Country Camper from the Dumpster at school. It had been in the girls' toy box, but the girls in his class totaled it and the teacher threw it away, deciding that it would be no good to anybody.

Innis had hidden from the bus when we were leaving to go home. He squatted in the group of kids after their teacher had counted heads, and then rolled into the shrubbery. He had to wait half an hour as his teacher got the room ready for Monday. But she finally left and he ran over to the Dumpster and crawled in. He found the Country Camper and walked home.

Innis brought the Country Camper home for his sister, Cynthia, but she didn't have a Barbie to go with it. The Camper became a fort for some of the Indians, and others attacked to try and get control of it. After one was counted dead, we set it aside, but only for a little while. Then it came back to life as someone else. There weren't too many Indians, so we had to bring the dead ones back to have enough people to fight.

When The Raleigh Man finally did show up, I almost didn't want to leave the battle, but Innis reminded me about the cat masks and the radio car. Maybe he'd drive the car this week.

He pulled up to his spot, and I ran into the house to tell Kay that The Raleigh Man was finally here. Kay's boyfriend, Peter, was in there with her. They weren't married, yet. They had just started seeing each other, so they were making out whenever they had the chance. I still have no idea how they met, since Peter was from another reservation a long ways away.

Wherever he did live, he came out to our res pretty often these days. They really did seem as if they were going to get married. I could especially tell when Kay said she didn't want to go see The Raleigh Man because she and Peter were busy. Her loss.

I ran back out and the trunk was already open. My Aunt Olive was there before me. Cynthia stayed in the house; she didn't like the cat masks. At first I thought that I must have taken longer than I thought, but then I noticed that Aunt Olive had her poncho folded over her arm. She was leaving for some place. She came and picked out a few things, paid for them with a couple of crumpled-up dollar bills that matched The Raleigh Man's suit, and sent Ace back to the house, carrying these things.

Innis and I were trying on our cat masks. They came in different colors, but most of them were either blue or red. They looked just like a cat's face, right up to the muzzle. There was no chin on the mask. But it had whiskers on the top and bottom, and big cat ears, and eye holes shaped liked cat eyes.

The masks were made of plastic and were shaped to fit kids' faces, perfectly. They fit Innis and me, but not Ace. He had a really round face, and the masks always just sort of sat on his eyebrows for a few minutes before the cheap elastic that held the mask on broke. Ours always broke in a few days, too. The Raleigh Man kept a stack of them in his trunk. He knew that when he showed up the next week, these would be broken and lost, too.

So for Ace, he always kept something else. Once it was a balsa glider, and another time it was a parachute man. Ace always tried the mask on, anyway, in hopes that this week it wouldn't break. This week, of course, the mask broke as usual. But before Ace could even receive what The Raleigh Man had especially for him, Auntie Olive had sent him into the house with her supplies.

Innis and I were looking at the radio-controlled car in the trunk with our cat eyes when Auntie Olive turned to The Raleigh Man and told him it probably wasn't a good thing for him to be on the reservation that day. She advised him that he shouldn't make his usual stops and to just keep going.

She sounded pretty serious, so Innis whispered to me that it looked as if we weren't going to get to see the radio car this week. Occasionally, The Raleigh Man hooked the car up and drove it around in the clearing, hoping one day someone would buy it for us kids. No one ever did, but we still liked to see him drive it every once in a while. He hadn't done it at all that summer, so it seemed like the time was right, until Auntie Olive spoke.

She quickly walked away and got in her car and The Raleigh Man seemed to have gotten her message. He closed the trunk up and got in his car. He pulled out even before Ace could come back out of the house.

We went back to war in the mountain, but that didn't last long. Kay leaned out the front screen door and yelled for me to come and get some shoes on. We were going somewhere. Peter was driving. Innis came running, too, but Kay said he couldn't come, this time. We were going down to the dummy burning, and she didn't want to be responsible for him.

Just before we left, I promised Innis that I would remember everything and tell him all the details. He said he'd try to make a little cloth dummy so we could act it out with our Indians once I got the scoop. I hopped in the car, and as we drove away, I watched Innis and Ace out the window. They were looking grim.

Peter was usually a really nice guy. As we pulled out of the driveway, he said he was taking us to get ice cream before we went to the burning. We drove by the site and a lot of people were milling about. Some were in the trees stringing up the dummies, and others were on the ground admiring the stuffed figures and the handiwork skill in some of the stitching.

We didn't see any white people on the road, but we got kind of a strange look as we cruised by. As we were almost past, a solid, hard noise came from the back end, then another, and another. We were being bombed with dwarf green apples. I knew what they sounded like hitting cars. I had hit some before.

Peter slammed on the brakes and, throwing it into reverse, plowed his car into the clearing. A big group immediately surrounded us. Some people held on to boards with nails in them, and others had baseball bats. Peter jumped out of the car, swearing at whoever was closest, asking them if they were nuts.

They all looked at each other and then shifted, moving a little closer. Kay figured out what was going on and opened her door. Peter stuck his head in the window and told her to stay inside. She didn't listen. In fact, she grabbed me and dragged me out her door. She began shouting even before we were halfway out.

By the time we got out, a few inches were all that remained between Peter and the other men. Finally, someone recognized Kay and yelled to the guys that it was all right. They backed right off and Kay started yelling at some of them. They hadn't recognized Peter's car as belonging to any Indian they knew, so they bombed it. I went and stood with my mom and auntie.

Before Kay could get too far into her rant, we heard the sound of more apple bombs going off. The kids in the bushes had been instructed to bomb any car they didn't recognize, especially any new-looking car. The only people who had new cars on the reservation were the chiefs and they were already at the protest.

The car being bombed went off the road and almost landed in the ditch. It came to a stop and the bombing started again. Some of the men headed toward the road to see what the driver was going to do. I could see through the bushes that the car was maroon, the same color as The Raleigh Man's car.

I moved to another opening and could see the car's window. It was The Raleigh Man. I could see his old blue eyes, bugging out behind his old glasses, his forehead looking furrowed like a plowed field. They had to stop. Why were they going after The Raleigh Man? He never refused to leave, or anything.

I started shouting for them to stop. I figured that it worked for Kay, and I felt as if I had to do something for him. But before I had gotten more than a couple of words out, my mom had magically appeared next to me and covered my mouth with her hand. She squatted down and whispered in my ear that I couldn't help him. He had to get out of this himself. Auntie Olive had warned him, but he didn't listen.

The Raleigh Man eventually recovered enough to get his car

moving again, but by then it was dented all over the place. It was getting a little darker outside, and I couldn't see his blue eyes anymore. I had closed mine, anyway, and twitched every time another apple smashed into his car.

As the shadows grew thick and more people arrived, some of the men went to the trunks of their cars. I heard the latches and almost felt that Raleigh Man excitement, but I knew they didn't have any cat masks or radio-controlled cars. They pulled out some five-gallon gas cans and set them near the ghostly dummies.

A few guys scrambled back up the trees, and when they were steady, someone handed them the cans. They poured the gasoline on the dummies, and after they climbed down, everyone gathered around for the lighting. The dummies danced in the igniting flames, then twirled like ballerinas as they burned.

Most everyone seemed to be having a good time, but no one mentioned the trailer guys. They talked only about what good times they used to have before the state changed everything. I thought about the good times I wouldn't be having anymore. Though it's usually the state's fault, this time it really wasn't. With a few more burnings, we finally got rid of the trailer guys, but I didn't even care anymore.

When we got home, Innis asked me to tell him everything, but I wouldn't say anything. Someone else must have told him, though. He didn't seem too surprised when The Raleigh Man didn't come by the next week, or the next, or the next. But I never spoke of it. I didn't want anybody to look back on that day with fondness.

Chris Fleet was born to Mohawk people and grew up in the rural area surrounding Syracuse, New York, where he still resides on the shores of a lake with his wife and cat. Fleet is a young writer whose works have only recently appeared in print. His first collection of poetry, entitled *The Geese Will Believe This Autumn,* was published in 1993. *Blood Quantum,* his book-length manuscript, was a finalist for the Native Authors' First Book Award and will be published in the near future. Fleet has completed a collection of exciting and original short stories, and he is writing stories for film. At twenty-five, he is one of the promising young contemporary Native American authors.

Chris Fleet

# Bagattaway

JACK WAS PLAYING IN THE 777TH LACROSSE GAME OF HIS life. He wasn't a great player, but he could run, he could catch, and he had a shot that made opposing teams hear rattles and drums. The fourth quarter hurried along, and his team was losing by two goals. He had to do something to change the momentum, but he couldn't focus on the game. His mind had been wandering all day, kept coming back to a comment somebody made to him at work the other night. Jack and this white guy at work were talking about good places to camp. The white guy insisted that no matter where Jack went he should take along a gun. Jack rebuffed him again and again at each suggestion. "What do I need a gun for?" he finally asked. The man said, "Because the only things out in the woods are bears, psycho nazis, and Indians. You need a gun out there, a real stopper. Believe me. I should know after having a camp in the mountains for thirty years."

A whistle blew and brought Jack's mind back into the game. He looked around and saw that his team was sagging. Their heads were down and their sticks were sagging. For a second he wondered why he should even care what happened to the team. For him lacrosse was more than a game; it was a part of his spiritual fiber. It wasn't a look or an attitude or a cool thing to do; it was ritual. So he wondered why he cared what the outcome was for a team that had not the faintest idea of the game's origins and why it was played. Up home they would light some tobacco and pray that the Creator would protect them from injury, but here at school they told him to get real and then went off to get stoned before the game. But here team member competed against team member to score the most goals because it would surely get them laid before the next game. But here he was, out of place and running out of time. A whistle blew again and he was running. A white boy with the ball tried spinning around him. Jack saw the boy's face and it looked like his coworker's face. "Outa my way, wahoo," said the white boy as he stiff-armed Jack to the throat. And then all the play stopped. Nobody ran. Nobody moved. Some of the players looked around with fright. Was that a gunshot they'd heard? "Oh my God. Call an ambulance!" yelled one of the referees. "Number seven! Number seven get the hell off this field. You'll never play in college again if I have anything to say about it. Fucking wahoo!"

Jack walked away, and as he walked away he looked at the circle forming around the crumpled white boy's body. He looked at his favorite stick, which was wrapped around both of the white boy's legs. There was bone protruding, there was blood. He had changed the momentum of the game, but he kept on walking because he no longer had place. Like always, he was running out of place. One thousand years of lacrosse and one less arena to play upon. To destroy that white boy was satisfying, but he knew it took a bad mind. One thousand years. And Jack walked away and could have sworn he saw the chagrined faces of George Washington and Sam Champlain selling beaver hats and popcorn to the stunned crowd. One thousand years. And it was one less place he could play this game for his Creator.

What did it matter anyway? There were only a few weeks left in the spring semester. He didn't care if they asked him back or if they told him to never come back. One thousand years and one less place to play.

What was place to Jack anymore? Was it the hills? He loved to sit atop the highest hills and look out upon the valleys as they rolled endlessly. Often his mind would wander back and he would be one of the first of his people to find this land so many thousands of years ago. Looking out upon it, the rivers and the lakes and the streams and the trees—yes, the trees—he could see why they came so far to this marvelous place. It was a land of power, especially in the winter, and he could understand just how it was and why he could never leave. Without this place he was nothing. And now one thousand years later he had no stick, he had no team, and he had no place to play. "I believed in what he taught me. I've done all that he's said to do. Lacrosse was the only part I had left. Lacrosse was my fire."

The crumpled Ford was waiting for him in the parking lot. It was always there for him, and he thought one day he would sing a song for it. For now, he threw in the rest of his gear. He would go north, back up home. But would he be welcome? He wondered what business he had throwing himself at his relatives. He and his family didn't live there anymore. Jack seemed unsure if he even existed in that place. Sure, he knew them and they knew him. But did he exist as a *WisWis*? Everything about his people seemed to be escaping him. He didn't remember dancing with them, and if he didn't dance with them, then he couldn't have been singing with them either. He had seen his birth in his vision, but all else was lost to him. Everything he had learned, remembered, and done had been with his grandfather. And now he was alone. Even Grandma Audrey didn't remember most of what Honeo had taught him. She didn't know the songs or the dances or the stories.

The Ford with no back window galloped past his dorm and didn't bother to stop. Nothing of importance was there, only a few shirts and a pair of pants. Jack didn't care about the books or the Walkman he was leaving behind, and he didn't have a computer or a TV or a Nintendo like the rest all had. Everything he needed, like his sticks and his tobacco and his pipe, was in the Ford. The more he thought about his life as a one-man ritual, the more vivid in his mind became the picture of his soul. It was branched and gnarled like the hands of his grandfather. Alone for one thousand years.

This is what it meant oh so long ago . . .

Playing lacrosse meant he was Indian. It tied him to his cousins, his brothers. His grandfather had made him his first stick. Well, actually he took an old one and sawed the handle down until it was the perfect weight and balance for Jack's little hands. And when the stick needed new thongs or new rawhide, his grandfather was on the scene repairing it. For years there was no place they wouldn't drive to see a good game or maybe catch a glimpse of some legend young or old. They grooved the highways and dusty back roads from Long Island to Ontario and all the way to Vancouver. Jack always could recall the reservation games. He knew the scores, the players, and the count of the wounded. Those box lacrosse games were the bloodiest he had ever seen, the bloodiest he ever played in. The place he learned to shoot and the place he learned to maim. A place to be a warrior. A place to give thanks. A place to be Indian. That was lacrosse.

Way back he wasn't allowed to play with white kids. Grandfather said those white kids insulted the Creator with their skills. Those kids would teach him bad habits. So every night Jack and Honeo would meander to a clearing not far from their tin can home where Jack could learn how to pass and catch, how to pick up a ground ball, and when to use all those little tricks that white kids would never know. When Friday came it was game time. Honeo took Jack up home, where he could get in a boys' game and either become a player or be forced to play softball and pitch horseshoes for the rest of his life.

Jack was a player. He was a player before he ever stepped onto a field. Honeo told him no one would pass him the ball unless he could rifle it through the net, told him that no one would respect him unless he knocked some people down, told him that those boys would beat him harder and harder if he cried or if he wasn't quick enough or smart enough to avoid their clublike checking, told him with his turtle eyes and fox mouth that he had to play his best because Great Mystery was watching.

Six-year-old Jack, scared for his life, walked out onto the packed earth of the box field and took his position. He looked around, saw four of his cousins were on his team, and tried to avoid the hawklike stares of the others. The last thing he wanted was to catch somebody's eye. Give them a reason to stalk him.

A whistle blew and Jack was running. He was chasing after the ball, and as the ball got closer and closer to him, he could feel and hear the wooden sticks slashing his arms and the backs of his legs. It stung, but he kept on running. His lungs burned and his sides knotted with cramps, but he kept on and on . . .

And then the ball was in his stick. He scooped it up through a mob of little boys. More checks rained down on him. Voices were screaming to him, "Pass it! Pass it! I'm open." But instead, remembering what his grandfather had told him, Jack pivoted back toward the goal. Opposing players started to stand in his way and then scattered after he ran over a few of them. A clearing opened in front of the cage. Some people later said they felt a burst of wind sweep over the field as this happened, others swore that they saw the face of all the dead legends, and there were those that simply would not argue about it at all because they had heard rattles and drums. Honeo would not say a thing about it, and Jack could only tell what happened on the field. He barreled over a few kids, saw that nobody else wanted to stand in his way, ran straight for the goalie, who by this time was standing firm against the pipe trying to cut down all the angles. Jack saw a crack of light in the upper left corner and let fly a swift, underhanded crank shot as he stayed on the run.

Now Jack couldn't have known this, but the goalie he was facing was pure and true. It was the infamous Blind Goalie, the one all the reservations were talking about. This Blind Goalie was actually blind, had been blind for the six and a half years of his life, and would always be sight-blind. Like most humans with such a special condition, the Blind Goalie had been blessed with other gifts. Gifts such as the ability to identify each unique individual by smell and therefore be able to tell at all times exactly where each player was on the field. He could hear the sound of the ball and know where it was and where it was going and its speed, but greater than that the Blind Goalie was blessed with a phenomenal quickness. He could cover the cage from post to post in what looked like a shrug of his shoulder. Nobody had ever scored on him. It was prophesied that nobody ever would . . .

Until Jack saw that crack of light in the upper left corner and let fly a shot from seven feet out. The Blind Goalie instantly moved to stop the shot in what looked like a shrug of his shoulder. He knew exactly where it was going. The sound of rattles and drums, the burst of wind on the field, the face of the dead legends, none of these distracted him.

Jack followed his shot straight to the shoulder of the Blind Goalie, who had made another famous save. The fans in the crowd, realizing that another historic save had been made, erupted into a roaring cheer. Everyone, that is, except Honeo, who never turned his head from the action and saw that the Blind Goalie stopped the shot from going into the upper-left corner but couldn't stop the shot from knocking him into the cage. The crowd took on a collective stoic face when it saw in super slow motion the Blind Goalie dropping onto his ass and the ball falling from his shoulder and trickling over the white chalk goal line. The force of Jack's shot dropped him. A whistle blew, the goal was good.

The Blind Goalie burst into tears when he heard the deafening crackle of the ball trickling over the chalk. He felt shame more than anything else, but he was just a boy. He couldn't have known that he'd allow only one goal per year for the rest of his life, those goals being scored by Jack in the identical fashion year after year. The Blind Goalie was the greatest goalie in the game's one-thousand-year history.

None of these events affected Jack too much. Sure, he hated losing to the Blind Goalie's team every year by a 2-to-1 score. No matter how great his shot was, he really didn't care that people only remembered it when he won games or did something fabulous with it like melting away the goal posts, as did often happen on a missed shot that skimmed the steel posts. Looking back on it, Jack knew it was that first goal which changed his life forever. He knew he had to get back to that place. That place of his first goal. That place where he could forever play *bagattaway*. Forever sing. Forever sing. Forever laugh. Forever cry. Forever remember and forever dream. That place, that place up home.

Chris Fleet

Kimberly M. Blaeser is a member of the Minnesota Chippewa Tribe and grew up on White Earth Reservation in the lake area of northwestern Minnesota. Currently she is an associate professor of English and comparative literature at the University of Wisconsin–Milwaukee, where she teaches courses in American literature, American nature writing, and Native American literature. She has written essays, poetry, short fiction, journalism, reviews, and scholarly articles. Besides Anchor Books' *Earth Song, Sky Spirit,* her work has appeared in *The Colour of Resistance, Returning the Gift, Narrative Chance: Postmodern Discourse on Native American Indian Literatures,* and *New Voices in American Literary Criticism.* She has also published in *Akwe-kon, Cream City Review, World Literature Today, Nebraska English Journal,* and *American Indian Quarterly.* Her collection of poetry, *Trailing You,* published by Greenfield Review Press, won the Native Writer's Circle of the Americas 1993 First Book Award. Her study of fellow White Earth writer Gerald Vizenor, entitled *Writing in the Oral Tradition,* is forthcoming from the University of Oklahoma Press. Blaeser lives on six and a half acres of woods, hills, and wetlands in southeastern Wisconsin with her husband, dog, and two cats.

Kimberly M. Blaeser

# Growing Things

"YOU HAVE TO GO DEEP TO DO ANY GOOD," SPANISH heard him say. He went on gesturing and explaining to her about fertilization. She found it hard to meet his eyes, so she turned small rocks over with her toes, half-alert for a fossil. Every so often she would look up at the old oak—seventy-five to a hundred years old, he had told her.

Now he was writing things down: formulas, brand names, equipment she would need. She wanted to laugh every time she looked at him. It was the way she'd felt ever since he'd come down the drive in that sporty Mazda. Like his shirt, it was some kind of blue she couldn't name—one of the designer colors invented in some laboratory, custom-made for yuppies. For this yuppie tree doctor.

She stood squinting, trying to superimpose some distinctive character over his smooth, round, dimpled cheeks. She tied a bandanna pirate-style over this head. No, that didn't work. She rolled it into a headband, but that looked silly on his close-cropped hair, made his little bald spot more prominent. Well, maybe a hat . . . an Aussie hat . . . or a scar across his cheekbone . . .

"Well, that should do it. Got it? I'd bring the mulch out to here if you don't mind the looks of it. Miss?"

"Hmmm? Oh, I think so. Mulch, fertilizer injections, pruning . . ."

"In the dead of winter."

"Right. But you say you can't promise it will do any good."

"Know in three to five years—if you're still here. I'll leave you my card if you think of something you forgot to ask."

And then he was bending over his notebook again. Suddenly she wanted to touch the little hollow on his chin, fill it with her finger. Feel the smooth curve of it. A tree doctor, after all. Some ancient blood, some spirit must have left its mark, somewhere palpable. Her hand moved to caress the cold smooth dip of the brown spirit stone in her pocket.

He himself had hardly touched anything. The bark for no more than a few seconds. A branch pulled down for a hasty look at the leaves. "*Bejou*, my friend Oak," her grandpa would say as he grasped a bare low branch in a handshake. "This here is my little Spanish." He would lift her giggling to the handshake, to the solemn introductions he used to make. "Good day, Mrs. Birch. What fine dress you wear." "Grandpa, her dress is torn," she would whisper, knowing he must pretend to correct her manners.

Because of her grandpa, the world of Spanish's childhood was furry, prickly, sticky with life. A place of rocks, cold and wet, their colors made vibrant by the waves breaking over them, rocks to be turned and admired in the hand, to be felt and heard with the hands. The world she knew was a place of sharp thorns, coarse or sleek animal fur, slippery bodies of fish. It was mossy forest floors upon which people and animals lay, bodies cushioned, remembering a nest of crisp fall leaves, imagining the soft bed of clouds.

To know the world by touch is to know it by heart. That, thought Spanish, was the single lesson her grandpa taught. Did he realize the many troubles she would encounter because she learned it so well?

Touch was of the devil—the lesson the nuns taught. Keep your hands folded on your desk in the classroom, in your lap when you sit, in front of you when you walk. Wear white gloves to church like nice young ladies do. Keep your hands clean. Don't play in the mud, don't put your fingers in the food, don't play with your hair, and don't touch boys—ever.

And yet, Spanish remembered how all the miracles in the Bible stories came about because of touch. Jesus touched the blind man's eyes, the dead, the lame, the sick. He blessed the loaves and the fishes. He broke the bread with his hands. The Bible knew the power of touch.

Was this power what the nuns feared? The reason Spanish spent so many afternoons writing one declaration or another five hundred times, saying in words what she wouldn't say with her heart, that she wouldn't hold hands behind the silo, wouldn't swing on birches, wouldn't touch the Host with her fingers. Wouldn't trail her fingers along the tree doctor's palm during their parting handshake until he looked up startled and laughed uneasily.

"Well, good-bye, then. Call me if you want . . . another checkup. If you have questions. If you . . ." He closed the car door on his own half-expectant mumbling. Spanish held up her left hand in farewell, her right hand again fingering the stone in her pocket. She stood squinting into the sun, watching the yuppie tree doctor drive off and wondering what she had expected.

Spanish had prepared for his arrival as if he were deserving of ritual honor, as if she had summoned him with a gift of tobacco—like a sucking doctor called to heal the sick. She had not completely settled in, so her preparation required she search the still-packed boxes for the odd group of items she thought appropriate. On the built-in side table she placed special teas and a tumbler of whiskey. She filled a kettle for the stove, set out a turtle-shaped bowl, matches and cedar. She dressed carefully, slipping a heavy silver bracelet onto her wrist, wearing the dream-catcher earrings given her by cousin Julia, and pulling her hair back in a beaded barrette with a thunderbird pattern she had designed herself. Dragon, her mixed-blood spaniel, she closed in the loft. "Sometimes them doctors need it real quiet." Her grandma's voice, consoling Spanish when she tied her old reservation dogs away from the house before a medicine man was due.

Old habits. She laughed now as she sat on the steps, her fingers buried deep in the hair around Dragon's neck, her caresses a peace offering for his recent banishment. The tree doctor—SHELBY MATHEWS, ARBORIST, his card said—had not come into Spanish's new log home, had not tasted tea or whiskey, had not made any offering, told any story, done any healing. Spanish told herself she was being unfair. She knew where she was coming when she moved here. The lake country of southern Wisconsin: rural, but still Middle America. Maybe her romps in the surrounding woods had tricked her, brought back memories, built her expectations. But Shelby Mathews was an arborist, not really a tree doctor as she had thought of him, certainly not a *djasakid* or conjurer.

"Still he has potential, eh, Dragon?" Spanish said, thinking of his hard-muscled legs and the quiet feel of his spirit. But then she laughed when she recalled his notebook and yuppie earnestness. "Should have asked him in for tea anyway. Maybe I could teach him what I know about the healing touch. Well, let's get about this mulch thing. Wanna ride in the wheelbarrow, Dragon?"

In the weeks that followed, Spanish would gaze intently at the oak, trying to see signs that her care was working. She felt what she knew was an inordinate amount of guilt for its threatened health. Even though she had fenced an eight-foot-wide circle off-limits for the heavy equipment during building, the oak's root system must have suffered.

Proximity, such a tricky business. Seven cousins layered together in the back of that old rusty pickup, their three moms crowded into the cab. Kids bouncing along singing to hear their voices jar and crack with the bumps. Going to town, going fishing, going visiting, just going along. Spanish thought about the close kin system of her childhood. Three generations sharing beds, clothes, chores, food, and fun, living together in tight quarters. What made it work? Living in Texas with cowboy Dale, the whole ranch hadn't been big enough for the two of them. She had fumbled through several relationships—the watercolor artist in Colorado, the schoolteacher in Illinois—always one or the other party began to feel threatened by the closeness. Claustrophobia. Not the classic panic in small spaces, but some fear of personal closeness. A need for freedom, for personal space—*my* space.

Last time, with Jim Snow, Spanish was the one who ran. She ran here. Built a cabin. Did freelance editing on her PC. Fished. Roamed the countryside. Looking for that space. Constantly reminded of the problems of proximity by this damn oak tree.

The arborist came back in late January—the dead of winter. Spanish had called him about the pruning. Small preparations this time and Dragon at her side, where she kept her nervous hands busy in his winter coat.

"How you liking it out here?" he asked while setting up. "Pretty quiet in the winter, isn't it?"

"I keep myself busy. I like quiet." Dumb answer, Spanish, dumb. She watched him find the rhythm of his pruning routine. Lotsa science in this guy, she thought, but some music too, maybe a little bit of magic he doesn't acknowledge yet.

It hurt her to watch the cutting, so she turned away, performing small duties about the grounds as she listened to his movements. Pruning wasn't in her blood. Not like it must be in the blood of the bonsai masters, and maybe in the blood of Shelby Mathews. She remembered the hollow feeling that came the first time she saw a woodchipper at work. Branches gobbled up by the shrieking machine, spit out as bits and sawdust. That was true modern magic, she supposed, but not for her. But this, this pruning for health, was a different kind of cutting, maybe an art. SHELBY MATHEWS, TREE DOCTOR, ARTIST. Spanish smiled as she conjured the business card in her mind.

He was done. It didn't look like art, not yet anyway. Poor stump branches, she thought. Together Spanish and Shelby carried the fallen pieces to her woodpile. "Come in for coffee or hot chocolate while I write you a check?" she offered.

"Sure, thanks."

He was fingering her chess set when she returned with the serving tray. He had removed his gloves and held an onyx knight in his hand, following its lines.

"Pretty set."

"Thanks. You play?"

"A little, sometimes."

"Want to?"

"What? Oh, play? Now?"

"Or . . . sometime."

They both laughed then at the awkwardness. "I'm sorry," Spanish began. "Out here, conversation, well, isn't my strong suit these days."

"No, I'm sure it's me. Pruning puts me in a bit of a trance, I guess."

A trance. It was a perfect answer. An arborist yes, but a tree doctor maybe a little too.

They didn't play chess. Just talked a little about the area, his business, her house, and about Dragon, when he demanded attention. Shelby didn't stay long, but he admired a lot of things in her house: the wood finishes, fish decoys, black ash baskets, books. Maybe one of them would bring him back, she thought when he left. Maybe she would.

Maybe if she knew about love medicines. Sympathetic magic was what the anthropologists called it when dolls were tied together to conjure a bond. Did those dolls break their leather ties when one of the lovers fled in search of personal space? What kind of love was it that created such a largeness in a relationship that no one became afraid? What kind of love had eluded her? Would this tree doctor who knew about root systems know about that magic?

As a child she had watched her old cat, Mrs. Tom, give birth and lick each newborn kitten dry. "Why does she do that, Grandpa? Doesn't she get tired?"

"She's waking up their blood, Spanish, the way you wake yours up each morning when you stretch. She's gettin' that blood to move around in their bodies . . . bringing them life."

Science would later tell her that that mother cat was stimulating her offsprings' circulation, but Spanish would always think about it as waking up their kitten blood. And when later she would lie with a lover whose hands gently petted and caressed her, who ran kisses down her neck and arms, she knew he was waking up her kitten blood, too, and filling the life vessels of her body. What stopped that magic?

The tree doctor came back a week later, pulled into the yard in an off-white four-wheel-drive Bronco. "Mazda's kind of impractical in this weather," he told her when she asked.

"I had a job down the road a ways, saw you in the yard . . ."

"I'm glad you came. I was just studying this tree."

"You won't know for a while, I thought I explained."

"You did, but I can't help searching for a sign." Spanish traced the bark pattern lightly with her fingers. "I try to encourage it, it's too grand to be destroyed by humans crowding in."

"I saw the tobacco."

"Huh?"

"The first day I came. You had some kind of ceremony."

"Made an offering. Appeasement, I guess."

"I wondered. And me? Hedging your bets?"

Spanish glanced up at his face and his raised eyebrows. But before she could respond, he laughed. "It's okay. I'm as used to skepticism as, well, as you are, I guess. After you've explained to forty people about some invisible fungus invading through the root system or tried to counter the story of some TV fertilizer wizard, you just accept it: some people are going to think you inhaled too much nitrogen or something."

She could have told him then, but he didn't seem in any hurry. If anyone did, he knew about waiting. Three years' healing for the tree if she helped it along. "Oh, I believe in science," she could have said, "just not by itself."

Someday she might show him the tamarack stands, the jack pines, the maple sugar grounds of her childhood. He might burn with fury when he saw the scars of clear-cutting in her homeland. Or they might sit together watching the waves of heat, wiping their foreheads with a folded red bandanna, and singing for rain to feed the rows and rows of saplings set before them. "Feel these furrows, child. They are the same on the great oak, on the marked land, and now on the forehead of your *mishoomis*." "Grandpa, are you turning to bark?" They laughed then. As Spanish did now with this smooth-faced tree doctor. She could almost see him turning to bark too. And waited.

Gerald Vizenor is Anishinaabe and one of the premier Native American figures in the world. He is professor of Native American literature in the Ethnic Studies Department at the University of California, Berkeley. He is the author of many books on tribal histories and literature, including *The People Named the Chippewa,* as well as critical studies. He edited *Narrative Chance,* a collection of essays on Native American literature. His autobiography, *Interior Landscapes: Autobiographical Myths and Metaphors,* and *Bearheart,* his first novel, were published by the University of Minnesota Press. *The Heirs of Columbus,* a novel, and a collection of short stories, *Landfill Meditations,* were published by Wesleyan University Press, which also brought out *Manifest Manners: Postindian Warriors of Survivance* and his most recent book, *Shadow Distance: A Gerald Vizenor Reader. Griever: An American Monkey King in China,* his second novel, won the American Book Award. *Dead Voices: Natural Agonies in the New World,* his fifth novel, was published recently by the University of Oklahoma Press, for which Vizenor is general editor of the series American Indian Literature and Critical Studies.

Gerald Vizenor

# Oshkiwiinag: Heartlines on the Trickster Express

## The Acudenturist

Lake Namakan never hides the natural reason of our seasons. The wind hardens snow to the bone, cerements over the cedar ruins, and hushed currents weaken the ice under the wild reach of our winter.

Overnight, the wild heirs are in the birch, the chase of wise crows. Higher in the distance, the bald eagles brace their nests once more with wisps of white pine, the elusive censers of the summer.

Everywhere, silence is unnatural in our seasons. Listen, the rivers cut massive stones to the ancient heartlines. Memories are more precise on the borders of reservations, nations, and the turns of creation. Trickster stories are the hidden currents of the seasons, the natural reason of our independence.

Gesture Browne is a trickster of precise memories, an esteemed tribal acudenturist, and the founder of the first reservation railroad. He was born in the summer, on an island near the international border, at the same time that Henry Ford established a modern assembly line to build automobiles. That industrial gesture, the coincidence of his birth, and his railroad adventures as an acudenturist were cause to mention the course of natural reason in trickster stories.

Lake Namakan, the memories of our seasons, the crows and bald eagles, the creation of reservations, and the revolution of automobiles were connected in a common vision of unrest and mobility. Gesture reasoned, as he probed a carious lesion in a molar, that the assurance of tribal independence was not a crown decoration of discoveries and treaties, but a state of natural motion. He shouted out, as his father had done from the water tower on the reservation, that sovereignties were movable stories, never the inactive documents of invented cultures.

## The Treatment

Gesture told me that trickster stories come out of the heart, not the mouth. "My heart hears the silence in stones, but teeth rot in the mouth, and what does a wimpy smile mean that covers rotten teeth?" His words warmed the air and brushed my cheek as he leaned over me in the dental chair. He smiled as he leaned, but never showed his teeth. Later, he revealed his crown.

Gesture was an acudenturist in motion, an acute denturist with a singular practice on his very own railroad. The dental chair was located at the end of the train, at the back of the luxurious parlor car. The train had been built for a rich banker who traveled on weekends to his country estate near Lake Namakan.

The banker, by chance of an abscessed tooth and a wild storm on the lake, gave his entire private railroad to the acudenturist and created an endowment to sustain the operation of the train on the reservation.

Gesture was born on Wanaki Island in Lake Namakan. He could have been a child of the wind and natural reason. The otters heard his stories on the stones in the spring, and he was more elusive in the brush than cedar waxwings. The islands were heard in the stories of the seasons, and seen in the everlasting flight of tribal memories. His relatives and the shamans come to the island in summer and winter to hear stories, to hear the stones and heal their presence in humor. His father was exiled and never returned to the reservation of his birth.

Ashigan, his father, was born on an island near the border. Six years later, his family was removed by treaty to a federal exclave, and then the unscrupulous agents ordered him to leave forever the White Earth Reservation. The order was a paradox; banished, as it were, back to the very islands his family had been removed from eleven years earlier. The sentence was truly ironic, as he had removed the United States Indian agent for crimes against tribal sovereignty, and held him hostage in a water tower. He told his son that "one removal must beget another in a stolen nest."

Ashigan shouted out the names of the criminal agents and told trickster stories on tribal independence several times a day for three weeks. Some people listened under the tower, others laughed and waited for the agents to shoot him down. He was a scarce silhouette on the tower, smaller for his age than anyone in his family, but his mouth was enormous, and his loud voice had been hired more than once to announce the circus and Wild West shows. He was no more than seventeen at the time of the removal and had earned the nickname Big Mouth Bass for his stories about the heinous incursions, assaults, larcenies, and murders on the reservation by the federal government.

Big Mouth Bass moved to the border islands and never mentioned the removal, the wicked agents, the twisted mouths of missionaries, or those tribal emissaries who had weakened his revolution in the water tower. The islands were sacred stones in his stories, and the avian shadows his natural solace, but he never shouted about anything ever again. At last, in his eighties, he returned to the reservation with his son, at the controls of their own train. He said the tribal railroad, *ishkodewidaabaan,* or the "fire car" in translation, was his "island in motion."

Since then, tribal people with terminal teeth, some of them with abscesses bigger than the one drained on the banker, drank wild rice wine in the lounge and watched the landscape rush past the great curved windows. They waited in the sovereignty of the parlor car to have their teeth repaired by their very own acudenturist.

"So, lucky for you this is not heart surgery," he said and then leaned over me, the side of his thick hand on my right cheekbone. Lucky indeed, were my very thoughts, but my heart was in my molars that morning. The silence was ironic. No one else has ever had permission to enter my mouth with various instruments, inflict pain, and then ask me questions that were not answerable. No silence could be more sorely heard than the mute responses of a crossblood journalist to the intrusions of an acudenturist, his unanswerable queries of me in a dental chair on a tribal railroad.

Gesture poked and scratched with a dental probe at the ancient silver in my molars. Closer, his breath was slow, warm, and seductively sweet with a trace of clove and commodity peanut butter. The leather chair clicked, a clinical sound, leaned to the side, and shivered as the train rounded a curve over the river near the border of the reservation. "Loose here, and there, there, there, can you feel that?" He pounded on my molars and we nodded in silence on the curve. Then, with a straight chisel he scraped the rough edges of the silver. I could taste the metal, the cold instruments, and his warm bare fingers in my mouth.

"Tribal independence is motion, stories to the heartlines, not the mere sentences and silences of scripture, not the cruelties of dead words about who we might have been in the past to hear our presence," he said and we nodded as the train leaned in the other direction. "Museums iced our impermanence, and the cold donors measure our sovereignty in the dead voices of their own cultures." He snorted and then explained that he would not be able to use an anesthetic because he was an acudenturist, "not a drugstore doctor." The silver was already too loose in my molars to wait on a licensed dentist at the end of the line.

"Instead, here are some scents of the seasons on the islands," he said and turned a narrow cone toward my face. The rush of air was moist and cool, and the first scent was a thunderstorm, then wet wool, a dog, and later on the essence of sex, but that must have come from generations of sweat on the leather chairs in the parlor car.

We nodded in silence and he turned the dental chair from the curved windows and the landscape to the power instruments. The other patients in the lounge turned with me from the rush of birch and white pine to the instruments. He started the mechanical dental engine. The drill was archaic, but the sound of the drive cables created a sense of contentment, the solace of an acudenturist in his own trickster stories. He drilled and cleaned the lesion, and then pounded real gold into the central grooves of my molars.

"Now, you are truly worth more than you were last night on the reservation, and we are both still free," said the acudenturist as he turned the chair back toward the curved windows.

## The Abscessed Banker

I was born on the reservation, but my father moved to the city in search of work. I quit school, bounced around for years, served in the military, and finally landed as a journalist for a large daily newspaper, the *Twin Cities Chronicle.* Naturally, the editors named me Big Cheep, a nickname they learned from me. A nickname based on the way Ishi, the Yahi man who lived in a museum at the University of California, said the word *Chief,* a personal reference to the anthropologist Alfred Kroeber.

I was assigned to cover any story that had the slightest hint of tribal presence, as if no one else could cover such events without a genetic connection to a reservation. For all that, and even the heartless celebration of essentialism over racial deverbatives, such as drinkers, drummers, and dancers, no one in my crossblood generation had a more exciting job. I would have it no other way, and was more than pleased to write about the unnamable tribes and such unbelievable characters as the acudenturist Gesture Browne.

My editors, however, as much as they liked my work from the unknown and exotic headwaters of the reservations, were never certain if my stories were true or not. The other reporters shouted out their rough humor in the newsroom when one of my stories landed on the front page. I heard their playful envy, to be sure, and the ironies of what was sold as daily news, but I would have laughed anyway at such racial quibbles as "You need tribal fishing rights to believe this story" or "The second coming of Christ is worth a page and a half, unless she's an Indian."

In the end, the distinctions between fact and fiction never really seemed to matter much to the editors or readers, and surely that must be the reason why tribal humor and trickster stories have endured the most outrageous abuses by missionaries and government agents and, above all other cruelties, the dominance of dead-letter anthropologists.

The city editor often said that my stories about tribal people on the reservation "may not be the truth, but his stories are truer than what we publish day after day about elected politicians all the way to the White House."

My editor bought the truth of the banker with the abscess who was lost in a thunderstorm, and he ran my story as a feature on the front page, but he would not believe the stories about my golden molars. These stories, and the leather dental chair in a parlor car, were not convincing. He even looked in my mouth, poked the bright molar with a pencil, and then shouted, "Fool's gold on a tribal railroad, now that is believable!"

He smiled, and then we nodded in silence.

Gesture never hides the natural reason of a thunderstorm on the islands at Lake Namakan. He waits on the massive stones for a burst of creation. I know, because when he hears that certain wind, the crash of thunder in the distance, he is transformed by the power of the storm. He told me that the most natural death is to be struck by lightning, "a crash of thunder and the human remains are a thunderstone."

Ashigan and his son were healed by the power of the west wind, the rush of water over the massive stones. Gesture looks at least ten years younger when he faces a thunderstorm. And it was a storm, one ferocious thunderstorm over the islands, that changed his life forever. Indeed, he was out in the wild wind, but he was struck by a banker, not lightning, in the end.

Cameron Williams, the wealthy banker, was out in a canoe that very afternoon, a chance to show his grandson the bald eagles near the international border. The banker had no sense of natural reason and, distracted by the rise of the eagles on the wind, he drifted on the rough water over the border and was lost in the many bays and islands of Lake Namakan.

Gesture saw a canoe turn over on the waves near the island. The banker was lucky that such a tribal man would stand in a storm and watch the lake catch the wind. The canoe tumbled on the waves, and then he saw the blue faces of children in the water, the faces that haunted him in dreams, the blue faces beneath the ice near the mouth of a river. He tied a rope to a tree and swam out to the canoe. The lightning hissed overhead, and the water was wicked on the rise in the wind. The child was ashen, blue around his eyes and mouth, and his ancient blue hands were closed on a miniature plastic paddle. The banker trembled—he was too scared to shout—but he held on to the canoe.

Gesture tied the rope to the canoe and towed the child to shore. Cameron nodded, the waves crashed over them, and lightning crashed in the trees on the island. Later, the child recovered near the fire, but the banker weakened; his eyes were swollen and lost color. The storm passed overnight, but the wind howled and the waves crashed on the stones for two more days. They could not paddle against the high waves.

Cameron was weakened because he had a canine abscess that distended his right cheek and ear and closed one eye. The swollen banker was delirious on the second night. He cursed women and the weather for his condition, and then he started to wheeze; his breath was slower, strained, and his thin hands turned inward to the silence.

Gesture heard the last stories in the old man. The lake was thunderous, and the waves were too high for a canoe, so he decided to operate on the banker, then and there on the island, and drain the abscess. That night he built a small sweat lodge and warmed the old man near the stones, and moistened his swollen mouth with willow bark soaked in hot water.

The next morning he moved the banker out to the boulders on the shore, turned his head to the sun, and told the child to hold his swollen mouth open with a chunk of driftwood. The child nodded in silence, and then Gesture wound a thin wire several times around the base of the canine, and with a wooden lever, braced in the seam of a stone, he wrenched the poisoned tooth from the banker's mouth.

Purulence and marbled blood oozed out around the tooth, ran down his chin and neck, and stained the stone. Then pure putrid mucus gushed from the hole of the abscessed canine. He choked and gurgled, but in minutes he could see. His swollen eye opened, and he turned to his side on the stone and moaned as the infection drained from his head. The child cried over the color of the poisoned blood, and then he gathered water and washed the pus from the stone.

Later, the child touched the dark hollow abscess with his fingers. That afternoon the banker laughed and said his mistake in navigation was "not much better than Columbus." Perched on the warm stones, he told stories about his childhood, and took great pleasure in his missing tooth, the natural imperfection of his weathered smile.

Gesture paddled the banker and the child in their canoe back to their vacation home on the luxurious western reach of the lake, a great distance on the other side of the border. The water was calm in the narrows, and the sun bounced over the scant waves. The eagles teased the wind and then circled closer and closer to the shallow water on the shoreline.

## The Feature Story

I was a journalist and convinced at the time that my stories created a sense of the unusual in a real world, even more in feature stories. Alas, the politics of the real are uncertain, and stories of natural reason and survivance in the tribal world were scarcely heard, and seldom recorded as sure historical documents.

Cameron Williams was one of my real features, a banker in the blood who reared his own documents and caused histories that touched on natural reason and tribal survivance. I was a reservation crossblood with a shadow of chance and the sound of oral stories in my ears, and he was a rich banker with several vacation homes and his own railroad. He was a serious stockholder in the very newspaper that employed me, and he traced his ancestors to the founding families of Puritan New England.

My editors at the *Twin Cities Chronicle* were too liberal for the banker, so it was even more difficult for me to track down any good information about the extraction of his abscessed canine in a thunderstorm. One of his assistants told me that he would not be interviewed for any story, and "certainly not about his exodontist."

I think it was my simple savings account at one of his banks that opened the door the first time. He was a pragmatist, to be sure, and he must have judged me by my documents, a savings account in this instance. Later, however, it would take more than my meager savings to overcome his suspicion of crossbloods. He told me that my genes were "enervated" and the "inheritance of a racial weakness has never been an honorable birthright." Crossblood or not, my recognition of one of his distant relatives earned an invitation to travel with him on his plane and train.

Cameron was a descendant of John Williams, a minister at the turn of the eighteenth century in Deerfield, Massachusetts. His family was captured one winter night, and his daughter, touched by the communion of the tribes, never returned. Eunice Williams renounced the dominance of her puritanical father and married a tribal man, and that historical document could not be denied by enervation. Twelve generations later, the banker is an heir to that crossblood union of Puritans and Kahnawakes in Canada.

"Sir, at our best we are crossbloods."

"At your best, you are a listener," said the banker.

"Indeed, and the abscess is your story."

"So, this is what you want to see, the hole," said the banker. He removed a false canine with his fingers and then smiled to show the hole. "The first thing my grandson did was touch the bloody hole, and he still does it when we tell the story together."

"How does an abscess become a reservation railroad?"

"Pack for an overnight and meet me in three hours at the entrance to the garage," he said and waved me out of the conference room. The scent of mint, an executive insinuation of nature in the carpets, lingered on my clothes for several hours.

Cameron was silent in the limousine to the airport. He only gestured at scenes out the window as we flew in his private jet over the lakes and landed at airport near his vacation home. From there we boarded a pontoon plane and flew close to the peaks of red pines, circled the many islands, and then landed on the smooth sheltered bay near Wanaki Island.

Gesture should have been there to meet the seaplane. How could he not hear the engines, and how often does company arrive by air? There was no dock on the island, so we waded over the massive boulders to shore.

"We were caught in a vicious storm and rolled over right out there," said the banker. "And here, on this very stone, a stranger saved my life, and he asked nothing for his trouble."

Gesture was reading in his cabin, a precise response to the curiosities and uncommon praise of a banker. Not even his mongrels were moved to denounce our presence on their island. "We never challenge bears or humans," he told me later.

The modern cabin was constructed mostly of metal, not what we expected to find in the remote pristine wilderness of the border islands. There were other surprises, such as skylights, a toilet that generated methane, and water heated by solar panels.

Gesture explained that the modern accommodations were a contradiction of tribal rights and federal wilderness laws. He had the aboriginal right to live on the islands, but he could not crap on the land or cut the trees to build a house. "Not because the trees have rights—that would be natural reason—but because the trees are on a pristine reservation," he told me. "So, we can live here in a natural museum."

Gesture and his father, their wives and several children, saved their money from treaty settlements, and income as guides for fishing parties, to buy modular ecological homes that were airlifted to the island in large sections and assembled in less than a week.

"I tried several times to remember what your house looked like, but my memory lost the picture," said the banker. The mongrels sniffed his ankles and sneezed several times.

High Rise, the white mongrel with the short pointed ears, moaned and rolled over at the feet of the banker. He rubbed his wet jowls on his shoes and ankles. The banker raised his trousers, and reached down with one hand to touch his head, to push him aside, but the mongrel moaned louder and licked his hand.

Poster Girl, the mottled brown mongrel that looked like a cat, was very excited by the scent of the banker and the moans of High Rise. She barked and ran around the banker in tiny circles. Her nails clicked on the wooden floor, an ecstatic dance. The banker was not amused by the mongrels.

"High Rise must have a nose for bankers," said the banker.

"Maybe, but he goes for the scent of mint. Yes, lingering from the executive carpets," said Gesture.

"Gesture, could we get down to some business?" the banker asked.

"You mean the mongrels?" Gesture responded.

"Would you like a paid scholarship to dental school?" the banker inquired.

"Dental school?" asked Gesture.

"Yes, an even chance to turn a mere instinct into a real profession, and you could be the very first dentist in your entire tribe," said the banker. His manner was earnest, but the invitation was an obscure pose of dominance.

"You flew way out here to send me to dental school?"

"A measure of my respect," said the banker.

"The measure is mine," said Gesture. He pointed to the books stacked near the wooden bench, and the mongrels moved in that direction. There were several novels and a book on dental care and hygiene. "You see, out here we are denturists with no natural reason to be dentists, our teeth are never the same, but denturists never turn mouths into museums."

"You saved my life," pleaded the banker.

"Maybe," said Gesture.

"You owe me the courtesy to recognize my everlasting debt to you," said the banker. "My grandson admires you more than anyone else in the family right now, he thinks you are the dentist of the islands."

"Denturist, and you had the abscess, not me."

"You are an original," said the banker. He moved to the bench and read the titles of books in several stacks. High Rise nosed his ankles, and Poster Girl posed beside him on the bench. There were new novels by Gordon Henry, Betty Louise Bell, Louis Owens, and Randome Browne, and older novels by Franz Kafka, Herman Melville, and Yasunari Kawabata. He was distracted by a rare book, the *Manabosho Curiosa,* the very first tribal book, published in the middle of the seventeenth century. The anonymous tribal curiosa of human and animal sexual transformations were discovered a century later at an auction of rare books in France.

"Gesture, this is a very rare book," said the banker.

"Poster Girl is a healer," said Gesture.

"What does she heal?" asked the banker.

"Whatever you want?"

"What do *you* want?" shouted the banker.

"What do you have?" shouted Gesture.

High Rise raised her head at the tone of his voice and sniffed the distance in the air. Poster Girl watched the banker on the bench. He was distracted more by the *Curiosa* than the mongrels.

"Basically, it comes down to this," said the banker. He laid the *Curiosa* on the stack of books, leaped from the bench, and turned to the window. "What would you accept that would make me feel better about this?"

"Make me an offer," said Gesture.

"Come with me and see!" shouted the banker. He turned and marched across the room to the door. The mongrels followed him out. He ordered the pilot to make room for one more passenger, but not the mongrels.

"Would you consider a scholarship to study at the university?" asked the banker. The pontoon plane bounced several times and then lifted slowly from the water.

"Why the university?"

"Say, to study literature," said the banker.

"I already do that," said Gesture.

"Anthropology, then."

"Anthropology studies me."

"You have a point there," said the banker.

"Natural reason is the point."

"You could be a pilot and have your own business on the lakes," said the banker. The plane circled the islands hear the border. The late sun shivered in wide columns on the water.

"Do you have a railroad?" asked Gesture.

"Yes, my own private line."

"Give me that, and we have a deal," said Gesture. He gestured with his lips toward the shoreline. Bald eagles turned their shadows over and over on Lake Namakan.

"Great idea, the first tribal railroad in the history of the nation," said the banker. He raised his hands and shouted nonsense in the air. "Did you hear that, Mister Crossblood, this is the return of the noble train."

## THE TRICKSTER EXPRESS

The Naanabozho Express, a seven-coach train, lurched out of the casino station on the White Earth Reservation and thundered into the sacred cedars on the last wild run to the White House in Washington.

Gesture Browne, the founder of the tribal railroad, or *ishkodewidaabaan*, in the memories of the elders, negotiated with the national native art museum the installation of a mobile cultural exhibition on the train, and then he summoned his heirs to declare motion a tribal island, a natural sovereign tribal state.

The trickster express ran on borrowed rails with a new museum, a parlor dental car, an acudenturist, a nurse with several nicknames, and the crystal trickster of tribal parthenogenesis. The express train was natural reason in motion, a nomadic survivance from a woodland reservation to the national capital.

Gesture never surprised anyone on the reservation with his uncommon transactions. His words rushed and bounced, one over the other with no connections or closures, but with that visual sense of transformations in his stories. Natural reason never ended, never in trickster stories, and never in his natural invectives. He was a wind in the best seasons, and his humor healed those who heard his stories on the trickster train. The man who conceived the first railroad on the reservation would not be caught unaware by his heirs on a wise run to tribal sovereignty.

The others, the educated canons on the bungee lines of reason, were astonished that an old man, who said he was once a woman, had stolen the sacred treasures of his own culture from a museum. The curators, on the other hand, were the dead voices of native museums, burdened with their obsessions, discoveries, heartless recoveries, and their mean manners of terminations and postindian tenancies.

Gesture reassured me that motion is autonomous, that natural reason and memories are motion, and motion can never be stolen. Bones and blankets are stolen; motion is a natural sovereignty. The museum commodities on the train had been removed, silenced, and unseen, as the tribes had been removed to reservations. He said the museum in motion was not stolen, but a revolution of native sovereignty. "Museums are the houses of thieves; the sacred objects were stolen in the name of civilization and are more secure than native communities on reservations. The museums are dead, and here we are, in revolution on a trickster train."

## THE CRYSTAL TRICKSTER

Cozie Browne heard that the west wind was lost, an ominous situation to consider that winter on the reservation. She heard the crows too, and rushed outside to warn the birch near the river. The ice waited in silence, hard-hearted on the blue summer mire, and even the cedar waxwings were uncertain over the late turn of the seasons. She overheard these stories as a child, and no one has ever been the same in her memories.

Notice of the lost wind was delivered by her cousin who lived in a cold basement apartment in the city. She was nine years old at the time and enticed by his wild urban manners. The mere mention of cities, that sense of distance and urban vengeance, molded the seasons in her memories. He was older and wiser about obscure tribal traditions and the enchanted stories of creation, and avowed that he could hear stories on the weave and wander of the wind.

Cozie was born in the summer at the same time that the first nuclear-powered submarine sailed under fifty feet of polar ice. The wind touched her head at birth with an ovate bunch of blond hair, a sign that tribal elders were reborn in their children. She learned to hear the bald eagles and to carry a sprig of white pine. She mourned in the presence of spirits, not humans, and no one but tricksters dared cross her trail to the fire.

Trickster stories tease a tribal presence, a chance to be heard between the reservations and the cities; otherwise, unseen, she would have shivered in silence over the insinuations of natural reason. Her uncle, a wise man of motion, rushed the thunderstorms on the islands, but the stories she heard would mend the absence, not the presence, of the west wind that winter.

Cozie earned four memorable nicknames in the natural service of the seasons. One name at birth, the second was shortened and secular, and much later she secured two more names as the first permanent night nurse at the public health clinic on the White Earth Reservation.

When she was born, Gesture Browne named his niece Minomaate, a tribal word that means a good smell, like "something burning" in the language of the Anishinaabe. The shorter version of her name was *mino,* a word that means "good," and that was translated as "cozy" by the missionaries. The two time-release nicknames, the first such postindian names on the reservation, were given when she became the night nurse.

Cozie is her heartline name, a trace to the ancestors, but the two other nicknames are essential in the stories of those who heard the seasons and were healed by *oshkiwiinag*, the crystal trickster in the dead of night.

She is touched by the sound of the wind, the distance of shadows, that rare presence of creation as the dew rises over memories, and the natural ecstasies of ancient rivers. Later, she is morose as the sun haunts the ruins of the night. She hears the tricksters of creation overnight, not in the bright light.

Sour is her nickname at first light, and later, seen closer to the sunset, she is summoned as Burn. The dawn and sunset determine the mood and manner of her timeworn names in the clinic on the reservation. Sour in the morning. Burn as the night nurse.

Sour was summoned one morning to the clinic. "Some sort of emergency," the director said on the telephone. She was not pleased, but there was a reported medical crisis on the reservation at Camp Wikidin near Bad Medicine Lake. The Girl Scouts had been ravished and were rumored to be in a state of post-traumatic ecstasies.

"Ecstasies are a medical crisis?"

"City Scouts . . ."

"To be sure, and the bitter light of day is upon me," she said and leaned over his polished desk for instructions. Sour covered her eyes and told him to close the blinds.

"Sour, you know we would never bother you in the morning, but it might cloud over and rain, so we thought you could bear partial light and examine the campers," said the director. "Who else could answer the emergency?" He closed the blinds very slowly.

"Heat rash?"

"No, more serious," said the director.

"Poison ivy?"

"No, more serious than that, it seems."

"Hornets in the shower?" said Sour.

"No, more serious, some sort of ecstatic hysteria brought on by something they ate, some allergic reaction, or whatever," said the director. "The camp leader said it might have something to do with the discovery of a statue."

"What statue?"

"No, no, this is not that myth of the trickster who transformed all the tribal women one summer in ancient memory," he said and then raised his hands to resist the rest of the story. "No, no, this is not one of those trickster diseases, these are young white Girl Scouts from the city."

"Why not?"

"No, the trickster in that story was made out of crystal."

"*Oshkiwiinag,* and plenty more," said Sour.

"Right, hundreds of women were pregnant that summer."

"My grandmother told me those stories."

"Never mind, get out to the camp," said the director.

"My uncle said the crystal trickster was a man and a woman at a circus that summer, and somehow, he teased, the population doubled in one year on the reservation," said Sour.

Sour packed a medical case with calamine, ammonia, baking soda, various antihistamines, and epinephrine. She drove the shortest route over unpaved back roads to the Girl Scout camp. The first giant drops of rain burst in the loose sand, and the black flies wavered in the slipstream. Splendid foliage leaned over the road, a natural arbor that reduced the light north of Bad Medicine Lake.

Camp Wikidin was built on stolen tribal land, a sweetheart concession to the Scouts on land that had been ascribed to the tribes in treaties. "Maybe the Scouts are allergic to the reservation," she muttered on the last turn. The camp director and two anxious assistant Scout leaders were marching in circles in the gravel parking lot.

"This thing is something strange, something sexual!" shouted one leader. Her cheeks were swollen and bright red, her gestures were uncertain, and she watched the shadows at the treeline in the distance.

"Wait a minute," said Sour.

"Really, some kind of sexual thing," the leader insisted.

"No, no, stand back and let me park the car."

"Dark windows," said the other leader.

"I hate the light," said Sour.

"Allergic?" asked the camp director.

"No, no, just hate what the bright light does to faces and the natural play of shadows," said Sour. "So, now about this sexual thing, where are the girls who need medical attention?"

"We locked the girls in the main cabin to protect them for now," said the camp director. "We thought it best, as they had the very same symptoms."

"Why?" asked Sour.

"Because, this thing *could* be sexual," said the director.

"Do you mean a man?"

"Something very sinister has happened here."

"Doctor Sour . . ."

"Nurse Cozie Browne," said Sour.

"Nurse Browne, we thought you would be a doctor."

"Perhaps you need a surgeon from the city," said Sour.

"Never mind, we have all been touched by something overnight," said the camp director. She turned toward the nurse, her face narrowed by one wide crease down the center of her forehead. She turned the loose wedding ring on her finger. She was worried, but not frightened. "Something that *could* be sexual, but we cannot believe our own words."

The assistants were closer to panic than the director. Their hands were unclean and trembled out of control. The assistant with the big red cheeks chewed on her knuckles. She could not determine if the "sexual thing" was the beginning or the end of her career as a Girl Scout leader.

Sour moaned at the last turn to the main cabin. The campers were at the windows, their bright red faces pressed on the panes. Their sensuous bodies had overheated the building, and a wave of moist warm air rushed out when the director unlocked the door.

Sour examined every camper in a private office with pictures of prancing horse on the walls. She soothed the girls with gentle stories about nature, images of lilacs, pet animals, and garden birds, but could not detect any allergies, infections, or insect bites. Most of the campers were shied by the heat of their own bodies, and mentioned their dreams, the unnatural sensations of soaring over water.

Barrie, one of the campers, had the sense at last to consider what had changed in their lives that might have caused such ecstasies. The girl described, with unintended irony, their habits and activities over the past few days, and then she revealed the secret of the Scouts, that the campers had not been the same since they discovered a statue buried on the other side of the lake.

Later, when the campers gathered to clean and examine the figure, their secret tribal treasure, some of the girls swooned and fainted right at the table. The emotions were so contagious that the campers buried the statue and worried that they were being punished by some demon of the tribal land who hated outsiders from the cities. These were signs of post-traumatic ecstasies.

Barrie, who was a senior Scout, drew a very detailed map of the secret burial site. She blushed as she marked the trail to the burial site near a cedar tree. Then she fanned her cheeks with the map. The mere thought of the trickster statue caused her breasts to rise and her breath to shorten.

Cozie located the crystal trickster in a moist shallow grave. She bound the statue in a beach towel and returned to the clinic. She was ecstatic on the back roads, certain that the treasure was the very crystal trickster that had transformed the mundane in so many tribal stories on the reservation.

She locked the trickster in a laboratory and reported to the director that there were no diseases to treat at the camp, nothing but blushes, short breath, and "mild post-traumatic histaminic ecstasies." Later, the camp leaders reported that the girls were much better and that a cookout was being prepared. The Scouts swore that they would never reveal to anyone the stories of the crystal trickster.

Burn unbound the trickster that night when she had finished her rounds in the clinic. The room was dark, with an examination light on the statue. She soaked the trickster in warm water, and as the mire washed away, the pure crystal seemed to brighten the laboratory.

The crystal trickster was named *oshkiwiinag* in the stories she heard on the islands and the reservation. The ancient statue warmed her hands and face. The crystal was smoother than anything she had ever touched. Smoother that a mountain stone, human flesh, otter hair, smoother than ice cream.

*Oshkiwiinag* was about seventeen inches high, and each part of the crystal anatomy was polished with precision. The arms, legs, head, torso, and penis were perfect interlocking parts. For instance, the bright head could not be removed unless both arms were raised, and the arms could not be removed with the head attached. The pure crystal penis was the most precise and intricate part of the trickster. She could not determine how to remove the penis from the crystal body.

Burn polished each part with such pleasure that she lost her sense of time and place. She carried the shrouded trickster home in the front seat of her car and placed the statue in a locked closet. She would consider how to present the trickster to her uncle and grandparents at Wanaki Island.

Cozie and the thirteen Girl Scouts who had touched *Oshkiwiinag* were pregnant, and nine months later their trickster babies were born at almost the same hour. The coincidence became a scandal in the media, and hundreds of reporters roamed the reservation in search of wicked tricksters. The tribal government was cursed with nonfeasance, and the clinic was sued for malpractice by several mothers of the trickster babies. Cozie was portrayed as tribal witch on several radio and television shows, a nurse who hated the light and caused those innocent Girl Scouts to become pregnant.

Cozie was forced to leave the only job she ever loved at night. At the same time, she had a clever daughter and an incredible trickster who could conceive a child with a crystal touch. She trusted that *Oshkiwiinag* was the real father of her child, because she had not been with a man for three years, two months, and nineteen days. Her uncle taught her to be precise with memories, and he said that "trickster conceptions were natural reason on the heartlines."

"Natural is not the reason," said Cozie.

Several months later, the state medical examiners concluded in their report that the conceptions were curious cases of parthenogenesis. There is medical evidence that ecstasies and even terror have been the occasions of innocent conceptions. Such trickster stories were heard in tribal communities centuries before the medical examiners were overcome by the coincidence of parthenogenesis.

## The Heartlines

The Naanabozho Express waited overnight at the station near the clinic. Gesture invited his niece to dinner in the parlor car. Cozie told him stories about *oshkiwiinag*, and the medical investigations on the reservation. He leaned back in the dental chair and insisted that she establish her own clinic on the train, "so you can practice trickster conceptions on women who would rather not bear the sensations and tortures of sexual intercourse."

Cozie moved to the train that very night and painted an announcement on the side of the parlor car. The sign read PARTHENOGENESIS ON THE NAANABOZHO EXPRESS and, in smaller letters, SOVEREIGN CONCEPTIONS IN MOTION WITH NO FEARS, TEARS, OR DISEASES.

The trickster express circled the reservation for several months, and in that time thousands of people had their terminal teeth repaired free by the one and only acudenturist in motion, and even more women boarded the train for a short time to touch *oshkiwiinag* and conceive a child without sex. Some women had their teeth renewed and touched the trickster at the same time, ecstasy on one end and a better smile on the other. The crystal trickster soothed those who would fear the pain of dental instruments.

Gesture is precise about memories and his mission to show the nation that tribal independence is truer in motion than in the hush of manners, that natural reason is heard in heartline stories of chance and coincidence, not in the cultural weave and wash of silence.

The Naanabozho Express lurched out of that lonesome casino station on the last wild run of natural sovereignty from the White Earth Reservation to the White House in Washington.

Laura Tohe is from the Tsenahabilnii (Sleepy Rock People Clan) and born for the Tohdichinii (Bitter Water Clan). She was raised on the Navajo Reservation in New Mexico and Arizona and is from Lupton, Arizona. She attended schools on the reservation, as well as Alburquerque Indian School. She completed her bachelor's degree at the University of New Mexico before earning her master's and doctor's degrees in creative writing and literature at the University of Nebraska–Lincoln. Her work has appeared in over a dozen anthologies and journals, including *The Colour of Resistance, Songs from This Earth on Turtle's Back, Calyx, Quilt, The Platte Valley Review, Wanbli Ho, Estuaires Revue Culturelle, Les Cahiers, Braided Lives, Nebraska Humanities, The Clouds Threw This Light, Callaloo, Reinventing the Enemy's Language,* and *Returning the Gift.* She is the author of *Making Friends with Water.* In 1993 the Omaha Emmy Gifford Children's Theatre commissioned her to write a one-hour play entitled *The Story of Me,* which was performed throughout Nebraska. Tohe is assistant professor of English at Arizona State University, Tempe.

Laura Tohe

# So I Blow Smoke in Her Face

IN THE MORNING I RACE Łį́į́'łITSOI ACROSS THE OPEN PLAIN near the windmill. The prairie dogs must duck into their holes when they hear the thundering of hooves passing. My mother watches us from the doorway of the house as she mixes the dough for tortillas. The dust swirls behind us and she thinks I'm just like her mother was. People used to say she could ride—"that girl could ride bareback with her little brother sitting behind her and the dust swirling furiously behind them."

My family owns horses. Just west of Tohatchi is where I'm from. From the north window are the dark blue Chooshgai Mountains rising above the dry plains and sand mesas on the southeast side. In the winter the holy ones emerge and cover the peaks with snow, bringing us water for our spring fields. Sometimes I feel their breath blowing down the slopes and I know they are alive as a newborn colt steaming with life.

My uncle teases me because my legs are bowed. I wear tight Wrangler jeans so they show. My boots are creamy tan, the color of sand. The tips are dark brown and my boots are sexy.

In the summer we go by horseback to look for our cows. We take a sandwich and a canteen of water. We ride all morning moving south past sagebrush and green tumbleweeds toward Gallup looking for our brand on the right shoulders of our cows. I've memorized their spots and faces the way some people remember their address. When the sun moves overhead, we ride west along the barbed wire fencing till we get to the bridge.

I like riding toward the Chooshgai best, toward the cool mountain slopes. By midday we stop under the cottonwoods near the silver water tank and eat our potato-and-Spam tortilla sandwich that Grandma packed. My cousin Viv and I scratch our initials into the water tank and when no one is looking I scratch in ER's initials.

We ride west toward the tall pine trees. On the way up we meet some riders who are also looking for their cattle and tell us they haven't seen our brand, so we decide to turn around.

We stop at the trading post and tie the horses to an old elm tree. While Uncle waits, Viv and I go in to buy three Pepsis and a Payday. Uncle doesn't eat candy, so Viv and I pass it back and forth until the left-over nuts roll around in the wrapper.

Viv and I race down the hill toward the highway. I pull my welder's hat down and give Łįį'łitsoi free rein. The wind rushes past us. It flattens our faces and the earth cannot hold us. We are flying over sage, chamisa and the little yellow and purple flowers that spread across this broad land. I want to go on and on like this but the horses begin to foam at the mouth, so we fall back into the horses and ride home slowly. They, too, know the exhilaration of a good run. Tonight I will give my horse extra oats and rub his back carefully with sand. Later, Uncle catches up and tells us we shouldn't tire the horses out like that. "Your mother won't like it," he adds to reinforce himself. My mother, the matriarch, is his older sister, who inherited the homesite and most of the cattle and horses from her mother, as is the Navajo tradition for daughters to inherit the family's land and property.

It's late afternoon and the drifting clouds give us patches of shade. We ride slowly in the direction of home while Uncle sings riding songs to carry us back.

So I don't care if some of the girls have named me Wishbone. At least it's not as bad as the names the school has labeled me: troublemaker, incorrigible, dumb Indian . . . One night they made me scrub the porches at midnight till my back ached. It's their way of shaming you, their way of taking control of you. They want you to know who's in charge, who's the authority. Like making soap flakes, they chip at you one flake at a time until your parts are lying in a bucket.

Then I light up a cigarette right there in the dorm. Soon the smoke drifts toward the ceiling like fog and the smell escapes from under the door and into the hallway, but I don't give anyone a chance to turn me in. I put on my jeans, navy blue sweatshirt, boots and stuff my pockets with the last of the money from home.

On the way to 7-Eleven I meet Viv, who is usually willing to go along with my schemes. In Navajo we're sisters because our mothers are sisters. She's also my best friend. We've hauled water, scrubbed our clothes on a washboard down at the windmill, learned to make tortillas and even thrown several batches of dough out into the brush behind the house because it was stiff as cold clay and we didn't want my mother to find out.

We walk across the campus, past the chain-link fence, ignoring the rules of signing in and out. Young pachucos in their low riders whistle at us. Usually we ignore them, preferring cowboys and their music. But tonight I want the company of wildness. So we enter their car and cruise up and down Central, two stomp Navajo girls and two Chicanos. We laugh and laugh until they get serious. We drive down Fourth and I tell the driver to let us out. They don't want to, but when I tell them we're government property and they could get into a lot of trouble, the door swings open. The sun is sinking behind the treetops when I think of Edgar. I tell Viv let's cut across the houses toward Tanoan Hall. We make it back as the last of the students are coming from dining room detail. We walk to Edgar's window, which is the fourth one down from the end, and look through the steel mesh that covers all the windows and that was installed after the dorm attendants found students crawling out at night after bed check to visit girlfriends in other dorms or to go to 7-Eleven.

"Shhhhd, Edgar." We give the Navajo signal. Someone jumps off the bunk bed and sees us. He pulls the curtain back. It's Jasper, Edgar's cousin. "Oh, hi, Jasper. Edgar *hágo bidiní.*" He leaves and brings Edgar. Edgar smiles at me from behind the mesh cover and says, *"Cigarette-ísh nee'hólǫ́?"* I pull out a pack of Winstons from my boot and we light up and exhale streams of smoke.

"Is it time for your bed check?" I tease. It's just an expression that we use to make a joke. Just something to laugh about living in these government boarding schools. The practice of making sure everyone is in bed at ten is another carry-over from the military life that these schools are modeled after. Edgar blows a cloud of smoke through the steel mesh and shows me his hands.

"I have dishpan hands," he announces and puts his fingers through the mesh to show us. Sure enough, the fingertips are shriveled and the nails are soft and pale. His fingers are those of a Navajo, long, slender, thin-skinned and brown. Some people notice faces but I notice hands. It was in the kitchen as he gathered trays to scrub that I first saw his hands. "I just got back from kitchen detail. They're so clean I could operate with them," he jokes and stares at his hands.

*"Hát'íílá naadeidą́ą́'* [Was it bear meat again]?" Viv asks. It's a joke because it's at least three or four times a week that we have Salisbury steak or roast beef, otherwise known as bear meat and rubber meat, respectively. The rubber meat could pass for beef jerky, seeing how all the moisture is cooked out of it.

Car lights pass down the street outside the fence and I remember my family going to the Chooshgai to gather wood in the fall. From the mountaintop we could see a thin line of car lights moving across the plain in the far distance below. It made me feel better just thinking about cutting and piling wood into my dad's truck and how Grandma would boil coffee and cook us mutton stew, so that by the time we had finished stacking the last log, the meal would be ready. I knew Viv and I shouldn't be here at Edgar's window but sometimes you just have to take control of your life and not let someone take it away from you. At home Viv and I took care of the cows the way Mom showed us, because most of the herd was hers. She taught us how to herd, how to vaccinate, how to rope and throw down the calves at branding time, and how to take care of our cattle. I had never gotten a summer job working as a clerical aid for the community or the chapter house the way others my age did. Taking care of my family's cattle was my responsibility when I was at home. Because I cared for the cows, Mom had given me a few of hers. I even had my own brand.

*"Nihíma nicháa'há'dooshkeeł,"* Edgar teases back. He jokes about Mrs. Harry, who is the head matron and who, if she catches us, will give us extra detail or ground us. On campus she has a reputation for being a mean woman, even though she's an Indian, a Heinz 57, an Indian who's from several different tribes.

" *'Éí lą́ą́'*. She's had it in for me ever since I got back late from Christmas vacation," I say as I inhale. Mrs. Harry, the woman who on my first day at the Indian School made everyone scurry away from the rear exit and back to their beds when they saw her car rounding the corner, breeds fear in the hearts and minds of the girls in my dorm. They avoid making her angry because she'll make you scrub, sweep or clean something even for minor infractions. She's always trying to catch me breaking the rules and sometimes she makes me do extra work around the dorm if she sees me talking in the hallway, like the time she told me to mop up the water in the showers when it wasn't my detail, or the time she told me to sweep the porch after Edgar walked me back from the rec hall. "No sweeping, no TV," she said. I said okay and went into my room. Ever since then she watches my every move.

Mrs. Chavez, the girls' dorm attendant, sees us at Edgar's window as she makes her rounds and tells us to get back to our dorm. "Mrs. Harry wants to see you, Vida," she says and looks at me.

"Another month in the salt mines," I say sarcastically and stomp out the cigarette. It leaves a black smear on the concrete.

I'm lying on my bunk bed and thinking about home. I'm thinking about the calves nuzzling their mothers. I'm thinking about Łį́į́'łitsoi and riding him across the dry plains, under the bridge and toward the Chooshgai. I'm thinking about tall straight pine trees and the cool breeze that drifts from the mountains. I'm thinking about the smell of sage after a summer rain. I'm thinking of Mom's warm round tortillas.

Viv sits beside me and dangles her feet from the top of my bunk bed. We take turns smoking my cigarette. Then there's the knock at the door and, sure enough, she has sent Apple Annie, her favorite, to get me. Viv and I exchange looks. I step out into the hallway by the bulletin board, where my name has often appeared with the other offenders. She's waiting there with hand on hip. The other girls are watching from their rooms as if this were a showdown. She's ready to tell me off, to shame and humiliate me again. But I won't give her a chance, so I take a drag and blow smoke in her face.

Yes, my mother thinks as she watches me riding outside the northwest fence where the cows graze, my daughter is just like her grandmother. She returns to her weaving. The design grows upward in layers of dramatic and geometric shapes.

Łį́į́'lítsoi and I move easily through the trees. We've been this way before. He picks his way steadily up the mountain slopes. The clean mountain air feels good. My horse is strong and happily we make the climb up into the Chooshgais.

Tiffany Midge received the Diane Decorah Memorial Award in 1994 for her *Outlaws, Renegades, and Saints: Diary of a Mixed Up Halfbreed.* The talented young writer has been an active performance poet, reading for the Red Sky Poetry Theatre, the Live Poet's Society, and Red Eagle Soaring. Midge's works have appeared in a number of magazines, and a selection of her poetry is slated for presentation at the prestigious Washington Metro Art Program in Seattle. In 1994, she was honored with her designation as a featured performer at the Bumbershoot Library Arts Program, one of the largest literary and art festivals in the United States. A professional writer living in Bothell, Washington, Midge is Hunkpapa Lakota and plans on attending the University of Montana, where she will major in Native American studies and creative writing.

Tiffany Midge

# Beets

IN FOURTH-GRADE HISTORY CLASS I LEARNED THAT THE Plains Indians weren't cut out to be farmers; that the government tried to get them to plant corn and stuff, but it was one of those no-win situations, meaning that no matter how hard the Indians fought against progress and manifest destiny, they'd never win.

This history lesson occurred around the same time the United States began its hyperecological awareness, which soon seeped into the media. Theories and speculations were developed that asserted that the earth was heading for another ice age. Whereas today scientists tell us that the earth is getting hotter. It was during this time that my father's convictions regarding the demise of the twentieth century began tipping toward fanaticism. *The Whole Earth Catalogue* took up residence in our home and he began reciting from it as if it were Scripture. He wanted us all to get back to nature. I think he would have sold the house and moved us all into the mountains to raise goats and chickens, but my mother, who didn't have much of a say in most of the family decisions, must have threatened to leave him for good if he took his plan to fruition. So he settled with gardening. Gardening is too light a word for the blueprints he drew up that would transform our backyard into a small farming community.

One day I returned from school and discovered my father shoveling manure from a pile tall as a two-story building. I couldn't help but wonder where he ever purchased such a magnificent pile of shit, and impressive though it was, I doubt the neighbors shared in my father's enthusiasm. I wouldn't have been surprised if they were circulating a petition to have it removed.

"Good, you're home!" my father said. "Grab a rake."

Knowing I didn't stand a chance in arguing, I did just as he ordered. And I spent the rest of the day raking manure, thinking the Plains Indians opted not to farm because they knew enough not to. I think my father would have kept us out there shoveling and raking till after midnight if my mother hadn't insisted I come in the house and do my homework. The next day I had blisters on my hands and couldn't hold a pencil.

"Hard work builds character," my father preached. "Children have it too easy today. All you want to do is sit around and pick lint out of your belly buttons."

I was saved from hard labor for the next week because the blisters on my hands burst open and spilled oozy blood all over the music sheets in singing class. The teacher sent me home, back to the plow.

"No pain, no gain," Father said, "Next time wear gloves."

The following weekend our suburban nuclear unit had transformed into the spitting image of the Sunshine Family dolls. I began calling my sister Dewdrop. Myself, Starshine. I renamed my mother Corn Woman and my father Reverend Buck. Reverend Buck considered it his mission in life to convert us from our heathen Hungry-Man TV dinner, Bisquick and Pop-Tart existence.

"Do you realize that with all these preservatives, after you're dead and buried, your body will take an extra few years to completely decompose?" Father preached.

"I don't care," my sister said, "I plan on being cremated."

As the good reverend's wife and children, we must have represented some deprived tribe of soulless, bereft Indians and he designated himself to take us, the godless parish, under his wing.

Mother resigned herself to his plans. And we trudged along behind her. When she was growing up on the reservation, her family had cultivated and planted every season, so gardening wasn't a completely foreign activity. The difference was, her family planted only what could be used. Their gardens were conservative. But my father's plans resembled a large Midwestern crop, minus the tractors. He even drew up sketches of an irrigation system that he borrowed from *The Whole Earth Catalogue*. It was a nice dream. His heart was in the right place. I'm sure the government back in the days of treaties, relocation and designation of reservation land thought their intentions were noble too. I kind of admired my father for his big ideas, but sided with my mother on this one. Father was always more interested in the idea of something rather than the actuality; to him, bigger meant better. My father liked large things, generous mass, quantity, weight. To him, they represented progress, ambition, trust. Try as he might to be a true renegade, adopt Indian beliefs and philosophies, even go so far as to marry an Indian woman, he still could never avoid the obvious truth. He was a white man. He liked to build large things.

"What do you plan to do with all these vegetables?" my mother asked him.

"Freeze and can 'em," he replied. Mother was about to say something, but then looked as if she'd better not. I knew what she was thinking. She was thinking that our father expected *her* to freeze and can them. She didn't look thrilled at the prospect. Father may have accused her of being an apple from time to time, even went so far as to refer to her as apple pie, what he thought to be a term of endearment, but Mother must have retained much of that Plains Indian stoic refusal to derive pleasure from farming large acreage.

Father assigned each of us a row. Mother was busily stooped over, issuing corn into the soil, as if offering gems of sacrifice to the earth goddess. I was in charge of the radishes and turnips, which up until that day I'd had no previous experience with, other than what I could recall from tales of Peter Rabbit stealing from Mr. McGregor's garden. I bent down over my chore, all the while on keen lookout for small white rabbits accessorized in gabardine trousers.

My sister was diligently poking holes in the soil for her onions when our adopted collie began nosing around the corn rows looking for a place to pee. "Get out of the corn, Charlie!" I ordered him.

Father chuckled and said, "Hey, look, a scorned corndog!"

Mother rolled her eyes and quipped, "What a corny joke!"

My sister feigned fainting and said, "You punish me!"

Yeah, we were an image right out of a Rockwell classic with the caption reading, *Squawman and family; an American portrait of hope.*

In school we learned that the Indians were the impetus behind the Thanksgiving holiday that we practice today. This legend depicts that the Eastern tribes were more reverent and accepting of the white colonists than any fierce and proud Plains Indian ever was. My father challenged this theory by suggesting I take armfuls of our sown vegetables to school. "It'll be like helping out the Pilgrims," he told me. I brought grocery sacks of turnips to class one day and offered them as novelties for our class show-and-tell activity. Everyone was left with the assumption that it was the Sioux Indians who were farmers and who had guided and helped the Pilgrims in their time of need. Mrs. Morton didn't discourage this faux pas but, rather, rattled on about how noble, how Christian, of the Indians to assist the poor colonists in the unsettling and overwhelming wilderness they'd arrived at. My classmates collected my offering of turnips and at recess we rounded up a game of turnip baseball. Lisa Parker got hit in the face with a turnip and went bawling to the school nurse. Mrs. Morton ignored me the rest of the day and sent me home with a note to my parents, which said, *Please do not allow this to happen again.*

At Father's suggestion, my sister engineered a baking factory. Every evening after dinner she would bake loaves of zucchini bread. These baked goods went to the neighbors, coworkers and the public just happening by. My father had suggested she sell them at school, but Mother firmly reminded him that the teachers weren't supportive of free enterprise in the elementary schools. "Well, she could organize a bake sale and the proceeds could go to charity," my father offered. So the following week Helen Keller Elementary School had a bake sale in the school gymnasium. Tables were loaded up with flour-and-sugar concoctions of every creed and color. Cookies, cupcakes, strudel, fudge, brownies and whole cakes. My sister's table was the most impressive and I felt swelled up with pride at her arrangement. She had a banner struck across the wall behind the table that read *zucchini's R R friends.* And then along with her stacks of loaves she also had our season's bounty of zucchini. I even snuck in a few turnips for color. The teachers milled around her table praising her for her fine ingenuity.

Mrs. Morton asked me, "How did your family ever come into so many zucchinis?" As if zucchini was old money we had inherited.

"Oh, zucchini is a fast-growing vegetable," I told her. "My father says that it breeds in the garden like rabbits, really, really horny rabbits that multiply exponentially."

Mrs. Morton ignored me for the rest of the day and sent a note home to my parents that read, *Please do not allow this to happen again.*

In school we learned about the fur trappers and traders who migrated all over the frontier trading with the Indians. We learned about the Hudson's Bay Company and how the Plains Indians bartered with them for the glass beads and shells that modernized and increased the value of their traditional regalia. We learned that before money, folks just traded stuff. Bartered their wares. But then gold was discovered throughout the West and bartering furs and beads took a backseat. The Indians weren't gold diggers.

Aside from the Trouble with Tribbles, zucchini problem in our garden, we had another problem to contend with. The beets. Some evenings I would discover my father stooped down over the beet rows, shaking his head and muttering, "Borscht . . . borscht."

My sister was encouraged to invent a recipe for beet bread, as she had done with the zucchini, but it kept coming out of the oven soggy and oozing red juice, as if it were hunks of animal flesh trickling trails of blood all over the kitchen counters. Not a very appetizing sight. Father had a bit more success with his beet experimentation. Inventing such delicacies as beetloaf and Sunday morning succotash surprise and beet omelets. He'd counteracted the red by adding blue food coloring, so we ended up with purple tongues after eating. My all-time favorite was beet Jello. And Mother packed our lunches to include bologna-and-beet sandwiches. We took sacks of beets to our grandparents' house and my German grandmother was delighted with our offering. "Oh, I just love beets!" she exclaimed. "I shall make borscht and pickles."

The beets were beginning to get on everyone's nerves. But there were other cauldrons bubbling in our household; my father's overstimulated dread of waste. He'd been raised by a tough and hearty Montana farm girl, who in turn had been bred from a stock of immigrant Germans from Russia who had escaped the banks of the Valga River after the reign of Catherine the Great. As if injected straight through the bloodline, my grandmother Gertrude instilled a heavy dose of "Waste not, want not," medication to my father. My grandfather also ladled out his own brand of practical conservation. But more out of his penny-pinching and obsessive attention to dollars and cents, not out of some necessity imprinted from childhood to "Save today, you'll not starve tomorrow." The examination of water and electric bills was one of my grandfather's favorite hobbies. Either wattage fascinated him or he was always expecting to get stiffed. The latter being more true, because he was one of *the* great complainers.

It didn't come as much of a surprise when my father promoted his newest scheme: of bartering our surplus beets door to door. The catch was, we were the ones doing the soliciting, he was going to stay home and watch the World Series. He furthered his cause by explaining to us that the Indians traded long ago and this would be our own personal tribute to an old way of life.

"Yeah, but they didn't sell beets door to door like encyclopedia salesmen," my sister retorted. "I'll feel so stupid!"

"Nonsense!" my father said. "It's a fine idea. Whatever money you make, I'll just deduct from your allowance. And if you make more than your allowance, you can keep the difference. Save up for a bike or mitt or something."

I couldn't help thinking that if only my mother had stopped my father when he'd decided to become Reverend Buck and toil and sweat in the garden, none of this would be happening. This was a bad episode from *Attack of the Killer Tomatoes,* and my father's ambition and insistence on doing things only on a large scale didn't seem to justify the humiliation and embarrassment that resulted when we were coaxed to distribute the fruits of our labor. However, his latest plan I was for the most part agreeable to, but only because I was so completely eager to do anything that would levitate me in his eyes as angelic and perfect and because, secretly, I enjoyed witnessing my sister's discomfort.

We filled up grocery sacks with surplus. Father had suggested we fill up the wheelbarrow, but Julie wouldn't hear of it. "For cripe's sake, with that wheelbarrow filled with beets we'd look pathetic!" she argued. "We'd look like Okies from *The Grapes of Wrath!*" My father was a fanatic about Steinbeck. He taught my sister to read "The Red Pony" before she entered the second grade. I, on the other hand, was considered the *slow* one.

We set out. Our own personal tribute to Indians of long ago. We weren't very conspicuous. Nothing out of the ordinary, just a couple of brown-skinned kids in braids walking grocery sacks down the suburban street. Indians weren't a common sight in residential neighborhoods, and my sister and I had experienced our share of racial prejudice. When my mother wrote out checks at the grocery store, the store manager was always called by the clerk to verify her driver's license. This occurring immediately after a white woman wrote a check to the same clerk but no verification was asked for. Once riding my bike, I heard some kids call me *nigger.* I don't know what hurt me more, the fact that they had called me an ugly name or that they had misrepresented my race. My sister during a Husky game at Hecht Ed Stadium was insulted by a black man when she was buying hot dogs. "Must eat a lot of hot dogs on the reservation, huh?" he told her. Later when we told Father, he responded with "Did you ask him if he ate a lot of watermelon?"

We had walked most of a mile to a neighborhood outside the confines of our own, so as not to be further embarrassed by people we actually knew. When we had come to a point where we felt we were at a safe enough distance, my sister told me to go up to the house with the pink flamingos balanced in the flower bed. "Only if you come too," I told her. So together we marched up to the door and rang the doorbell.

A woman with frizzy red hair answered the door. "Hello?" she asked. "What can I do for you girls?"

My sister nudged me with her elbow. "Would you like to buy some beets?" I asked.

The woman's brows knitted together. "What's that? What's that you asked?"

"BEETS!" I shouted. "WOULD YOU LIKE TO BUY SOME BEETS?!"

I yelled so loudly that some kids stopped what they were doing and looked toward the house.

The woman was having a great deal of difficulty disguising her perplexity. Her brow was so busy knitting together she could have made up an afghan. Finally, some expression resembling resolution passed over her face. "No, not today," and she very curtly closed the door in our faces.

I wasn't going to let her go that easily. "BORSCHT, LADY!" I yelled. "YOU KNOW HOW TO MAKE BORSCHT?!"

My sister threw me a horrified look, shoved me and ran down the street. "HEY JULIE!" I called after her. "YOU SHOULD SEE YOUR FACE, IT'S BEET RED!"

We didn't sell any beets that day. Our personal tribute had failed. After I caught up with my sister, I found her sitting on the pavement at the top of a steep hill, with her face in her hands. I didn't say anything because there wasn't anything to say. I knew that she was crying and it was partly my fault. I wanted to make it up to her. Though I wasn't bothered by her pained frustrations, tears were another matter entirely. When she cried, I always felt compelled to cry right along with her. But on this day I didn't. Instead, I took the grocery sacks filled with beets and turned them upside down. The beets escaped from the bags, and as we watched them begin their descent to the bottom of the hill, I noticed the beginning of a smile on my sister's face. When the plump red vegetables had arrived at the bottom of the hill, leaving a bloody pink trail behind, we were both chuckling. And when a Volkswagen bus slammed on its breaks to avoid colliding with our surplus beets, we were laughing. And by the time the beets reached the next block and didn't stop rolling but continued down the asphalt street heading into the day after tomorrow, my sister and I were displaying pure and uncensored hysterics—laughing uncontrollably, holding our bellies as tears ran down our cheeks, pressing our faces against the pavement and rejoicing in the spectacle that we viewed from the top of that concrete hill.

Ralph Salisbury, who is of Cherokee, Irish, and English ancestry, served as a professor of English and ethnic studies at the University of Oregon from 1951 to 1994. He is a well-known poet, storyteller, translator, and editor. He has been a Fulbright Scholar in Norway, where he studied the cultural and oral traditions of the Sami, and he is currently lecturing in Germany. Salisbury has published several books, short stories, essays, reviews, and articles of criticism. Some of his best-known works include *One Indian and Two Chiefs, A White Rainbow, Going to the Water, Spirit Beast Chants, Pointing at the Rainbow, Ghost Grapefruit and Other Poems,* and *Trekways of the Wind.* His short stories have appeared in Anchor Books' *Earth Song, Sky Spirit,* as well as *Earth Power Coming, A Nation Within, Literary Olympians,* and *Songs from This Earth on Turtle's Back.*

Ralph Salisbury

# The Last Rattlesnake Throw

"IT'S THE WAR." THOUGH I WAS ONLY TEN THE YEAR fighting ended, I remember my teachers' words, because I heard them often. A former student's sticking his knife between the ribs of a soldier at a dance was due to "the war," though recollection informs me that the former student was the older brother of one of my numerous Navajo classmates, the soldier an African American. I also recall that there was located just outside the dance hall a store whose front wall was all glass, even the door, and the floor-to-ceiling shelves behind the counter were lined with bottles, their labels as colorful as cartoons on TV.

Marijuana smoke mingled with the smell of creosote brush surrounding our school at the edge of our little town, and the war was to blame. One of the older girls had missed something her tittering friends called "her period," and when she also missed having her graduation picture in the paper, showing up in the bridal section instead, a teacher said to another, "At least this will keep him from going to war." When the front page exposed the SNAKE CLUB THRILL SEEKERS CLUB, the words below our faces, all in a row, quoted the principal as saying that nothing like this had ever happened before the war.

The war, to me, was a first-grader's blurry awareness of my real dad's going away and being killed at its beginning, and of the man my mom had followed from Oregon to Arizona's being trained to do something and, then, being sent to do it, in Asia.

"Married, I could draw an allotment from the Army," I remember my mom pleading quite a few times, right up to when her friend left, still saying he'd only be going somewhere in the U.S. and would send money to bring us there.

Probably because rent was cheap, and our address the only one to which Mom's "friend" might conceivably write, we stayed, Mom with the only bedroom all to herself now, and me with a pad on the kitchen floor, so used to cockroaches scurrying across my face in the dark I would just swat without waking, until a scorpion got back at me for all those I'd shook out of shoes and squashed. Mom's pay kept us eating, since she could buy wholesale where she worked. When I came home with a concussion after a big kid pushed me off a swing, there wasn't any money for the doctor, but there was a kind of extra-strong aspirin in the REMEDIES section of the store, and after a week or so I could go to school again.

TV never said we were losing, even when, months later, it showed the last Americans escaping off roofs into helicopters, but you could tell that the war was getting worse and worse because the base became more and more crowded with troops being hastily trained to replace those killed, and as more and more black kids and blond kids and brown kids crowded our school, there were more and more fights on the playground.

Our teachers may or may not have been right that the Snake Throwers Club started because of the war, but, for sure, the war brought a new boy, called Breed, who caused the club to end a few months before the war itself ended. Breed's dad was the new blond military policeman we often saw dragging some drunk soldier out of a bar, but Breed's mom was Indian, and Breed's black hair blew in desert wind over eyes as blue as the sky I'd see through holes a bird had pecked in the bathroom roof's thin shingles. Breed's family lived in what had been a garage just half a block from the former garage Mom rented, and because Breed considered me Indian even though my real dad had been only half Cherokee and my mother was blond, we became friends. Kids began to notice that my eyes were as black as the stones called "Apache tears," and for the first time in my life I heard the schoolyard chant "Redskin, Redskin, starts fights but never wins" directed at me. Actually, because I was small for ten, I didn't have many fights, but because Breed was big for twelve, older boys thought they could beat him up without being teased for fighting "a baby." Tough sons of tough soldiers who'd been slammed into the guardhouse tried to take family revenge, but, his dad having taught him boxing, wrestling, judo and karate, Breed held his own with fifteen-year-olds.

Whether the eighth-grade gang's inviting him to membership meant they respected his courage or whether they were planning to kill him for being his father's son, or for being Indian, I don't know. The nine boys who stopped Breed and me on our way home were all white, but all were laughing and acting friendly. They even answered Breed that, sure, I could come along "and watch."

It was my second time to watch. My home being on the way to hills where rattlesnakes crawled higher into sun as evening came, I'd tagged along, unasked, on what was to be the first throw. It started with the gang captain's trying to snap off the head of a bull snake by swinging it like a whip, as the gang lieutenant claimed his granddad had done to a rattler. The head staying on, despite some energetic whipping, the captain spun the mottled length faster and faster and let it fly, writhing and twisting, to land, with an explosion of yellow pollen, on the canyon's other side. The lieutenant tried his luck at decapitating a small garter snake and, finally, threw it, only to see it drop, its striped body writhing in pain, on spines of a cactus below the canyon rim. Next, finding one of the rattlesnakes the gang had come to shoot with BB guns, the lieutenant first pinned its head with a forked stick, then, amid silence, whipped the snake around so fast it couldn't twist to strike him, and threw it farther than the leader had thrown his bull snake. The captain stayed captain by throwing a rattlesnake even farther, and from then on, every boy had to throw a rattler to be in the gang.

. . .

"THRILL SEEKERS", the headline read, meaning, I guess, the exuberant, sometimes cruel recklessness with which manhood tears itself out of the womb of childhood, a tearing that makes for youth crime and makes for the warrior tradition of history's great names, "humane, democratic soldiers" being victorious only on TV.

A few weeks back, Breed's dad had volunteered for combat and avoided going to the guardhouse, where he'd put so many others, after first confiscating their drugs. For the first time since his dad's disgrace, Breed acted proud, sticking his big chin out, as he'd do before a fight, and when he asked that I come along and watch his throw, I thought he wanted me to see that, even though he'd cried a few times, he was a kid with plenty of guts. It turned out he wanted help. He'd grown up in the city and had never even seen a rattlesnake. On the way to the canyons, I told him about using a forked stick to hold the head and then spinning around to get the snake stretched in a fast whirl before it could twist to strike. I even took off my belt and showed him how I'd seen it done.

"It's the war." Teachers meant the high cost of rent and food, meant high taxes and low salaries, meant drugs, meant boys who, imitating TV crime shows, masked their faces with mothers' or sisters' nylon panty hose and ganged up on two girls walking home from a movie.

"It's the war," Mom said, meaning her friend hadn't written a single letter after leaving.

"It's the war," Breed's mother's people had probably said, meaning the blond soldier would never have taken their daughter away with him, unmarried, if the previous war hadn't caused the reopening of an army base. The war. Meaning the old tribal ways of love and marriage would not have been destroyed except for whites' invasion of Ute land. It's the war, my Cherokee people must at one time have thought, seeing their daughters pregnant by the invaders, seeing each generation lighter-skinned, seeing the old religion destroyed by the armies of the new.

Breed did everything I'd whispered he should, picked a small snake with less power to resist his whipping, poked it out of its coil, and pinned the head with a forked stick while he grabbed the rattling end and stretched the body straight before going into a whirl, which had to end just right, with the snake flying head-first over the canyon edge.

I'd stayed as close as I dared, so I could warn Breed if the fangs got too close to his shoulder. The gang was lined up twenty feet away.

Breed might have had a special enemy not even he knew about, a kid whose dad had been put behind bars or a kid who hated brown skin. It might have been what journalists would call "a prank gotten out of control," no enmity at all but heedlessness. Whether someone had a plan or only an impulse, he certainly had a blowgun, fashioned from one of the hollow reeds abundant along the little river that made both reptile and human life possible in this desert, made gardens fertile and made an army base possible. Bubble gum, from a cheering or jeering mouth, was balled inside the pithy tunnel slick with spit. Inside the gum was imbedded a sandburr, its spines about the size of a rattle-snake's fangs.

The aim accurate, sandburr struck brown neck. Breed's response was equally accurate. The snake flew, its rattling echoing off canyon walls, its body convulsing for self-defense.

A boy screamed. The scream was like one I'd heard and thought a cat's cry, the scream really that of a girl being dragged into bushes. The stones of the canyon and all of the gang touched or nearly touched by the snake echoed the first scream, but a doctor would discover no snakebites.

The gang had probably never intended a membership picture, but they had one, even including an uninitiated, and never to be initiated, member, me, all of us in an all-American team victory row, grinning, glorying in our fame, only Breed among us solemn, that week's news about his dad the last news he'd ever get.

My mother, terrified of snakes, borrowed from Grandma and moved us back to Oregon, where, eventually, a forwarded letter informed her that her friend wouldn't be marrying her or anyone.

In a war that secured oil to fuel more war, Breed became, for the second time in his short life, a news item, and my right arm, which had never thrown a snake but had thrown grenades—one of which was thrown back—became something rare in a desert, fertilizer.

Having to paint left-handed caused me to become what I'd sworn I'd never be, a teacher, teaching, amid orderly rows of study desks. The psyches of millions propagandized into war-lust. "Democracy," we teachers say to our pupils, so as not to lose our jobs, afraid to say what General and President Eisenhower said about a conspiracy of big business leaders and military officers.

"It's the war," my paintings awkwardly say, from the hallway walls of my hometown library's small basement, a model's beauty doomed to remain in her flesh, in her slowly, inexorably aging flesh, my brush leaving whatever I have of beauty a prisoner, a prisoner of war, in what's left of my body and in whatever may sometime grow from desert sand.

D. L. Birchfield is Choctaw, born and raised in Oklahoma. He received his bachelor's degree at Western State College in Gunnison, Colorado, and earned his law degree from the University of Oklahoma. Birchfield is a prolific writer and an energetic editor. He is an editor for *News from Indian Country, OKC Camp Crier, The Raven Chronicles,* and *Moccasin Telegraph.* He was coeditor for a special issue of *Callaloo* focusing on Native American literature, as well as associate editor of *Durable Breath: Contemporary Native American Poetry.* Birchfield edited a number of Native American entries for the *Gales Encyclopedia of Multicultural America,* including those on Choctaws, Apaches, Navajos, and Pueblos. He published a short story in Anchor Books' *Earth Song, Sky Spirit,* and he has produced a novel based on "The Little Choctaw." He recently authored two books for children, including *Tecumseh* and *Jim Thorpe.* He has also completed *Rabbit,* a book dealing with animal lore and legend. Birchfield is the executive secretary of the National Caucus of the Wordcraft Circle of Native Writers, and he is a member of the Western Writers of America, Science Fiction and Fantasy Writers of America, and Romance Writers of America. He lives in Oklahoma City, where he mentors young native writers about the art and magic of publishing.

D. L. Birchfield

# Never Again

It was late Friday afternoon, the weekend before Thanksgiving, which meant that deer season would begin the next morning.

I was alone in the living room, idly watching the local news, weather, and sports. Mom and Dad were out in the backyard. My kid brother Delbert was back in his room. My other siblings were scattered all over the planet.

I wasn't watching the news for any particular reason. Certainly deer season was the furthest thing from my mind, until I heard the weather.

We'd been having balmy, seventy-degree weather, beautiful days, pleasant nights. But now a blizzard was barreling down the plains straight toward us. "This will be a major winter storm," said the weatherman. "It's got it all—snow, sleet, freezing rain, bitter arctic wind. We may get a foot or more of snow." It would hit the Oklahoma City area the next day, on Saturday evening, and would hit southeastern Oklahoma late Saturday night. They were warning all creation to take cover.

I tiptoed down the hallway and peeked into Delbert's room to see if by any chance he might be watching the local news on his little TV. He was sitting at his desk reading a book, with a set of stereo headphones clamped to his ears. I could see by the setting on his stereo that he was listening to a local FM rock and roll station, one that didn't even give the time of day, let alone any news or weather.

I looked out in the backyard. Mom and Dad were engaged in a spirited discussion, pointing at the crazy quilt of flower beds and vegetable garden plots the backyard was divided into. I didn't need to hear what they were saying to know what they were talking about. "This space gets just the kind of full sunlight that I need for my creeping phlox," Mother would be saying; and Dad would say, "But that's where I plan to plant my okra next year."

It was an old war, and this skirmish wouldn't be over until it was nearly time for them to go shopping for groceries, which would get them out of the house during the critical time necessary to get packed and get gone, if Delbert could be enticed into one more outdoor adventure—if he hadn't heard about the change in the weather. Probably Mom and Dad had heard about it.

I popped my head into Delbert's room and said, "Hey!"

He looked around, took the headphones off of his head, and said, "What?"

"Did you know that deer season starts tomorrow morning?" I held my breath. He had vowed never again to follow me off into the woods, and he had meant it too.

"Deer season?" he said. He looked out the window at the spectacularly beautiful weather. He said, "You want to go?"

He didn't know. *He didn't know.*

"I'm thinking about it," I said. "If we run over right now and get our deer tags, get back and get packed, we can be at Grandpa Crowder's old place by about midnight and camp there at the edge of the woods. Tomorrow we can hike up into the McGee Valley, deer hunt along the way, and camp tomorrow night up on the Potapo. Nobody else will be way off up in there. We're bound to get a deer."

"I loaned out my backpack," he said. "And we ruined that old tent."

"We won't need a tent," I said, walking to the window and looking outside. "We can take that old tarp out in the shed and use it to keep the dew off of us. I've got my backpack, and you can carry my old Marine Corps duffel bag."

A half hour later we were buying our deer tags. By the time we got back home Mom and Dad had left to go shopping. We left them a note telling them where we were going and that we'd be back probably Monday or Tuesday.

While Delbert was throwing his things together I ran over to a buddy's house and borrowed his heavy-duty, U.S. Air Force, arctic sleeping bag. Delbert, I noticed, packed a lightweight cotton sleeping bag that didn't even have a waterproof shell.

When he saw me packing my winter hunting coat, gloves, and insulated underwear he looked real thoughtful for a moment, then packed his too, saying, "It might get a bit nippy around daylight."

We packed enough food for a few days, packed a campfire cooking kit, gathered up our deer rifles and ammunition, and left the city well after dark, barely getting away before it was time for Mom and Dad to get back home.

We talked about deer hunting all the way on the drive down, and I changed stations on the radio every time one of them started to do a newscast. It was after midnight when we pulled up in front of our great-grandfather Crowder's old, abandoned home place, way back in the foothills of the Ouachita Mountains, at the end of the road.

Our great-grandfather had lived to be very near a hundred years old, maybe older. We guessed him to be at least ninety-eight when he died, based on the age of his children and on things he could remember about his early life (he didn't know what year he had been born). Recorded by the Dawes Commission as a three-quarter-blood Choctaw, he was actually a Chickasaw/Choctaw mixed blood, descended from a white man named Eli Crowder, who settled among the Choctaws and intermarried, probably sometime in the 1780s or 1790s, and who fathered large families of mixed bloods, first by a Choctaw wife, then by a Chickasaw wife, from whom our great-grandfather was descended (though the Chickasaw blood had been forgotten until some of the family got to digging around in old history books).

Eli Crowder and his in-laws had been a part of Pushmataha's eight-hundred-man Choctaw army that fought engagements with a faction of the Creeks in the War of 1812, where Eli won the name Muscokubi (Creek Killer) in an episode told at some length in H. B. Cushman's *History of the Choctaw, Chickasaw, and Natchez Indians* (1899). Some of Eli's descendants became prominent in tribal politics during the nineteenth century, one of them becoming one of the principal interpreters in the nation. But our great-grandfather preferred the solitude at the edge of the McGee Creek wilderness, where he and his son, our great-uncle Bunnie, lived for most of the twentieth century. They had finally died one winter, within a few weeks of each other, a few years earlier. Our father had been their favorite relative. Dad practically lived with them, off and on, when he was growing up. Dad said Grandpa Crowder was a white-haired old man when he first met him.

As we pulled up and parked, even by moonlight Granddad's old place looked changed almost beyond recognition. Planning was well advanced to build a dam on the McGee, and people who specialized in ruining remote areas were already at work. Somebody had bulldozed all the timber across the road in front of Granddad's place. We had intended to camp in that timber.

Now we could see for a quarter of a mile to the north across the new pasture, all the way to the new treeline, which we knew was where the land fell away down a steep mountainside to the McGee below. We decided to hike across the new pasture to the treeline to make camp. It was not quite 2 A.M. when we crawled into our sleeping bags and fell asleep under a bright canopy of stars, the kind of sight that's simply unavailable in the light-polluted atmosphere of a city.

We were up at first light, in time to cook a big breakfast and be packed up and ready to go by the time it was light enough to see how to hunt. Deer season had now begun, so we eased our way into the woods, hunting as we went.

Looking back across the new pasture at Granddad's old place I could barely believe it was such a short distance away. Where we had camped was about halfway from Granddad's house to the McGee. When I was a kid, it had been a pure wilderness adventure to go to the McGee. The world seemed suddenly smaller and not nearly as interesting. There had been a maze of different trails through the pine forest leading from Granddad's house to different places on the McGee. It seemed it had taken half my life to learn those trails, and they passed through many different environments, different visual experiences, different places. Now anyone could find his way across the pasture, and it all looked pretty much the same.

Neither me nor Delbert could figure out exactly where we had camped in relation to that old network of trails, and rather than cast around trying to find one of the old trails we just headed down through the timber on the steep, rocky hillside. We came out on the McGee a little upstream of where we usually did, but that was all right, as we had to go upstream quite a bit to wade the river at the shoals.

I noticed that Delbert was having some trouble trying to find a comfortable way to carry the duffel bag, with its single heavy strap. It didn't work very well trying to sling it over one shoulder, the strap wasn't long enough to sling it across his back, and it was too heavy and bulky to try to carry by its hand strap. Carrying it up on top of his shoulder seemed to be about the only way to do it, which didn't look like much fun. In fact, it looked downright awkward, as he was also trying to carry his deer rifle and a chopping axe.

When we got to the shoals just below the mouth of Crooked Creek, at the exact spot where the McGee Creek dam now sits, we met a fellow on horseback wading the river and coming toward us. When he got to our side he danced his pony around a little bit and said he had missed a good shot at a big buck about daylight up near the mouth of the Potapo. When we told him that's where we were heading he wished us luck, saying as far as he'd seen we'd have the whole woods to ourselves.

The river gurgled and splashed as it raced through the rocky shoals, spring-fed and clear and not quite knee-deep. We pulled off our boots and socks and rolled our pants legs up to wade it. The day was already warm, with bright sunshine, and the mountain valley was sprinkled here and there with the very last of the autumn colors.

After crossing the river Delbert stood drinking in the sights. He said, "You know, this is how it ought to be, two brothers out doing the things that brothers ought to do. I'm really glad we made this trip."

I nearly broke down and told him about the blizzard right then and there. Just hearing him talk like that brought a catch to my throat, and it was all I could do to keep from getting all misty-eyed.

He asked me if I remembered the time that summer after we had moved up to western Colorado, when I had been in college up there only for a year or two and he and our kid brother Ernie were just little brats, when we went backpacking up the side of the Grand Mesa that time with Billy Burch, up the Kannah Creek trail, and after we got camped that night came one of the heaviest rainstorms they'd ever had up there. Did I remember that, and did I remember how we'd just about gotten situated that night where we could sleep about half-dry under that rain tarp when that big American water spaniel of ours came crawling under the tarp with us and got us all soaking wet before we could stop him.

Yes, I said, I remembered that, as I scuffed my boots on the ground and then studied the marks I'd made in the dirt, and wasn't it a surprise when it started raining, and rained hard all that night and all the next day, and it had been such pretty weather and all.

Ten minutes later I had a stroke of inspiration. Our plan, after wading the McGee, was to head west for about a half mile, following the trace of an old logging road until, way up on the hillside, there was an old fenceline that led straight to the mouth of the Potapo about a mile away to the north. That fenceline crossed some little creeks that fed into the McGee to our right. It occurred to me that on that route we would come to another old fenceline that would connect with our fence at right angles, coming from the west. If I remembered right it would join our fence in a dense stand of pines, and it might be possible to get old Delbert off on that other fenceline, heading west instead of north, heading out of the watershed of the McGee Valley, heading toward the Muddy Boggy River, where the little creeks we would cross would be flowing to our left toward the Boggy, rather than to our right toward the McGee.

I wondered how long it might take old Delbert, who knew the way to the mouth of the Potapo about as well as I did, to figure out that something had gone wrong. It was not far to the Potapo, but it was several miles to the Muddy Boggy. If a fellow was concentrating hard on deer hunting he might not notice the change in direction. I wondered if I could get him all the way to the Boggy before he figured out where we were.

After wading the McGee we followed the trace of that old logging road up the hillside, came to that old fenceline, and started following it north. Pretty soon I saw that dense clump of pines up ahead where the other fence would be joining ours.

I said, "Hey, we ought to hunt that cover pretty close, don't you think? How about we get over on the other side of the fence and you slip out there a ways, and I'll ease along here by the fence, and maybe one of us will flush out a deer to where the other one can get a shot."

Sure enough, we climbed over the fence and Delbert eased off out into the woods about fifty yards. I got a little bit ahead of him and started angling toward the west. He used me as a bearing, thinking I was walking along the fenceline, and I gradually got him headed due west just about the time I came upon that other fence. Pretty soon we ran out of that clump of pines, and he came over to where I was, and we proceeded down that fenceline, hiking straight out of the valley of the McGee.

It was uncanny how that one old fenceline looked like the other one, and the terrain was all pretty much the same. I noticed this when we topped the little rise that separated the McGee watershed from the Muddy Boggy, but Delbert was intent on his deer hunting and was paying no attention at all to where we were going.

We slowed the pace considerably. We did some still hunting through the woods, sometimes on one side of the fence, sometimes on the other side. Time ticked away. It was getting on toward the middle of the day, and we had already gone far enough to have gotten to the mouth of the Potapo when we crossed the first little creek. It was flowing off to our left, off toward the Muddy Boggy as pretty as you please, but Delbert didn't give it any mind.

We'd gone about another half mile before Delbert said, "Shouldn't we already be at the mouth of the Potapo by now?"

"Well," I said, looking all around, "it does seem like we've been at it for a while, doesn't it? I've kind of lost track of time and distance the way we've been concentrating on deer hunting so much."

The sun was high overhead, standing in the noon post, so we decided to stop and heat up some soup. We'd hardly gotten started again when we came to a place where the fence went right through the middle of a bunch of tall boulders.

Delbert, standing in the middle of the boulders, looking up all around, said, "I don't remember any place like this."

On down the trail we came to another little creek. Delbert stopped and stared at it for a long time. He said, "Am I all turned around, or what? This thing's flowing off in the wrong direction."

By then the valley of the McGee was far behind us. We were up near the top of the watershed that separated the Muddy Boggy drainage, to the south and west, from the valley of the Potapo, which was just the other side of a little rise to the north. The water in that little creek was barely a trickle, but it was definitely flowing downhill, and that was definitely to our left, and Delbert definitely stared at it for a long time.

He said, "Something is not right."

I said, "You don't suppose somebody moved the mouth of the Potapo on us, do you?"

We finally decided we must have come upon one of those little creeks that went first one way and then another, and we just didn't remember it.

I said, "I'll bet the next time we cross it, it'll be flowing the other way."

But he knew those big boulders were not on the trail to the mouth of the Potapo. He said, "Man, this is spooky."

Another quarter of a mile brought us to another creek. It was a little bit bigger than the other one, and there was no doubt about which way it was flowing either.

"We're lost," he said. "I don't believe it. We should have come to the mouth of the Potapo a long time ago. I don't know where we are, but we're nowhere near the mouth of the Potapo."

It was a complete mystery, and we spent a considerable period of time discussing it. Finally, Delbert said, "I think we've been going toward the west."

The sun was beginning to dip toward the west, and it was becoming more and more obvious that we were hiking straight toward the sunset.

I said, "Do you suppose we might have been concentrating on deer hunting so hard that we got on the wrong fenceline somewhere?"

We decided to give it one more try down the fenceline. About another quarter of a mile brought us to another little creek, and it was flowing off in the wrong direction just like all the others.

"This is as far as I'm going," said Delbert. "If we camp here, at least maybe we'll be able to find our way back. Dad never will stop laughing if he finds out we got off up here and got lost."

The little creek had just enough water flowing in it to use it for camp water, so we followed it downstream until we found a good place to camp. We pitched camp and then went out deer hunting until it got nearly dark.

We hadn't seen a deer all day, and we weren't real sure where we were, but that didn't dampen our spirits. It was a beautiful evening, and a big supper cooked over a campfire tasted pretty good.

We sat around drinking coffee, just enjoying the evening and the campfire, until finally we spread out that old tarp, rolled out our sleeping bags on top of it, and bedded down.

We lay there awhile, just gazing up at the stars and talking. We'd almost dropped off to sleep when we heard geese honking.

"Do you hear that?" said Delbert.

"I sure do," I said.

Before long they came flying directly over us. They were flying so low we could almost reach up and touch them. They were straggled out in the most ragged-looking V shape you ever did see, a bunch of dead-tired geese barely able to flap their wings, hollering and complaining and protesting, making the most awful racket. It took a long time for all of them to finally pass over us.

Delbert snorted. "Ha," he said. "Uncle Bunnie said when you see a flock of tired geese flying low like that it's a sure sign there's a blue norther right behind them. But look at it. There's not a cloud in the sky."

The Uncle Bunnie that Delbert was referring to was our dad's youngest brother, who lived not far from Grandfather Crowder's old place. It was one absolutely beautiful, balmy night, and it was still warm well after dark. We had a good laugh about our Uncle Bunnie's cornpone Choctaw country wisdom and then dropped off to sleep.

We woke up an hour or two later with a cold, hard, driving rain hitting us in the face. The sky had turned pitch black, and the campfire was nothing but embers, so we had to turn on a flashlight to see how to get the tarp out from under our sleeping bags, throw it over them for a shelter, and crawl back into the sleeping bags beneath the tarp.

Delbert's cotton sleeping bag got wet before he could get it covered up, and we both got wet running around getting things situated. I was able to get snuggled up again nice and cozy in that heavy, waterproof, arctic sleeping bag, and would have been able to drop right back off to sleep if Delbert hadn't started complaining.

He complained about the holes in the tarp. It did have holes in it, about as big as your hand, every few feet all the way across it. He said about all the tarp was doing was collecting the water so it could run down the holes and get him soaking wet.

Then the rain turned to freezing rain, with a howling, shrieking wind, and he stopped complaining about being wet and started complaining about being cold.

The next thing I knew he'd gotten up and gotten dressed and was building a bonfire to end all bonfires. By then the freezing rain had turned to heavy snow.

The first bonfire he built didn't work very well. He built it over on the other side of the creek up against some big rocks where it was a little bit sheltered from the wind. It burned well enough all right, and the pitchy old pine limbs he piled up made a big, hot fire that threw a lot of heat. But he failed to notice that the flat slab of rock he'd built it on top of had fissures and fractures running all the way through it. When the fire got real hot, and when those fractured pieces of rock had expanded as far as they could expand, they exploded up out of those cracks all in one big boom.

I woke up to what sounded like a mortar attack, with fire raining down everywhere and Delbert running for his life, with the explosion scattering rocks and bonfire and blazing limbs from hell to breakfast.

I told him I would appreciate it if he could make a little less racket, that some people were trying to sleep.

I drifted in and out of sleep all night long, waking up now and then when he would come in from the woods dragging a bunch of firewood.

When I woke up at daylight it was still snowing hard. There was at least a foot of it on the ground, and it had drifted three or four feet deep in places. The wind was howling out of the north at least twenty or thirty miles an hour. Delbert was standing in front of his bonfire, stamping his feet, flapping his arms. He looked about as frazzled as a man can get.

I got up and got dressed quickly. I said, "This may be just the lucky break we've been needing. The one thing you can count on on a day like today is that the deer will be someplace where there's some shelter from this wind."

He just glared at me. He said, "If you think I'm going anywhere except straight to the car, you're crazy."

We had some coffee and cooked breakfast. After he'd finished eating he felt better. He said, "Where do you figure they'd be on a day like today?"

I said I wouldn't be surprised if we were a little bit south of the Potapo, about a mile, maybe, and if he would remember, along the south side of the Potapo were some steep hillsides, almost cliffs, with some deep cuts in them that ran way back up in the hills for about a half mile. Down in those cuts, out of the wind, was where I figured the deer would be.

I pointed upstream on the little creek we were camped on. I said I'd bet it wasn't more than a quarter of a mile upstream to the crest of the watershed, and just the other side of it was probably the top of one of those cuts. In this high wind the deer wouldn't hear us coming, and they'd be upwind of us. We might both get a nice buck.

He wanted to know how I expected us to carry out a deer through the snowdrifts. "It's been all I can do," he said, "to carry in firewood."

I said if we got a deer we could field-dress it, hang it up in a tree to freeze, and come back and get it when the weather cleared.

The more we talked about it the more we liked the plan, and Delbert was ready to do some deer hunting by the time we got all packed up and broke camp.

We hiked upstream to the fenceline and left our packs there. We stacked them almost on top of the top strand of the wire, as the snow had drifted almost all the way over the fence.

Not long after crossing the fence we crossed over the watershed and found a little depression that soon turned into a deeper and deeper gully, heading northeast.

We soon found ourselves descending into a deeper and deeper canyon. When we saw a thick stand of evergreens up ahead we eased up close to it. We settled in to wait and watch, figuring we had a pretty good deer stand.

We were out of the wind, but the cold was miserable, a damp, humid cold. The longer we sat there the colder we got. The temperature must have been at least down in the teens. Before long our teeth began to chatter.

"I think stopping was a mistake," I finally whispered.

"I think not going back to the car was a mistake," Delbert whispered back.

"I think you're right," I said.

We stood up.

Deer exploded all around us. There were so many white flags bobbing up and down in so many different directions that all we could do was stand there, dumbfounded, and stare.

"Well," said Delbert when the last one had disappeared, "we found the deer. I'm not sure where, exactly, we found them, somewhere in Oklahoma, maybe, but we did find them."

Hours later, after slogging our way through the snowdrifts, feeling the constant bite of that howling wind, we finally retraced our route all the way back to the McGee. It was still snowing hard.

As we stood there at the edge of the water, not wanting to wade out into it with our boots on, and not wanting to take our boots off either, Delbert was in a foul mood. On the way back he'd pretty much worked out the little bit of trickery about those two fencelines in that dense clump of pines and was beginning to have his suspicions about the weather.

Neither one of us could quite work up enough nerve to take off our boots before wading the river, so we had to climb that long, steep hillside to get on up toward Granddad's old place with wet, squishy, freezing feet.

It didn't help any that the lock on the car door was frozen full of ice and had to be thawed out with a cigarette lighter before we could get it open.

"Well," I said, "at least we can drive over to Uncle Bunnie's and get dried out and warmed up before heading back. I'll bet he's already got a deer."

Delbert wasn't much company on the way over to our uncle's house. He just slumped down in the car seat, shaking his head, saying, "Never again."

Duane Niatum has been in the forefront of Native American literature for years, and he has produced an impressive body of literature, including poetry, short fiction, essays, and reviews. He was born and raised in Seattle, and he is currently completing his doctorate at the University of Washington. His books include *Songs for the Harvester of Dreams, Digging Out the Roots, Ascending Red Cedar Moon,* and *Drawings for the Song Animals: New and Selected Poems.* He has edited *Harper's Anthology of Twentieth Century Native American Poetry* and *Carriers of the Dream Wheel.* His fiction has appeared in numerous magazines and literary journals. Niatum's work has also been published in scores of anthologies, including Anchor Books' *Earth Song, Sky Spirit; From the Belly of the Shark; The Remembered Earth: An Anthology of Contemporary Native American Literature; This Song Remembers: Self-Portraits of Native Americans in the Arts;* and *Recovering the Word.* Niatum is a member of the Klallum Tribe and one of the most prolific writers in the Greater Northwest.

Duane Niatum

# Talking Things Over with the Boiler Man

FOR MONTHS I HAVE RETURNED TO THE OLD MAN'S BASEment almost out of habit. It is loaded with hiding places, quiet and solitary, and he has never accused me of intruding upon his private world of supervising the heating in our apartment house. Of course there is more to it than the fact that it is in the basement where I live. I enjoy the old man's jokes. Ian is funny and wise in a way that speaks of the genuine. Also, my father would be about his age, if he were still alive, and he does have the same penchant for telling tales as my father did. And he is the only one who will listen. What friends I have turn a deaf ear whenever I try to talk it over with them. He listens; they think there is no battle of the sexes and don't want to hear otherwise. But more to the point, in my mind, he has secretly become an adopted father into my Coast Salish Clan. Grandfather, my other father, more a presence than my real father ever was, would welcome Ian into the tribal family without question. He once told us that the Irish are pretty tribal themselves, particularly in the drinking, partying, and storytelling area. And there he is, sitting before the dark like the Rock of Gibraltar.

I will be quite surprised if he does not try to play a few tricks on my jumping rope. My father certainly would have, and called it the funniest thing going on the block, if not in the city. He could not let a week pass without at least one practical joke on someone.

I say, "Hi!"

He says good-naturedly, "Hello, Young. You're still a little jumpy? That sweatband of yours is oozing worry beads and love notes."

"You guessed it, Ian. But I've decided your boiler room's the best place in the city for me to skip out on my anger and dread. Like jumping up those stairs backward for the hell of it. I hope you don't mind I ended up here after running around the block a few times." He smiles and waves his arm for me to jump right on. And says, "Lad, you're entirely welcome. Not enough people in this building appreciate healthy, oily dirt and dust; my round-the-clock boiler. Yes, I'm glad you came down for a visit. I'd thought of giving you the honor of being my number one guest. How are you and the feisty woman doing? It's hide-and-seek in the garbage room next door? No? Splendid! I prefer guests who bring the snappiness of willows and sea winds. My father told me many lives ago, 'Don't snub your nose at youth. They help you age with class.' Like bells, like storms, like pub jigs, Young. It's a fact; occasional visitors break up this sweat house routine."

He sounds more like a father every minute. I know for a fact that it is impossible for me to be related to this old man—a man who proudly claims he is the Blackest Irishman in the city—but life does reveal stranger truth serums. Then I say, "Do me a favor, Ian. Tell me it was not a mistake when I told Holly I'd sleep with a mummy before she'd hear me knock on her door again. I can take it. I skip five miles of rope between her apartment and my own."

He seems unwilling to answer, glances here and there. The corners of his mind seem preoccupied with more important issues. Finally, he says, "You're sure?"

"About every three minutes and then I'm on guess row."

"You appear fit; all that skipping and sweating has you lean as your rope."

"Yes, I give it a little effort. I swim a little too. Swim to the bed; swim to the toilet; swim to the wall; rush to the door, then to the bar."

"A rope and run and splash man. With muscles shaped in the arena of love. A man of grief and sweat asking for a little time to organize the next strategy."

This last remark of his proves why I began thinking the old man has a third eye. I say, "We try. Just you ask these feet. We trip only when it's fun."

"I can tell. The evidence is plain for all to see. Those sneakers look new but well stretched. Pinched and torn for the rough roads.

Anyone can see you're a man who dances best on the wire of the unexpected. A man who can weather the skids and the wraparound bruises."

"I will, I will! But, Ian, please answer me one haunted question?"

"At your service, lad. If I must and the weather's calm."

Then it hits me that the whole damn world must know that I am not doing well. I look down to see something crazy about my feet. I say, "Wait. Who untied my shoes? I'm all tripped up!"

"See. You're not that delighted with the idea of singing love songs beneath her window. Making that long run back."

"Ian, I would like very much to say yes, but a blue jay said that would be like wearing a hornets' nest for a hat."

"Young, pull yourself together. That's shatter talk. Stop right now and do twenty push-ups for the spirit. One can see you've lately watched the windows shut out the light like burnt offerings. Heard the women you lost riot in your sleep and on your runs. Those'll be the days and nights you'll need your rope. Maybe even a spare set. Ah, but the dear woman with the Aida voice said you hardly looked out anyway. Swore you were blind-mouthed."

"She did?"

"Only last week."

I pretend to act unalarmed. I ask, "Would it do to look out? It's slowly dawning on me that I've spent my whole life looking out the wrong window. Every new look out another window shows me a life beating by in the other direction, taking my little moon goddess with it."

"You could look for what's been canceled today purely for the shock. Even the latest generation courting self-destruction do that. Lad, would I tell you life's simply what it seems? That's the cellophane line of politician, undertaker, and doctor. As for this basement, you can feel powerfully at ease because this stack smokes!"

"Ian, you're just an old pro-stack peeling off the paint of the city of Bedlam."

"Am I that blatant? Coaching the game of your last resort?"

"Yes!"

"Let's hope you're wrong, son. It looks to me as if you're just a little tangled up in where she doesn't want to be. Stop dialing her number and wishing upon her star if she won't live with you in the give-and-take parlor of friendship and sex. Don't tell me you've forgotten our last talk? She's only one part of the trial."

"She is?"

"There's no denying it. So starting tomorrow, maybe you should ask yourself if you want those love boils to heal, part with the pain they just love to give to you. Today you're talking as if everyone on the street's gossiping about your canoe-in-a-tree romance, that they're all saying, 'Oh, Oh, Young's lost in the scabby patch. Been down in the boiler room so often the rats have chewed their way into his soul, poor Scabby.' "

"What am I doing? This basement's my last resort?!"

"You've known all along this is no game for wimps. I'm merely suggesting it's not easy to run out on your story. You must skip on and on with it or choke. We learn how to jump for the choices that may never be there. And more or less lose it like a puff of smoke up a chimney."

"What a plot! I think it's about time I climb up those stairs four or five steps at a time for the park, the lake, and a little fresh air!"

"Young, you know we Irish don't believe in plots unless you mean those with the stony markers. Have you forgotten already that you can't breathe what air's left without a trial? You help write the story even if you've nothing to do with where it goes or how it ends. And don't forget that life has its own way of adding pages and pages of little surprises. Wasn't it your choice to run through her maze reciting her name and how it had put a spell on you? Whether it's her maze's or the world's, there'll always be the faithful rat on the left. Rat on the right. Rat, rat, rat all the way home! So perhaps the time's come for you to welcome them as family."

"I can't right now but I'll skip miles and miles of rope."

"Is this why you tell me this has to be the day?"

Still holding to the rope, I say, "Would I be this far down if the boiler wasn't here and she wasn't jumping like a beanbag through my mind? She's going to do it, old man. I can hear her broom banging on the pipes, banging on the door, banging on my head, and down those stairs."

"Young, I've heard that broom in action a time or two myself and I'm not exactly your next-door neighbor. But didn't you hand her the broom the other night?"

"You would mention that."

"Sorry. Sometimes I can't help myself."

"Ian, I know she's going to do it."

"What, skip your rope?"

"Until we never skip again."

"You're learning little by little one of the trials."

"I hang by its knots."

"There's no doubt about it. She's got you worried all right."

"Old man, it's her silence one day, her absence another, and when she returns grinding her teeth and sneering, I feel winter coming on."

"A cold, cold block."

"Some days it's a rack."

We swap a few more episodes and then he asks if another failure would be worth adding to the diary? Can I accept the new gray hairs on my left temple that are waving frantically to their neighbors on the right? What about the storage locker of the heart? Is there any room left to mark on its fracture wall? He asks, how prepared am I for the really big show?

I say what I know I'll immediately regret: "You're one to talk of gray hairs and crumpled dreams. Two or three of your sea chanties I wouldn't wish on my worst enemy."

"Now don't throw mud, son. Who asked for this show anyway? And how about showing some respect for your elders? I told you I was sailing to China before your father was born. But back to your story. My point is, if she can't show you love's rainbow or garden, maybe another woman can. Find that fishing pole, Young. It's a wide, wide, wide sea out there. Or for the moment does she have you too thoroughly by the beast pouch?"

"Firm and determined."

"Well, where's she now? It's been awfully quiet on your floor. Such silence makes a boiler man very uncomfortable."

"Bird-watching by the ocean with a woman friend."

"What happened? Even my boiler thought you two sounded like the perfect family, a couple who had been married for years; every fight echoed through the walls and to the basement."

"She said she needed to practice living more in her own space. Get more into herself. Make herself a feeling fan for the hot nights and cold sweats. That she could relax and let me in if I kept my apartment and she kept hers. That way we'd be sure and have plenty of space in between. As a result, the closer we came, the louder she demanded extra distance. When I asked her if she thought we'd ever live together under the same roof for an entire week, the rest of the night tripped her total alarm system, all forty-eight buzzers and gongs!"

"Sounds like she's riding at a gallop that little fear that grows."

"Right on through her roof and mine. If it had been a plant, Ian, we'd have had to cut a hole in the ceiling for it to escape. Trying to break through her denials is like trying to make a concrete floor a peacock pillow. She has made it the law of the court that we continue to live on opposite ends of the city and visit one another two or three times a week. When I reminded her that that was not what she originally told me she wanted, she said, 'Can I help it if I'm so creative in my social arrangements?' "

"No wonder you're down here so frequently. Your problem's proving to be our age's tiny shard that's making everything impossible. The idea whistling like a wind across America's that we're about as intimate with one another as two gas pumps in an abandoned station. This reminds me of a story my grandpa from County Cork told me during the Depression: 'There never was a fear that lost a beat that I've wind of.' "

It is becoming quite clear that the old man wants me to let him return to his business. He is now seriously contemplating his boiler. I get the hint when he tells me the boiler looks as if it needs a new coat of paint and that he better start back to serious work. To make my exit easier, he says, "Want to rest? You're going to burn up that rope. How about a game of chess? A toss of the dice? Cards?"

"Too numb."

"Think positive, lad. You're this apartment house's break-in champion. But if that's not enough, you could try two slow but steady laps around the lake; take in the sun and rose-petaled air. Those laps should keep you in shape for another round with your sweetheart when she does show up. A few laps should do the trick."

He says he hates to mention that my face appears to be wrinkling in her memory. And after piecing together my story from what I've told him, he believes it would be best that I not wait for a choice. But the scene looks brighter than I realize. He can tell that I'm not going to fold up like a paper bag. Thus he thinks I am doing a fair job of keeping the lid on my boiler. I might still be caught—I think these are his exact words—but I am jumping for more than the splitting of nerves.

"It's the trial?"

"You can't skip it."

"Will I run again?"

"The question's to where."

"To her, to her."

"On recalling your last midnight drama, I distinctly remember her shouting from the far end of your hallway, 'Someday, I'm going to forget how to come back!' "

"So you think I'm learning to tumble and be a sport about it?"

"At the first step, at the second step, at the third step."

He then says I can visit anytime and I have his sympathy but he doesn't envy me my youth and hot pursuits. The more stories he hears from the younger generations, the happier he is being at an age when the daisies and cornflowers sing constantly to him of the last hurrah.

It is after this I tell him I am giving my rope a good rest and will he please, please deal us a game of cards. His face lights up with gambling spirits. He glows in aces because no jokers are playing tricks with his deck: "Now you're talking, Young. That's why I'm your buddy, the boiler man. Cut the deck and let your luck shuffle in!"

Richard G. Green was born at Lady Willingdon Hospital in Ohsweken, Grand River Territory, commonly known as the Six Nations Reserve. As a student of writing, in 1973 he began contributing short stories to *Indian Voice,* an urban Indian publication based in the San Jose Indian Center, San Jose, California. His stories have appeared exclusively in native publications and literature anthologies in the United States and Canada. In 1987 he became a regular contributor to the "Our Town" column in the *Brantford Expositor.* He is writer-in-residence at the New Credit of the Mississaugas First Nation Library, where he gives writing workshops to beginning and emerging talents. He lives on the Reserve, where he creates material for the North American Indian media.

Richard G. Green

# A Jingle for Silvy

MY BEST FRIEND, SILVY LONGFISH, SAYS I'M JUST A BACKward Indian. She says she wonders why I never call her a forward Indian. Whoever heard of a forward Indian? She got that way when she moved to the city. Silvy's the best friend I'll ever have. I just wish we were still dancing together in powwows.

I wonder what Silvy'd do if she were here right now watching me beading my new moccasins? She'd probably smell them; deerskin's always so fresh and clean. I remember last year, when we were in grade five. She said she'd make the prettiest ones she could. Silvy's got this *thing* about pretty. Probably because she's so pretty herself. To cover it over, she said she'd enter them in the fall fair. She said she'd probably win the red ribbon. Come to think about it, Silvy's got this thing about winning, too.

These moccasins are going to go real good with my new jingle dress. Like Silvy would say, I'm going to be color-coordinated. For the first time in my whole life everything's going to match. I'm trying hard not to go superfast. I don't want to lose my beading rhythm. After a whole morning's work, I've got only one moccasin done. Luckily, it's the last one. Good thing the Creator gave us only two feet.

Silvy gave me these tiny seed beads when she left. They're the old-fashioned kind with the weeny holes. I've already stuck my finger twice. Silvy probably knew that's what I'd do. She's smart like that, don't cha know.

Thinking about Silvy is making me impatient. I've used two beads that are the wrong shade of green. Now I've got to pull out the whole leaf. Silvy never used to be impatient until she moved to the city. Her mum got her a new dad. He's even got blond hair. Now they got lots of money and a new motor home.

The day she told me, *she* was impatient. She said, "Well, I'm going to the city now. I'm outa here. I'm going to be an *up*town Indian." Didn't matter a whole lot to me, though. It's not like I'd never see her again. I knew she'd be back. Even if it was only for the powwow. Maybe this time she'll stay. At least for the summer. Sooner or later everybody comes back to the res.

In runs Delbert, my twin brother. I don't know why people call us twins, on account of he's a boy. He's such a dweeb but he can make really good jingles. He gets Grandpa's snuff lids and shapes them into cones. Normally, this takes a lot of skill and patience. But Delbert's not normal. Tota says he's a natural. He makes money selling jingles to other dancers. He even charges me. But I don't pay him any money. I'll just do his homework for the month of September or something. Good thing we're in the same class. I mean school, not quality level.

"Here's your three new jingles," Delbert says. He's puffing like he just ran in the Tom Longboat marathon race or something. He drops them right in my bead bowl. "I couldn't fix the old ones. They were too flattened."

"Those old cones were real brass jingles. Gramma gave them to me. That's why I wanted them fixed, dweeb."

"These sound just as good . . ."

"That's not the point. They're a different color."

"So?"

"So you can't put silver jingles with brass ones."

"Why not?"

"They aren't color-coordinated."

"Well, leave them off, then. You all ready got 250 jingles anyways . . ."

"Two hundred and twenty-nine! I need 232 to make my outfit perfect."

"Tota says you're not s'posed to make things perfect. Only the Creator can make perfect things." He smirks. "That's why I leave a little space when I bend the tin."

"Grandpa doesn't dance in the powwow this afternoon. I do."

"You can just put them in the middle of the V. You know, where you got them ribbons coming into a V at the top. That way, everybody'll think you done it on purpose."

"Everybody but me."

I decide to make Delbert invisible. I didn't hear what he said on account of when you're invisible nobody can hear you. It worked, and by the time I put three more beads on my leaf, he was gone. I took his advice about putting the tin jingles on the top row in the center. On account of Delbert's got expertise. I made the moccasins perfect, though. I figure now that my jingle dress is screwed up I'm still on the Creator's good side.

On the drive to the powwow, Mum gives me some gum to chew. I didn't want to chew it on account of my loose tooth. But I didn't want to hurt her feelings, either. When somebody gives you something, you're not supposed to make them feel bad and not take it. Ever since Mum quit smoking she's always chewing something. Sure enough, out pops the tooth. I pick it out and put it in my jeans with my spending money. Then I put my tongue into the hole. Yecccch! It's all bleedy. I hate when this happens.

When we drive over the bridge next to the powwow grounds, I see the sun shimmering on the river. The water looks like a giant jingle dress. After we get to the parking lot, I figure it's one o'clock because the loudspeaker guy says, "Grand Entry in thirty minutes. No Indian time allowed." I don't know why we have to always start on time. You'd think this was TV or something.

Being skinny comes in handy at these kind of things. When you have to put fancy clothes on, it's lots easier to get dressed. I know one of Delbert's tubby friends who has to start getting ready a whole hour before Grand Entry. Trouble is, after all this work I never know what I finally look like.

Mum's talking to this white woman with a camera who's come over to admire me. I hate when this happens. I also hate being number

124. That extra digit makes my sign bigger, which means it'll cover up more jingles. Mum tugs at my number to straighten it. Like it's going to stay that way. She's always tugging at something. Sometimes she even makes my eyes water. Like when somebody distracts her while she's doing my braids. Like now.

"*A:ki,*" I say, fighting back the tears. "Ow! Ow! Owwww!"

What can I do? You can't run away when somebody's got your braids. All I can do is hope the woman isn't going to stay and take my picture. I'll bet I've been photographed a zillion times. Silvy gets her picture took lots. Even when she doesn't have her outfit on. Nobody ever takes a picture of me when I'm just normal.

Mum and that woman are talking about me like I'm invisible.

"She's really quite shy except in school and at powwows," Mum says. "Yes, she likes to play ball with the boys, but no, she doesn't have any boyfriends yet . . ."

I'm so embarrassed I hope I *am* invisible. I'm beginning to feel like an object when good ole Delbert runs up.

"See? I told you," he says. "Those silver jingles look great." He inspects one of his new jingles and then flicks my nose. "Gotcha. Ha, ha."

"Okay." Mum snaps her gum. "You're ready now."

"Could I have a pict—"

"Ha, ha. Better hurry up, dude." Delbert whisks me away with his hand. "They're already lining up."

Normally, I'd smack him but he just saved my life.

I shuffle off toward the assembly area. All my jingles are gleaming and swishing. I sound just like rustling leaves in the fall. Silvy always meets me over by the garbage can.

"Attention all dancers," the public address system cracks. "Would all dancers*queeee* . . . please go to the assembly area. All dancers please go to the assembly area for Grand Entry. If you haven't registered yet, they'll take you over there. Last call. All dancers to the assembly area."

I wriggle to settle everything. I hope none of Delbert's jingles fall off. I saw somebody's eagle feather fall off once. They had to stop the whole powwow and do this lost-feather dance thing. On account of he was a *rohskenhrakehte,* warrior, I asked Tota all about it. I'd hate to have the whole powwow stop on account of me.

He said you can't insult a spirit. When a feather falls, it's the spirit of a fallen warrior. So four veterans, representing the four directions, sing two verses to the Creator and the spirit of the fallen warrior.

Then they sing four verses and charge the feather on the downbeat of the drum. Those who have not taken coup will use an eagle fan because they are not strong enough to touch the spirit. After six verses, the honored veteran picks up the feather in his left hand. He lets out a whoop to signify that the spirit of the feather has been captured.

Lucky for me all anybody has to do is give back my jingle cone if it falls off.

"*Squeee* . . . Okay dancers. It's powwow time."

One of the Drums starts up and its shrieking singers begin their song. *Boom, boom, boom, boom-boom.* Six beaters mix their being in unison with the spirit in the hide. It creeps out to the dancers. I can *feel* it.

I'm really proud of these new moccasins. I can tell they're happy. They like to be at a place where they're more welcome than shoes. I'm happy they will keep me connected to Mother Earth. I pray they will keep me on the good path.

In comes the Eagle staff bearers. Then some old guys with dark blue uniforms and medals on their chests. They carry the U.S. and Canadian flags. They go clockwise to be in harmony with Mother Earth. Everybody is preparing to join the dance and enter the circle. There must be a zillion people here to watch. I adjust my number and look for Silvy.

I see her over with the men's fancy dancers. She looks like a boy in her short, streaky haircut. She's also got on leather hot pants with lace edging and Luscious Red lipstick. It clashes with her dark complexion. It *must* be Silvy. I run up to her jingling away.

"Silvy?" I hope she doesn't get all emotional. "Is that you?"

Silvy casts a cold stare, the kind you see on statues. It's like her eyes are dead or something. She looks at my jingles and her eyes begin to soften. Here comes the *real* Silvy. I back off in case she's going to hug me. No sense getting all your jingles crushed.

"So." She cracks her chewing gum. "How you been, 124?"

Silvy says she *loves* it in the city. Silvy says her mother's new boyfriend's got lots of money. Silvy says he takes her out to dinner in places with candles on the tables and stuff. Silvy says he's got yellow hair all over. Then she giggles. I wonder how she knows this.

I'm consumed by curiosity, just like a cat. So when Silvy squeezes through the crowd and goes over to the river, I follow her. The powwow can wait. I wonder if she wants to borrow my stirrups?

"You got any boyfriends, dude?" Silvy picks up a stone and throws it into the river. "I got about five."

I look for a log to sit on. "Do you really have five boyfriends?" I fluff my dress and sit down.

"Yeah." Silvy giggles. "They all like my brown skin."

"Wow." I think about having five Delberts running around. "How do you keep track of them all?"

"It's hard. Sometimes I get them mixed up. Sometimes I call them by the wrong name. But they don't seem to mind. Like the time when I was having sex with Johnny"—she covers her mouth and giggles—"I called him *Joey!*"

"*You* were having sex?"

"Well, of course, dude. Don't you? Or are all you Indians too backward around here?"

There she goes again talking like she wasn't from here. She was born here and went to school here and lived here all her life. She knows everything I know about our tradition because *onkwehonwetsher-aka:ion,* old-time Indians, taught us. She knows when you marry outside you're outside the sacred circle. She knows you shouldn't die outside the circle, either.

"I thought about it once," I say. "Me and Kevin Sky got into some really radical kissing. Then things turned icky. He wouldn't take the gum out of his mouth."

Silvy looks at me like she's disgusted. Her eyes go all cold again. Then she looks at her reflection in the river. I give her one of my rocks to throw. Instead of seeing how far she can throw it, she fires it right at herself. Rubs her whole reflection right out.

A boat full of people comes splashing down the river. Its motor sounds like a giant mosquito. When they see the tipis and all the people, their motor changes its pitch. Silvy comes out of her trance and looks at me. Heck, she's my best friend. I've got to know.

"Do you like it?" I don't know why, but I look down and giggle. "Doing it?"

Suddenly, I'm very uncomfortable. I'm not sure I really want to hear her answer. I wish I'd never asked. Silvy must be looking at me; I feel my face flush. She's close enough, maybe she'll smack me or something. I decide to change the subject but I can't figure out nothing to say. It's like when you're in a bad dream and you try to holler for help. Nothing comes out.

I sense something happening. I look up but Silvy isn't even looking at me. I must be invisible again. She's looking over my shoulder and I hear footsteps coming. I stand up.

"Oh shit," Silvy says. Suddenly, she reaches over and starts fondling my jingles. "These are really nice. How many of them do you have on your dress?"

"About 232," I say. I turn and here comes this dreamy blond guy. He looks like somebody from a men's clothing ad. He's walking right at us.

"Oh, here you are, Silvia," he says. "Who's your beautiful friend?"

I put my hand up to shade my eyes. I definitely want to see this guy better. "Marcie Henhawk."

"Well, Marcie. You'll have to come and visit us sometime. Isn't that right, Silvia?"

Silvy looks away like she's focusing on the boat. "Yes, yes, of course."

All of a sudden Silvy sounds like some kind of maid or something. She's definitely talking in this English accent. I figure he's got her going to debutante school or something.

"Do you think your little friend would like to come with us to the motor home? Maybe she would like to have a few drinks." He turns and looks at me. "Have you ever had a mai tai before?"

"Oh, of course," I say. This just blurted out.

"No," Silvy says. "She can't. She's got to dance in the powwow. Don't you, Marcie?"

"Well . . ."

"*Don't* you, Marcie?"

"Yeah," I say. "Maybe we can have some My-Lai's later. After I finish dancing."

They're behind me when we walk back toward the arbor. The crowd noise and my jingles drown out some of the things they say. I hear Silvy utter two or three "don't"s but when we separate she goes with him. I watch them walking up a steep hill in the woods. Silvy must need some help because the guy's pushing her up the hill with his hands on her bottom.

*Boom, boom, boom, boom, boom, boom-boom.*

I stand in the crowd and watch a blur of fluorescent red, blue, pink and chartreuse feathers. It's the men's fancy dancers. They step high, twirl and fall into leg splits to the beat of the drum.

"How about those fancy dancers," the announcer says. "Let's put our hands together and let them know we appreciate them. All Nations

Intertribal next! The Creator likes it when we're dancing, so let's keep Him happy. Everybody dance."

I pick up on the singing. I wait until I feel the spirit of the drum. I ease out into the circle. No sense attracting all kinds of attention. I'm supposed to lose points for not being in the Grand Entry. Maybe I'll get lucky and they didn't notice. There's zillions of dancers here. I'll bet I wasn't even missed.

I've got my jingles swaying in a nice rhythm when Darrin Beans comes up. This is the first time I've seen him since school let out. But I know he's had his eye on me. I've had my eye on him, too. I pretend not to notice him. No sense appearing anxious. Especially with all these relatives and people around.

"*Sek:on,* Marcie."

I'm trying to move like a cloud. "*Sek:on,* Darrin." I keep my step clean and sure.

"*Kia'tara:se.*"

Suddenly, I'm glad I know the language. He says I have a nice appearance. "*Katoria:nerons,*" I say. I am moved.

"*Kattats,*" he says. I present myself.

He increases his step and draws away from me. He looks so handsome in his traditional outfit. He's got eagle feathers bursting from the top of his head like a bonnet. A full-circle eagle bustle sways in unison with his manly stride. Traditional dancers tell a story when they dance. I wonder what kind of story he's telling me. He turns and sways toward me, then swooshes away like an eagle in flight. He pretends not to notice me but I know he did this to get my attention. Maybe he's telling me a bedtime story. I giggle to myself.

Suddenly, Delbert runs up. "I got some real bad news for you," he says, standing directly in front of me.

"Get out of my face," I say, craning to look at Darrin.

"Silvy got drowned."

*Boom, boom, boom, boom, boom, boom-boom.*

I just stand there, unable to move. I feel Delbert's arms around my shoulders. Good thing he does that, because my legs are all rubbery. "Don't crush my jingles" is all that comes out. Everybody must know about Silvy, because they stop the dancing.

Delbert takes me over to Mum. She's really puffing away on her cigarette. She lets me sit in the folding chair and hugs me. I smell stale tobacco. I feel water from her tears on my neck. I try to talk to her but my throat's got this big lump in it.

"We thought you drowned, too," she whispers. "Somebody said they saw you with Silvy and her stepfather-dad at the very spot where she drowned."

"I was with them," I croak. "They wanted me to come to their motor home and have some My-Lai's with them. I went to dance instead."

"Silvy's stepfather-dad was really upset. They found him asleep. They said that when they brought her body to him, he threw up and almost fainted."

Powwow committee members took a long time to decide about the powwow. They even left their trailer office and went into the woods for spiritual guidance. Their leader finally came out and told the loudspeaker guy what was going to happen. They decided to honor Silvy by dedicating the whole powwow to her. They said she came from far away and wouldn't want this festive occasion to stop.

"Ladies and gentlemen," the loudspeakers crack. "The powwow will commence after an honoring dance for Silvia Longfish."

Silvy got honored by almost everybody. Before her dance ended, there were even white people going around the circle. I guess when you drown it's a big thing. Even when you know how to swim.

I go over to the river. I stand where Silvy stood. A tear falls off my cheek. I pray to the water spirit not to be too harsh with her. She was my best friend. I pull off my center jingle. I drop it into the water. I hear the drum start up.

Barney Bush is Shawnee, and he has been an active writer for years. He is a poet, short story writer, storyteller, and teacher. His books include *My Horse and a Jukebox, Petroglyphs,* and *Inherit the Blood.* In 1978 he earned a master's degree in English and fine arts from the University of Idaho, and he has been a visiting writer for the state of North Carolina. Since 1989 Bush has been performing and recording his music throughout Europe. His CDs *Remake of the American Dream,* Volumes I and II, have received high critical acclaim both in Europe and Japan. His most recent work, *Left for Dead,* is a double CD released in July 1994 by NATO Records of Paris, France. Currently, Bush teaches creative writing at the Institute of American Indian and Alaska Native Arts in Santa Fe, New Mexico.

Barney Bush

# Roma and Julie: Indians in Duality

"MUST YOU BE REAL ALL THE TIME?" SHE ASKS, SOAKING, alternately chewing on the marijuana stem, the last vestige of relaxation in her house. She is worn out and uncomfortable listening to the bums of reality all the time. "We don't have a world here!" she screams at him.

He is unmoved by her frustration. The spirit in him has suffered uncommon deaths, and keeps coming back like the dream of the panther that walks up the creek near his house. He tells her this dream, the words to her heart, her womanhood, her silence that is more than the body, from where she responds, "Do you run from the panther, or with the panther?"

"I was a child, forty years ago, when the dream first came looking for me. I was in the dirt road, front of the school, waiting after dark, the small dark before the full moon. His sleek body was tiny mirrors of yellow light, and blue. He was elegant beauty guarding, prowling for the first signs of fear or panic that come to some children in the night."

She is trying hard to listen now. There are sounds of unborn children moving around inside her. She doesn't want to hear them or the cracking in her skull when the confusion comes galloping in. What can she say to him, either politely or rudely, to shut him up?

The wind makes a sound like water running out of the deepest soul, the kind that whispers to its own offspring, the kind that makes oppressors tremble and rush to move the old timbers from the forest . . . before it cleanses the hearts of their own children and evicts the greed, traditional gods brought here from their own ancient homelands to suck the beauty from native souls and the veins of Turtle Island.

Julie knows that she has been affected, even though her face and blood say she is a native spirit throughout the circle. Her turmoil is a compromise to survive with less agonizing, a powerlessness to halt a rape that seems to be without restraint, inevitable. "What good is it if the oppressor will not change? How do you get his oppression to lighten up?" she asks from her first mind, the one to which conception was given some thirty years ago.

These questions, she realizes too late, should not be asked. Why in the hell can't she shut her own mouth and let him believe what he wants? She knows he is too fucking serious—that old dream blood is eating him up. He will die never tasting the bittersweet compromises—the thrills of Vegas, the cut of barbed-wire nights in Vancouver, the full moon dark on the Champs-Élysées or the Eiffel Tower, whose fairground glow—whose petroglyph was never in the movies like this. And, damn, he's watching me, she thinks, from that silent world that doesn't have a place in this America. People laugh at him and call him a witch, but never to his face. Why are people afraid of him? What is there in his old harmless world that makes people nervous? "Shit," she says aloud.

Of course, he's watching her. And he's heard it from the outside world, "Accept me as i am." He's choosing his words, to tell her about the two sides—who she is and who she is not; that she is not the affectation that comes only from the darkest side of white people . . . that oppressive side that wants to colonize, reshape our own clarity of what is right and what is wrong behavior—that when you go among the whites, you must pray first and ask your invisible guide to accompany you so that world cannot beat your manhood or womanhood out of you, and make you an addict to their darkest sides, where right and wrong are taught in reverse.

Roma (the nickname from the chronic's wine, Roma Tokay, which will stay in the back of the throat for days) is recovering from addictions, impatience, and self-destruction. He has sweated, steamed himself in cedar smoke, sweet grass, tobacco, and sage. He has been prayed over, washed in the creeks and oiled by the hands of the faithful, what white folks say they get from baptism. He has returned to the sun and moon of his homeland, where the white people dig his relatives from their graves, strip-mine the earth for eternity, steal respect from his living relatives. And the local whites talk their old games, gossip first among themselves, take advantage of his relatives who need their jobs, those already hooked to the dark economics. Whites whisper that somebody ought to shoot him, and they search for the "right" person to do it.

He knows all this and more. Even their dictionaries of English cannot come close enough to the truth. You have to watch what they do. He whisks back his mane of midnight hair and speaks to her in the first voice.

"The oppressor lightens up when he has made you a defeated victim competing for his attention, a mirror for his vanity. And for this he will rub your belly, and you will call him whatever he desires, whatever he impresses upon you, male and female. His hands will fondle the genitals of your wildest dreams, and make your passions invisibly sweat for the darkest alibis."

"So what happens if I come to live with you?" Julie feels this whirlwind inside, from her stomach up into her brain. It's almost too much. She wants a toke badly. She wants to get out of here, but cannot bring herself to cut the cord that is attached to his heart. "Well, what the hell happens? Do I wind up pickin' fuckin' blackberries, stretchin' greasy deerhides to the smokehouse, beadin' belt buckles and bolo ties, sweatin' my fat ass off out hoein' corn, and sittin' on my fat ass at Greencorn and powwows? Is that what I do? Tell me, Roma! Is this what you expect?"

"You forgot to mention the children. You forgot to mention the faces of our children. How handsome they look in our dress and how proud they will feel when the old point them out, and nod to them, and to us. We will do the things that men and women do." Roma doesn't speak of the voice between a man and a woman that is never anyone else's business, needs no words but "that language" that belongs only to the bond.

"The keeping of the word"—where it comes from. Now she recalls the dimness in her own family. Now she's listening to reality shit again. Every time she's fallen for this and tied her hair back for one of these bastards, she hears about his sleeping around . . . and he'll act as if nothing were going on.

"What am I doin'?" she screams. "Why can't I just get out of this bullshit now? You guys never stay serious . . . you always act like you have nothin' to lose. This is too fuckin' complicated!"

Through the window, she sees the bare light of dawn—a smoked light darkened by the wet cover of swollen clouds. Corn, left to the stalk for seed, is hardened and ready to be brought in before the squirrels know it. They both know it's time to cut wood, even though it's only late summer. The blackberries are gone. Spiders have webbed every open space. It's the dusty chill before autumn, even with the light rain falling.

She has left him sitting inside, with his panther dream and the pungent odors of braided tobacco leaves and the breath of cedar smoke. This night has made her flesh feel heavy, her head stuporous at the edge of exhaustion. She's out of pot. Her teeth clench these episodes of survival, old records, like fingernails up a blackboard scratching through the grooves.

With folded arms, she walks the garden like a tourist. She sits wearily on the largest stone in the sculpture of rocks. Her eyes scan the forest that shimmers mirage-like behind the rain. She rests her head onto her knees. Her body convulses, not because of the rain, not even because of the emerald-eyed sentry that rests in the black veil of the moon, matted with damp leaves. But because she has a gun.

Gloria Bird was born in Washington State in 1951, and she is a Spokane Indian. She received her bachelor's degree in English from Lewis and Clark College in Portland, Oregon, and her master's degree in literature from the University of Arizona. She is one of the founding members of the Northwest Native American Writers Association, which has contributed significantly to furthering native writers from the region. Her award-winning work is always thoughtful and well crafted. She has had a short story appear in *Talking Leaves,* and her first collection of poetry is entitled *Full Moon on the Reservation.* Greenfield Review Press published the volume, which won the Diane Decorah Memorial Award for Poetry. Bird teaches literature and creative writing at the Institute of American Indian and Alaska Native Arts in Santa Fe, New Mexico.

Gloria Bird

# Rocking in the Pink Light

SOMEONE IN SQUEAKY SHOES BRINGS HIM IN, ROLLS HIM into my arms. The smell of Safeguard lingers pungent in the wafted air. All I can see initially is a ball of thick white flannel dabbled with blue elephants and pastel baby rattles, and where his head should be only the tip of the loose sock that covers his head, the first thing I remove. There, like a spindle, his hair turns in whorls back on itself, a single black swatch points upward, while the rest of his head is covered over in long, unruly fur that surrounds a squished-in red face that I am already in love with. There, on his nose, white dots—evidence of the diet that fed him—which have not yet worked their way out of his skin. I unwrap him. Arms as long as the legs, both curled up tightly close to his body, his arms are red as sunsets, as wrinkled as the skin of Grandma's armpits, but soft as buckskin, and the peeling transparent covering that smells of woodchips in rain, the earthy smell I will forever associate with childbirth.

Because I came in during the late stage of my labor, I was given no dulling medication for pain—I had barely taken my place on the coldest of tables when the waters broke—so that my son, newborn, opened his eyes blinking up at the nurses, at the light from the window, alert. His eyes are fiery black balls in which stars live and make him appear as holy as an ancient man; he moves, then puckers his lips, which are minute hearts of deep, deep red. I open my shirt, position his head to rest on the crook of my arm, the slight weight of his body supported by the remaining bulge of stomach, which, I am told, will go down in a few days' time. My little suckling machine with his perfect heart-shaped mouth shakes his head instinctively back and forth, back and forth. Between two fingers I position a nipple too big, it seems, for his mouth, but he finally grasps it firmly in his open mouth. We stay like that, bundled together. I lean against the pillows and backrest of the bed for what seems like hours. Even after he is asleep, I do not move him.

I want to embrace his magic, let it spin me motherly toward his small frame and perfect face, his nose pressed to my left breast, which I must hold so as not to smother him, but the ache spreads outward from my tender belly, the mother blood escaping from between my legs. I can feel the layer of dried sweat on my forehead and clinging to loose strands of hair. I ease the backrest of the bed nearly flat, scoot down to sleep with my son, who breathes in and out irregularly next to me and whose tiny heart I feel through cloth and layered swaddling fluttering like the hooves of ponies over dry grass calling me home.

My son's shape is a diamond; the skin flap covering his cranium rises and falls with his breath, his beating heart. The tip of the diamond reaches nearly to his forehead of thin fuzz and backward to the spiral of long straight black hair in which the unruly strand perches like a knowing flag, marks some line of demarcation that predicts the sleeping infant's temperament and predilection; at its greatest width, it is about an inch and a half. When later, at two months, the old lady we call Auntie Etty sees him for the first time, she acknowledges our kinship by offering to hold him. She begins to unwrap the yellow blanket, removes his socks, his nightgown. We are sitting in the P.H.S. Clinic waiting room. I dare not protest, however weakly, how the baby could catch a chill but watch her deft wrinkled hands silently as they move over his body: two long perfect feet (she appears to count his toes); two hands as delicate as marble, the chiseled details of which outline the miniature moons of his nails (counts fingers); the sleek roundness of his head. There. She stops at the soft spot while he wiggles in her lap, attempting to pull his limbs back in. She rings the ridge of skin flap with her fingertip. *Diamond,* she says. *What does it mean? I used to know, but I have forgotten. Let me see.* I can see in her eyes in their overt goodness that she knows but is weighing the consequences of her action, decides against putting words where no words need be. I already know. She caresses the smooth of his stomach, pulls his gown down, hands him back in pieces: body, booties, blankets. He knows things already, which I don't say, but instead, *He makes no fuss, is a good baby,* to which she smiles and nods and pats my hand.

I am dreaming my son, resting in the warm spot away from the metal bars the nurse pulled up *so the baby will not roll off,* though my arm is draped over him while he sleeps, my body already keyed in to imperceptible movements emanating from the sleeping baby. We are caught together in the most basic of needs—his, simplified and crystalline; and mine, operating as refracted and reflected rays of light from moisture to create a rainbow opposite the sun. I sense that my will is no longer my own, the way it has been for eons for women who have birthed nations. I release my youth, my wandering eye, my solitude, the very corpuscles that rattled through my veins for this infant who is dependent on me, my body continuing to provide his nourishment the way it did while he still rocked inside me, his added weight swelling my ankles, and as he grew seven, eight, then nine pounds and two ounces by the time he emerged. While still inside of me, stretching, he pounded against rib bone, the weight of his head pressed against my pelvis until I ached. My feet grew one size larger, and a filling from a calcium-depleted tooth fell out.

We dream together: my lips moving, my fingers curling around the curious sway of his backside. *I am rocking in the pink light, swaying with sensations that tickle under my foot; through the membrane I see my mother's face, her eyes large and round, a halo of light emanating from behind. She coos and ahs, removes the dampness from my bottom, and I am dry, my belly full.* Someone is in the room.

I open my eyes and see the baby's father, the one from whom I am estranged. He stands in the entrance of the room, hat in hand, *Hi,* he says, *are you awake?* I tell him to come in, pulling the front of my robe to cover my exposed breast, the soft nipple slipping from the baby's mouth, the awkwardness acute in the cool air of the room in which we negotiate our new relationship to each other, sterile and unfamiliar. His face is as round as his son's, his eyes wide, too pretty for a man's, I think, as brown as tree bark and well lit with intelligence. I can still feel his love for me, aching and hesitant. He smiles. I respond by motioning him to a chair next to the bed. *Want to hold him?* I ask, placing our son between us on the hospital bed, where he can lift the baby without the intimacy of touching my body, of which I am aware he is aware, the air of our proximity thin as cotton this dance of separation remembers.

*I can't believe you slept with him,* my best friend had said that next morning over coffee. Neither could I. We were too old for reckless pawing, the slobbering tongues, the ridge of his teeth as sharp as the razor edge of his need. Sometimes on the street he pulled me in, possessive in front of other men; he came to my work to talk domestics that built a wall around me so thick that "they" could see I was a monitored possession. Against my will, he would peck my cheek, ask, *What time will you be home?*, stressing the last word in such a way that there could be no mistaking our living arrangements; then, when I did return, I returned furious over his transparent behavior, his draping insecurities, his puppy dog looks of repentance.

He sits here, between my newborn son and me, beaming his fatherhood as if he were the one whose guts were split open, whose body had betrayed him in spasms of pain and humiliation in front of strangers who prodded at the tenderest of skin in private places, and whose center of being imploded in a single struggle to release the plug from which life was held precariously at both ends: the cord around his neck, the placenta refusing to dislodge. The baby's nose and throat were suctioned; I was scraped clean. His grin is the final rope with which he draws me in, and he knows I hold no malice toward him. That though it is not love but care, duty-bound, I will never keep him from our son. And though I have put him out, I cannot shut him out completely. He will take the scraps; he would savor the remembered juices of my bones; and he will pretend that there is something *more* between us.

I watch as he strokes the shock of thick black hair on the baby's head, and as the tiny fingers curl around his. He is pleased by the clarity of our son's distinctive coloring, the obvious similarity of the baby's features to his own, and in particular, as he removes the diaper to assure himself of our son's gender, a reality pinch that puffs up his manhood. When he says, *My son,* I see my future wavering like wet, heavy laundry hung in the wind, as flimsy as a door on rickety hinges. The inarguable terms of parenthood lie stark black-on-white, as simple as the papers imprinted by our child's footprint above a golden seal, and in the too eager movements of his thick hands as he signs on the line marked FATHER with his full given name, claims responsibility for the hospital bill and, later, signs the forms for my release.

*We are a family now,* he says. Though my eyes say no, my mouth remains closed, my head is nodding yes. An awkward finality pulls us together, at the center of which is our son, who at this moment lies sleeping the sleep of infants who wake at three or four o'clock in the morning, whose cries wake the neighbors, and who suckle in those early hours desperately as if starving for touch, for comfort . . . who begin to put the pieces together at five years of age, suddenly cognizant of changes around them, who are jolted by the suspicion that something is missing, something amiss, whose eyes remain dry yet distant and full of questioning that incomprehensible death touched down . . . and in the swirling black hole is contained a creeping harboring of cancers, dark and mean . . . that one day will suck his father through to the other side . . . a child wanting to remember . . . but, who?

*Was I released then? And am I released now?*

But in the room, the quietness evaporates as his scratching boots on slick linoleum suggest hesitation. I look up. I cup my baby's head in the palm of my hand, the palm of my heart. I am still reveling at the body's fertility, the division of cells, and the truest mystery of procreation. I am kept awake by the sheer force of adrenaline, though I am fatigued, my face puffy with water weight and aged by incredible pain.

He wants to come back. I watch him, handsome, clumsy, child-like in his inability to articulate what he wants. Remembering how to read him, how he changes with the slightest scrap of hope, I tell him, *We'll see.* He takes my hand, placing in it a stone *for love:* an electrifying crystal of the deepest amethyst, its sharp edges as jagged as the way my intuition has formed its defenses. He leaves before I am able to protest, before I am able to register what he has in fact resorted to in a last desperate attempt to change what is not within his power to change.

Once the father of my baby leaves, we return to our sleep. *I enter the pink light floating in liquid, call through the membrane that is as tight as a drum around me, "Is this how you come, Love, transfixed from an outside source, a white witch's doing?" The question fills me with anxiety; I struggle to change the direction of the dream. I am following a purple string of light; one end I notice is attached to my son's navel, another to mine, and a third, trailing off to the horizon, where the baby's father is sitting too close to a plum-colored bonfire. I can hear a soft chanting, move in closer to discern the words, only to discover too late that as he makes a circling motion with his hands, he is reeling us in, the baby and me.*

The room is dark when I awaken. A telephone down the corridor rings. A cart rattles its metal clutter against the walls of braced nerve endings, stops at the door. A nurse enters, flipping on the light switch. I close my eyes against the brightness. She checks the baby's bottom, disturbing him. She turns back my blankets and begins massaging the sore muscles of my midsection, pressing down hard, rubbing. She moves my hand up, makes me continue rubbing, rubbing in circular motion *so the uterus will contract.* I feel cramping. She hands me a green-and-white pill, *a stool softener,* then a large white *pain killer* that sticks in my esophagus. She exits in a clatter of rattling metal. I am to be released in the morning.

I move the baby to the other side to feed him. He is sleepy and I have to push on his cheek to remind him to suckle, and the sensation of emptying relieves the pressure that has gathered there. As he becomes sated, the movement of his mouth slows to an on-and-off feeding. A clear liquid puddle forms at the edge of his mouth. I try to pull away; he won't let me, sucking faster in his sleep, already possessive, the bond of splitting cells that binds us all.

On the edge of sleep, I move my arm out to stretch, touching the cold metal of the sidebar, when the thud of the stone hitting the floor jars me awake. On the windowsill, wrapped in a shiny ribbon, is a potted plant of fat mauve-colored blossoms that stink like weeds. I slide from the bed to retrieve the crystal to plant it deep in the soil of the plant that will not come with us when we leave. It glitters like diamonds in the moonlight but is as cold as city streets. I mean no harm, know I am not cruel enough to bait frail superstition like a fishhook. I make my way back to the bed, feeling in the blankets for my son before climbing back to the still-warm spot next to him. My last thoughts before I fall asleep jumble together: that our relationship is like a parabola, a conic section taken parallel to an element of the intersected cone; that humans' feeble abilities *would* conceptualize a mathematical formula to express only a portion of the whole; yet, recognizing my basic mathematical illiteracy, that the formula has more to do with the theory of projectiles than imaging; that still, all of history, both sides of our lineage, could make up the shape of the parabola that contains us in its cone like a cradle in which we are rocking toward that pink light, toward morning, when I will name the baby Xavier.

Guadalupe J. Solis, Jr., is a native of Wisconsin, born of mestizo parents in the town of Neenah. He is completing a master's degree in creative writing at the University of Wisconsin–Milwaukee. Solis is a young native writer whose short fiction has appeared in *The Cream City Review*, *Hayden's Ferry Review*, and *The Mixed Bag*. Solis is bilingual and has used his language skills to write bilingual stories for children, including works for Book Production Systems of San Diego, California. Solis lives in Milwaukee, where he creates his literature and plans his future as a professional writer.

Guadalupe J. Solis, Jr.

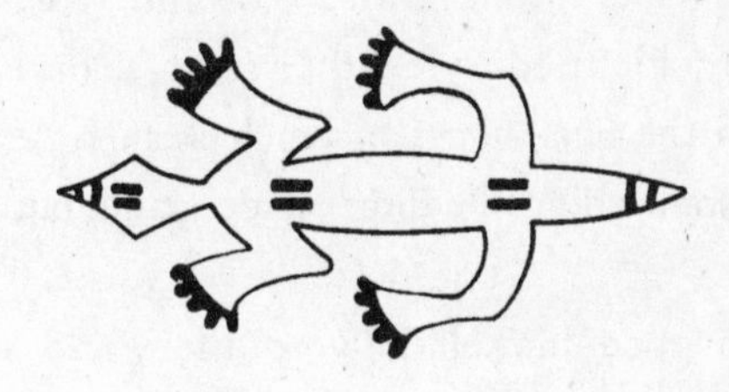

# El Sol

LYING NEXT TO THE TREE WITH HIS EYES CLOSED, HE imagined himself blind. The warm fingers of the sun danced across his hairless legs and chest, touching his face in tentative caresses. He listened to the rustle of tall grass and the rhythms of his heartbeat. His hands squeezed the moist earth, trying to see the greenness with his skin. The leaves above him chattered in the stronger gusts of wind. In the distance he heard the rumble of a train, probably dropping boxcars off at the paper mill.

The late August rays felt good on his almost naked body; in his well-worn sneakers and cutoffs, with his T-shirt lying next to him, he felt like a castaway. He tried to feel the world, as his *tía* had asked him to do. She was in the final stages of her leukemia. At twelve he knew some things and some things he didn't understand, but he was sure that his *tía* was dying.

He tried to open himself fully to the world around him, the whoosh of cars from the distant street, the smell of the grass, the audible thump of birds beating their wings against the wind.

His body was starting to itch, defeating his senses. Sighing, he sat up and brushed the grass from his arms and back, feeling the indents left on his skin—a reminder that he was only a visitor here and not a resident. He stood, threading his T-shirt into a belt loop. It struck him again as he looked at the distant street how two different worlds could exist so close together. He lived a block away in a place of people, houses and cars. Here, he felt small. Once he crossed the railroad tracks, he was alone with the fields and the sky.

He turned his back on the houses and ran into the wild. His legs never tired; he ran and ran and ran. In some places the grass was taller than he was. The trail he followed had been worn down by others seeking escape, too. At times he dashed into the towering grass, leaping higher and higher as his strides grew stronger. The clouds above paced him, racing him to the lake.

. . .

He let himself quietly into the room he shared with his *tía,* careful not to disturb her in case she was sleeping. She was awake most nights now, in pain, and any kind of rest was welcomed and respected by the family. He looked at the bunk beds he shared with her; the bottom bed was empty except for a rosary hanging above her pillow. His *tía* was sitting in a rocking chair by the open window.

"*Tía,*" he whispered to the back of the rocker.

"Daemy," her voice rasped, "come here, I'm not sleeping."

He went to her, grass-stained and dusty.

"You have a good run, Daemy?"

"Yes."

"Rolling in the grass, too?" She inhaled with a wispy smile.

"Yes."

"How is the sky . . . when you ran? Did it follow you?" Her hand waved the air in front of her, a summoning of him and his day.

"Yes," he said again.

He knelt by her feet, resting his head on her knee—completing their morning ritual.

"The ducklings at the marsh are getting big," he said into her skirt.

"Of course. Soon autumn will be, then they will fly." Her hand lightly touched the back of his head; he could feel the heat of her fervor. "I smell the grass . . . and the marsh, of course, but something else, too . . ." she whispered, then coughed. Gaining control of her voice, she sighed, "Tell me, Daemy."

He told her all about his morning: how his legs seemed to stretch forever when he ran, the marsh grass bending before him, the birds fighting the wind, and how the train's engine growled in his chest. Staring sightlessly out the window, she asked him to repeat parts in more detail—drawing from him pictures of his day.

Every morning he was her eyes, ears, fingers, nose; every morning he pulled out a piece of himself to share with his *tía*. She had been with his family for two months. His *tío*, her husband, had run out on her and she had nowhere else to go. His dad had brought her home to live with his family in their small house. "Dameon," his dad had said, "your *tía* is *enferma—muy, muy*. She must stay in your room . . . with you."

At first he was upset at the thought of someone sharing his room, but once she was there, he began to understand. Then, a month ago, she went blind because of her sickness. She didn't complain. Even at night she tried to muffle her pain so as not to disturb his sleep. Before bed, she would pray to God, thanking Him for another day.

Once, he had asked her why she prayed. He wondered why the more she prayed, the sicker she became. Didn't God hear her? And if He did, why was she so sick? She told him that God was helping her with her faith. "What is faith?" he asked her. She didn't answer, but asked him, "When you play tomorrow, will you do something for me?"

"Yes."

"Will you remember everything you see and tell me about it?"

"Okay . . . I'll try," he answered her, confused.

"Good, Daemy, that's all we can do."

Since then, every morning, he had a mission to *try*. He neglected his friends and began to discover the world beyond the tracks. Every day he changed for her.

The second week in September, he was up late one night listening to her labored breathing, her quiet pain. He shut his eyes tight and prayed to God to help her. Feeling nothing, he rolled to his side using his awakened senses to share in her suffering. When he finally fell asleep, he was drained of all his energy. He slept later than usual and was awakened by his *tía*'s soft crying. His mother was by her side.

"Mama . . . ?" he started.

"Shh . . ." his mother whispered, as if she needed to. "Your *tía* has lost her hearing."

From then on she sat in her rocker by the window, humming to herself, smiling. He wondered if he should keep up his morning runs for her. Out of habit, he left that morning and ran down the street and over the tracks.

He lost himself.

He came back later and knelt by her chair as before, resting his head on her knee.

"Daemy," she whispered, "how was your run? I can smell the grass and your sweat; you ran hard." Her hand touched his face, his lips. "Speak, Daemy. I can't hear you, but I can feel."

So he spoke as before. He told her about his hard run. Her hand moved gently back and forth across his face and lips. She rocked slowly, smiling as if she saw and heard. Her nostrils expanded, inhaling his day. He didn't know if she understood him, but she was happy. He continued his morning runs.

One morning before he left, his father stopped him. "Dameon, it won't be long now." Dameon sprinted out the front door and headed for the tracks. He stretched his legs out and reveled in the wind and smells of life. He wondered, as he ran, if in some way God was telling his *tía* things. The look on her face was at times happy, yet sad. His legs pounded the ground harder.

Now as he came to her, he brought her things. Once, a pussy willow. She ran her hands up and down the stalk, touching the soft, downy top. After a while she smiled: "Pussy willow." He nodded his head against her knee. Sometimes he brought rocks—the kind you skip across the water. Other times he offered flowers, a milk pod and, once, even a grasshopper. Each day he found something different to offer. She would sit for hours, smelling and feeling every gift he presented to her.

When he was out in his new world, he'd sit and pretend he was blind and deaf. Closing his eyes tight, he would force air into his eardrums, shutting out every sound except his breathing and heartbeat. In front of him, laid out on the ground, he would have the things he was bringing to his *tía*. He'd grasp an object and try to see with his fingers what he was holding. Or, hold it to his nose to identify it with smell.

He came home one afternoon to find a note saying his mother and father had taken his *tía* to the hospital. And, for him to stay home until they came back.

He went into the bathroom, stripped off his dirty T-shirt and cutoffs, and climbed into the bathtub. He lay there soaking, trying to imagine what else God could take away from her. As he lay there with eyes closed, a soft familiar voice in his heart asked him to run one last time. Run hard and fast—for me.

He dug his dirty clothes out of the hamper, not even bothering to dry himself, and put them back on. Forsaking even his sneakers, he burst out the front door and headed for the tracks with his wet hair sticking to his forehead. He ran along them, stretching his legs farther than ever.

The sky was an icy blue and the wind held a breath of autumn. He turned to the tall grass, and the lake beyond, breaking stride only to leap the tracks.

He picked up speed.

He thought if he could jump high enough, he could break through and grasp the sky. For the first time, he could see over the tall grass. As he leapt higher and higher, his legs loosened and he fixed his eyes on the sun. Fire burned in streaks across his face and pooled into his ears.

He raised his arms and caught the wind.

His feet left the ground.

He was free.

Guadalupe J. Solis, Jr.

Vee F. Browne is from Cottonwood and Tselani, Arizona, and a member of the Navajo Nation. She belongs to the Bitter Water and Water Flows Together clans. She is a journalist, educator, and fiction writer. An award-winning author, she has received much acclaim for her children's books, including *Monster Slayer,* winner of the Western Heritage Award, and *Monster Bird,* winner of a Rounce & Coffin Club–Los Angeles 1994 Western Books Award of Merit. Her books on Navajo folktales have been published by Northland Press. Her new books, *Maria Tallchief,* published by Simon & Schuster, and *Owl Book,* offered by Scholastic, appeared in 1995. In addition, Browne's short stories have appeared in *Neon Powwow,* and she has won the Buddy Bo Jack National Award for Humanitarianism for Children's Books.

Vee F. Browne

# The Mystery of the White Roses

DRIVING ON ICY ROADS DURING THE WINTER IS UNPREDICTABLE and as full of tension as an unsolved mystery. Now, returning home from a Christmas shopping trip to Gallup, there's a misty fog covering the slick road like a star patchwork quilt over a love seat.

As I blink my eyes in disbelief, near Window Rock, home of Diné Native Tribe, a faint figure appears in the distance . . . Looks like a transient with a backpack . . . N-n-n-no, a serviceman . . . that's his duffel bag . . . He's thumbing a ride . . . Oh, I know the warnings about picking up hitchhikers . . . Mm-m, he's handsome, with a knockout smile . . . NO, I mustn't. Hm-m, he's about my age. Should I stop? . . . O-o-o-h, why not! He's a marine. Dad was a marine, a Navajo Code-Talker. I brake carefully and pull over.

"Hi. Where are you headed?" I call out through the lowered window.

He leans forward, holding his head near the open window. "Hi. Going near Ganado?" His eyes avoid mine.

"Yeah, Sergeant, jump in. That's on my way home to Chinle." He tosses his bag in the back, slides into my Blazer, and we take off as he clicks his seat belt. "Are you coming home for the holidays, Sergeant?"

"Oh . . . yeah! Uh . . . yep . . . you might say, I'm coming home. Thanks for the lift. My name is Stuart."

"Stuart, you can call me Vi."

"Vi, do I know you? Have we met before?" We exchange glances.

"You remind me of an old friend, a basketball player at Holbrook High."

He shakes his head. "Not Holbrook. Window Rock . . . maybe?" We drive on, and I blush. He doesn't know. He has this candid smile, creamy ivory skin, and splendid legs, quite revealing through his camouflage pants.

"Well, where did we meet?" I ask. "Perhaps, a writers' workshop?"

"A dance . . . perhaps?" He lifts his shoulders, as well as his eyebrows.

Ahead of my blue Blazer, snowflakes begin swirling in a hypnotic, heavenly twister. But soon we drive into a beautiful Southwest dusk with mauve hues of twilight descending, silhouetting these snow-dusted ponderosa pines.

We jam on KISS, the rock radio station from Farmington, as I sip a diet Coke. "Would you like one?" I ask.

Stuart nods his head. "No, thanks."

"What's your protocol, Stuart?" I try to sound light, while hoping he's not of the Bitter Water People's clan. He pauses. Most of the cute guys turn out to be either a distant cousin or married to a best friend. I just hope that isn't the case this evening. I glance at his left hand. No ring! Being a single parent can be pretty lonely and frustrating at times. It would be nice to have a friend, especially a marine.

I glance at him, awaiting his response. He returns the glance and says, "I come from the Coyote Pass clan, and part Irish from my dad's side. Any relation?"

"No, I'm of the Bitter Water People's clan," I say, tickled with ecstasy. I know he is the one for me. We both know it. "By the way, where are you stationed?"

"I'm being transferred, but I can't disclose where. I work in Intelligence."

I am impressed. "That's neat! I once tried writing to Sergeant Clayton Lonetree. I found his address through NAU's library news bank in Flag." With the road conditions worsening, I do not look at my passenger. "Did you ever run into him? He was a double agent in Intelligence arrested for espionage."

He nods. "Uh-uh."

Several miles onto the Summit Peak Overpass, we pass a black Trans Am that has just skidded off the road. Someone has already stopped to assist. Suddenly, Stuart clenches his fists and beads of perspiration trickle down his forehead. "Some people drive too fast on black ice," I say aloud as I watch the road closely, keeping a firm grip on the steering wheel.

Stuart slaps his chest with both fists and exhales slowly.

"Are you all right?" My voice is unsteady. I wonder if he is in a flashback. I ease up on the slick road, driving cautiously.

"Hey, uh, I'm sorry! . . . Oh, man." His face is pale. He wipes his brow. "I . . . I just happen to . . ." He starts to say something, but just stares ahead. "Never mind . . . I don't think it matters now, anyway. I'm all right." After ticks of silence, he mumbles, "Say, what's your favorite NFL team?"

The change of subject is welcome, and the road is improving. "The Cowboys!" I squeal. "Michael Irvin is the best wide receiver because of the precision of Troy Aikman's arm." I feel rather embarrassed at my outburst. Stealing a glance at his reaction, I'm impressed with his facial contours. He looks like Karl Malone from Utah Jazz. He doesn't respond.

"Are you okay?" I ask softly. He is hauntingly handsome. I'm curious to know if he has a girlfriend, but I do not ask.

Now it's sleeting lightly. I flip on the windshield wipers, and they click in tempo with the music on the radio. My new friend sighs in relief.

"Music helps . . . I'm okay," he says and rests his arm near my shoulder. I've been warned about picking up strangers, but I truly like Stuart. I feel the warm sensation of our chemistry and the excitement of finding each other. He is my Christmas angel.

As we're nearing Ganado, Stuart suddenly shouts, "Stop! Stop! That dirt road there leads to my home." So I brake and pull over. The sleet has subsided. He unclasps his seat belt, but I can see he's not in a hurry to leave. He taps his fingers on his knee. He wants to say something. "Sorry about my behavior . . . Forgive me." He lowers his head and taps his fingers on the dash. "Vi . . . may I give you a hug?" He extends his warm arms. What a gentleman.

I undo my seat belt and turn to face him as his eyes travel down my long dark hair and caress my breasts. I feel drawn to him. I don't know, but it just happens. I slowly wrap my arms around his neck. His strong embrace clinches our new friendship. For a moment we become one, quivering as we create passion with our awaiting lips.

His fingers lift my chin to meet his. His mouth closes over mine. Our lips touch with gentle kisses. The Navajo moonlight reveals our mystic presence of love through steamed-up windows. Minutes melt. The motor is purring. "What a hug," he says, with half-closed eyes. I sigh and wipe my lips with my tongue. He squeezes my fingers and says, "Gotta flee . . ." Then he clears his throat.

I manage a smile and look into his sad eyes. "I know." I wish it weren't so.

He gently runs his fingers through my hair and returns a sad smile. "You're the one, sweet one." His voice trembles as he squeezes me comfortably close to him now. "Although we'll be a world apart, I'm glad we met tonight."

"Me, too," I whisper. I check my Citizen watch and look up at the brilliant, silvery moon, which seems to be winking at us.

"I know . . . I know, time to go," he says, reaching for the door. We must part. Although my daughter is staying overnight at her grandmother's, I know I need to get on the road to Chinle and home. It's an hour's drive. This fiery night closes the first exciting chapter. Wonder if there'll be another.

"By the way, do you have a phone?" he asks, now running his fingers through his own thick, ash-blond hair.

"Yeah!" I give him my number. Bingo! Another romantic chapter to come. This is it! I think.

"Time is up," he says. "Thanks for the ride. I'll call you." Then he writes his name on the steamy window with his index finger—STU—and draws a heart around it. He smiles and asks, "Do you like white roses?"

"Why, where's your garden?" I say. "Yeah, I love roses!" He responds with a parting fond kiss.

"Take care, Stu. Bye." I get this lump in my throat. I never did like good-byes. I feel as if I'd known him a long time. The door shuts, and he disappears into an ebony night with star-filled sky. After adjusting my seat belt, I turn on my lights and begin to glide out onto the pavement without checking my rearview mirror. Suddenly, a fast-approaching car swerves, and honks! *B-E-E-P!* I feel frightened with a nervous chill.

"Great!" I finally zoom safely on my way. I miss Stuart already.

I'm almost sorry to reach the Chinle turnoff. An acoustic guitar pitches a sad melody, "Last Dance with Mary Jane," and I touch the passenger's seat. I see Stu's heart has disappeared from the side window.

Home, at last. I reach over to the backseat to retrieve my Christmas packages, and there on the floor is my Knight in Shining Armor's duffel bag. "OH NO!" I whimper at first. But, on the other hand, now I have an excuse to see him soon.

Four days pass before I receive my check from the *Observer News*, where I'm a stringer. This job keeps me in gas money in between book contracts. Now that I finally have money for gas, I'm going to see Stuart today, and I'll invite him to go to Gallup with me to pick up the novel I ordered, *The Death of Bernadette Lefthand*.

I'll remember the dirt road where I dropped off Stuart. But what was his last name? I'm not sure I heard it. I grab his duffel in search of his last name and unzip the bag. I reach inside the dark, cold bag . . . What's this? A bouquet of dried white roses! A chill comes over me. Next, an engraved dog tag turns up—STUART CHEE LOVE. That's it! Still puzzling over the white roses, I take off. I step on it. I need to be back before school bus time.

I slow down at the dirt road, turn left, and drive up to an old log house. I'm eager to see Stuart again. I sit in my Blazer and honk, waiting for someone to come out. I'm nervous. I want to see his smile. I squeeze my fingers. I can't breathe and my stomach turns. In our tradition, it's unacceptable to go up to the door, knock, and expect to be asked in. Not around here. The Diné elders will come out to meet you. With this respect I wait, and in a few minutes a small woman in a long red skirt comes to my assistance. I roll down the window. "*Ya-a'teh.*" I extend my right hand.

"*Ya-a'teh,*" she responds. "What brings you here?"

I clear my throat and say clearly, "Where can I find Stuart Chee Love?"

The middle-aged woman lowers her eyes to stare at a frozen blue bird, lying under a bush. She says, "He is not here. Stuart was my sister's son." She looks toward a tall, charred tree, not too far away.

"Where did he go? I must see him. He left his duffel bag in my car last week."

She pauses and then says, "Why, you must not talk that way, my daughter. My sister used to dwell over there." With her pursed lips, she points to the burned tree. "Last winter my sister lit a match near a leaking butane bottle, and it exploded."

She nods her head. "Stuart was her only son. We called him home from service." Tears brim up in her eyes and fall like raindrops. "He caught a train to Gallup that night and hitched a ride in a black Firebird that hit a black horse. Stuart died in that accident, near Tse Bonito, between Window Rock and Gallup."

Last winter! I'm wordless. My heart beats against my breast. I stare at the duffel bag and the aunt's haunting eyes. She says, "I can't help you. *Ha gone'.*" This is the Diné way. She walks back inside.

For my people, it is taboo to speak of the dead. I lean on the duffel bag, my eyes swelling with tears, and ask myself, "Now what do I do with Stuart's bag?" Slowly, I reach into the duffel bag and pluck two dried white roses from the bouquet . . . For remembrance . . . I inhale the faint fragrance.

Finally, I get my misery together and carry Stuart's duffel to the charred tree. There I hang it on a blackened branch. "You are home, Stuart," I say with my arms wrapped around the bag, choking on my words. Salty tears help to soften the lump in my throat as I sniff my roses. Suddenly, snowflakes swirl about and sweep ashes out of nowhere into the air. I feel a heartbreaking sadness in a memory of his image. Slowly, I walk back to my Blazer, climb in, and gently hang the roses on my rearview mirror.

As I exit down the snow-packed dirt road, I change my plans. I'm not going to Gallup today. Not today.

At long last, I pull into my own driveway and, in grief, follow the path toward my entry door. I hear the phone ringing inside. I make an effort to move faster; I move like one in loss. I think it must be Stan, my editor. Once inside, I pick up the phone. "Hello!"

"Vi, you're the one, sweet one . . . Thank you . . . ou . . . ou," resounds a far-away familiar voice. Then I'm cut off. Still holding the phone, I sink slowly into my desk chair. Then I walk outside and get into my ride. I fall apart, kissing the immaculate white roses, recalling the unforgettable ride with destiny in mystery of walking the twilight of unanswered love.

*Taa'kodi!*

Georges E. Sioui is Wyandot-Huron from Quebec and a member of a leadership family that includes his mother, Dr. Eleanor Sioui. He is an associate professor of history and dean of academics at the Saskatchewan Federated Indian College at the University of Regina. Sioui's books include *For an Amerindian Autohistory, La civilisation wendate,* and *Les Wendats, une civilisation méconnue.* Sioui has been a research fellow at the Newberry Library, as well as a tribal leader, protecting the rights of First Nation peoples. He has been a spokesperson of native people several times before the World Court and the United Nations, and he maintains a close relationship with tribal elders throughout Canada. His works have appeared in the *American Indian Culture and Research Journal, Revue d'Histoire de l'Amérique française Recherches amérindiennes au Québec, Indigna,* and *Anthropologie et Sociétés.* His book *Les Wendats* was nominated for a Governor-General's Award for the best nonfiction book of 1994. He is currently editing a collection of short stories by Native American writers and plans to expand his work in native literature. Sioui lives in Regina, Canada, with his wife and son.

Georges E. Sioui

# A Belated Letter to Christopher Columbus

Dear Christopher:

How touching and honoring it was for the whole world to see your living image on satellite television last night, and for me to be addressed by you personally, in my quality of First Supreme Chief of the newly recognized Indian Nation of America, on the occasion of the 500th anniversary of your landing in the "New World" (which, as you justly declared, was "just as old and civilized, in 1492, as your own 'Old World' ").

This letter is to seek your very important moral support in a most special request dispatched yesterday (please find copy attached) by our government to the Prime Minister of India. My Council and myself recognize that our overture to the government of India corresponds in all major points to the declaration you made last night concerning the very sad fate of our People after your first arrival here in 1492.

Also, our government hereby expresses to you its wholehearted acceptance that you be present at our Nation's inaugural session at the World Assembly of Nations. In fact, we see your presence at that session as a potent expression and a lasting symbol for the foremost goal we have committed ourselves to as a Nation: the attainment of genuine world unity around the Sacred Circle of Life honored by our People, and of which you have spoken so convincingly to the world.

Last, we realize and accept, though with profound regret, that your time back here on Earth will not be a long one, as you have told the world, and for this reason, we are looking forward to help make it as spiritually gratifying as possible—during your stay on what you have termed "the Sacred Land of America."

Assured that this second meeting, five hundred years later, will be the true meeting of our hearts, minds and spirits, we are awaiting you, Dear Christopher.

THE SUPREME CHIEF OF THE INDIAN NATION OF AMERICA
Place of the First Peoples of America
World Assembly of Nations Headquarters
Washington, D.C. 0004
U.S. of North America

His Excellency the Prime Minister of India
Legislative Assembly Building
New Delhi, India

Most Honored Prime Minister:

First allow me to greet you in the name of the most newly recognized Nation on earth, the Indian Nation of America, of which I am the first Supreme Chief.

Last year, prior to the official declaration of the recognition of our Nation by the World Assembly of Nations, I had proposed to our National Council, of which I was the Vice President, that our first official diplomatic gesture, of which the present letter is to reveal the subject to you, be directed to Your Excellency. The National Council had then wholeheartedly accepted my proposition.

My Council and myself know full well that our overture will appear strange to Your Excellency, but I shall say right from this moment that it is in no way any stranger than the fate which our

People have known in direct relation with the reason for the request which is the subject of our overture.

Five hundred years ago today, an accident occurred which almost instantaneously changed the course of history, as well as the very description of the world as a whole: a European sailor named Christopher Columbus found himself lost on the shores of our Continent.

That accident, as willed by the Great Power of the Universe, Master of all things, was a blessing for most other peoples of the world, but meant ruin and complete disaster for our ancestral Peoples.

I do not think it necessary, very dear President, to instruct you about the highly harmonious social and natural state in which the first peoples of America lived. I shall only say on this point that Christopher Columbus, as he himself said, had landed in an Earthly Paradise, which he took to be the Indies. Strangely, it never occurred to him then, any more than he cared to admit to any of his innumerable followers, that the land of riches which he was searching for was, in reality, poor in comparison with the one he "discovered."

To come closer to the subject of the present address, Christopher Columbus, and thereafter other Europeans who undertook to appropriate our Continent and to save our souls in the name of we know what (which produced the effects which we continue to know), named our land *Indies* and universally called its aboriginal inhabitants *Indians*.

It is with the most authentic respect that we utilize this name, which we share with your people, knowing well that your country took a long time in learning about this history and becoming aware of the affliction of our Peoples, and never helped in bringing it about. Furthermore, we hope and we firmly believe that our Nation has never affronted the dignity, the sense for beauty and the capacity for Peace which the name *East Indians* has come to symbolize: for these virtues and qualities, the admiration of our People is forever yours.

Please allow me a few more remarks and explanations, dear President, before I unveil to you our request, which will also contain a proposal to your people which you shall perchance accept.

Our Nation, all through these five hundred years, has lived, and continues to live, a fundamentally demoralizing and weakening dilemma: that of existing without having a name of its own. I shall illustrate the gravity of this fact by explaining that by attaching a false name to our entire Nation, the oppressors created the notion that we did not have any right of existing, physically or culturally, in any part of our Continent. We were *Indians,* consequently without rights, anywhere, in our own land.

Although we are rejoicing over the fact that the World Assembly of Nations has taken this decisive measure for our protection, we still are, dear brother President, after five centuries of constant exposure to all forms of aggression, a People without a name. One needs to have humaneness and compassion to understand the misfortune of a People so united by history, worldview and aspirations, but without a name to define and designate itself. Assuredly, every Indian throughout history has felt this void and has attempted to imagine a name, a better name. No one, however, has been able to invent or discover a name truly apt to identify and signify the Nation.

Dear brother, the only name which, after all this time, has become natural to our minds and ears is the name *Indian,* and this is why that name, excepting the names of our loved ones and of our tribes, is to us the dearest sound which ever will be. It is probable that never has a word more characterized a People than that one. There is not a single contemporary inhabitant of our Continent who, upon hearing the word *Indian,* does not think about our People, and few who are not socially conditioned against us by some of the innumerable unfavorable preconceived ideas which this name evokes.

Brother, we most respectfully affirm that the name *Indian* has since long become more generally associated with our People than it is with yours. A proof of this is that if someone wants to refer to your people, he (she) must specify the origin by affixing the word *East* to *Indian,* or else say: "from India." Besides, we are assured that inside the wide Asiatic world, it is more appropriate to refer to your people by a name belonging to a dominant language in your country and by which you should, in all logic, become universally known.

Dear brother President, the essence of our request is that your country officially make the gift of the name *Indian* to our newly recognized nameless Nation. This name, which we cherish and desire, would remain ours through a gift from your part, in memory of the hard fate known by our People during five centuries, and as a reminder of the essential moral values for the sake of which we have unconditionally resisted. This recognition, especially coming from your country, would leave a well-auguring mark upon the birth of our Indian Nation of America and would also officially seal the already ancient, tacit alliance between our two Nations.

If this very special alliance between us should materialize, we would in our turn propose that you oblige us in the following way. The Indian Nation of America will establish preferential economic and political relations with your country, with the free-access road to the common American world market which has thus far been closed to you. You and your trade partners of the so-called Third World shall have a first take in our resources available for trade; you shall be free to establish your diplomatic quarters in our cities and territories; the Indian Nation of America shall intervene against all and any racist or otherwise unjust manifestation reported by any member of your Alliance; the Indian Nation of America shall in all circumstances provide all possible material and moral support to the members of your Alliance, for as long as they shall not be engaged in war actions.

As I have suggested at the beginning of the present letter, our overture, however strange it may appear, is part of a process of correcting an act which still needs to be repaired and which, when examined in its original intent, appears infinitely stranger than the action which we are taking. Having said this, dear brother President, must I add that our Council, our Senate and myself are anxious to receive a reply from you?

In closing, may I request, dear President, that you transmit our fraternal greetings to the members of your government and to the people of India when you submit to them the present overture? And whatever they should decide, tell them, if you please, that we are waiting for the occasion to go and visit the people of the country which we have since long wished to see, and shall soon see.

May the Great Power of the Universe bless you and your people.

Sincerely,

Georges E. Sioui
(Wyandot-Huron)

Lee Francis is from Laguna Pueblo and grew up in New Mexico. He earned a Ph.D. in 1991 and has worked at the University of California, Santa Barbara, San Francisco State University, and California State University, Long Beach. In recent years Francis has worked in Washington, D.C., for the Bureau of Indian Affairs and American University. He is well known in Indian country as a man who helps and encourages other Indians to research, write, and publish. He is editor of *Moccasin Telegraph* and was guest editor of *Callaloo,* a collection of Native American literature produced by Johns Hopkins University Press. He recently completed a major book for St. Martin's Press entitled *Native Time: An Historical Timeline of Native America.* Francis is the national director of the Wordcraft Circle of Native Writers, an international organization that promotes the ancient responsibility of educating and informing native peoples and others about Native Americans. Francis lives in Fairfax, Virginia, with his wife, son, and cats.

Lee Francis

# The Atsye Parallel

CLOUDS OF DUST BILLOWED IN MARTHA'S WAKE AS SHE swerved around another pothole on the dirt road like an award-winning racetrack driver. The shiny-clean car she had rented at the airport in Albuquerque looked as if it hadn't been washed in months. Serves the rip-off artists right, she thought as she continued speeding down the dusty one-lane road to the Old Village. She smiled at the thought of returning the rental car and telling the smug agent that it needed to be washed. "Probably tell me that it was clean before I rented it," she muttered.

Martha slammed on her brakes to avoid hitting the rabbit as it bounded across the road. The car spun and skidded into the shallow ditch. Well, they did say the brakes were good, she thought. Serves me right for thinking such mean things. When the blizzard of dust had settled, she got out of the car to check for any damage. The hot mid-morning sun surprised her. It's going to be a scorcher today, Martha thought as she started to walk around the car. Out of the corner of her eye she saw the mottled brown rabbit perched on its hind legs looking at her and sniffing the air. "Thank you, sister rabbit," Martha said to the motionless creature. "I needed to be reminded to be careful with my thoughts." As if in agreement, the rabbit took one last sniff, then bounded off in the opposite direction until it disappeared in the distance.

Martha turned slowly in a circle looking at the land where she had been born and raised. Sparse wild grass grew in scattered, disconnected clumps in all directions for as far as she could see. In the midmorning sun, the land looked bleached and dry, with only a sprinkling of stunted piñon and scrub trees to break the dreariness surrounding her. Far off in the west, Blue Mountain stood silent and majestic. Martha stared at the mountain for a moment. I know my place, she thought, here in this world so far from the center of power in Washington.

Looking at Blue Mountain, Martha smiled to herself: Those fools in Washington don't know what power is, brother mountain. If they could see you as I do, then they would know what power really looks like. Shaking her head, Martha got back into the car and slowly backed it out of the ditch. She turned off the air-conditioning and rolled down the windows. After listening for any strange sounds from the car, Martha shrugged her shoulders and decided that the car, like Martha, had survived the encounter with the rabbit.

Martha resumed her drive to Old Village at a much slower speed. "I'd best watch my thoughts," she admonished herself aloud, "especially here at home." With one hand on the steering wheel, she fumbled in her purse with her other hand for the Pueblo songs audiotape she always carried with her. "I'm really glad this car has a tape player," she said aloud while shoving the audiotape into the opening and turning it on. For the remainder of her drive to the Old Village, Martha sang along quietly with the ancient songs of the people. It was almost noon by the time she arrived at her brother's home.

As she got out of the car, her brother came out to greet her. "*Qu-wah-t'si, ka-zí-zi* [Hello, my sister]!" he said, a broad smile on his leather brown–colored face.

"*Tru-chi-muh, ka-dyú-ma* [And how are you, my brother]?" Martha responded automatically as she returned her older brother's polite hug.

"*Ma-meh tá-wah* [Very good]. You're just in time to eat."

"That's me. Always in time to eat," Martha said, laughing.

"Everyone is here" was all her brother said as they walked into the modest adobe-and-rock home.

The front room was filled with people quietly sitting and eating at a long plank-board table covered with a lime-green linoleum cloth. "Nyah!" shrieked Martha's five-year-old granddaughter, Rose Ann, with unmistakable jubilation. With arms outstretched, she bolted toward her grandmother as fast as her chubby legs would carry her. Martha bent down like an expert baseball catcher to clutch the small bundle of energy that hurtled into her arms.

"Rose Ann" came the disapproving voice of Martha's daughter,

Charlotte. *"P'bish-ti-i* [Shame on you]. You know it's not polite to be so loud."

The joyful delight in the small girl's eyes faded as her eyes began to fill with tears. Rose Ann looked at her grandmother for support. Martha hugged her granddaughter, and seeing that the child was not going to burst into tears, Martha slowly stood up. As if picking some invisible lint from her faded blue cotton dress, Martha looked directly at Charlotte.

*"Tau-y-eh, sa-mák* [Thank you, my daughter]," Martha said without a trace of emotion in her voice. "It is good to remember not to be loud." She paused for the slightest moment, then continued, "Especially when correcting another."

*"Ka-zí-zi, Cí-na* [My sister, Like-A-River] . . ." interrupted Martha's older brother, Joseph Malcolm, before Charlotte could respond. *"Ti-chu-qa-ya ah-mu-u ch-o-peh* [Come sit here and have something to eat]."

*"Ha-ah. Tau-y-eh ka-dyú-ma. Niupesíh* [Yes. Thank you, my brother. I shall eat]!" Martha replied, the tone of her voice returning to normal with each word spoken. He's good, Martha thought as she watched her brother make room for her to sit at the table and eat. If only I could be as tactful and diplomatic. Of course, Martha continued her thought, if I were, then I'd probably be the Governor instead. Martha couldn't help but smile to herself.

*"Ma-meh rahí-wa tá-wa, Yanúi Nyah* [It is good that you are here, Yanúi Nyah]," Martha's younger brother, James Anthony, said.

*"Ha-ah, tau-y-eh,"* Martha responded aloud. She wondered to herself why her younger brother used the formal title for their mother. *"T'sah-tsi* [I am not] . . ." she started to protest, but the rest of the thought died before it was born. Her mother had passed over. Martha, like all the others, had come to bury her mother in the ancient way of the People. That was why they were all there. "I am not," she repeated,

"as tired after the plane trip as I thought I would be," she finished, hoping that no one had noticed her distress.

"You should come back home from Washington for good," said Martha's youngest sibling, Florence.

"*Ha-ah.* I probably should," Martha quickly replied. But we all know I won't, she thought to herself. She looked at the adults sitting at the long table all intently focused on the meta-conversation going on. She remembered trying to tell her husband, Robert, about the silent way of talking. He just couldn't understand how everyone in her family always seemed to know what the other person was thinking or feeling or was going to do at any given moment in time. He was convinced it had something to do with "being an Indian," as he phrased it. Martha still loved him, even though he had been dead four years. He was a good man, she thought. In Martha's mind, her husband had been the most compassionate and caring man ever elected to be in the United States Senate.

Robert Edwin Wellborn and Martha Rose Atsye had been married when she was twenty-one and he had just turned twenty-three. Fresh out of Georgetown University Law School, where they had met and fallen in love, he had no trouble getting a job with the most prestigious law firm in Washington. Martha remembered teasing him, saying that the only reason he got the job was because of his rugged photogenic good looks, thick black hair and the emerald green eyes of his Scots and French ancestors, which captivated one and all. Now, some forty years later, Martha still wondered why he had asked her to be his wife.

"Auntie." A voice to Martha's left brought her abruptly back to the present. "Auntie, *quees-t'che aitya'a bá:ha* [would you please pass the bread]?" Martha fumbled for an instant, then reached for the basket filled with bread freshly baked in the *orno.* Handing the basket to the young man, it took Martha a moment to realize that it was her brother

Michael Albert's son, Kevin. "Nephew!" she exclaimed. "I almost didn't recognize you! Your mother said you had grown but she didn't tell how good-looking you'd gotten."

Kevin's pale-colored face turned pink with embarrassment. "Ah," he stuttered, not knowing what to say. "Thank you, Auntie," he mumbled, with his eyes looking down at his plate.

Wickedly, Martha continued, "So when are you going to be getting married? I'm sure that any girl in the village would say yes to a marriage proposal from you." The instant she finished her sentence, Martha knew she had committed a major blunder.

Her nephew, defiance blazing from his pale gray-blue eyes, looked directly at Martha. Before he could respond, Kevin's uncle James Anthony, sitting next to Martha's right, said quietly, "*Wink-te.*"

In a voice filled with unmistakable sincerity, Martha looked at her nephew and said, "Well, good for you. It's nothing to be ashamed of, is it?"

"*Hee-ouh* [I don't know]. Not if you don't think so, Auntie."

Looking at everyone else seated at the table before looking directly at her nephew, Martha said deliberately, "It isn't so much what I think, nephew. What is important is what you feel in your heart. Do you understand?"

"*Sù• ton$^{ih}$, Yaúni Nyah* [I understand, Yaúni Nyah]."

There it is again, thought Martha. The title for the Clan Mother. Yaúni Nyah [Mother of Rock Clan]. Without speaking, Martha got up from where she was sitting. Her face was a mask devoid of emotion as she walked into the small front guest bedroom and quietly closed the heavy oak door.

Only after she was safe behind the closed door did Martha let the tears flow unashamed. The thought of a world without her mother was unimaginable. I should have been here, Martha silently berated herself. I should have been here to help Mother pass on. As the tears continued to stream down her cheeks, Martha remembered their last conversation.

"Soon, daughter," her mother had said, "I will pass over to another wonderful adventure." Martha remembered saying, "Don't be silly. You'll be here for a long long time." Burned into Martha's memory was the surprised look on her mother's face at Martha's response. "*Cí-na, sa-mák* [Like-A-River, my daughter]," Martha's mother insisted, "my time is almost here. Soon you must take on my duties."

"*Ha-ah, senaí-ha* [Yes, my mother]," Martha said aloud to the empty room. "It is time for me to take up your duties." Then, pulling several sheets of Kleenex from the box on the dresser, Martha dried her eyes. Looking into the mirror above the dresser, she removed the beaded barrette that held her shoulder-length jet-black hair in a tight bun at the top of her head. After refixing her hair into its original tight bun, Martha reinserted the silver-and-turquoise barrette. Her composure regained, Martha opened the door and went back to her place at the table. Only her oldest brother, Joseph Malcolm, remained. In silence, Martha continued eating until only small bits of her meal remained on the plate. When she had finished, Martha looked up at her brother.

Almost in a whisper, he said, "*Há-no sanaí-is o-wi-chi-kom-mi* [The mothers of the People are waiting]."

Martha knew what her brother was telling her. She nodded in acknowledgment and stood. Carefully she moved the chair she had been sitting on back into place. She glanced at her brother and was startled to see him staring intensely at her.

"*Yémas* [What]?" she asked, her hand unconsciously brushing her coal-black hair to make sure it was not out of place.

"I want to remember you."

"Am I so easy to forget?" she bantered lightly. Her brother's focused intensity made Martha uncomfortable.

"You were too small to remember when our mother took on the duties of her mother. But I remember how she changed after going to that gathering of all the clan mothers." Taking Martha's hand, he held it a moment. "I will miss you, my sister," he said in a voice filled with deep sadness. "Soon you will be the center for all of us. I will be your son and you will be our mother. *Ko-sha t'si-ano-ah há-no.*"

"It is the way of the People," echoed Martha quietly. "*Sh-row hi-wah* [Yes. Let us go and greet the clan mothers]."

They walked out into the yard and watched the children playing under the giant oak tree. The mongrel dogs, which seemed to understand the game, were yapping and cavorting with the children. The game remained a complete mystery to the two adults as they walked east to the home of their younger brother, James Anthony. During their twenty-minute walk they told each other the latest Indian jokes interwoven with news about the members of their far-flung family. Both avoided talking about Martha's impending meeting with the clan mothers, who were waiting for Martha at the home of James Anthony.

Although James Anthony had never been married, he was definitely not *wink-te,* a word Martha liked better than *gay* or *queer.* Still, some thought, as a traditional spiritual authority of the Old Village, he should get married so that no one could spread untrue gossip about him. Not that it would matter. James Anthony was completely oblivious to mean-spirited people. His heart was open to everyone. Given that he had the name of Maiyá-ni, or One-Who-Knows, it was fitting that all the clan mothers would gather at his home.

As they approached the front door, Martha stopped. She was suddenly overwhelmed by a dread of the unknown and could not bring herself to move another step closer. She clutched her brother's hand in a truly rare instance of intense physical familiarity. "*Ak'ko-á'e* [What shall I do]?" Martha lamented.

A shocked look rippled across Joseph Malcolm's face and instantly transformed into calm determination. "*Sacsí, Cí-na* [Be strong, Like-A-River]," he replied, using her Indian name. "Remember, my sister," he said as he tightly squeezed her hand, "I will always be there whenever you need me."

Recovered from her paralysis, Martha released her brother's hand and smiled shyly. "*Cú-nyes-i, ka-dyú-ma Kókopah* [I am ready, my brother Owl]," she declared quietly. Looking at her brother for a moment, Martha walked the last four steps to the door and knocked lightly on the screen door.

"*Ti-s'tcha* [Is that you]?" said someone from inside the house.

"*Ha-ah* [Yes, it is me]," responded Martha.

"*Haw-eh-oup Cí-na, Kuyutha samák* [Come in, Like-A-River, daughter of Singer]," another's voice said.

Martha turned to look at her brother, who had not moved. And while she knew he was not permitted to accompany her to this gathering, she wished that he would. A vivid childhood memory suddenly exploded into Martha's consciousness. In a flash, she remembered that Joseph and she had been fighting. She had wanted to do something that was forbidden and Joseph had told her no. Martha remembered screaming, "Why are you always such a Goody Two-shoes?" The look on Joseph's face then was the same she saw now. "I'm not a Goody Two-shoes," Joseph hotly retorted. "It is the way of the People. We must keep to the ways of the People or else we won't be human beings anymore. Is that what you want?"

In a final gesture to her brother, Martha raised her right hand and, with the palm facing him, slowly spread her five fingers. In silence, Joseph Malcolm mirrored the gesture. As he turned to walk back to his home, Martha opened the screen door and walked into the home of her brother James Anthony.

The front room was distinctly different from her oldest brother's. Where Joseph Malcolm's had a cluttered, lived-in feeling, James Anthony's front room was sparsely furnished. The smell of damp earth and white chalk permeated the air from the glowing white walls, which had been freshly calcimined.

In the northern corner sat the eldest clan mother in an overstuffed chair, which looked out of place in the otherwise sparsely furnished room. As was proper, Martha greeted the elder first.

*"Qu-wah-t'se, Ishkay Nyah. Qu-wah-t'se, Nyah há-no."*

*"Tru-chi-muh,"* they responded.

*"Ma-meh tá-wa,"* Martha concluded as she carefully sat on the floor close to the overstuffed chair. It was several minutes before the silence was broken by the eldest clan mother.

"We grieve with you and we are filled with happiness for our sister who has passed over," said the frail old woman to Martha.

*"Ha-ah,"* agreed all the other women, sitting on cushions placed in a loose circle around the large room.

*"Tau-y-eh, Nyah,"* Martha responded somberly.

*"Maiyá-ni? Haw-e-ma* [One-Who-Knows? Please come here]."

*"He-uh* [Yes]?" responded James Anthony, who seemed to magically appear in the doorway leading into the kitchen. *"Sé'e hi-ti* [How may I help]?"

"We must be alone now, my son," said the eldest of the mothers. Her English was clear and precise. It came as a result of having been kidnapped from her home and taken away from her parents and family when she was six years old by the United States government's enforcers at the Bureau of Indian Affairs to Carlisle Indian School in Pennsylvania. At Carlisle she was forbidden, like all the native children forcibly brought there, to speak the language of her People. Any child caught not speaking English was severely punished, with the school wardens insisting it was for the good of all the children.

*"Ha-ah,"* he responded. Nodding to his sister, James Anthony walked to the front door and quietly closed the door behind him.

The sun had long set when Martha left her younger brother's house. The hot, dry air had cooled somewhat but she didn't notice. Martha was in a state of mind-shock. All the ancient stories, lessons, teachings, and the reasons for the ways of the People had been given to her in a matter of hours. For an outsider, it would have seemed like a gathering of elderly women sitting around and having a social visit. For Martha, the reality was substantially different. How have they been able to keep silent about all they know? Will I be able to keep silent?—the questions whirled around in her mind, repeating over and over.

The oak tree creaking in the warm summer breeze startled Martha out of her deep contemplation. Disoriented, she took a brief moment to realize that she was leaning against the oak tree in front of John Malcolm's. The light from the windows cast golden shadows and Martha could hear the voices of her family talking mixed with the sounds of canned audience laughter from a TV sitcom. How like us, Martha thought, acting as if this were just another ordinary family get-together. Suddenly Martha remembered her encounter with the brown mottled rabbit. "Yes," she said aloud, "I will remember to mind my thoughts." The loud laughter from the house confirmed for Martha that she had correctly understood how she must behave. Martha forced herself to smile and started walking toward the house. The laughter from the house continued, and by the time she opened the screen door, Martha's smile was genuine.

"Mother!" exclaimed Charlotte, her eyes wide in disbelief. At that instant everyone in the room turned to look at Martha standing in the doorway.

"Nyah!" shrieked Martha's granddaughter Rose Ann. "What happened?"

Martha was mystified. Looking at the faces of everyone in the room, she could see that they were all in various stages of what seemed like shock. "Nothing happened," Martha, still baffled by everyone's reaction, said to Rose Ann.

"Sister . . ." began Florence. "I mean . . ." she stuttered, "Yaúni Nyah. You must . . ."

"*P'bish-ti-i, zí-zi* [Be still, sister]. Who are you to tell our mother what she must do?" demanded Joseph Malcolm.

Without being told, those who were sitting silently stood. The only person in the room not looking at the floor was Joseph Malcolm. Someone turned off the TV as he crossed the room to where Martha stood. It seemed to Martha that with every step her brother seemed to age a decade. "Mother, please come," he said softly as he started to gently guide Martha by her elbow toward the front bedroom.

"*Kókopah, yémas* [Joseph Malcolm. What is going on]?" demanded Martha, her voice rising in anger.

"Yaúni Nyah," he pleaded, "please come into the other room."

"*Ha-ha, sa-mu-ti Kókopah, há-no Ho-chin, hí-nome e'aú skanaí-ha s'á cúunyesí* [Yes, my son Owl, Governor of the People, I am your mother and I shall go with you]," Martha retorted as she jerked her elbow away from her brother's gentle hold.

No one spoke as the two made their way to the front bedroom. After Joseph Malcolm quietly closed the door, he slowly turned to face his sister, who was looking at herself in the mirror. Joseph Malcolm watched the tears streaming down his sister's face for a moment, then opened the door and quietly closed it behind him.

When her tears had stopped, Martha turned away from the mirror and walked over to the bed and lay down. The night chant of the cicadas lulled her into a deep dream-filled sleep.

Resting on a branch of a red oak, she watched the man and woman slowly walk toward the bank of the river. The woman's white-silver hair looked like strands of silver glittering in the sun. They stood there for a moment and then the old woman took off one of her moccasins as if to shake the sand out. Suddenly a herd of antelope and deer and buffalo and all the other animals of the forests and plains sprang into existence. The man, shaking with fright, hurriedly guided the old woman across the stream and the pair continued their journey. She watched for a long time until they disappeared in the distance.

Vaguely curious, she wondered where the man and old woman were going. With that thought, she was suddenly standing on top of a large boulder thirty feet from the ground. She looked down and could see the old woman and man standing on the bank of a second river. She watched the old woman take off the other moccasin, and as she began to shake the sand out, all different kinds of birds appeared, each singing their own songs. As they disappeared once again into the distance, her interest in the old woman and man became more intense.

In an instant she was slowly circling high above the man and old woman, who stood on the bank of a third river. Again, the old woman took off her moccasin, and as she shook the sand out of it, reptiles of all kinds suddenly materialized. The man was visibly shaking in utter terror of the old woman and urgently hurried his companion as they continued their journey.

She was not surprised to find herself somehow magically transported to the bank of the fourth river. This time, when the old woman shook out the sand from her moccasin, thousands of insects of all kinds appeared. Clearly in a state of panic, the man seemingly floated across the water to the opposite bank with the old woman in tow.

She was filled with an irresistible desire to see the faces of the man and the old woman with the glittering white-silver hair. In that instant she was standing in front of the old woman, who smiled at her. The face belonged to Martha.

The shock of seeing her own face staring back at her jolted Martha awake. It took all her energy to slow down the wild beating of her heart. "Calm," she said quietly. "I must become calm." It was several minutes before the adrenaline quit surging throughout her body and her heart resumed its regular cadence. Slowly Martha sat up. After several more minutes she got out of bed and walked to the small adjoining bathroom. Not turning on the light, she turned on the faucet and splashed cool water on her face. After taking several deep breaths and slowly exhaling, Martha dried her face. Carefully she folded the small face towel and placed it back on the towel bar. Midway on her way back to bed, Martha thought she heard someone in the front room. Quietly she opened the door.

Joseph Malcolm sat in his recliner. Martha could see in the light of the small table lamp by his chair that her brother was lost in deep thought. Not wanting to disturb him, Martha began to close the door.

"*Nyah, ti-s'tcha* [Mother, is that you]?" Joseph Malcolm whispered.

"*Ha-ah.*"

"*Sé'e hi-ti?*"

"It's nothing. *Kowuh-wuka* [A dream]."

"*Ui-pán'ri* [May I listen]?"

"*Key-yo Kah-peh.*"

"You dreamed of the sacred one?"

"*Ha-ah. Ak'ko-é'e* [Yes. What shall I do]?" Martha faltered.

Joseph Malcolm vaulted from his chair. "*Sá* [No]!" he pleaded. "*Sé-wa kuaienikúya cá-cih tá-wa yémas* [I ask you not to speak anymore]."

"*Cicí-pa* [But I want] . . ."

"*Hí-nome có-tyu. Rahí• wa cá• cih tá-wa yémas* [I must go. Now is not a good time to speak about this]," he said in a voice filled with terror. With his hands pressed against his ears to shut out the sound of Martha's voice, Joseph Malcolm rushed out of the house, the screen door slamming behind him.

Shaken by her brother's explosive reaction, Martha wanted to run as far away from the place of her birth as possible. "My duty," she spoke to the empty room. "I will do my duty but I don't have to like it." As she went back to the bedroom, a song from her childhood echoed in her mind. What were the words? she asked herself while getting back into bed.

As she lay on the bed, Martha remembered the words and quietly sang the childhood song. "*Key-yo Kah-peh, koh-t'chuu-ma. Key-yo Kah-peh, koh-t'shu-ma. Kaahts-oh-ee-tu-i-nah. Koh-wah-schum-ma s't-cha-ah. Ai-kut-to-ri-nah. Ai-kut-to-ri-nah. Key-yo Kah-peh t'cho-sto* [*Key-yo Kah-peh,* the sacred one. *Key-yo Kah-peh,* the holy one. Tens upon tens of years come and go. And they did reap what they had sown. Cursed by troubles every day. Cursed by troubles every day. For the brutal murder of *Key-yo Kah-peh*]." Her last words were barely audible as Martha drifted off to sleep.

Darryl "Babe" Wilson has been writing for years and is best known in his native California. He is Achuma-We on his father's side of the family and Atsuge-We on his mother's side. Wilson was born to the people of the Pit River of northeastern California, and he has spent his life preserving the oral tradition through his speaking and writing. His essays, poetry, and short fiction have appeared in *News from Native California, Talking Leaves, Red Ink, Looking Glass,* and Anchor Books' *Earth Song, Sky Spirit.* In 1992, Wilson edited a volume entitled *Dear Christopher,* and he is currently under contract from the University of Arizona Press to edit the oral traditions of his own people in a book entitled *Yoken A-aswi Yusji: Necklace of Animal Hearts.* Wilson completed his bachelor's degree at the University of California, Davis, and his master's degree at the University of Arizona, where he is finishing his doctorate. He lives in Tucson with his twins, Hoss and Boss.

Darryl "Babe" Wilson

# Grampa Ramsey and the Great Canyon

IT WAS A SUMMER BEFORE I KEPT TRACK OF TIME. IN OUR decrepit automobile, we rattled into the driveway, a cloud of exhaust fumes, dust and screaming excited children. A half dozen ragged kids and an old black dog poured from the ancient vehicle. Confusion reigned supreme. Uncle Ramsey (after we became parents, his official title changed to "Grampa") was standing in the door of the comfortable little pine-board home just east of McArthur. Aunt Lorena was in her immaculate kitchen making coffee.

Just as quickly as we poured from the vehicle, we disappeared. There was a pervading silence. Always the crystal bowl rested on Aunt Lorena's kitchen table. Usually it held exotic, distant, tasty objects: oranges, bananas, store-bought candy! There seemed to be three hundred black, shiny eyes staring at the contents of that bowl, but we knew that we must wait for Aunt Lorena to say "when" before we could have the contents—which we instantly devoured.

I cannot remember if we had any cares. It was before I began the first grade. I didn't care if I had shoes or clothes. I didn't care about anything—except not to allow my brothers and sisters to have something that I couldn't. And when I did not know that they got something more than me, it didn't matter, really.

It seems that my "thoughts" were already focused upon some other objective. I listened to the old people. I remembered what they said, the tone of their voice, the waving of the hands. My mind registered the long silences between their choppy sentences and between their quiet words.

They spoke in our languages, A-Juma-wi and Opore-gee, and they used a very crude and stumbling English. The English words were strange. I preferred the "old language." As our lives moved into the world of the English-speakers, and our "old" language became less and less important and less and less used, something within the old people hesitated.

His employment as a "cowboy" came to an end when a shying

horse threw him and he landed on his neck, nearly breaking it. After his days in the saddle faded, he worked on various ranches in the Fall River Valley until his retirement.

He spoke to us in Opore-gee (Dixie Valley language), giggling when the twins would say the words correctly after he explained them. We would have to go visit him many times before he would tell us a "real, not fake" story of our people and our history. During these times I took notes because a tape recorder "spooked" him and it mattered little what he was trying to say; the "ghost" inside the tape recorder affected him—he was occupied with the "ghost" instead of the lesson.

Close to the time of his "departure," he spoke of being "so old that I no longer think about the end, but think about the beginning, again."

As a silent, powerful, unseen ship passing into an endless sea in the darkness, he moved into the spirit world to join his wife and others of our shattered little nation. He departed during the full moon of October 1986. Aunt Lorena preceded him by sixteen years.

Discard the rules of English kings and queens. Suspend logic. Grampa speaks as he learned to around campfires and in a distance so long ago that he claimed, "I didn't have enough good sense to listen good."

Grandfather's story:

## HOW THE GREAT CANYON WAS MADE

[This canyon is between Fall River Mills and Burney, California, on the Pit River. Grandfather interchanges Qon and Silver-gray Fox occasionally. They are the same being in his thought.]

. . .

"Qon [Silver-gray Fox] worked to make the world from a mist and a song long ago. He and Makada [Coyote] set to making things on earth. Makada was constantly trying to change things. Qon had the power to create. Makada had the power only to change things. He was always jealous because he could not create—he could only change. Qon created things. Makada always tried to change them. Qon persisted. Makada insisted. Sometimes he made a go of it. Sometimes Makada got his way. He sure was insistent, that Makada. [Smile, twinkle and gruff giggle.]

"This was the time when Qon put his place, his home—maybe you say 'office'—on the Pit River/Hat Creek rim near Hogback [a small mountain]. From that place he could watch everything. This was before there was a Great Canyon, so Da-we-wewe and It-Ajuma [streams, including the Fall River and Pit River] could make it to the ocean, so salmon could come up there. Fall River and Dixie valley are the valley drainage.

"It [the office] was like an umbrella that you can look through but you could not see it—like a bubble or something but you can't see him [it]. When it rained, it did not rain in there. When it snowed, snow could not get in. Wind must go around. Storms and lightnings bounced off. I don't know just how to say—as if an arch. Like a thinking or a thought or something.

"I dunno. You couldn't touch it or see it. Anyhow, it was there so the Power could watch. Qon wanted everything just right. He knew he had to watch old Makada. It was bad. Qon needed help from Makada. Makada was insistent.

"Qon molded earth like *wa-hach* [a form of bread made in an iron skillet without grease], flattened here, raised there. Everywhere not the same. It was when Chum-see-akoo was being made. Some call it Ya-nee-na [the small area where the Hat Creek and Pit River come together and create a small peninsula in a shape like Argentina. Highway

299 East runs through it]. It was made. Qon wanted to name it. Makada wanted to name it. They talked. They argued.

"Qon said, 'Let's make some other things and get back to this place.' So they did. They roamed and made *a-hew* [mountains] and *da-wi-wiwi* [streams] and *a-ju-juji* [springs]. Qon named these places. They returned to Chum-see-akoo/Ya-nee-na. Makada said, 'You, brother, have named all of these other places. It is my turn to name this place right here.' [A gruff giggle from Grandfather because Coyote called Silver-gray Fox "brother."]

"Qon said, 'No, you will call it by any name but a real name. Sometimes when you talk you don't make much sense. Let's go and make some more.' So they did. [Silver-gray Fox was in the process of making the Pit River Country into a livable place.]

"Watching from a high bluff, Qon saw the insistence of Makada. He waited. Meanwhile he forgot to make a place for the Pit River to run and drain the upper valley. He forgot to make a canyon. There was a mountain of solid rock. No canyon.

"They returned to the small valley again. Again they got in argument. This time Qon give in. He give up. He got tired of arguments.

"Makada called it Chum-see Akoo [Mice Valley] because he liked to eat mice. He really liked the taste of fresh mice. Today that is what we call it. Mice Valley. But what about the canyon that was filled with solid rock? The Pit River cannot run through it. The salmon must come so peoples can eat.

"Qon looked and saw a wide spot below rock mountain. Rock mountain must be made into a canyon for Pit River. He spoke to big bass-sturgeon. 'You must do this so river can run to the ocean.' Sturgeon said, 'Okay, but I am not strong enough to break that mountain.' Qon said, 'Tomorrow I shall tell you what to do after I think.' Why did Qon have to think? I dunno.

"Next day Qon said, 'Go to top of mountain [Mount Shasta] and get power.' He went, then he swam back from mountain. He got back and got a run at it and hit it [the rock mountain] with his head. BANG! Again and again, BANG! It hurt. He got tired and it hurt. Qon said, 'Go back to the mountain for more power.'

"Meanwhile Makada was off doing something. He could not create. He was changing something. Always changing, Makada.

"Sturgeon struck the mountain, BANG! Again and again. Again he got tired. Again it hurt. He went back to the mountaintop and got some more power. BANG! Old mountain rock he began to break. It got weakness. He cracked it! He got more power in a hurry. He broke it! Rocks were everywhere. Later they found some rocks clear up in Dixie [Valley]. Rocks flying everywhere. He broke through. He did it! He came out to Bo-ma-ree [Fall River Valley].

"Qon said, 'Good.'

"Meanwhile Qon found Makada. He was up at the hot springs cooking quail eggs and looking with his head down seeing himself in the water. [Gruff giggle.] Makada always thought he was real cute.

"When they came back, Makada noticed the great canyon. Qon looked at Makada. Makada looked away, with his tongue hanging sideways from his mouth, and said, 'I didn't do it [make the canyon]. I was gathering quail eggs to boil in hot springs.'

"Looking to the rim, today, you will see power [the "office"] is gone. Qon and Makada ran east up the canyon that was rushing with water [the Pit River]. There were more things to make. Maybe it was then that people was made, but that is another story. Not for today."

We left Grampa Ramsey in possession of a "real, not fake" story. At times it seemed as if it was a story about creation in general, but it was, for the most part, a story of the Great Canyon. For this time spent with Grampa we are made richer. Richer in knowledge and in understanding. Richer in language and the function of that language. Richer in the spiritual connection that binds us to the earth.

Andrew Connors lives and works in Milwaukee, Wisconsin, where he is closely associated with the American Indian community. He is editor of *Migizi,* a newsletter for the native community, and he teaches at the community Indian School. Connors also teaches drama at Spotted Eagle High School. He takes particular interest in mentoring young native students in history, theater, and creative writing. He also enjoys spending time with elders. Connors is a Bad River Ojibwe, born in Ashland, Wisconsin. His short story "Avian Messiah and Mistress Media" appeared in Anchor Books' *Earth Song, Sky Spirit,* and he has had a lyric poem, "Traveling Thunder," and a short story, "Like a Snowflake," appear in *Dreaming History.* "Avian Messiah and Mistress Media" also appeared in *Re: Dux,* published by the University of Oregon. His play *The Wind Whispers* was produced by First Stage. Connors heads the Woodland Nations Troupe, and he lives in South Milwaukee with his two children, Eric and Anna.

Andrew Connors

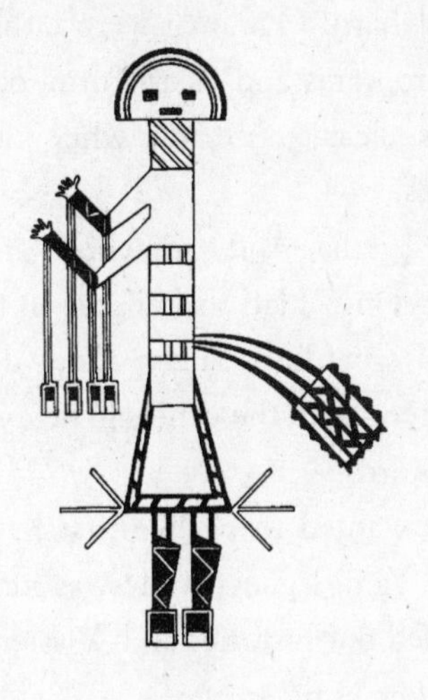

# Looking for Hiawatha

SNOW DANCER TALES . . .

"Do you remember when that anthropologist met the Snow Dancer?" Two Dogs says. Laughter erupts, noggins nod, the child questions, Grandmother smiles.

"Oh, long ago, this was, long ago and hard," Two Dogs continues. "They called it the Great Depression, hard times, but to us it was just another in a cycle of hard. Our men were either loggin' or gamblin', stakin' government programs and clear-cuttin' our dreams."

Everyone agrees, clear-cut dreams, while Grandma gently wrestles the child to her knees.

"Well, this young fella, Andy somebody, I think, was fresh from college," Two Dogs begins. "Had this degree in this new science called anthropology. Now, I don't know much about this anthropology, but I guess they were different than the others. They weren't after our bones, they were after our words.

"Anyway, Andy wanted to be like that Kroeber fellow out west. The man and his last Yahi. I guess Andy was lookin' for his Yahi. This was before Radin raided our histories and Wissler's reformist pity fell on deft ears. We remember him."

Grandmother nods. "Looking for Hiawatha," she says as the child skitters under the table and plays by Auntie's feet.

"So he comes here lookin' for Hiawatha, badgering the Shinaabs to fill him in on what he believes is tribal truth."

"He goes to Aanakwaad. 'No,' Aanakwaad says, 'Hiawatha don't live here no more. Left him on the shores of Gitche Gumee a long, long time ago.' Andy scribbles notes, scratches his head, thanks Aanakwaad, and moves on over to Misakakojiish.

" 'Kojiish, Old Badger, would hear none of it, and chased that poor Andy off with curses flung backward in the wind. 'Kakojiish Animosh added his piece, and then it was a sight. Talked about it for days. Thought that'd be the last we saw of Andy.

"But no, he moved on to the DeFoes. They weren't home. I think all the Shinaabs planned this once word got around that an anthro was here again. Words travel fast on the tribal winds. From house to house, lodge to lodge, he ranged lookin' for Hiawatha until the Shinaabs grew tired of his questions, which were wrong, and sent him to the Snow Dancer.

" 'Is Snow Dancer a shaman?' he asked. He shook slightly from shaman power tales he read in North American Aboriginal Pagan Studies 101.

" 'No,' the Shinaabs coyly replied. 'The Mission threw out our shamans when they taught us the Our Father who art in heaven, the value of money, true civilization. No, the Dancer is a storyteller, teacher, and gatekeeper, to some she is known as the Little Drum Weeper.'

" 'Huh,' Andy stumbled. They sent him on his way, sayin', 'Snow Dancer may be down by Gitche Gumee walking the same paths Gitche Hiawatha once trod.' Which excited him no end, and off he traipsed dreamin' of the thesis that would grant him tenure and a place in anthropological history.

"Andy crested the hill and fell down a slope, finally restin' on the shore covered with rocks and twigs. He looked up one side, down the other, spyin' a shawled figure standin' near the water.

" 'Snow Dancer,' he whispered, and approached her quietly, as though clompin' through the surf would disturb imagined powers and shamanistic hoodoo. He quickly recalled the questions he'd ask, misplacin' his enlightenin' ones for book ones.

"Still, Dancer stood by the shore, swayin' with the waves and singin' to the wind.

" 'Excuse me,' he politely began, standin' behind the woman in the shawl. Odd how these Shinaabs managed to keep their hair so younglookin', he thought, studyin' her backside. Snow Dancer was small and looked as though one good blow of lake breeze would topple her and send her flyin'.

"Dancer turned slowly, eyein' the voice that interrupted her songs. 'Yes?'

"Andy was startled and momentarily misplaced his speakin' voice. 'Uh' was all he uttered while starin' at the young woman before him. She couldn't have been more than twenty, twenty-three at the most, and though she was small and as red as he imagined Indians should be, he was smitten by her beauty and the racial discrepancy of her gambolin' gray eyes.

" 'Er,' he began, fumblin' with his notes. Strange, what he was feelin'. Who would've thought this colonial bookworm could feel the stirrings a woman puts in a man as he gazes at her realizin' she is his Helen, a Shinaabe Pocahontas to his John Smith.

"But why should he feel as he did? She was just an Indian princess who couldn't possibly be old enough to answer his tribal inquiries. Hell, she couldn't have been any older than he, and was she Christian, and if so, Protestant?

"Someone must be puttin' him on, for surely as God's in Heaven, this couldn't conceivably be Snow Dancer. Somewhere in his studies he'd read about Indian humor—a paragraph or two—then he smiled, broadly exposin' pearly whites as he realized that he was the butt of a tribal joke.

" 'Yes?' Little Drum Weeper asked again, wonderin' about this man. She smiled: just another wanderer lookin' for Pontiac and Hiawatha on the shores of Gitche Gumee.

" 'Excuse me,' said Andy again. 'But I was looking for someone called Snow Dancer. You haven't seen her perchance?'

"Dancer suppressed a laugh. 'Yes, she's been around here and now she's off somewhere. I think she went down the shore a ways. Looking for Makwa. Returning a favor, I think.'

" 'Makwa?'

" 'Yes, the Bear.' Andy looked nervously about. Dancer calmed him, sayin', 'Don't worry about Bear. There was once a time when everyone could talk to Bear. You see, Bear has a power that can't be tamed by missionaries and holy rollers. Some say Snow Dancer can still talk to Bear, and we know for a fact that Niimi can.'

" 'Niimi?'

" 'Geget!' Dancer was on a roll. 'Niimi dances madly backward with Bear and does an Irish jig when the moon is full and the waters are high. Some say Niimi is a direct descendant of Nanaboozhoo. But I'd have to question that, since I know for a fact he's my cousin. Though Nanaboozhoo runs in the blood, we can't claim him as a direct descendant, since he's related to all of us.'

" 'Er, yes,' Andy started, dismissing the tribal maiden's pontification. 'I'd like to ask Snow Dancer about this Nanabojo.' He studied his shoes. 'Did I say it right?'

" 'For a white man,' Dancer said.

"The waves lapped the shore and tight shoe tongues lapped at his feet. Self-consciousness was new to his heritage, though he imagined his lineage meldin' with hers. He quickly fumbled through his pockets for the cross he kept there. These thoughts wouldn't do him any good in his quest for Heaven, so he reminded himself to pray to the anthropological god who classified tribal ghosts and dreams into linear tangibility and beg absolution.

" 'How is it you speak our language so well,' he asked.

"Should she tell him about the school? He'd never understand. She let it ride, said she was Catholic—which was somewhat acceptable —and that's where she learned English and *chimookamaan* meanings in the tribal world.

"This last sentence he didn't comprehend at all, but what he did discern was an instinctive stirring and her eyes drawin' him in. He clutched the cross tighter.

" 'I understand your people believe that everything has life,' he began, after the cross reassured him he was still a God-fearin' man, and she a pagan princess. 'For example, I read that your people believe everything has a spirit. Is this true?'

"Dancer strolled along the shore, watchin' a fish leap from the water and a gull swoop up the fish. Life went on as the spirit of the fish joined the spirit of the gull, while the spirit of the young man released male hormones that got lost in the spirit of the wind.

" 'Do you see that tree?' Dancer said, stoppin' quickly and directin' Andy's gaze toward a hilltop and away from her body.

" 'Do you mean that cedar tree?'

"Dancer nodded. 'That tree has a spirit. If that's what you're looking for.'

"Andy saw nothin' but a tree stretchin' skyward. Nothin' extraordinary, and he wondered if he should mention the great sequoias he'd seen in Washington State. Now, those trees had spirit, not like the cedar, although it was a magnificent specimen. But he bit his lip and nodded, askin', 'How so?'

" 'As our people moved around,' Dancer began, 'we would make camp wherever we found cedar growing. This was a good sign. The cedar gave us nearly everything we needed for survival.'

" 'I thought it was the birch tree,' Andy remarked.

" 'The birch is a good tree, too,' Dancer replied, 'but the birch will bend and break in a strong wind, while the cedar just bends and takes it.'

"Andy found it interestin'.

" 'The cedar gave us nearly everything, like I said,' Dancer continued. 'Cedar helped us build our lodges, gave us moss for our baby's bottoms . . .'

" 'You used cedar moss for diapers?' Scribble, scribble. Andy's hand flew across the page.

" 'Sure, why not? It's there and available. There are some parts of cedar that are edible.'

"Scribble, pause, edible, incredible!

" 'Also, we knew that wherever cedar grew the land was good land,' Dancer said. 'That's why we made our camps near Grandmother Cedar, and that's why Grandmother has a spirit.'

" 'Interesting,' Andy feigned. 'Now, you claim that your people could once talk to the bears. Did your people talk to other animals, like, say, an otter or a muskrat?'

"Dancer embarked along the shore again, Andy trottin' right behind. 'The animals are always talking to us, but lately people have lost the power to listen to what they have to say.'

" 'How so?'

"She shrugged. " 'I don't know, but somewhere the paths crossed and no one understood the *chimookamaan* words we now spoke.'

" '*Cha-MO-ka-man?* That's the second reference you've made to *chamokaman*. Who is this *chamokaman?*'

"Dancer nodded at Andy. 'When your ancestors came upon the Anishinaabe, they brought the cross with them and the cross didn't believe in animals as living spirits.'

"Andy tensed. This wasn't true, how dare she belittle the faith. To his credit, he said nothin', consumed with his thesis, and followed Dancer along the shore, scribblin' notes.

" 'Animals, the Fathers said, were to serve man as food,' said Dancer. 'We knew this, but we also knew that animals told us about life. So the healers listened to the animals, the trees, the winged creatures, the water, the land.'

" 'Fascinating,' Andy said. But he tired of this discourse. A few more notes, then off he'd go lookin' for that woman that danced in the snow. She was a pretty little thing, though. He drew away from her sexuality, and scanned the area for Snow Dancer.

"As they walked, they talked, or Dancer talked, tellin' Andy things that couldn't possibly be true. She talked about how the people came from the east—he believed it was the Bering Strait (read that in a book somewhere). 'Did you know,' she said, 'that Longfellow had it all wrong about Hiawatha? Hiawatha wasn't Ojibwe, he was Mohawk, Turtle Clan. He helped form the Iroquois League with the Peace Maker. Oh yes. Did you know that in the Iroquois Confederacy, women are the power. But the English couldn't fathom dealing with women as tribal leaders. Though they forgot about the English queens.'

"As they walked, Andy got the impression that there was no Snow Dancer, ancient tribal storyteller, *aye.* 'Tell me,' he said. 'I once read that your people also believe that rocks can speak.'

" 'Ah yes,' said Snow Dancer. 'The one about the farmer and the rocky field. Written by some anthropologist who heard it from the Flambeau, I think.'

" 'Er, yes,' he continued. 'Anyway, we know rocks are inanimate, lifeless objects, not like animals, which do communicate, in a way. But rocks?'

"Dancer stopped. Andy stopped. Dancer watched the lake. Andy studied Dancer. He spread his arms over the shoreline, pointin' at the stones, rocks, and boulders clutterin' the surface.

" 'So tell me,' he said slyly. 'Do these rocks tell you anything? I mean, do *all* these rocks speak?'

"The stones, rocks, and boulders sang to her. 'No,' she answered, shakin' her head.

"Andy beamed triumphantly. He'd exposed a tribal fallacy. A fallacy because it wasn't written by the learned in hardbound college texts, oral tales based in myth because science and the word of God Himself proved life was for the livin' man, and everyone knows rocks, stones, boulders, animals, birds, fish, water, the land, and, yes, women were not the livin' man.

" 'No,' Dancer said again. 'But *some* of them can.'

" '*Some* of them can . . .' "

Andrew Connors

. . .

Two Dogs roars with laughter. Everyone around the table joins in. "No," Two Dogs says, choking back tears. " 'But *some* of them can,' she said." He wipes his eyes, smiles at Grandma, and the child sitting on her knees looks around the table wondering what the joke is.

"That Andy somebody never did find Hiawatha," Grandma says, and everyone breaks up again, sipping hot cocoa late into the night.

Jason B. Edwards is a mixed-blood Blackfeet-Blood who was born in Ann Arbor, Michigan, spending summers on reserves in Montana and Alberta. His grandmother was a traditional storyteller who instilled in him a love of stories and the magic of words. Edwards is a combat veteran of Vietnam, where he served fifteen months before attending Michigan State University. He has written a novel about Vietnam entitled *Hard Road to the Sun* and another dealing with a returning veteran of the war entitled *Dreamland*, a chapter of which has been adapted for his short story in this volume. He has published in *Cavalier*, *Way Station*, *Lansing State Journal*, and *Carlysle Communications*. Edwards is a professional writer who lives in East Lansing, Michigan.

Jason B. Edwards

# Dreamland

I DON'T LIKE IT HERE.

One of these days I'll go down to the bus station or train depot, buy me a one-way ticket, and leave this damn place. Go back to Montana. That's where I was born and raised.

Did you know they call Montana "The Big Sky State"?

Well, they do. And it's true.

In Montana the sky's so big and clear it makes you dizzy with all that endless space goin' on forever in all directions. Out there, freedom ain't just a word on the lips. It ain't some hazy ideal tied to a flag or a piece of paper. In Montana, freedom's a place made of wide-open spaces and endless sky. A place where the spirit can dream and roam and wonder.

Here in the city, you hardly ever see the sky. There's walls and buildin's keepin' it "out there." And what little sky manages to slip through is usually dirty and gray. Even when it rains, it's like mud drippin' outa the sky. Nearly everything's paved over, like the city can't stand to touch the Earth.

Ugly damn place, this city.

Yep. I wanna go back to Montana. But I'm still here.

Oh, I tried goin' back a few times. Got all the way to Helena, once, before I turned around and came back. I knew I wasn't ready, yet. The Faces and Voices that live in my head don't like it out there. They like dirt and darkness and death, and Montana's too open and sunny and alive. They like it here in the city just fine. But *I* don't like it here, and someday I'm gonna leave all those Faces and Voices behind. I'll get better and go home, back to the res'vation and my people.

Folks say, "Chief, why you wanna go back there?" They call me "Chief" 'cause I'm a full-blood Indin—Blackfoot Nation, Pikuni Tribe, Small Robes Band. Even when I tell 'em my name's Tom Losteagle, they still call me "Chief." They say, "Ain't nothin' out in Montana but grass and trees and mountains. And it gets cold out there—thirty, forty, even fifty below. Why you wanna go back, Chief?"

And there's truth to what they say. Montana gets real cold. It gets so cold you can hear the trees pop. Sometimes the trees even shatter 'cause they're all froze up inside.

Believe me, that's some serious cold.

But in Montana, it's only cold in the winter. It's the ice and snow and wind that's cold. Here in the city, everything's cold all the time. It's like mosta the people have ice in their souls and winter in their hearts. Even when it's in the nineties and the asphalt's sticky-hot, I hear 'em poppin' and crackin' like Montana trees in winter. They're all froze up inside, and their eyes're pulled way back deep in their heads so they don't have to see anything around 'em.

People here don't wanna see or think or feel. Sometimes I think maybe they ain't people at all. Maybe they're machines with springs and cogwheels and clockwork stuff under a layer of phony plastic skin. If you listen real close, maybe you can hear the *whirrr-click-click* of their works as they pass.

Maybe that's my problem: I ain't a machine.

I used to be a machine, but I didn't like it much. A machine don't do nothin' but what it's designed to do, and it just keeps on doin' it over and over again. Mindless. Emotionless. Without a thought or a care. And when it breaks down and can't be fixed anymore or a newer model comes out, it gets tossed on the scrap heap and forgotten.

So I became a person again.

A person sees and thinks and feels.

And, of course, that screwed everything up. There ain't many places left where you can be a person these days. And there's the machines. They don't like people, and they're always out to get you.

'Course, that's not what the VA shrink says. He says I got that post-traumatic stress over in Vietnam, that the war scrambled my brains, and The Faces and Voices belong to people I killed or saw get killed.

Maybe.

But I was a machine, then, and it didn't bother me till I became a person again. Then The Faces and Voices came to haunt me with memories of bein' a machine.

The VA shrink don't understand 'cause he's still a machine. He doesn't think I know, but I have good ears. I can hear his little wheels goin' *whirrr-click-click,* the cogs goin' *ca-ching, ca-ching,* and his batteries hummin'.

It don't bother me, his bein' a machine. But you gotta be careful. Machines don't understand people too well. They don't understand how easy we break. Still, I have hope for the shrink. If I can become a person, anybody can.

The VA shrink says my brain's all fucked up from the war and all the things I saw and did over there. That's what he wants me to believe, but I don't think it's true. Not all of it, anyway. I think a lot of it's this place, this city. It makes a person feel smaller each day till he's invisible, and you wonder if maybe you don't exist. If you ain't a machine, the loneliness and hopelessness gnaw away at you like cancer.

The city ain't made for people.

Lucky for me there's Dreamland.

Dreamland's an old amusement park down on the waterfront. It's a ghost town of old rides and run-down buildin's piled up on a peninsula in the bay. It's all boarded up and fallin' apart, and the old roller-coaster ride looks like a giant dinosaur skeleton. Nobody goes there no more but us and the seagulls and rats.

The machines leave us alone down there.

"Us" is me, Boom-Boom Benevides, Mama Ski, Papa Doc, Ms. Doc—no relation to Papa Doc—Kit Katz, Sweet Willie, and Jenny Lake—also known as Marvella Tush.

Other folks pass through from time to time. This past winter we had whole families comin' through—folks thrown outa their apartments and such 'cause the rent was too high, farmers who lost their farms, all kindsa folks pushed off their land and outa their homes just like us

Indins. But, like I said, they were just passin' through, tryin' to track down what's left of the American Dream. Boom-Boom, Mama Ski, Papa Doc, Ms. Doc, Sweet Willie, Kit Katz, Jenny Lake, and me—we're the regulars at Dreamland.

Roberto "Boom-Boom" Benevides was a top-ranked welterweight back in the sixties. He was famous for his hand speed, heart, and his ability to take a punch. Unfortunately, he took lotsa punches, and now his brain's a little mushy. He gets real bad headaches that make him babble and moan in Spanish. Sometimes he forgets things like what day it is, or why he went someplace in particular, or who I am. They say he made a few million bucks in the ring, but Boom-Boom never saw much of it. I hear his former manager lives in a big house and drives a fancy Mercedes.

You figure it out.

Mama Ski's real name's Laura Kaszlowski, but she don't mind us callin' her Mama Ski. She was a normal housewife lookin' forward to what folks call "the golden years" when her husband got real sick. Their insurance didn't last long, and Mama Ski had to sell everything they owned to buy med'cine and pay doctor bills. When her husband finally died, she didn't have a penny left and she ended up out in the street. So much for "the golden years," I guess. It was Mama Ski who discovered Dreamland and claimed it for herself and people like her, just like Columbus did when he discovered America. 'Course, we know it ain't *really* ours—which makes us a little smarter'n Columbus, if you ask me.

Papa Doc ain't a Haitian dictator in exile. He ain't even a doctor. We just call him that 'cause it's like his real name, Papadakis. Stavros Papadakis. He's a Greek sailor who jumped ship 'cause of trouble back home, I guess. We don't really know much about his story 'cause he don't talk much English, but he's welcome here at Dreamland.

Ms. Doc *is* a doctor—the M.D. kind. I guess she worked at some big hospital when, one day, she just flipped out. Nobody knows why 'cause she don't talk about it much, and at Dreamland, we respect folks' privacy. All we know is she chucked it all and wandered to Dreamland, and she's been here ever since. Sometimes she gets a little foggy in the head, like Boom-Boom, but it's okay. We still like her just fine.

When I was in Vietnam blowin' things up and gettin' medals for it, Kit Katz blew things up right here and got the FBI after him. I guess it made 'em plenty mad when he blew up a buncha their offices and about six draft boards. It's been over twenty years, now, and they're still after him. We won't turn him in, though—even though he talks kinda snooty and acts hoity-toity sometimes. You never know when you might need someone who's good with explosives.

Sweet Willie's a hustler, always lookin' for a quick way to make us rich, cookin' up scams that almost but never quite make it. Willie's lived all his life on the streets. It's all he knows. When I talk about Montana, he thinks I'm talkin' about Mars. He can't imagine a place that ain't all city.

Jenny Lake, a.k.a. Marvella Tush, is our newest resident, and nothin's been the same since she came. She's young and real pretty—for a white woman—and everybody likes her. But Mama Ski and Sweet Willie say she's trouble. I think maybe they're mad at me for bringin' her to Dreamland, but what else could I do?

Since I became a person, I see things, think, and feel. And when I see a girl gettin' beat on by some mean dude, I feel mad and think, I'm gonna do somethin' about this.

That's what happened, you know.

I was out in the city, huntin' up some food. What we used to call "foraging" in Nam. I knew this restaurant where every so often they throw out food that's been around too long—packages of cheese, containers full of chili, heads of lettuce, stuff like that. It ain't bad, neither. I only been sick once from eatin' what they throw out.

Anyway, I started down the alley to check the Dumpster, my mouth already waterin', and that's when I heard it: fightin' sounds, a man's voice all mad and mean, and a girl's whimperin' cries.

"Fuckin' bitch!" the man hissed. He sounded like he wanted to shout and whisper at the same time. "Stupid honky who'e! Razor Reggie say you gonna do it, you gonna fuckin' DO it . . . !"

I heard slappin' sounds and more girl cries.

Well, I slipped into Careful-Creeper Mode. You know, like in Nam, when you know Charlie's around. In Careful-Creeper Mode, I sorta float over the ground, quiet as fog. The alley was dark, but my eyes soaked up light like a Starlite scope and wrapped it around whatever I looked at.

What I saw was a VC torturin' one of our nurses. He was slappin' and shakin' her real hard and bouncin' her off the wall, and I saw her mouth and nose bleedin'.

I went to raise my rifle, but it wasn't there. I couldn't find my .45 or K-bar knife, neither.

That was real dumb, I thought, goin' out on night patrol without a weapon. But then I remembered what the DIs said back in boot: a marine is never unarmed 'cause HE is a weapon, every part of him. A good marine can kill you with his attitude.

And I was a good marine. That's why the brass kept sendin' me on these missions. They could count on me. I always did the job and came back alive. Even that one real bad time in Laos.

So I Careful-Creepered my way closer, never lookin' right at the guy, you know, but just over his left shoulder. People can feel you lookin' at 'em, just like a deer can feel the hunter's aim, so I never look right at a dude I have to waste.

This guy was pretty tall for a VC, I thought as I moved closer, but that didn't bother me. I knew my job. In two quick, simple moves, I could shatter his spine and break his neck, or I could rip out his windpipe with a jarhand grip, or I could just poke my thumb through his temple into his brain. I'd done those things plenty of times, so I wasn't worried. Killin' people ain't so hard, once you get the hang of it.

But then I came outa my brain fog and realized I wasn't in Vietnam. The girl wasn't a U.S. nurse, and the guy wasn't a VC. Sometimes, when I'm under pressure or in danger, the tuner in my head flips the TV of my mind to The War Channel, and I'm back in the jungle. See, I knew what to do back then and over there, and I was real good at it. The best. But back here, I just get confused. Back in Nam, things were simple and there was only one rule: survive. Here there's just too many rules to keep straight in my head.

I couldn't kill this guy 'cause he wasn't a VC. He was a black guy beatin' on a red-haired white girl.

I don't have nothin' against black people—even though the only time them and whites ever got along was when they were killin' Indins. Most of the black folks I've met are okay. But this one wasn't.

He needed to be fucked up a little.

But, see, that's a problem. When you're trained to kill, it's hard to stop short. It ain't easy to pull back from that dark edge, and things get outa hand real quick.

So I just grabbed the guy from behind and threw him across the alley. He hit the other wall pretty hard, fell down, shook his head, and got back up kinda slow.

"What the FUCK!" he shouted. "You in a worl' uh shit, now, muthahfuckah!"

Then he got a good look at me. For a moment, we just stood there, starin' and sizin' each other up.

I saw a tall, lean black guy with fancy alligator shoes and lotsa gold jewelry. He had mean eyes and looked like he could move pretty fast.

He saw a 6′4″, 250-lb. Indin with braids to his chest, fists nearly as big as his head, and wild black eyes. My bein' over two feet wide through the shoulders seemed to impress him. He suddenly looked like he'd rather stand in shit up to his armpits than be in that alley with me.

"Yo, now listen, dude," he said. "Ain' none uh this yo' bidness, dig? This 'tween me 'n' the bitch. Y'all jus' step aside 'n' ever'thang be coo'."

"Sorry," I said. "Can't do that. Why don't you go away and leave the lady alone?"

"LADY! Shit, man, she one uh Razor Reggie's who'es! She ain' worth aw this." He pointed a finger at me like he was aimin' a pistol. "You don't step aside, maybe ol' Razor Reggie be comin' faw YOU, dig?"

"I don't think that'd be too smart. If he comes lookin' for me, he just might find me. And then I'd have to stomp his head out his ass. Maybe you two think you're real tough guys, but I ain't no girl. You fuck with me, and I'll unscrew your head and shit in your chest cavity."

The guy pulled somethin' from his pocket. There was a clickin' sound, and I saw light dance along the blade of the knife he now held.

"I'm through fuckin' witchu, Tonto!" he snarled. "You just move on, or I'm gonna cut you up. Now whatchu thinka that shit, man?"

I laughed, and that really seemed to bother him. I guess he was used to scarin' folks, and havin' a guy laugh in his face musta been a new experience for him.

"I think," I told him, "you ain't gonna like the steel enema you'll get if you come any closer."

He blinked at me and looked confused. Then he turned to the girl behind me.

"C'mon, now, Jenny, girl. You stop this booshit now an' c'mon back to work, we fawget aw 'bout this. You split, an' Razor Reggie gonna come aftah yo' honky ass. An' he be pissed, you dig? This time he just might do some slow cuttin' on you . . ."

"Leave me alone, Leon!" the girl cried. "I'm through with this shit! Do you hear me? THROUGH! You can go fuck yourself! And you can tell Reggie to go fuck HIMself, too! I ain't doin' no more of that whips and chains and torture bullshit!"

"Yo! Who you think you talkin' to, bitch?" Leon took a step toward her. "I'm gonna . . ."

"One more step," I warned, "and you ain't gonna do nothin' but fall down and bleed a lot."

Leon gave me a wary look. "Man, you don't know who you messin' with!"

I shrugged. "Far as I can see, you're just a greasy little shit who likes to beat on women. You don't scare me, Leon. But you ARE startin' to piss me off."

I took a step toward him, and Leon stepped back.

Maybe he'd forgotten all about that little knife he still held. Suddenly he didn't look very tough at all.

I took another step, and he backed off farther.

Maybe it's my eyes. Kit Katz says my eyes look real scary when I'm in one of my moods. He says I look wild and crazy, like I really wanna smash things and hurt people.

"Both uh you's dead meat!" Leon hissed. "Dead fuckin' meat!"

And then he took off, runnin' outa that alley like his ass was on fire.

I turned to the girl and smiled. "You feel like dead meat?"

She wiped blood from her face with a torn part of her top and shook her head.

"Good. Neither do I. C'mon. I know a doc who can fix you up. Can you walk okay?"

She nodded, but her top was all tore up and she tried to hide her titties with her arms.

But I didn't look.

Well, yeah, I looked a little.

Then I took off my field jacket and gave it to her. It covered her completely from her neck to below the knees.

"Who are you?" she asked as I led her away.

"Folks call me Chief, but my name's Tom Losteagle."

"You a for-real Indian?"

"Hundred percent."

"What kind?"

"Big and friendly."

It's always the same. Folks see a real, live Indin walkin' down the street, they stare at him like he's a dinosaur or saber-toothed tiger or somethin'. We're s'pose to be extinct. At least they think so. And seein' one of us on the street makes 'em scratch their heads and wonder how they fucked up and let one get through the genocide machine.

"No," she said. "I mean what tribe? You an Apache or Mohawk or somethin'?"

"Or somethin'. I'm Pikuni."

She shook her head. "Never heard of 'em."

That didn't surprise me.

"Where you from?" she asked.

"Duck Lake, Montana. That's on the Blackfoot Res'vation."

"I thought you said you were a PeeKUHnee."

"I am. Pikuni Tribe, Blackfoot Nation. There's Pikunis, Kainahs, and Siksikas in the Blackfoot Nation. I'm a Pikuni."

She looked me up and down. "You sure are a big mother. Are all Blackfoot men as big as you?"

"Naw. Some's bigger, some's smaller. I'm about middle-sized. Back in the old days, our enemies called us 'The Tall Ones.' "

"Well, I'm Jenny Lake, from Le Croix, Wisconsin."

"Lake. That's a good name—pretty, deep, cool, a place of life. Lake. That'd be a good Indin name."

She giggled. "You're a weird dude, Tom Losteagle."

I laughed. "So folks tell me."

Her face turned serious. "Thanks for what you did back there. That took guts. Weren't you afraid?"

I shook my head.

"What if Leon'd had a gun?"

I shrugged. "Then I woulda had to kill him."

"You gotta gun?"

"Don't need one."

"If Razor Reggie comes after you, you'll need a gun, believe me. He's a mean sonuvabitch."

"I can be mean, too, when I have to. But who's this Reggie guy? Why's he after you?"

She sighed. "That's a long story. I guess you could call him my manager. Pimp's more accurate. I make skin flicks and turn tricks for him. Leon makes the movies. You know, I didn't mind much, at first. Sometimes it was even kinda fun. But then they started gettin' into all this leather and whips and pain shit, and I didn't care for that at all. I ran away a few times, but Reggie always found me, beat me up, and put me back to work. But tonight I'd had enough. I'm sick of lettin' those pricks beat on me."

She looked up at me kinda sheepish-like. "Do you think I'm awful? You know, for makin' nasty movies and all?"

I shook my head. "We all do some whorin' to get by. But nobody should have to put up with beatin's."

Jenny sighed. "Reggie's sure gonna be mad. I'm the biggest moneymaker in his stable."

"He'll get over it."

"Yeah, maybe," Jenny said, but she didn't sound very convinced. "I still think he'll be real mad. Reggie doesn't like losin' things."

I stopped and turned her to face me. I saw the fear and confusion in her eyes, and I smiled, tryin' to put her at ease.

"Listen to me, now. You ain't a THING. You're Lake. A place of life. Think about that. You're part of the Mother's blood, a livin' part of the universe. You're where the animals come to drink, where the plants grow thickest, where the fish and otters and beavers live. You ain't a THING. Understand?"

She stared up at me, still lookin' confused and afraid. And then her eyes sparkled into a smile and she laughed. It was a nice sound, like water, and it made me smile.

"You're a weird dude, Tom Losteagle. But I like you."